Binding
Book Three of Millennial Mage
By J.L.Mullins

Copyright © 2023 by J.L.Mullins

All rights reserved.

No part of this publication may be reproduced, distributed, or transmitted in any form or by any means, including photocopying, recording, or other electronic or mechanical methods, without the prior written permission of the author, except as permitted by U.S. copyright law.

The story, all names, characters, and incidents portrayed in this production are fictitious. No identification with actual persons (living or deceased), places, buildings, and products is intended or should be inferred.

Contents

Chapter: 1 - I'm Going to Become an Archon 5

Chapter: 2 - Are You Heavier? 21

Chapter: 3 - Flow 35

Chapter: 4 - Worth Every Copper 49

Chapter: 5 - This Won't Kill You, Directly...................... 63

Chapter: 6 - Yay, Me… 77

Chapter: 7 - Already Lost to the World 91

Chapter: 8 - Group Breakfast Deal 105

Chapter: 9 - Mana 119

Chapter: 10 - That Has Merit 131

Chapter: 11 - A Hodgepodge Foundation...................... 145

Chapter: 12 - Fleeing the Madness of Reality 159

Chapter: 13 - She's a Scary Lady 173

Chapter: 14 - Watching for a Trap................................. 189

Chapter: 15 - About Time You Finished 205

Chapter: 16 - A Taste of Human Blood......................... 221

Chapter: 17 - Wish Me Luck? 235

Chapter: 18 - The Real Work... 247

Chapter: 19 - What the Rust?... 261

Chapter: 20 - False Choices 275

Chapter: 21 - Plentiful and Free..................................... 289

Chapter: 22 - The Crux of the Matter at Hand.............. 303

Chapter: 23 - In Ancient Times 315

Chapter: 24 - That's a Bit Embarrassing	327
Chapter: 25 - To End a Very Long Day	343
Chapter: 26 - Progress is Progress	355
Chapter: 27 - More Questions	369
Chapter: 28 - Mistress Odera	383
Chapter: 29 - Only a Mage Protector	395
Chapter: 30 - Crystal	409
Chapter: 31 - A Calm, Uneventful Evening	421
Chapter: 32 - I'm Hardly Standard	433
Chapter: 33 - A Start	449
Chapter: 34 - Fool's Folly	461
Author's Note	465

Chapter: 1
I'm Going to Become an Archon

Tala was in her own room, that she had paid for herself.

She had a lucrative, if unideal, contract with the Caravanners' Guild as a Dimensional Mage, and she was starting to make a few friends.

In fact, one of those friends was renting her this room. *Lyn really has been amazing to let me stay here.*

Sighing, Tala took one last look around her room before turning around to see Lyn standing in the doorway.

"Gah!" *How did I not hear her?* She thought back and realized that she had, in fact, heard her arrive but hadn't registered it. *I'm going to have to figure out how to control that better...*

Lyn smiled. "I know it probably feels even smaller now, after the Wilds…"

Tala smiled, her stance softening. "It's wonderful, Lyn. Thank you, again."

Lyn's smile widened. "So… you're sure you want to stay?"

"Absolutely."

The older woman stepped forward and gave Tala a quick hug. "Good." After the brief contact, she pulled back. "How about I go grab us some dinner?"

Tala brightened. "That sounds fantastic! How about some more of Gretel's meat pies? I feel like I could eat a dozen… maybe two." She felt her stomach rumble slightly.

Millennial Mage, 3 - Binding

"Make it three? And anything else you think looks good…" *I lost a few earlier, rather violently…*

Lyn gave her a questioning look.

"Holly said I needed to eat, a lot."

She shook her head. "Fair enough. I'll do that. Take some time, settle in. I'll be a bit."

"Sounds good. Thank you, Lyn."

"See you soon." She left without another word.

Tala stretched, again. "You know, if I'm going to be without my salve for a bit, I should enjoy baths more often."

Terry looked at her skeptically.

Tala coughed, looking away. "You have no idea how often I've taken baths before."

Terry let out an oddly deep, seemingly disbelieving, chirp.

"Fine, well, I'm going to ready a bath." She grabbed one of Holly's books and her review notebook, using the latter to narrow down what to study in the former as she strode from the room. The digestive system was her first focus. A smile tugged at her lips, and she glanced back, seeing the terror bird on her bed and the tools on her writing table. It looked horribly bare, but it also looked right. *Not that I'm going to leave it like this.* She smiled.

Time to relax.

*   *   *

Tala's bath was not quite ready before Lyn returned with food.

Tala had forgotten that a fire had to be built to heat the water in this place, and she hadn't wanted a cold bath. *I'm getting spoiled, it seems.*

She had filled the tub and just stoked the fire when Lyn called out to her. "Dinner!"

"Coming." Tala walked out, moving carefully as she continued to read, only to find Terry already sitting beside Lyn, eyeing the basket full of mini meat pies. Another basket of food sat off to the side, the contents wrapped in linen.

Lyn smiled up at Tala. "Can he eat one?"

Tala shrugged. "I've seen him eat worse."

Lyn smiled and tossed one to Terry. The bird devoured the mini-pie quickly.

Tala grinned. "Watch this." She grabbed one of the pies, then looked to Terry. "Up for some showing off?"

Terry tilted his head, eyes on the pie, and gave a slight nod, hunkering down, almost dancing from foot to foot.

Tala tossed the pie to the side.

Lyn opened her mouth to protest but stopped. "Where'd it go?"

Tala had had her eyes on Terry the whole time, and still, she'd only seen the barest flicker. The only difference was that he'd changed position, slightly, and was now wolfing down the little pie.

"Tala..."—Lyn focused on Terry—"how old is that terror bird?"

Tala grinned, devouring her first pie. *So good! Garlic and yams, and is this beef?* "Not young."

"The shortest cool-down I've seen between teleports was in a dimensional rabbit. It could jump every three seconds or so."

Tala shrugged. "Not too different."

Lyn had a serious look on her face. "It was hundreds of years old, Tala. My understanding from my passing curiosity is that the time is halved every decade or so, for non-sapient users, and the time increases the larger the thing teleported." She narrowed her eyes, examining Terry more closely. "Is he a dwarf terror bird? That might explain some, but he'd still need to be close to a hundred and fifty years old, at least."

Terry looked inquisitively to Tala, but she slightly shook her head. "Could be, I suppose. Who knows for sure?" She ate another pie. *Oooo! Parsnips and beets? Nicely blended flavors, too. I wouldn't have thought those would go with pork so well.*

Lyn stared at her for a long time, then sighed. "Fine…" As she took up and began eating her first pie, she was watching Terry. She finished her first and started on her second, suddenly throwing another off to the side.

Terry seemed to instantly shift positions, again eating the newly acquired pie.

"Less than an eyeblink…" She examined Tala, again, and sighed. "Fine… I won't dig."

Tala smiled. "Thank you for dinner. What do I owe you?"

Lyn waved the question off. "Welcome home, that's what you owe me." She smiled. "I assume you want to get back on the road as soon as Mistress Holly's done and you have your chat with the guild?"

Tala hesitated. "Maybe…" She thought about the training that she'd been doing, as well as the mounting advice to create a sufficient Archon Star. Plus, she'd promised the Guardsman's Guild she'd give them some time. "What would it mean for our contract if I became an Archon?"

Lyn froze, a new bite of meat filling her mouth. After a long moment, she began chewing once more, and eventually, she swallowed the savory treat. "Tala. How likely is that?"

Tala shrugged. "Depends on the answer?"

Lyn sighed, deeply, scratching beside her right temple, her eyes squeezed shut. Under her breath, she muttered, "Give me strength." After another long moment, she opened her eyes and smiled. "Tala, dear friend, that would constitute a material change to the services you could offer the Caravan Guild."

Tala thought back. *There was a clause about something like that...* "Sooooo...?"

"So, at the very least, we would retest you and alter the arrangement accordingly. The most common result would be that you'd be allowed to take on two contracts at once, being considered a Dimensional Mage *and* a Mage Protector of the wagon train—assuming you'd be capable of that."

Tala perked up at that. "So, half my inscriptions would be covered? And I'd earn a gold ounce for each arcanous encounter the wagons survived?"

"You'd earn that for your team, but basically, yes," Lyn confirmed.

That would be so utterly fantastic. "How does that work, anyway? If one thunder bull attacks, versus a herd of ten, is that the same pay because it's one encounter?"

Lyn sighed, again. "Depends. If there's any indication that you personally caused the encounter, then you get nothing additional. If it is unavoidable, then it depends on the quantity and power of the beasts in question. Ten thunder bulls directly defended against would be three ounces gold, added to the payment of the protectors."

Tala was nodding. "That sounds fantastic."

Lyn was giving Tala a very wary look. "What are you planning...?"

Tala gave the other Mage a quizzical look. "I'd think that was obvious. I'm going to become an Archon."

Lyn groaned, putting her head in her hands.

Tala popped another meat pie into her mouth, and Terry flickered just slightly, then held very still. She turned to regard the bird, its dimensional magic burst obvious. "You know, I can sense when you do that."

Millennial Mage, 3 - Binding

Terry looked her right in the eye, then tipped back his head, opening his mouth and allowing the four meat pies he'd snatched to slide down his throat.

Tala just laughed, and Lyn looked up in confusion. "Terry, I'm going to feed you. Is human food so much better than what you're used to?"

The bird locked gazes with her and bobbed up and down, letting out a low, resonating squawk of affirmation.

Tala cleared her throat, handing Lyn another meat pie. "Now, my room. What can I do in there?"

Lyn looked between her two housemates and sighed. "This is my life now, isn't it...?"

Tala grinned. "Just when I'm in town."

"Right! You never answered my question."

"Oh... you're right." Tala thought. "I just did two contracts, so I'd be good for four months, right?"

Lyn nodded hesitantly. "Yes, but it would look bad and lower your priority for taking contracts."

Tala nodded. "Understandable. A month then? I think I can do what I need to by then... Though, I've no idea what becoming an Archon requires. I'll try to have that at least started in a week and a half. I shouldn't do anything too crazy until Mistress Holly's done."

"That goes without saying." Lyn took another bite, speaking around the food. "And don't forget your meeting with a senior guild official."

"Right... Assuming my contract isn't dissolved—"

"As I said, I should have been informed if they were going that route."

Tala nodded. "Assuming that's true, a month should be a good amount of time, but I'll know more in less than two weeks?"

Lyn sighed. That was becoming a habit. "Alright, Tala. I won't start looking for your next trip, yet."

"Thank you. Now, my room?"

"Do what you like with it, just please don't break down any walls or destroy the furniture. If you want something different, let me know, and I'll pull out what's in there." Her eyes twinkled just a bit. "You can buy whatever you want to put in there."

Tala rolled her eyes. "Yes, with my thousands of gold ounces, I shall customize this room to perfection."

Lyn just smiled back at her. "If you so choose."

Tala ate one last meat pie, feeling a bit past half-full as she swallowed the final pieces. Her eyes fell on the other basket. "What's in there?"

"My, you weren't kidding." Lyn grinned. "This"—she picked up the basket, handing it to Tala—"is a selection of desserts. I certainly don't need them." She picked out a chocolate puff pastry. "So, you should take them before I eat them all." She winked.

Tala rolled her eyes. "Thank you." She took the basket and began eating, savoring each bite. "Mmmmm... Thank you." She sighed contentedly. "Well, I've a bath on. I should get to that. Good night, Lyn."

"Good night, Tala."

Tala walked back and placed the basket of pastries in her room. Then, leaving her books beside the basket, she moved to the steam-filled room, undressed, let her hair down, and climbed in.

Terry didn't join her, but she sensed him from the direction of her room through the collar, with no added feeling of warning. *Close. Likely on my bed.*

With her next few days already planned out, she simply relaxed in the water, allowing the embers below the tub to keep it just below her maximum temperature.

This is nice.

* * *

Millennial Mage, 3 - Binding

Tala woke early, her window still showing no sign of morning's light. Even so, she knew it was time to rise.

No nightmares last night. She would have thought that all the fees she'd been forced to pay the day before would have made the nightmares more prevalent, not less. *Don't knock it, Tala. Just be happy.* So, she put them from her mind.

She glanced under her covers and felt herself smile at the subtle, yet obvious, glow. True to her guess, the light didn't even illuminate the blanket above her, but she could clearly see herself, fully covered in the magical lines.

She stood slowly, then, with careful deliberation, she moved through her wake-up routine: stretching and exercising her mind, magic, spirit, and muscles.

The last was expectedly surprising.

I knew there would be improvements, but this seems incredible. Every single exercise, she had to shift towards harder variations, and even so, she struggled more with proper form and balance than with the strength required for the movements. In the end, she was left frustrated with her lack of control more than any missing strength.

A clear way to improve, I suppose.

Her room wasn't really big enough for the longer range calling of her knife, so she simply did a couple dozen summonings from around five feet, at which point, she had to lie down due to dizziness. *That's right, Tala. Overwork your soul. That seems wise.* She'd still been focused on how much her physical strength had improved that she hadn't been as careful as she should have been. *I'll be more careful next time. I swear…*

While she was trapped on her back, the spinning room holding her prisoner, she contemplated the day's tasks.

Charge the cargo-slots, go to the Guardsman Guild's training yard, go to the Constructionists' Guild, massage… then Mistress Holly. She felt tension grow at the last.

Maybe, I could skip today? At the thought, a memory of Holly's visible aura of power surfaced, and she shuddered. *Maybe I won't skip...*

Still unable to stand, she made random noises, playing with what sounds she could make. *I'm bored...* She looked to the side, and even the act of turning her head brought her near to retching. She stared at Kit from across the room. "Must get book…"

The pouch did not respond.

"Terry?"

The bird shifted in his corner, opening one eye to regard her.

"Can you bring me my pouch?"

Terry tilted his head, regarding her. Then, he was suddenly beside her on the bed, the dimensional magic blip unpleasant in her current state, though less so than she'd expected.

She felt a light pressure on her arm, then Terry let out an oddly indifferent, low, thrumming squawk. The bird vanished back to his corner and curled back up.

"You're no help." She raised her arm lightly, looking where she'd felt the pressure. "Did you just try to cut me?"

Terry chirped happily.

"Still happy with your decision, eh?"

Happy chirps were her only reply.

"Won't help with the pouch?"

He settled back down, closing his eyes.

"You're kind of mean." *Hey! Moving my arm didn't make it worse.* She flexed, bringing her arms up in front of her, her hands clapping together with surprising force. She felt the last vestiges of the endingberry power left in her system drain away, and a crack like thunder exploded through the room. She felt extra power shunt to the inscriptions around her ears, protecting them from the incredibly loud sound.

Millennial Mage, 3 - Binding

Terry jumped up, looking around in alarm.

Tala felt a fresh wave of dizziness at the loud sound despite the dampening scripts.

Lyn's voice floated their way. "Tala? Is everything okay?"

Tala groaned, and she heard Lyn hurrying to her door. "Can I come in?"

"Sure…"

The door opened, and Lyn stood in it, regarding her for a long moment. "Tala."

"Yes?"

"Why are you naked?"

"It's my room." *And… I forgot to get dressed.*

"I asked if I could come in."

"And I answered."

"Usually, that question is to determine decency."

Tala groaned. "Decency can wait for my head to stabilize…"

"Are you ill?"

"No, I just overworked my soul."

Lyn sighed. "From anyone else, I would assume that to be a joke."

"From anyone else, it just might be."

"What do you need?" Her tone had taken on a maternal cast.

"Apparently, a blanket…"

Lyn snorted, striding into the room and moving the blanket that was bunched up beside Tala to cover her. "There."

"Thanks…"

"So…" Lyn sat down on the bed beside Tala. "What was the noise?"

"I clapped."

"You clapped…"

"Yup."

"Is that a metaphor? Some obscure training technique based on the heroes of yore? Or…?"

"No, I just clapped."

Lyn looked at the other Mage's palms, seeing the subtly glowing scripts, just like those that covered the rest of her. "Seems like it was a hard clap."

"Yeah."

"Please refrain? It was quite loud, even out in the living room."

"Will do, boss."

Lyn shook her head. "Do you need breakfast? The work yard is expecting you to drop by this morning, and I've written down the information for your other appointments. The sheet is ready for you."

Tala groaned, again, and sat up. Surprisingly, the room remained steady. "I think I'm ready."

Lyn stood, keeping her back towards Tala. "Well, get dressed first, please?"

It took barely any time for Tala to pull her clothes back on. She decided to go with the immortal elk leathers again, given she was going to the training yard this morning.

Terry appeared on her shoulder as she stepped out of her room. With a smile on her face, Tala took a moment to look around herself.

To her right, directly beside her at the end of the hall, was the door to Lyn's room. Across the way was the door into the bathroom, and beside the bathroom door, closer to the living room, a window let in the beginnings of the first light of day.

The building was a simple construction, with poured stone floors, lightly textured and most likely sealed. The walls were painted plaster over stone. *Heavily built.* The floor was dark, the walls light; it produced a pleasing atmosphere.

Why have I never just stopped to take it in?

Millennial Mage, 3 - Binding

She felt herself smile. She didn't have any deadlines. Nothing was demanding she become ready. Sure, she had tasks that she wished to do, but that wasn't what she meant. She had no obligations on her overall time, not at the moment.

She moved down the hall, which was wide enough for her and Lyn to pass each other quite easily.

Tala came out into the living room and saw Lyn sitting at the table off to one side, food laid out. "I thought food wasn't included?"

"Well, I figured two meals wasn't quite a pattern." Lyn smiled. "I was informed that you developed a... liking for coffee."

Tala was *quite* sure that 'liking' hadn't been the word Lyn was going to say. She was about to comment, but then she saw the coffee in question, in a mug beside the other place at the table. Tala immediately forgave Lyn all implied slights and sat down, taking a deep pull of dark, decadent deliciousness.

So smooth, so dark, so perfect.

They ate quickly as both had many things to accomplish that day.

Lyn and Tala left at the same time, saying their goodbyes as they went in different directions: Tala to the work yard, Lyn to the Caravan Guild's main office.

Tala took her time walking through the city, enjoying being back in Bandfast.

It had a different feel to it than Alefast—more relaxed, less... imminent. *I suppose that's what happens when you're one wall away from the Wilds.*

There were similar mixes of architecture, and the people didn't really look different, save Bandfast citizenry seeming a bit more relaxed. *Maybe a bit heavier, too...* It was an interesting notion. *Does safety lead to weight gain?*

That couldn't be the only factor, obviously, but it was entertaining to consider.

Many people gave Terry odd looks, but no one seemed particularly alarmed by him. Tala fell back into her habit of reading, sketching, and jotting down her thoughts as she walked, both to keep her mind occupied and to prevent her from sprinting through the city. Mostly, though, she read. *I have to get through my anatomy review, after all.*

She was still having a bit of an odd time moving, each of her movements more powerful than she was expecting. Interestingly enough, the method of walking, learned at Adam's suggestion, lent itself marvelously to the task as she was used to careful, precise movements, and her enhanced nervous system adjusted to the changes in her power quite rapidly.

As Holly had implied, and Tala had discovered the night before, she felt ravenously hungry, and she was sure it was her new inscriptions that were causing the hunger, even if not directly. They were working on reshaping her at a fundamental level and that required nutrition.

Towards that end, Tala bought no less than ten pasties of various kinds for the wonderful price of a single silver. As she walked, she occasionally tossed out bits of jerky, noticing the instantaneous, slight shift of Terry's weight when he moved out and back, always having caught the meat.

She did not share the pasties.

Terry did not hold it against her. Much.

Finally, she reached the work yard and the waiting cargo-slots.

The first one, to her surprise, charged incredibly slowly, taking a full minute to reach its maximum. She frowned. *The mental construct is right...* After a long minute of thought, and ten bits of jerky flicked randomly, she had a realization. *I've just been using my leftover power flow to charge these up. And my scripts are using most of that, now.*

That actually reminded her of her items. She had charged them as part of her training earlier that day, and it *had* taken longer than usual. She'd just attributed that to the city being utterly devoid of free-floating power. *Maybe it was something else?* Since she was already thinking of them, she decided to top them off. *If I can be hungry, why not them?*

That done, she moved to the next cargo-slot and concentrated.

She formed the mental construct, just as before, but now, she reached inside. She saw, as well as felt, almost all her power pouring from her gate into her spell-forms. She grabbed the entirety of that flow and channeled it down her right arm, through the mental construct, and into the second cargo-slot.

She exhaled.

The indicators flickered to life in rapid succession.

Blinking in surprise, Tala pulled back her hand. *Less than two seconds?* The cargo-slot in front of her was fully charged and ready to go.

Hesitantly, she moved to the next one and repeated the process.

Done.

She moved down the line, charging the remaining seventeen with little more than the time it took to touch them and take a quick breath.

That was... amazing! She had noticed a slight dip in her internal reserves during each charge, as her active scripts continued to use her power. That store of power had needed to be refilled by her gate, once the inflow was available again, but it was a minimal dip.

She heard the sound of a single person clapping, approaching from behind. "Wonderful! I can see you took my suggestions to heart and have improved remarkably."

"Master Himmal!" Tala turned around, giving a slight bow. "It's wonderful to see you again. Thank you, once again, for your advice."

He smiled, folding his hands before him. "Think nothing of it, Mistress Tala. You have progressed tremendously in just two short weeks."

She smiled. "Thank you." As she focused on him, she saw the same oddities in his aura as before but more clearly this time. The underlying color was suppressed but obviously red. What she could see of it was fractured, somehow broken, and as she examined it closer, she could see that parts of it were much closer to orange than she first realized. *Not uniform?* From what little she understood, that seemed… bad. *Well, he did say that he'd broken something with his gate. It's probably related to that.*

"Now, I can see that my hopes were not unfounded. We are nearly done with your custom set of cargo-slots, and I am glad that I added the ability for the larger capacities to be enabled. We should be able to get you a set close to four times those measly constructs, with added additional benefits for more fragile and valuable cargo. With those sizes, you'll be able to have some outfitted as passenger and bunkhouse variants. You'll be able to have a full caravan in just two or three wagons, depending on the Mage Protectors." He shook his head. "The cooks will never leave their own wagon behind." He smiled whimsically, speaking under his breath. "I would so love to examine one of their chuckwagons one day."

I knew it! That wagon and what the cooks could do within never made sense. Brand hadn't just been messing with her after all. She smiled. "You and me both."

Chapter: 2
Are You Heavier?

Tala passed a bit of time with Master Himmal, but eventually, she bid him goodbye, promising to come by to test out the custom cargo-slots near the end of the week.

She had been surprised that he hadn't commented on Terry, but she supposed arcane pets weren't too uncommon. She fell back into her routine as she walked to the training ground that Adam had indicated. She was almost done with the first set of topics she'd noted for review. *Good thing, too. Holly's got to have something to work on, or she's likely to be cross.*

When Tala arrived, she was startled by what she found.

It was a sprawling compound, with the training yard open to the street so that passersby, or the curious, could watch the training. *Good for recruitment, I guess?*

The training yard was at least a hundred yards long and half that wide. There were sections of grass, dirt, and paved stone of various sizes interspersed throughout. Across the entirety, hundreds of men and women were stretching, sparring, practicing techniques, or otherwise working their muscles.

To her surprise, her magesight picked up the ebbs and flows of power throughout the yard, and not just from the healers, ready to help if those sparring were injured. Power moved through these people in a manner that she could only equate to that of the arcanous creatures she'd seen. *Not the elemental magics, obviously.*

Millennial Mage, 3 - Binding

Even so, she could see that, to a variety of extents, these guards would be stronger, faster, and more durable than the average citizen. *How are they doing that without inscriptions?* The power was clearly coming from their own un-inscribed gates, but she couldn't see anything directing it.

Something to investigate, I suppose. She'd seen hints of it in Adam, before, but it was being fully brought out as those before her worked to push themselves.

Around the training yard were quite a few buildings. Some appeared to be additional training halls, either to allow for more private or more sheltered training. It was a cool morning but not painfully so for the average person. *Probably why most of them are outside.*

Other buildings seemed to be instructional classrooms or administrative offices from what little she could see. Overall, it looked more like a school, which emphasized physicality, than a barracks and muster yard. *I suppose that's what I get for assuming.* She felt a smile tug at her lips.

The sparring drew her attention, and she noted that those who were using weapons were using wooden or padded varieties, though they didn't seem to be pulling their strikes, whether armed or barehanded. In fact, as she watched, one of the combatants broke a training sword over another's shoulder, the strike drawing blood and breaking bone, if the deformation of the shoulder that she could see, even at this distance, was any indication.

Before the man's first scream had died down, a healing Mage was beside him, the healer lighting up to Tala's magesight as he quickly repaired the injury. *Clever. So they can train at full power, get used to injuries, and not lose much training time.* She thought for a moment. *I wonder if they ever let the injuries stand? Might be useful to practice fighting while impaired.* That was a question for another time.

Quite a few citizens were standing along the road, either individually or in groups, watching the goings on. Many more slowed down as they passed, mixtures of admiration, envy, and contempt across their faces. *There is someone who will look down on any endeavor, I suppose.*

Without slowing, Tala walked forward, crossing the almost invisible line between street and training yard. Immediately, one of the nearby Guardsmen stood and came her way.

"Mistress? How can we serve?"

"I am searching for Guardsman Adam. He'd asked me to come by today."

The Guardsman bowed. "Would you be willing to wait here? I can go and inquire on your behalf."

Tala simply nodded, and the guardsman jogged off, ostensibly to do just that. Many of the others in the yard were glancing her way, but no one seemed to pay her much more attention than their initial glance.

As she continued to look around, she could see parts of many of the techniques that Adam had taught her demonstrated in the movements of those across the yard. It was fascinating to observe how a simple striking pattern was altered for use with a spear, mace, or sword, and also how each of those differed from the others. *There is such depth to the practice.*

A few minutes later, the guardsman returned, gesturing towards one of the central buildings. "Guardsman Adam is expecting you, and he awaits you there. Would you like a guide?"

Tala shook her head. "No, thank you. I can find my way just fine."

He bowed. "Good day, Mistress."

"Good day, guardsman."

Millennial Mage, 3 - Binding

He returned to his practice, and she strolled through the training yard, weaving in wide arcs to avoid interfering with anyone.

As she walked, she took in the beautifully clear sky above and basked in the morning light. *Many are likely still rising, and here I am, already at my second task of the day.*

There were, of course, the sounds of exertion and cries both of attack and pain filling the air around her. As she walked, she saw no fewer than twelve healing Mages spaced around various parts of the yard, and she might not have spotted them all. *A healer for every twenty people or so? Seems excessive but must work for them.*

She came to the building in question and looked up at the simple, sturdy architecture. There was a beauty in its utility, and she found herself smiling at that.

"Mistress Tala!"

Her gaze dropped, and her smile changed just slightly to one of greeting. "Guardsman Adam. Seems I found the right place."

The guardsman was wearing loose-fitting clothes, clearly meant for exercise, and he had a light sheen of sweat to him.

Spent the morning training? She stepped forward, into the building.

"Mistress Tala. This way, please." He led her deeper into the building and down a series of interconnecting hallways. As they walked, he used a cloth to wipe much of the sweat from his head and arms. "Thank you for coming."

"Thank you for being willing to train me."

He grinned. "This is a rare opportunity. Master Rane is already here." He added the last as an afterthought.

They came to one of the instructional rooms and entered together. Some thirty men and women, all in their twenties, sat facing the front of the room. They were all dressed similarly to Adam, and they each seemed to have a notebook and a means of taking notes, and each was doing just that.

A much older man, at least in his fifties, sat at the front of the room, also facing the last remaining occupant.

Rane was just finishing his sentence as they walked in. "—the force is therefore redirected, or avoided, without actually being guided."

In the silence that followed, Rane waved to Tala, smiling, and she waved back.

The older man stood. "Thank you, Master Rane. Can anyone tell me a key take-away from his last point?"

A woman near the front spoke up. "He doesn't have to concern himself with dodging because his opponent's attack causes him to be moved out of harm's way."

The older man frowned. "Yes and no. He will not need to focus on taking the action, that is correct. However, if any attack met by that defense, no matter how small, causes him to alter direction to mitigate the damage, that means that Master Rane is constantly subject to forces outside his direct control. He would have to be even more aware of the incoming attacks than if he simply moved out of the way beforehand or braced to take the blow."

The woman frowned in turn. "Then, why is it better?"

A man in the back of the room spoke loudly in response, "Because unexpected movement is better than unexpected injuries."

A few people smiled at that, and Rane nodded, responding, "Precisely. I could close my eyes and simply stand still and be fairly safe. I'd be utterly ineffective but safe from mundane attack."

The main instructor smiled. "So, you will each write up a basic overview of a fighting style for Master Rane, and in coming classes, we will compare it to what he has actually been using."

Rane smiled. "I hope to learn something. I make no claim at perfection."

The instructor had noticed Tala and Adam entering, and he turned to them now. "This is Mistress Tala, and you all know Instructor Adam."

Those present returned a chorus of greetings.

"The central project of the next two weeks will be creating, then perfecting, a fighting style for Mistress Tala here. That portion of your assignment for today will be to construct a series of tests to determine the scope and limit of her abilities so that we can build a style that maximizes her effectiveness. Mistress Tala."

"Yes?"

"Would you give us a basic outline of your combat capabilities?"

Adam whispered, "Including physical and defense, please."

Well, I guess I have good timing, at least. Tala cleared her throat, suddenly feeling nervous as she walked out in front of the gathering. "Hi." She waved.

A smattering of 'Hi,' 'Hello,' and 'Greetings' came back to her.

"So, as an Immaterial Guide, my abilities differ slightly from Master Rane's." She nodded to the other Mage. The listeners were already writing. "As I am able to alter non-tangible properties of the world around us, my defenses mainly involve the increased strength of humanity's natural traits."

The same man in the back of the room called out. "What does that mean?" Several students grinned at this comment or chuckled.

Tala cleared her throat, again. "Well, just as a stickpin would not easily enter your skin, my magic makes that resistance more potent. It takes a much greater force to split my skin cells apart or to harm them directly. Similarly, all my underlying structure, both bone and soft tissue, is strengthened and reinforced. If those bonds are broken, my natural healing processes are accelerated to repair the damage nearly instantaneously."

"Does that apply to your muscles?" It was a different questioner.

"It does."

"So, does that mean you can work out and see immediate results?" Yet another.

"Not immediate but much faster, yes." She smiled. "Also, my power does not create matter. I must eat to provide material for that healing, and thus, I can't heal from unlimited damage as I would quickly burn through my body's supplies."

"Why not alter your body to store more?" A fourth speaker.

"Great question. That is another of my inscriptions. My adipose tissue, and other similar portions of my body, are now inscribed to store more, more efficiently. I can effectively have much larger reserves without seeming to have such." *Though, the appetite that brings on might cause issues with my coin pouch…*

Two questions came in at nearly the same time: "Does that mean you eat way more?" and "How are you not too buff to move?" She stopped trying to identify the individuals asking the questions.

She smiled. "I do have to eat a lot more, though that will slow down in time—at least until I pull from those increased reserves and have to refill them. As to my muscle mass, my inscriber is quite clever, and my muscles, when they do repair, do not change size, simply becoming denser and more powerful."

"How much stronger than normal are you?"

"I've not tested, specifically, but in the range of four to five times what I was without the inscriptions."

Millennial Mage, 3 - Binding

There was a chorus of mutters through the room at that. "Are you heavier?"

Tala laughed. "I suppose I am—and will continue to become—heavier until the reworking, strengthening, and reserve filling is complete." She cleared her throat and glanced towards the door where Adam and Rane waited. She smiled, feeling much more confident now that she was so far into it. "Offensive-wise, I have gravity alteration spell-workings and a knife, which can become a sword for short periods of time."

There was silence at that.

The instructor waited a moment, then asked, "What sort of gravity alterations?"

Tala nodded. "I can either restrain or crush. My restraining magic lifts the target from the ground and alters the effects of gravity on them to keep them aloft."

"What?" Another listener.

"They will float there on their own." She smiled, simplifying. "Crush will increase the force of gravity upon the target four-fold. If the target is not killed or fundamentally altered, usually leading to death, it is increased four-fold, again. This continues until the target is dead or fundamentally altered."

Absolute silence filled the room for a long moment. Finally, a woman near the front swallowed visibly and asked, "So… why do you need to fight hand to hand? Why not simply use magic to crush your enemies, see them driven before you, and to… be done with it?"

The instructor looked incredibly relieved that someone else had asked that question and smiled. "Excellent question, Cona."

Tala nodded. "First, I can have only a few targets before I must be re-inscribed. Thus, I cannot use that to deal with large numbers of enemies, and if I am near the beginning of a venture, I must be sparing. Second, there are some beings who can operate under such conditions, at least for a while, and it burns through a lot of power to take them out in this manner. That also reduces the number of targets I can affect."

The girl was nodding, seeming to understand. "So, you need to be able to fight lots of weak creatures or incredibly strong beasts, but those in the middle you can simply crush?"

"Well, I would prefer to crush the most powerful as well, but that is generally correct."

The group seemed to better understand.

She had an additional thought. "Oh! I also have a repeating hammer."

"A what?" Some of the listeners seemed to know what that was but not all.

"A repeating hammer is a magical hammer, which redirects force from the striking face back away from the tool. It effectively can break through anything that a hammer could damage at all, in a single blow."

The instructor nodded. "That is sufficient, I believe. More can be revealed by the testing they will devise." He looked to Adam, then back to her. "You will be available for testing tomorrow?"

She shrugged, smiling. "Sure. How long will you need me for?"

He thought for a moment. "If you arrive when you did today…" He seemed to be contemplating deeply. "Let's say four hours on the outside. We'll spend the time before you get here weeding out all the duplicates and refining the plan. So, that should be enough time."

She grunted. "That should work."

The instructor relaxed visibly. "Then, after that, I think we will need a day without you to compile the first ideas. We can begin testing them the day after?" He hesitated. "I can assure you, Mistress Tala, I will be overseeing the entire process, along with several other experts, and we will have a truly spectacular result."

She smiled. "That sounds wonderful. Thank you."

Tala waved to the group as she departed. Rane walked out with her.

"Hey."

She glanced his way. "Hi."

"Are you still mad?"

She frowned. *Mad? Oh! Right...* She sighed. "No, Master Rane. It isn't worth the effort."

He grunted at that. "Well… I'm glad."

She shrugged.

"So… what are you up to today?"

"I've got a *lot* going on today."

"We could grab lunch? You're looking a little pale…" He shook his head. "Sorry, that's not really relevant."

I guess he noticed my missing iron salve. That was fine, she wasn't trying to hide the fact. She shook her head in response. "I really don't have time."

He seemed to deflate a bit.

With effort, she kept from either sighing or rolling her eyes. "I'll have more time tomorrow, but just a bit."

He perked up. "Lunch, then?"

She quirked a smile. "After whatever crazy assessments they come up with? I'll probably need it."

"It's a plan then." He smiled.

"Sounds good." She glanced ahead, to the archway back out onto the training grounds. "I really do have to go, but thank you for asking."

He smiled and waved her off. "See you tomorrow."

* * *

Okay, Tala. Avoiding it won't help. Let's get this over with.

Tala held herself stiffly upright as she walked into the Caravanner's Guildhall, marching straight through to one of the main desks near the back of the atrium.

"Good morning, Mistress. How can I assist you today?" The young man, sitting behind the desk, smiled warmly at her.

"I'm Mistress Tala. I was informed I needed to meet with a senior guild official?" *Come on, come on. This is not what I want to do...* No. She needed to be here. This had to be dealt with.

"Mistress Tala..." He looked through a large appointment book on the desk in front of him. He turned the page, beginning to frown. "Mistress Tala... I'm sorry, I'm not seeing you in the collated calendar. Who is your appointment scheduled with, and when did you schedule your appointment for?"

Tala hesitated, then felt herself coloring. "Oh... I didn't know I needed to schedule it. I was simply told one was needed." *Whenever I was ordered to attend a disciplinary meeting, I had to go right away, and I was seen right away...* This, apparently, was different. *I have to schedule my own session to be reprimanded.* She almost snorted a laugh. *I guess I should have expected that.*

The young man checked a few more pages, then looked up, apologetically. "It doesn't seem to be here, and no senior official is available today. Who were you supposed to meet with, again? Perhaps, I can get you in tomorrow."

Tala opened her mouth to answer, then closed it. *I have no idea.*

The young man seemed to understand. "I see. That's more than fine." He nodded, consolingly. "I'd recommend reaching out to your guild handler, or point of contact, and asking them to schedule the required meeting."

Tala nodded, feeling incredibly embarrassed. "I'll... I'll do that. Thank you."

"Happy to assist, Mistress. I wish I could have done more. You have a good day."

*   *   *

Ten minutes later, Tala had shaken off her embarrassment and was again walking the streets of Bandfast, this time heading towards the Constructionists' Guild. As she was walking, she realized that the pace of her reading was much faster than expected—faster than even on the recent caravan trip.

I guess the enhancements made my movements easier, freeing up more of my mind to focus on reading? It was as good a reason as any other she could think of.

The books were a masterwork in and of themselves—at least the one she was currently referencing was. It contained detailed schematics of each organ or organ system as they were discussed, coupled with cleverly rendered schema, illustrating their three-dimensional nature, along with how they would accomplish what they did. It was, unsurprisingly, incredibly detailed on the how. If Tala didn't understand what, and how, the magic was supposed to work, it wouldn't function. In the worst case, it could malfunction and destroy the parts of her body inscribed.

I didn't really expect to delve back into anatomy and physiology so deeply, so soon…

She'd always preferred physics, hence the nature of her offensive spell-forms, but the work Holly would be doing now was *incredibly* dependent on Tala's second favorite subject, just as she'd suspected it would be.

I'm just glad that I already had specific interest and knowledge in the muscular-skeletal system, along with the vascular, or I'd have to have done a bunch of research before even yesterday's inscriptions…

She sighed. It was fascinating, and Holly had gone out of her way to make the writing engaging, but it was still a dense subject matter.

How did she even have time for this?

Tala supposed that the general overviews would be common to anyone getting any given organ inscribed, so those would just have to be copied over.

And it's not like I'm the first person to have my organs enhanced. This is probably just an amalgamation of those techniques, slightly modified for my particular make-up.

She hesitated, even stopping in the middle of a stride. *Wait… how did she know the exact dimensions of all my organs to make properly shaped spell-forms…?* She placed a hand on the back of her neck.

How much is this script analyzing and recording?

She thought back. *Holly said that it would monitor everything about me…* She groaned. *Well, I did understand what it would do… I suppose I just didn't assume it would be literal…*

She sighed, continuing on her way and returning most of her attention to the current portion of this book.

Tala finished the first subject on her list to review by the time she reached the Constructionist Guild's local office. Closing the book with a satisfying *thunk,* she tucked it into Kit and looked up at the beautifully designed façade. *Rust me, they really didn't spare on the expense of this place.*

While highly detailed, the elements were tastefully interwoven to give an overall inviting, if humbling, atmosphere. Tala smiled as she walked up to the large front doors.

There weren't a lot of other patrons at the moment, but that made some sense. This guild didn't have as much to do as the Caravanners. *Though… are the wainwrights a subsidiary?* That made sense, and most guilds worked in that way. *Guilds of guilds… ah, society. How wonderful your complications.*

She found herself grinning.

As she stepped across the threshold, she felt a tingle in her keystone, indicating magic had been directed her way, and a wave of power pulsed out from behind her. There was no specific spell-form to it, but it had the overpowering sense of an infrared aura. *Did the* door *just scan me and announce my classification?*

An attendant appeared, entering from the side. "Mistress, how can we serve you today?" His eyes glanced to Terry, and there was definite curiosity, but he didn't comment beyond his initial question.

Tala pulled out the sheet that Lyn had written up for her. "Hello, yes. I was sent here by Mistress Lyn of the Caravanner's Guild. She said I should ask for Master Boma?"

The attendant paused, power rippling over his face as he looked at her. "I apologize, Mistress, but Master Boma usually does not attend to the needs of those below Archon…" He was clearly torn. "Mistress Lyn sent you, you say?"

Tala nodded.

"Very well, let me check with him and see if that name changes anything for him."

"Thank you."

"You may find it more comfortable to wait in there." He pointed off to one side. "There is a waiting area through that archway, and you'll find refreshments available while you wait."

With a smile and slight bow, the man turned and went back the way he had come.

"Well, Terry, let's see what refreshments they have for us."

Chapter: 3
Flow

Tala sat in the nicely appointed waiting room.

The furniture was comfortable, but not so much so that she wished to stay here for a long time. It appeared robustly made and didn't creak or budge, even when Tala, herself, shifted. It was mostly a dark wood in construction, though she couldn't tell if that was the wood itself or a stain. Heavy canvas, a darker blue in color, covered the cushioned portions, and she had little trouble imagining the pieces lasting for years, or even decades, with moderately heavy use.

She ignored the somewhat bland art of the walls, choosing instead to begin the next topic of review from Holly's books, a mug of coffee in her hand. *If this is available every day, I might need to come by more often…* Though, she doubted they would be happy with her dropping in just to get coffee… *I wonder if they have wine available later in the day?*

As she thought about it, the freely available beverage did not make her hopeful for reasonable prices for their services. *Ah, well. We'll have to see.*

The coffee was well-brewed, as far as she could tell, and filled a happy little void in her chest. She smiled as she drank. *This is nice.*

There was nothing for Terry.

He was only somewhat mollified by a few chunks of beef jerky, which Tala tossed out randomly. *I wonder if he minds? Maybe I should just give him the pieces...* She shrugged to herself. "Terry, do you mind me tossing the jerky?"

He gave her a clearly confused look.

"I mean, do you want me to just hand it to you, instead?"

He seemed to consider, then shook himself, his eyes moving back to her empty hand.

She grinned. "Fair enough." She pulled out another chunk and tossed it in a random direction. *Well, there we have it.*

As she waited, she continued to read and absently charged her magic items. *I could forget later; might as well keep them topped off whenever I think of it.*

After close to a quarter-hour, a short, stocky Mage walked in. "You're the one Mistress Lyn sent?"

Tala stood, her keystone tingling, indicating magic was directed her way. "I am." Her magesight showed the man to be an Immaterial Guide, just like her.

Unlike her, he had inscriptions that very closely mirrored those she'd seen on Master Himmal and his assistants. *Focused on analyzing and working with magical items.*

His aura was a deep yellow, just far enough from orange to no longer truly be that color. It was contained, somehow, and seemed to almost be held up for display. *How does that make sense?*

His magesight was already active, even though the inscriptions she could see indicated that it wasn't always on like hers was.

"I assume that you are Master Boma?"

He grunted. "I am. Why did the Caravan Guild think you needed to see me? You clearly aren't an Archon, and any mortal work can be handled by..." He trailed off as Tala drew and held up her knife. "Girl, what, by the stars, have you done?"

Tala just smiled. "I read that I can merge items of power into soul-bound artifacts to increase their base power. Is that true?"

He gave her a long look, then took the offered knife, examining it critically as he spoke. "Of course it's true. That's the primary way to alter and shape such. Otherwise, you have to use an item in very specific ways for… well, it depends, but it's always a long time. That can cause the power to shift and grow to better suit you." He shrugged absently, clearly talking from a depth of experience as he examined the weapon. "Some are more fluid than others." His gaze flicked to her eyes. "Child, this knife is starving, even while bound to you. You don't have the strength of spirit to support this bond properly." He gave her a hard look. "I assume you were told not to bond anything else? How did you even bond this so weakly?" He gave her a long look. "You're not bound to…"

Tala simply waited as he rambled on. After all, the man wasn't leaving room for her to answer any of his myriad questions.

"Ahh, so you came to the spell-form without proper guidance and didn't know what to do with it?" He looked back at the knife. "This has to be the weakest Archon Star I've ever heard of. How is it stable?" He shook his head. "Doesn't matter, it clearly is. So, you want to increase the power of this item then?" He finally stopped there, awaiting a reply.

"Yes. I'm building the power of the bond daily, and I have a host of harvests that I think will be compatible with the knife."

Boma grunted. "Well, we'll see about that." He sighed. "Come on, then."

"Umm… I'm sorry, but how much will this cost?"

He gave her a long look, then sighed. "It completely depends on what we're working with, but the absolute cheapest it would be is one ounce gold. If you have some insanely complex things to work with, it might be a hundred. I won't know 'til we're in the room."

Tala frowned.

Master Boma sighed, again, shaking his head. "I won't do anything that will cost you even a copper before we discuss and agree to a price. Alright?"

She smiled just slightly. "Thank you. That sounds quite acceptable."

He gestured back towards the room's exit. "Let's go."

Terry flickered up to her shoulder, and the Archon paused.

"That is an interesting creature. Secondarily bound to you via that collar, yeah?"

Tala nodded. She'd recharged the collar along with her other items every time she topped them off.

"You're not fooling anyone, birdy."

Terry cocked his head.

"Well, fine. I'm sure you fool most people, but not those who know what to look at." He moved his gaze to her. "Your defenses must be insane, child. I've never seen a terror bird that old, and they universally grow in power over time… Still, he seems to like you. Don't loose him on the city, please?"

She smiled a bit guiltily. "It's a training collar, so he has to stay close to me."

"Small mercies. I don't want to have to hunt the two of you down at the end of a trail of blood. That sounds *very* irritating." He looked back to Terry. "As for you, I'd have just killed you, had we met in the Wilds. You mind your Mage. Understand?"

Terry crouched just slightly, eyes narrowing.

Master Boma squared up with them, relaxed but clearly ready. "This won't be a test, creature. If you make me, I'll break you like an egg. The city is no place for a wild animal. Know your limits and mind your betters."

Terry hissed but settled down, turning away from the Archon and tucking his head under a tiny wing.

Tala, for her part, felt like Boma wasn't just posturing, even though she couldn't discern any explicitly offensive spell-forms from his inscription. *If nothing else, he probably has a host of items to use… somewhere.*

Master Boma shook his head but didn't comment further. He strode from the room, carrying Tala's knife. She followed without complaint or comment.

They went back through the entry atrium and down a side hall into a large room, closed off by heavy, iron-clad doors. Inside, the stone walls and ceiling were coated with overlapping iron plates, which seemed to be lacquered. *To keep them from rusting or from getting iron dust on anything?* Probably both.

Boma closed the heavy doors behind them, dropping a bar across to prevent unwanted entry.

The center of the floor was blank, flat stone, but Tala's magesight showed her that under the top six inches or so was an incredibly complex interlacing matrix of currently inactive spell-forms. *How can I see them so clearly, even while they're inactive?*

It was far more complex than what she could easily understand, even with her magesight providing some insights. Below those appeared to be more iron panels—if she understood the odd reflection effect that she saw correctly. They seemed to be designed to be removed from a room below. *What is that for?* She decided not to walk on the floor over the dormant magic, just in case.

"Now, girl, I assume that you have the harvests in that dimensional storage?"

Tala nodded.

"Put them over there." He pointed to the center of the room.

So much for not walking on that portion of the floor... She sighed and did as he asked, taking the pouch off of her belt, opening it, and pulling out the feathers and talons.

Boma followed her and began examining each piece as she pulled them out. When she finally finished, he grunted. "Well, you weren't wrong. These should be compatible, but they aren't going to expand the versatility of the knife. They'll just make its magic more potent, more efficient, more effective."

"Meaning?"

He gave her a flat look, then sighed. "Meaning, if done correctly, it will be able to cut through harder material, even some magics, and stand up to more abuse. It looks like this weapon can shift shape. That will likely happen more quickly, and with less effort on your part. We can likely use the feathers to help strengthen the blade's connection with you, as well, so the poor artifact will stop starving from a weak, unsupported soul." After a moment, he shook his head. "That might be too much to ask. Even so, the melding will allow you to feed it more easily as your soul grows in strength."

"Fair enough."

"Do you wish to incorporate all of this together?"

Tala shrugged. "If you think that's best? I'm not exactly an expert."

He gave her a long look before just shaking his head again. "This knife is bound to you. Assume that's forever, as the alternatives are worse than death. Trust me on that. I think it reasonable to put this investment in."

"Then, I'll bow to your experience."

He snorted. "It'll be two gold for the working, and that's the guild-to-guild rate. If I treated you as an individual, it would be five." He gave her a hard look. "You did come because of a guild representative, correct?"

He's giving me the choice? Maybe he has to tell someone, somewhere that this is a guild job or that he reasonably assumed so? She didn't care, really. "Yes, sir."

He nodded, a slight smile tugging at his lips. "Good." He began arranging the feathers in a circle, overlapping them to make continuous steps, the quill angled slightly inward. "Drive the knife into the stone here." He drew a line on the stone with his finger.

How did he do that? As she did what he asked, the blade easily pushing into the hard stone, she analyzed what she'd seen. *He altered the reflectivity of the material, changing its color.* It was a clever use of Immaterial Guiding, but it seemed a bit frivolous.

With the feathers and knife in place, he placed the talons in a smaller circle, the hooked blades pointed outward within the circle of feathers. That done, Boma stood. "Your bird will need to wait by the door."

Terry flickered over without the need for additional prompting.

Boma quirked a smile, looking at Terry. "Thank you for not wasting everyone's time by pretending ignorance." He turned to Tala. "You will stay in the center, here." He stripped off his Mage's robes, tossing them on the floor back near Terry and leaving himself in only short pants, which ended near his mid-thigh.

He took a deep breath, seeming to center himself. Then, to Tala's magesight, he exploded outward, a flood of magical tendrils lancing out from countless places on his now-exposed flesh, entering the floor to interact with the intricate mesh Tala had previously detected below the surface. Magic danced through a thousand intricate patterns on his skin. He seemed to control each individualized thread as it, in turn, manipulated those below the stone floor.

Portions of that hidden inscription activated, harmonizing with Master Boma's spell-forms, and the stone shifted, portions sinking downward to form a detailed spell-form seemingly engraved into the floor. This shifting wasn't the moving of joints but the stone itself, moving as if carved, shaped, sanded, and polished into form.

Further activations on Master Boma's part caused liquid copper to flow through the channels and depressions, clearly guided by the forms below the surface.

I wonder if that's a more complex version of how the teleportation rooms function, hidden spell-forms below the stone. "Won't I be caught in the working if I stay here?"

He looked over at her, clear bemusement across his face, even as he continued his work. "Girl, you are soul-bound to the knife. You could be on the other side of the city, and this would catch you. It'd just take more power and more metal, so you'll stay there." After a moment, he added an additional command. "Sit cross-legged around the knife, and place both hands upon the hilt."

She complied. "Wouldn't the iron keep the working from leaving this room if I was elsewhere?"

"If you weren't soul-bound, yeah. Magic doesn't need a pathway through physical reality to flow across a soul-bond." He paused again, seemingly moving through a more difficult manipulation of his magics before he gave her a level look. "I'll forgive your ignorance because these are all Archon-level concepts, but please, make a proper star and elevate yourself soon, yeah? Your lack of understanding is *painful*, and I'm forbidden from correcting your deficit as you are now."

Tala stopped asking questions. *I am so, incredibly glad that I didn't attempt this on my own.* Seeing Boma's work, the very idea seemed laughable. *The more I learn, the more I realize how much I don't know.*

The spell-form was now complete and filled, Tala sitting in an open circle in the middle. The lines of the spell-form ranged in size from thread-thin to as large as her little finger. It was all copper. If she had to guess, she'd have said it was at least four or five pounds of the metal, and that was just what she could see on the surface. *I'd have thought gold would be preferred...* She hesitated. *No, that much power would be a waste and likely much,* much *too expensive to be practical. And with copper, when not all the metal is used up, they can still deactivate the spell and reuse that material.*

She knew that this spell-form likely had depth, meaning there were layers below what she could see. Thinking back, she remembered seeing holes in the stone, likely the pathways towards those lower portions. *Plus, this is using the material from the spell-form below the stone and using up Master Boma's inscriptions, too...* Two ounces gold was sounding like a better and better deal as she contemplated all that was involved here. *Might be barely more than cost...*

She looked up, noticing a secondary circle, closer to the door, fully inscribed, prepared, and intermeshed with the main circle surrounding her. Master Boma sat down in that circle, tendrils of power still connecting him with the workings.

Tala looked around herself, trying to take in all she could.

"Mistress Tala."

Tala looked to the older Mage.

"When this activates, the magic will flow through you, the knife, and your materials. You will be given choices on how the integration will occur. I *strongly* recommend that you choose the one you came here for. Don't be tempted by the other things presented. As much as you've been a bit annoying, your ignorance is understandable, and I'd hate to end the morning by killing an inhuman abomination."

She frowned. "What? I don't understand…"

He sighed. "I know, child. Please just remember what I said."

She nodded, hesitantly, and he reached out, placing his hands on perfectly sized imprints to either side of him. The threads of power seemed to collect, moving across his skin until they all seemed to originate from his hands, flowing into the stone. His gate opened wide, the power flowing outward became a torrent, and Tala's magesight was instantly overwhelmed by a wave of refined power.

Her vision went white as a torrent of magic slammed into the knife and, through it, into her.

* * *

She was outside herself, without form, looking into a white void.

It wasn't bright; it wasn't dim; it simply was, and it was white.

An instant, or perhaps a decade, passed without anything violating the purity of the void.

Then, there, before her bodyless gaze, stood… herself but different.

Tala stood, wings stretching from her back; her hands and feet ended in razor-sharp talons, and her eyes were solid black: inhuman and predatory. As she watched, the wings and talons retracted, fading into her flesh as if they'd never been, but the gaze remained the same: hungry, barely intelligent.

Tala moved back from that visage of herself and saw another standing nearby.

The second form was her as well but covered with short, black feathers. Her legs were more like Terry's, with reversed knees, and her torso was hunched forward, arms reaching to tear at her victims. Her talons were wicked-looking, clearly designed to shred that which she attacked, and her eyes...

How do these eyes look even more feral?

She was not behind those eyes. Well... of course, she wasn't because she was looking from the outside, but there was no humanity in that face. What she beheld was a beast of basic hunger and predatory need.

She shuddered—or she would have if she'd had a body.

The third version was a human-seeming Tala, but her arms were replaced by wings of sharpened metal. She somehow knew both that this version of her could fly and the wings were a permanent feature. *No retracting these for normalcy...*

The next Tala looked mostly normal, a knife in hand, her knife. As she watched, power flowed into the knife, and the arm holding it changed into a huge, winglike blade, incorporating the knife and making it an extension of her physical form.

The body incorporation looked like a medley of silver and black metal, interwoven into a symphony of death and sharp edges.

That looks interesting. It looks almost like one of the wings from the third option.

Next to that was a similar manifestation, but this time, the sword changed into a monstrosity, completely separate from her own physical body. The blade was nearly a dozen feet long, the hilt growing to be more than large enough for two hands to grip it with ease. Despite the tremendous size, the mirage of her seemed to wield it with effortless ease.

Hah, it's light as a feather. She considered for a moment. *It looks like it would cut more like an ax than a razor. That could be a pain. Also, I can't imagine fighting in close quarters with that or near anything, no matter how light it was.*

She moved on.

Finally, after dozens more, the last figment she saw was of her as she was, holding the knife.

In the figment, power gushed into the weapon, and it instantly flowed into the shape of a familiar sword—just as it had looked to her before. Though, there were now hints of a feather-like texture to the hilt, as well as the field of heat within the wire outline of the blade.

Somehow, she knew that the lack of increase in size and reach had been translated into *power* within the blade itself. She felt an overwhelming, instinctual cry from this final version, a hunger and unified purpose. This weapon existed to be wielded by her to hunt, kill, and protect herself from harm.

Yes. The weapon, the extension of her will, resonated with her very soul.

She looked at her options, for she knew that was what they were, and she understood what Master Boma had meant. The first options somehow integrated the two physical forms and her basic nature lost. She was not strong enough to fully unify with this weapon and stay as she was. *Does that mean I could get wings later? If I was stronger?*

Maybe.

It might be worth asking… once she was an Archon and people would answer her questions.

Do I want wings? She shook her… soul? *I don't have a head to shake... But now is not the time for such considerations either about my headless state or whether or not I want wings.*

She approached the last manifestation and indicated acceptance.

Power shattered through her and the knife; her very self felt as if it was being scraped raw.

* * *

Her vision splintered back into normal sight, and she found herself sitting cross-legged on the smooth floor of the room, the knife resting in her palms.

All traces of the arcane harvests and spell-forms were gone, and Master Boma was standing over her.

"Good, still human." He turned and walked towards the door. "I'll work up the exchange tablet. Take your time."

Tala looked down at her hands and the weapon resting atop them. She felt more connected to the tool than ever before. It felt like her heart beat within the knife, though the tool didn't pulse. It was as if the knife was her long-lost love but also someone who had been her companion for decades.

Yet again, she was struck with how it felt more a part of her than her own arms. *Strange... Yet, obviously as it should be... somehow.*

There was a hint of feather-like texturing in the pattern of the blade and handle, making the metal, at least, look like a form of patterned, folded steel.

She extended her blade to the side and poured power into the blade, watching it flow outward, taking on the shape of the sword more quickly and easily than ever before.

She still couldn't maintain it for more than a handful of seconds, and even that would be a strain, but it was a marked improvement, regardless.

She brought the extended blade in to look at it, lifting her hand to grip the blade, before she hesitated, realizing that that would be foolish. *Don't burn your hand, Tala, or stress your inscriptions.* Even so, as she'd brought her hand close, she'd noticed something.

In a direct line with the blade's edge, she felt her power being pushed back, driven back into her defensive scripts and away from the flesh itself. As the edge came closer, the scripts themselves seemed to be straining, as the magic in them was put under stress. *This will cut so much easier than before, even through magically defended materials.* She found herself grinning. *The power just flows away before it.*

Flow. That seemed fitting. "I will call you... Flow."

Chapter: 4
Worth Every Copper

Tala hadn't moved, and Terry was sitting with her when Boma returned, stone slate in hand.

"Here, this should be in order."

Tala stood and walked to him, Terry appearing on her shoulder after she was up. "Thank you." She took the tablet and looked over the short bill of sale before retracting her power from her finger, pricking it, and certifying the transaction. "There you are." She handed it back. "Oh! What would it cost to get one of those?"

Boma accepted the slate back, seeming to contemplate. "For transactions? Or do you want it connected to any specific archive or library?"

"I mean, I'd prefer it to be as useful as possible."

He grunted. "Probably wise. Adding additional connections isn't really that expensive, but more useful means more used, so you'll have to get it re-inscribed quite often... Five gold? With a recommended two-month re-inscription timeline. That would be an additional four gold each time."

Tala's eyes widened. *That's crazy!*

"Don't give me that look, child. It's a complex schema, and it takes a lot to ensure the connections don't muck up the archives they link to. We could do it in an artifact format, but that would be..." He blew out a breath, considering. "Fifty gold?" He nodded to himself. "Yeah, fifty gold ounces for one of those."

Fifty gold!? I could buy an apartment for that… Wait… Tala frowned. "One moment; you can make artifact-style items? With that specific of properties?" *They can interlink with archives. That doesn't seem like something that could happen randomly, even if the randomness was guided…*

Boma stiffened, freezing in place before he turned to look at her. "No. No, we cannot."

She sighed. "Fine. I'll ask again after I'm an Archon."

He seemed to relax a bit, still obviously a bit off-kilter. "Well, sure… If you think that would change anything."

She did. "I have a question regarding dimensional storage items, specifically of the artifact variety."

He turned a bit more towards her. "Very well."

"Well, I have two, actually. Questions, that is. First, how can I determine if it is safe to be in my dimensional storage after it closes? And second, how could I expand its internal size?"

Boma looked away, seeming to contemplate. "Well, your first question implies that you know your dimensional storage changes sometimes. That isn't rare for artifact-style items, but the most common dimensional storages are uniform and constant. Open or closed, they are the same inside."

She nodded. "Mine alters its shape, seemingly based on my more basic goals. It will also offer up the item I reach for, so I don't have to take it from a specific location inside."

He was nodding. "Not common, but not that rare. There are two subtypes of item that function in that way, that I know of. For one, all unoccupied space ceases to exist when closed. It is theorized that the unoccupied space never existed at all, and any perception of such is an illusion, meant to convey various things to the user."

That's a disturbing thought... When I climbed in, I may have been completely surrounded, engulfed, but didn't know it?

"In the other, the internal space is amorphous but relatively static. It alters itself to give desired items to the user and reshapes towards its user's needs, but it holds its form in the meantime. In those cases, they function much like standard dimensional storage items: closing them doesn't change the inside in the least."

"Huh, thank you. How would I determine which I have?"

Boma looked at her hip, where Kit hung, for a long moment, his magesight inscriptions activating. "There is something blocking my direct view of your item. I can tell it's a dimensional storage because of the flavor of the power coming out the top, but the rest is difficult to see. May I examine it?"

Tala handed him the pouch. He had no trouble grasping it. *Did Kit allow that, or did he overcome its attempts to avoid being grabbed?* She might ask after she got her other answers.

He opened it, looking inside for a moment, then pulled it closed and handed it back. "You have the second type. The internal space will remain in existence when the pouch is closed. It only reshapes to meet a sensed need from you."

Tala smiled in relief. She wasn't quite sure how much of a difference it would make, but she found herself happy that it was the second. "Quick question. Was it difficult for you to grab the pouch from me?"

He grunted. "Not really. Nice little defense, though."

So, it did try to avoid him, but it wasn't very successful... At least, that was what she interpreted from his answer.

He looked at his hand quizzically for a moment, then a flicker of power caused a puff of dust to rise off his palms. "You coated the outside in iron? A bit rude, that."

Tala swallowed. "I apologize. I didn't really think of it." She smiled in what she hoped would be an innocent way.

He grunted. "Don't hand that to a Mage. You might cause all sorts of... unpleasantness." He shook his hands, then sighed and wiped them on his robes. "Now, as to your other question, how to make the space bigger." He gestured expansively but not really indicating anything in particular. "The quickest way would be for you to soul-bond the item. That will give it a boost to storage capacity relative to the strength of your soul." He hesitated. "So, I'd wait until you're a bit stronger in that regard." His gaze hardened, briefly. "You should wait either way. Become an Archon before soul-bonding anything else."

"Understood. That was my plan."

"Good." His eyes narrowed for a moment before he grunted, seeming to accept her word for it. "Once you are an Archon, and you bond that pouch, if the increase in capacity isn't to your liking, we can do a similar working to what we just did. You'll have to provide other, compatible storage devices to combine with the pouch, but that should increase the working capacity."

Tala found herself nodding. "That seems simple enough. Thank you."

He gave her a long look. "Simple? No. Relatively easy? Sure."

She shrugged. "Fair enough. Oh!" She'd almost forgotten. "You do lensing items, too, right? Incorporators?"

"We do. Why?"

"Well, first off, why do I have to recharge his collar if it's a lensing item?" She patted Terry's collar.

"Quick answer is: you don't." He held up a hand to quiet her objections. "You are 'flavoring' your portion of that collar—if it is the type it appears to be. That allows it to be bound to you but doesn't actually use that power. No power store can be infinite, so you have to refill that tag every so often. If you were in an area of high enough magic density, it would fill on its own, the incoming magic being automatically flavored by the remnants of your power already in the collar."

I suppose that makes sense. "Thank you."

He nodded. "Sure. Anything else?"

"Well, I'm interested in buying incorporators. I have one for water, but it's cold water. Could you do one for hot water? Like near boiling? I'd also be interested in any generic ones that you might have available." After a brief moment, she had a thought. "What about coffee? I'd *definitely* want a coffee one."

He laughed. "Hot water is easy—we might even have one on hand. If not, we'll have the diagrams in place to make one quickly. Coffee? That is a rather complex substance." He looked away, not meeting her eyes. "It wouldn't be easy to make, and coming up with such a diagram, such a device, would likely cause friction with the Grower's Guild, which cultivates that crop in parts of the cavern complex below this very city."

Tala found herself grinning. "You already have one, don't you." She thought for a moment. "That's where the coffee in the waiting room comes from. How do you keep it from discorporating?"

"Mistress Tala, your conjecture is unwarranted. I'm afraid we cannot easily create such a complex incorporator."

She cocked an eyebrow at him. "I'll bet you can't."

He gave her an exasperated look. "I do apologize. The research required to create such would be extensive and prohibitively expensive. Even if you had the funds to commission such, we simply do not have the time."

"Fine, fine. I won't push. How much for the hot water one?"

"Thirty silver."

She didn't know how to feel about the price. It seemed both too expensive and too cheap. "Why? And how did you know the price already?"

He shrugged. "Why the cost? They are useful devices to some, but overall, they are inefficient. How do I know it? One is no harder to make than another once the details of its construction are known. All incorporators I can sell you will cost basically the same."

She grunted. *I can spend up to a gold ounce on a few of these. They're good training for my accumulation rate and useful besides.* "Which ones do you have in stock? I'll want a hot water one, whether I have to come back or not."

Boma was nodding, working on the tablet they'd used for the earlier transaction. From what she could see from her angle, it looked like he was going through a manifest list of items and materials this guild had on hand. He then manipulated the information, combining it with a secondary list. "Here are all the incorporators that we can create on commission for a certified Mage. If we have it on hand, that is indicated here." He pointed to a column of Xs and blank spaces to one side of the slate. "Take a moment to have a look."

She smiled, accepting the tablet. After a moment, she looked up in confusion. "This one says diamond. You can make a diamond incorporator?"

"Not as useful as it sounds. Any jeweler worth their metal will be able to tell it's not quite right. Plus, incorporated material degrades based on the connected mass exposed, along with various other factors. The more rigid the creation, the faster it discorporates as well."

Tala grunted. "Ah, so diamonds don't last very long."

"No, less than a minute." He shrugged. "Though, some of our clients have said it's quite fun to send out a spray of diamonds."

She smiled, opening her mouth, but he cut across her.

"Before you ask, no, it is not a harmful spray, nor can it be made to be so. I understand that there are some industrial applications for diamond dust." He indicated another incorporator listing. "If I remember right, it is a *very* effective material for grit-blasting to clean various items. The fact that it discorporates so quickly afterwards is a benefit as well." He hesitated. "To be clear, the incorporator, itself, does not do the blasting. That's an entirely different device."

"Huh, I suppose I can see that."

There were a surprising number of options, but they were all for unified materials, in one state or another. Only homogenous incorporations were available.

"This one says 'hot air.' How hot? And just… air?"

He smiled. "We can make it as hot as you desire, though efficiency drops exponentially. So, it can't even create more than a minor burn, even if you held it flush to your own arm. As to the chemical composition of what's created?" He shrugged. "For those, non-toxic in roughly the ratios found around us all the time. Mostly heard of them being used to speed drying or curing times. Some Mages who had baking hobbies have tried to make ovens from them, very precise temperature output and all, but the throughput was never sufficient for their purposes, given the point was incredibly precise temperatures over an enclosed space. Similar for a crazy lad who tried to use one to inflate some large cloth bag to fly; he claimed the same issue with output volume. Don't know that any Archons ever tried either of those tasks, though."

"This one, here, says 'flame.' That would burn something, right?"

"That is the idea. Ludicrously inefficient, as expected. I, myself, can only create about a four-inch, very thin flame for a short time."

So, worse than my inscribed item and more than four times the price. Not that I've used that outside of starting the fire under Lyn's tub... "But what does it actually produce?"

"A gaseous fuel at a high enough temperature to combust virtually instantly. And before you ask, the amount of fuel that can be produced at lower temperatures is equally minuscule, and it doesn't last very long; it's too complex a material for a durable incorporation."

These are not as useful as I'd hoped...

He smiled. "I imagine that you're a bit underwhelmed, yeah?"

"Just a bit…"

"Well, you don't see these everywhere, do you?"

"I suppose that's true." She sighed. "I'll just take one for water, as close to boiling as reasonable, one for hot air… at whatever temperature you think is reasonable for drying everyday items when wet, and one for coffee."

He gave her a long-suffering look. "The hot water and hot air incorporators will cost you sixty silver, together."

She nodded. *That's a lot, but I should be able to use them to good effect.* She decided to not fight him on the coffee. *For now.* "When can I pick them up?"

He took the tablet, working up a sales agreement before handing it back. "Tomorrow? These are well-known designs. I'm glad you didn't have too specific of temperature desires because if we haven't worked out formations for exactly what you're looking for, it'd require starting from scratch."

"It's not just a minor adjustment?"

He shook his head. "No, it is not." He didn't elaborate.

"Alright then." She confirmed the bill of sale. "That's all I can think of, right now."

"Well, it's been a pleasure. Do come back, once you're an Archon. I think we'll have a more productive time." He smiled.

She nodded, respectfully. "Thank you. I think we did all I needed us to. Truly, thank you for all your help."

He gave a slight bow and strode away, slate in hand.

*   *   *

It had been a very productive morning, and Tala was quite ready for some lunch.

With Kit mostly empty now, she decided to swing by home to load up the jerky, though she didn't particularly want that for lunch.

Terry didn't seem to mind the detour or the bits of jerky she regularly flicked out for him.

While she was home, after the jerky was stored, she looked around Lyn's kitchen. There was a very simple, inscribed hot plate without any means of powering it, and there was a large fireplace in the living room, though she'd never seen Lyn use it.

In the fireplace itself were wrought iron fixtures for hanging pots or kettles over the flame and others to allow skewered meat to be turned over the heat. There were heavy doors set into the brickwork beside the hearth that were clearly intended to be ovens, of a sort.

I have no idea how to use any of this. She let out a long-suffering sigh. *It would have been nice if the academy actually taught us practical skills...* Now that she thought about it, hadn't there been a cooking class available? *I didn't really have time...*

She'd have to seriously consider figuring out how to cook if she was going to be around the city much of the time. *Or, I could just go on more caravan trips and pay off my debt faster...* That was probably a better choice.

"Now, Terry, where should I get food?" She locked the door behind them and turned towards the nearest group of restaurants. *I wish I could practice some while eating...* She could read, at the very least.

She ended up choosing a new place, drawn in by the scents.

Twenty minutes and half a silver later, she exited the eatery, bearing what appeared to be a small log, one end easily the size of two of her fists. It was two-thirds as long as her forearm. *What was I thinking? This is huge!*

The meal was composed of an incredibly thin, flour flatbread, wrapped around a layer of melted cheese, then another layer of the incredibly thin bread. Inside that double layer of goodness was a medley of tender chicken, heavenly pork, fluffy rice, fried beans, perfect spices, cooked vegetables, mild cheese, and swirling, complementary sauces...

She sat down at an outdoor table, just staring for a long moment. The menu inside had listed this one as the 'Biggest Cheesy Little Caravan.' As that was a *much* too complicated name, Tala just thought of it as a food log.

Terry appeared on the other side of the table, and she took a moment to get a larger-than-usual chunk of meat for him.

He ate it just as quickly as usual.

Well, here it goes.

What followed was truly something to behold. Each bite was a subtly different combination of flavors, textures, and scents.

It. Was. Glorious.

Her mind was bent entirely towards the consumption of her lunch, her book forgotten as she simply enjoyed.

She ate the whole thing.

Leaning back, she let out a contented sigh. She pulled out her water incorporator and took a careful drink. *Hey! I didn't gag myself. I'm getting better control.*

Terry was stretched out in the sun on the other side of the table, ignoring her.

She glanced towards the eatery. *Should I get another?*

It was a tempting thought. Her stomach objected. She couldn't remember ever feeling so full.

No, Tala. That should have fed you for days. You don't need another... not right now... Maybe, she could reward herself with a second after her visit to Holly later this afternoon. *Yeah. That's a good plan.*

She groaned contentedly as she pushed herself up into a standing position. *Yeah, not another now.*

Terry blipped to her shoulder as she pulled out Lyn's sheet once more. *Now, where to for my massage?*

Her belly full, she wandered through the city.

It was alright that she was taking this day a bit easier than she had the last three weeks. She was due for a break.

I can train tomorrow.

Lyn's directions led her to an unassuming building without a sign out front. If it had been in the inner circle, she'd have assumed it was a house. As she thought about it, she realized that it could still be a home. *It's not like the guards do sweeps of the buildings, ensuring people only sleep in one part of the city.* She took another moment to compare her location to Lyn's directions. *Is this the right place?*

She checked Lyn's sheet again. *This seems to be the right place...* Still uncertain, Tala walked up to the door and knocked.

A decidedly feminine voice called from inside. "One minute, please!"

Tala waited.

Millennial Mage, 3 - Binding

The door opened to reveal an older woman with gray-streaked, black hair. She was smiling, highlighting the pleasantly warm smile lines and crow's feet on her face. She was just slightly taller than Tala and petite. "How may I help you?"

Tala glanced down at the paper she held once more. "Are you Emi?"

The woman's smile deepened. "I am! You must be Mistress Tala. Come in, come in." She stepped back, her long skirt swaying about her as she gestured for Tala to enter.

Tala stepped across the threshold, processing what her magesight was telling her about the woman.

Emi, like most people, had a gate through which power flowed into her body. It was a bare trickle when compared to any Mage. Lacking a keystone inscription, Emi wouldn't be able to alter or control the flow consciously. Even so, the diminutive woman had gold inscriptions set into her shoulders, arms, forearms, and hands, all focused on increasing the strength and dexterity of the limbs and preventing that increased strength from causing harm.

As Tala contemplated what she was seeing more closely, she saw that, underlying the inscriptions, indeed surrounding them and encapsulating them, was more magic of the same type but based in the woman's flesh, rather than the inscribed lines. *Again, it's like arcanous beasts in the wilds or the guards.*

It appeared as if Emi, through the years, had somehow acquired naturally occurring magics directly correlating to her inscriptions. *That can't be a coincidence. Do human bodies adapt to the inscriptions?* She realized that, if that was the case, it would explain why Mages who'd been getting the same inscriptions, consistently, for years, seemed more powerful than others.

Emi tilted her head. "Have I lost you, Mistress?"

Tala blinked, returning to the present moment. "I apologize. Your inscriptions are fascinating, and you seem well practiced in their use."

Emi smiled happily. "That is a kind way of saying I'm quite old."

Tala's eyes widened, but before she could respond, Emi chuckled.

"Oh, I know that's not what you meant, Mistress. Now, come with me. You are my whole afternoon."

Tala followed Emi through the simple building to a back room. "Mistress Lyn didn't tell me what the cost would be."

"The kind Caravan Guild functionary? Right, that was her name. Well, I have you for three hours, so we'll do eight silver. If, at the end, you don't feel it was worth it, we can discuss alternatives."

"That seems more than fair."

The room Emi had led her into had a waist-high, padded table in the middle, appointed much like a bed. "Have you received a massage before?"

"Not really?"

She barked a soft laugh. "Well, we'll talk for a bit, then you'll undress and get under the sheet, face down, and I'll see what I can do."

"Alright."

"So, tell me what's bothering you."

Over the next ten minutes, Tala explained what she was feeling from her back and limbs, as well as some of the changes that she'd noticed over the past weeks.

That done, Emi left so that Tala could undress and get in place on the table.

When the woman returned and began to work, Tala slipped into heavenly bliss as, through the early afternoon, each muscle was slowly cajoled into giving up its tension and pain.

Millennial Mage, 3 - Binding

Worth every copper.

Chapter: 5
This Won't Kill You, Directly

Tala floated in hot water, luxuriating as the heat helped her body rid itself of the lingering nastiness, which Emi had worked from her muscles. She could feel her own power, flowing along channels inscribed by Holly's machine, sweeping away the toxins more efficiently than her own body could have naturally.

It was fantastic. Her muscles felt like they were free for the first time in her life, and the magic flowing through her was rebuilding them. Somehow, she knew that this time was taking longer than it ever would again, as every loosened fiber was reforged under the heat of her power.

The density of magic in her body was slowly dropping and had been since this process started— despite her gate being thrown wide, drawing all the power into herself that she possibly could.

She didn't quite know what would happen if the magic ran out before the process was complete. Something told her it wouldn't be great.

She was in an artificial hot spring, in a secondary room inside Emi's building. She tried to distract herself. *I wonder if she has more than one of these rooms.* The pool had been shaped to resemble natural rock, with hot water constantly flowing through and being refreshed to maintain a perfect, almost too hot, temperature.

Terry, who had slept in the corner while Tala was being worked on, now floated in the water nearby, his feathers keeping the moisture out to enough of a degree that he had no trouble staying above the surface.

He looks like the world's most vicious duck…

Tala's everything felt smooth and unrestricted.

Emi's hands had been strong and experienced, tracing each clenched muscle to the source of the issue and relieving the tension. Tala had paid before being escorted to this idyllic, private oasis, and Emi had left her with a command to soak and relax for at least an hour before leaving.

That woman performs the real magic. I'm just messing with gravity; she truly affects the soul. Tala let out a contented sigh. The light feeling of nausea, brought on by the release of so many overworked muscle clusters, had finally fully dissipated, and she was left simply feeling content.

There is no way I can justify doing this regularly… Maybe shorter sessions? She would have to consider the expense if the need arose. *She should not have been able to do this much correction in just three hours…* Tala snorted. *Magic, Tala. It's an amazing thing.* As she considered it, she realized that her own inscriptions, now integrated with her muscular system, had likely helped the prolonged session be even more effective. *Hopefully, it will allow the results to be longer lasting as well.*

Terry tapped her on the head with his beak, and Tala's eyes popped open.

As the bird stared down at her, floating above her head, he let out an inquisitive, cheeping squawk.

Still feeling the colossal drain within herself, she decided that she'd waited long enough. "I need to deal with this, don't I…?"

He bobbed an affirmative.

Tala sighed, turning the gaze of her magesight inward. Her focus was immediately pulled entirely into the torrent of power rushing through her. She was used to her internal reservoirs being like a placid ocean. This was like a hurricane.

Even so, she fought through the distracting flows of power, examining exactly what was happening.

For most humans, muscles were anything but smooth. Throughout their life, each person collected countless places where their muscles locked up, refusing to unclench. These were trigger points or knots within the muscle tissue. Each one was both a weakness in the muscle and a lessening of the capacity. At least, this was Tala's understanding.

Tala's daily stretching and exercise had kept the largest of these at bay, while making innumerable smaller ones that were scattered throughout. It was these points that felt relief in a good stretch or were worked out with proper massage. Now, with the help of Emi's expertise, and Holly's deeply incorporated inscriptions, Tala's body had released them all, and those broken down, overworked, underutilized muscle fibers were being rebuilt: better, stronger, and more responsive.

Her energy stores, so recently overstocked, were being drained for the resources needed in the reconstructions. If it continued on for too much longer, her reserves, both physical and magical, would be utterly depleted.

Thankfully, at long last, it seemed that the process was coming to an end.

Four hours, give or take, to fundamentally alter my muscular system. It both seemed like much too much time and altogether far too fast. *Make up your mind, Tala. Is your magic too fast to make sense, or is it painfully slow?* She quirked a smile. *Both, it seems. I've not gotten used to what I can do, yet.*

Terry was still looking down at her, but he seemed fairly nonchalant in his inquiry.

"You could feel it wrapping up, couldn't you? You knew I was almost done." She smiled up at the bird. "Ready to go?"

He bobbed an affirmative.

"Fair enough. We do need to get to Holly's shop." She felt a bit of apprehension at the thought of more inscriptions, but her relaxed state kept it from growing into anything more. *Besides, these have already been amazing… and I need more food.*

She drifted over to the side of the large, inset pond and dunked under one last time before climbing from the water.

Thick towels waited on a shelf to one side. After running her comb through her hair to dry it thoroughly, Tala availed herself of the towels, drying the rest of herself off fully. She then dressed, braided her hair, and strapped on her belt, her knife and pouch hanging in counterpoint to one another.

True to what she'd seen, she felt the consumption of her magic slowly lessening to a noticeable degree, to the point that, after a few more minutes, her reserves began to slowly refill. *Down to about half. Not too bad.* The hunger also seemed to settle in deeper. Food was now a must, on the journey to Holly's. *I guess I fully processed the food log, then…*

Terry was still basking in the water.

"Ready?"

He let out a series of happy chirps.

Tala gave him a flat look. "You wanted to be done."

He hissed a happy reply, then appeared on her shoulder, perfectly dry.

She stared at him for a moment. "So, do you leave the water behind?"

He bobbed.

"What if some water got under one of your feathers, would it be brought along?"

He shook himself.

"How does your magic know what to bring and what to leave behind?"

He turned his head, meeting her gaze with both of his eyes.

"Right, much too complex a question."

Terry chirped once, shimmied slightly, and settled down on her shoulder.

Tala smiled, unlocking both doors into the room and pushing open the one that lead outside. "To Mistress Holly's shop, we go!"

The short walk passed by with reading and flicks of jerky for Terry, her eyes also nearly constantly looking for a source of food. The jerky she also just ate wasn't enough, though it helped. *I'm glad I have so much of that, now… What am I going to do when I run out?* She gave the bird a glance out of the corner of her eye.

He seems content, and I guess he can't really hurt me. Could I stop him if he decided to kill one of these people we're passing? She was quite uncomfortable with the obvious answer. *I suppose that's something to work on…*

She had a brief mental flash of Terry eviscerating everyone on the street with his previously demonstrated efficiency. *That would be… a lot of blood.* She swallowed involuntarily, and Terry popped open an eye, regarding her.

"Glad to have you on my shoulder, Terry."

The bird cocked his head, regarding her. She had no idea what he was thinking, but regardless, he closed his eyes again, settling back down.

I think he's actually made himself smaller than before. To better fit my shoulder? She didn't know. *I wonder what his range is. Could he become as small as a finger?* Might be worth it to figure out, but it wasn't like it would matter in the end.

She returned her attention to one of Holly's books and passed the remainder of the walk without distractingly macabre thoughts.

Tala was almost to the warehouse when she finally spotted a little eatery. *Yes!*

This establishment seemed to specialize in soups, and she almost groaned in pleasure as she stepped through the door. The overpowering ecstasy of scents washed over her, and she felt a bit weak.

"Mistress? Are you alright?" The proprietor was a middle-aged woman, a look of concern obvious on her prettier-than-average face.

"I'm just very hungry. What's your most filling soup?"

The woman nodded with a smile. "We have a sweet-potato cream chowder with bacon, along with other vegetables, spices, and meats, for a perfect medley of flavor."

Didn't I eat something like that on my trip? "That sounds wonderful! How much for…" She thought for a long moment. "A gallon?"

The woman smiled but seemed a bit bemused. "A gallon, Mistress?"

"As I said, I'm *very* hungry."

"Let… Let me ask." The woman turned, walking towards the kitchen. "Brand! How much for a gallon of the sweet-potato chowder?"

Brand? No way.

A familiar voice responded from the kitchen. "We don't usually sell it by the gallon. Are they looking for a discount, ordering the same soup for the whole group?"

"No, dear. I believe she wants it for herself."

"Herself? No…" The expected figure of a man came from the back room and stopped in the doorway, a wide grin blossoming on his face. "Mistress Tala! I didn't expect to see you in my shop."

"Brand? You have a wife?"

His smile slipped, the man stopping for a moment, color rushing over his face. "Of course I do! I told you so. Didn't I?"

His wife was frowning at him. "What's this now?"

Tala quirked a smile. "We had a misunderstanding, and when he thought I was going to kill him, he said he had a family as he begged for his life."

Brand frowned, grumpily. "That's not a very dignified way to express it."

"Inaccurate?"

He hesitated, then sighed. "No..."

Tala found herself grinning. "You know, I should have asked where you worked, when you weren't on the road, but the idea didn't cross my mind."

Brand shook himself, his good humor returning. "So, a gallon of soup? What, are you on a diet?"

His wife's eyes widened in obvious horror, but Tala laughed. "When the food's not free, I can't eat as much as I would like."

Brand nodded, understanding. "Too true. Well..." He seemed to be considering. "One and a half silver seem reasonable?"

Tala shrugged. "Looks like a cup would be a bit more than ten copper, so yeah. Sounds good to me." She smiled.

Brand's wife looked back and forth, then shook her head. "No, Brand. This is Mistress Tala, from the caravan?"

Brand nodded.

"Then, she should get two gallons for that price, at least this first time. We can charge her the regular price when she comes by later."

Tala's smile widened. "That is very kind of you, but I'm not sure I can eat two gallons. Also, I don't think we've been introduced. I am Tala."

The woman gave a slight bow. "You may call me Lissa, Mistress."

"A pleasure to meet you, Lissa."

Tala spent a few minutes talking with the two as Lissa served up the soup. They decided that Tala should eat at one of the tables off to the side, and so, she was given a large bowl, which was refilled as needed.

As Lissa placed down the first bowl, she spoke softly to Tala, then winked. "I simply must see if what my husband said about your capacity for food is true."

Tala felt a little embarrassed, but it had gotten her a bunch of extra food, so…

Several other customers came and went as Tala ate, but it wasn't a very busy time, being about mid-to-late-afternoon. Finally, Tala pushed her bowl back, scraped clean for the last time. "Amazing. Thank you."

Brand had returned to the kitchen some time ago, but Lissa smiled happily. "I'm glad you enjoyed." She set down a large jug with the amount she couldn't finish contained within.

Did I really eat more than a gallon? Tala stood, Terry appearing back on her shoulder from the other chair where he'd been curled up. "I definitely did. Say goodbye to Brand for me!" She slipped the jug into Kit and set her used bowl and spoon into the dirty dish bin off to one side.

"I will. Take care, Mistress. We look forward to seeing you again soon."

Tala gave a slight bow. "Definitely."

Back out on the street, Tala stretched expansively. *No more delays.* Her hunger had been addressed, at least for the moment, and she felt truly stuffed. Her strengthened abdominal muscles kept her from manifesting a food-baby, but she doubted she'd ever been this full before in her life. It was mildly irritating to feel like she could still eat more, from a hunger perspective, even if she really didn't have the internal room. She'd even eaten relatively slowly, taking nearly an hour and a half to eat everything. *At least I have almost another gallon, for after my stomach empties.*

A short walk later, she was at Holly's building. Tala entered the warehouse and was met by one of Holly's assistants. "Mistress Tala! Welcome. I'm to take you back to Mistress Holly." The woman hesitated. "Umm… May I pet your bird? He's quite cute."

Tala glanced to Terry. The terror bird's eyes had opened, and he was regarding the woman with what seemed to be curiosity. "Will you behave, Terry?"

He looked at Tala briefly, then gave a slight bob.

"If you wish? Just one pet, though; I don't want to overwhelm him."

The assistant smiled happily and gave Terry a slow stroke from the top of his head to the end of his short tail. "He's so soft!" The woman stepped back and gave a slight bow. "Thank you. Right this way."

Holly was waiting, with her contraption, in a back room.

"Ahh! Good, you're here. How far did you get in your reading?"

Tala thanked the assistant, who left with surprising alacrity. She then detailed to Holly which organs and systems she'd finished brushing up on.

"Hmmm… Good, good. Then, let's begin!"

"One moment…" Tala had been thinking and needed to ask. "How did you come up with this device, and make it functional, so quickly? I wasn't even gone a full two weeks."

"Hmm? Oh, we've had things *like* this for years. The Constructionists use a less precise version for inscribing softer materials." She smiled happily to herself. "They use my needle design all the time." She shook her head. "No, this is just the perfecting of that and alteration for using on souled entities."

Millennial Mage, 3 - Binding

So… I'm being worked on by industrial equipment. That wasn't quite right. *But, Tala, it's been modified for human use.* Tala sat on a stool with a sigh, lifting her arms above her head; Terry stretched out in a corner; and Holly slipped the expanded automatic inscriber over Tala's upraised arms, settling it around her torso.

"Now, I've modified the device to monitor your breathing and pulse and anything else that might displace or shift your insides. That way it can account for movements or slight variations. I don't want to have to knock you out again, after all. Even so, you need to remain as still as possible. Do you understand?"

Tala nodded. *Okay, Tala, you can do this.*

"Begin."

* * *

Ten minutes later, they were done, and the weird, internal-swelling pain was already a mere memory.

Tala stood, and the inscription machine was removed. Her stomach felt… odd somehow. Given they'd done her digestive system as part of this session, that wasn't unexpected. *Is it processing the food faster?* That was the intention, but she hadn't expected to feel it working. "Why did that take so much longer?"

"It had to work slower to account for your movements, both voluntary and involuntary."

Tala shrugged. *I suppose that makes sense.* "So, you wanted to discuss my idea for inscriptions in my mouth, throat, and lungs?"

Holly nodded, pulling out a tablet. "Yes, yes. They would have to be additional to those we'll add tomorrow. I worked up a schema." She handed over the tablet, showing a brief description of how it would function. "Basically, it will maintain the coherence of any spell-form or magic within your mouth, throat, or lungs, keep it from activating or penetrating deeper, and forcibly expel it when you exhale. That should prevent anyone from affecting you magically via the air you breathe, unless they can entirely overpower you, regardless. Those we just gave you on your digestive system already protect you against intrusions on that front, both mundane and magical."

Tala was nodding. "I think I'd like that. Yes."

Holly gave her a long look. "Why do I get the feeling you are going to do something marginally insane if I give you these inscriptions?"

Tala thought for a moment. *Why not tell her?* "Well, I did figure out that I can create spell-forms within my lungs, so long as I am holding my breath. I was hoping I could use these to help in the stabilization and expulsion of such."

Holly stared at her for a long moment, then started laughing.

Tala frowned at the woman.

Holly pulled up a stool, sat, and got herself under control.

Tala rolled her eyes and waited.

"Mistress Tala…" Holly shook her head. "My dear, the spell-forms required to create a specific effect would change depending on the exact composition of the air. It could be different from one breath to the next!" She shook her head again. "No, it *would* be different from one breath to the next, would vary if you held your breath for a different length of time, would be dependent on your heart rate, and so many other factors."

"So, you're saying it's impossible?"

"Impossible? No, not really. I've written scripts that analyze and calculate exactly what spell-forms need to be used before infusing a Mage's breath upon exhale, but they are *devilishly* complex, not to mention expensive. You are talking about doing that *manually*." She shook her head.

"And before you ask, no, I can't give you those inscriptions. They would take up a large chunk of your flesh, so we'd have to remove some of the vital, interlinking inscriptions for your other functions."

Tala frowned. "Couldn't I learn how to make it work manually?"

Holly held up a hand, palm down, waggling it back and forth. "With practice, and I mean a *lot* of practice, you could probably get to the point of creating a general effect with reasonable consistency, but it would never be something I'd advise you to count on."

Tala thought for a long moment, then shrugged. "Well, I'll try, so long as you don't think it will kill me."

"Oh, this won't kill you, directly. What I predict is you'll practice and think yourself 'good enough.' Then, you'll depend on the skill in a moment of crisis, and it will fail."

"I never planned to rely on it. I just wanted another tool."

Holly waved her off. "The scripts I'll give you will be useful, regardless. If you wish to practice this oddity, be my guest, but it will never be a reliable tool." After a moment's consideration, Holly shrugged. "If you do choose to go this route, which I again state is insane, I suggest first learning mastery of sensing the composition of the air in your lungs. That would be a good foundation."

Tala frowned. "I can do that?"

"Not yet. That's why you need to learn and practice it."

Tala rolled her eyes. "You know, that reminds me, Mistress Holly: When I tried to look up the spell-form modifications for air, it stated that that was the realm of Archons. Does that mean this won't be a limit once I take that step?"

Holly scrunched up her face in irritation, then shook her head. "No, not really. Archons often work effects into the air around them, such as shielding their aura from observation. That is likely what was meant. Air around us is much more consistent than air drawn into our lungs."

Something about Holly's demeanor made Tala think that that wasn't all entirely true, but she decided not to press for the moment. *I suppose the core of it makes sense, regardless.* "Well, it will be an interesting thing to try."

"Your other insanities have worked out better than I'd have foreseen. So, who knows? Maybe you'll dazzle me again."

Tala smiled, slightly, at the compliment, whether intentional or otherwise.

"And these scripts should keep you from killing yourself with your experimentation."

And good feeling gone…

"Now, go eat something, dear. Your body is screaming its need for sustenance."

She frowned. *I do feel pretty hungry… What happened to the gallon of soup? Has it already been processed?* "How can you tell?"

"Now that I've re-established the link, whenever you enter this building, and while you remain in it, the script on the back of your neck connects to my central archive, updating me on how your inscriptions have functioned, as well as how you've been doing overall. You obviously know that it will keep me informed of your status or it wouldn't work."

Tala sighed. *Yet again, I underestimate what's been done to me.* "Very well. Thank you, Mistress Holly."

"Hmmm? Oh, sure thing, dear."

Chapter: 6
Yay, Me...

Tala was turning to leave Holly's workshop, and Terry had already flickered up to her shoulder, when Holly grunted.

"I forgot. For your other hand, I want to do something a bit more esoteric for you. It will require practice, but it should be incredibly useful if you can make it work."

Tala turned back towards the Mage. *The Archon.* "Harder to use than my current offensive scripts?"

"Yes. By quite a bit, actually."

"Harder than creating spell-forms in my lungs?"

Holly gave her a flat look. "Don't be tiresome."

Tala found herself smiling. "Do tell."

"I want you to have a constantly-active, gravity-manipulation inscription."

Tala blinked. "That sounds… dangerous? My current offensive abilities are locked behind a hand gesture."

"If you need that crutch for a while, I can incorporate it, but I think, eventually, we can get it to a simple state of mind. Your cognitive and nervous system enhancements should be able to sustain that."

Tala frowned. "Let's keep it locked behind a hand gesture for now, but I think I like the idea of something a bit more utilitarian."

"It will, by necessity, be weaker than your crushing attack, especially after we enhance that, and much less precise than your restrain, at least at first, but I think that, in the end, you might lose the need for those pre-scripted functions."

"Alright. I'll give it a try." *She's an Archon, after all. I should listen to those wiser than me... when I can.*

Holly nodded, smiling. "I'll finalize the scripts then, and we'll add them tomorrow." She turned back to the slate in her hand.

Tala found herself frowning, looking at the back of her hand. *Wait a moment.* "Mistress Holly? Where are the detailed scripts for my crush and restrain? I don't exactly have much of me free and open for such workings."

"Hmmm? Oh, the bulk of those are in your right breast."

Tala blinked at her a few times. "What?"

"The three-dimensional scripts that enact the specifics of those effects reside within the tissue of your right breast. I'll be putting this new one in your left. Activation scripts and most of the metal reserves are, and will be, in your hands, of course."

"But..." Tala frowned. "Why there?"

"Well, around the regenerative inscriptions, you had room. I saw no need to fundamentally alter the internal workings of the tissue there." She quirked a smile. "Even when you have young children, we don't need to radically increase your ability to produce and hold milk, and I assumed that you didn't want your breasts to feel like someone had strapped rocks to your chest, so stiffening and strengthening the internal structures was unnecessary. Hence, free space for your other workings."

Tala didn't really know how to process that. "I... suppose that makes a sort of sense."

"Good,"—Holly responded in a monotone—"I'm glad you approve of my work. Now, I'm very busy, and you aren't my only project. Be off with you and eat something." After a moment, she elaborated. "Eat a lot of somethings. You read the book. Your digestive system will be able to hold and process much more, far more efficiently. I want you to test its limits. Goodbye." With that, she turned and sat at a workbench, continuing her work across several slates.

Tala shrugged and departed, Terry a comfortable weight on her shoulder.

Having finished with Holly for the day, Tala made her way back through the city to acquire another food log from the restaurant at which she'd eaten lunch. It wasn't a long walk, and she used the time to contemplate her new inscriptions, along with Holly's thoughts and ideas. No breakthroughs presented themselves, but Tala felt better for having taken the time.

When she arrived at the eatery, following Holly's promptings, Tala bought two of the delicious things. *How have I already processed all that chowder...?* She had to laugh at herself. She hadn't even considered the fact that she had been filling up her stomach before it was to be inscribed. *I'm glad I didn't puke again. That would have been wasteful.*

Thankfully, that hadn't happened, and now she felt empty and hungry once again. The new inscriptions in her digestive system were efficient it seemed.

Wait... One of the inscriptions was to prevent the vomiting of non-toxic food... Was that one activated first? That would be just like Holly.

She caught a whiff of the food sitting before her and returned her attention to the meal.

Terry watched with what Tala interpreted as slight amusement as she devoured both 'Little Caravans.' Tala even used the remainder of the chowder as a drink, to wash down the food logs.

"What are you looking at, bird? I've seen you eat so much more than this."

Millennial Mage, 3 - Binding

Terry shook himself, almost seeming to roll his eyes before he stretched out in the last vestiges of evening light.

Tala found herself smiling. *This is sooooo good.* To her delight, she found that she still felt a bit hungry, even after she finished. *I get to eat more?* She hesitated, the implications sinking in. *Well, this isn't going to be very good for my money pouch...* It seemed that the free food on caravan ventures might be a more valuable perk than she'd ever guessed. *Though, I should slow down eventually, right?*

The inscriptions in her body's storage mechanisms were similar to those on her muscles. Her fat could store dozens of times more calories without changing size, and she would need all of it. Her regenerative inscriptions pulled from those stores, and the scripts were interlinked so that her healing wouldn't be dependent on biological mechanisms to get the needed energy and compounds from her stores to the part of her in need of healing.

Eat more, survive more. She grinned. *I'm my own regenerative potion. I just need to be sure to stay topped off.* That was proving more problematic than she would have expected. *If only such potions weren't just the stuff of myth...* She hesitated. *Well, endingberries seem to be behind some legends, maybe something else is behind healing and regenerative potions?*

She could go in search of the origin of those myths... but now was hardly the time. Needing more food, she wandered the area near the restaurant and bought a large selection of inexpensive foods. *Another silver spent.*

She was torn, obviously. She needed to be saving up to pay off her debts, but she also knew that if she encountered something truly dangerous to her, a few extra calories in her system could keep her alive. *My debts don't matter if I'm dead...* She decided not to camp on the uncomfortably comforting thought.

In the end, she decided that she would allow herself the budget to eat six robust feasts a day, instead of three light meals, as she had been accustomed to before these changes.

So, three silvers a day, then. When not in a caravan. It was a painfully large amount when she contemplated it. Even after she realized that she'd spent more than that this day, without much consideration. *Easier to spend in the moment than with intention, I suppose.*

She licked her fingers clean of her last purchase—a deep-fried pastry that had been filled with a heavy, savory cream sauce. *Delicious.*

With a satisfied sigh, she turned towards home. *I need to do my practice, and there's really no good place to do it within the city.* Maybe the guards would let her use a space off to the side, so she wouldn't get in anyone's way? It was worth asking.

Some of those auxiliary buildings looked unused this morning. Maybe I could use one of those.

Terry seemed content to snap up the oft-tossed pieces of jerky as Tala meandered home. He hadn't been willing to eat the other food she'd offered him. *In time, Terry. I will teach you the amazingness of all human food.* That got her thinking about Terry, in general.

"Do you need exercise, Terry?"

The bird regarded her for a moment, then blinked away and back, allowing a little longer delay than usual to ensure she noticed.

"That is exercise to you?"

He bobbed a nod.

"Huh. Good to know, I guess." She smiled. "Sorry to make you sprint for treats."

He let out a vibrating almost-whistle: soft, low, and pleasantly melodic.

"Don't mind, eh?"

He shook himself, settling back down.

"Fair enough." She pulled out the current book for review and filled the last of the walk with silent reading.

* * *

Tala sat on the floor of her room, her body pleasantly worked and stretched.

Now, let's see what difference there is with Flow.

She drew the knife but remained seated.

She tossed the weapon at the wall before her and immediately called it back. As if on a string, the knife jerked to a stop and whipped back into her waiting grasp.

Tala grinned. *Yes!* It felt so much easier than before.

What followed was a series of fast throws and retrievals. She tried calling the knife back and moving her hand out of the way, but the weapon unerringly came into her grasp.

She could change which hand it came to, and she could even cause it to slap into any part of her that she wished, but she couldn't cause it to miss or fly past her. *So, I can't use this as a method for propelling it into an attack...*

Or could she?

She searched around until she found a cutting board in Lyn's kitchen; the other Mage wasn't home, yet.

The knife rested on the living room table as Tala held the cutting board over her right palm. *Here it goes!*

She pulled the knife to her right hand.

The weapon whipped across the intervening space and *thunked* into the cutting board, driving its point in and sticking in place.

That was effective. She frowned. *Well, if it didn't strike with enough force to go through the cutting board, it probably wouldn't penetrate an arcanous creature very deeply.* So, still not an effective weaponization of the ability. *I'll have to think of something else.*

She continued her soul workout until she started to feel weary in that regard. *Okay. Let's not overtax.*

She returned to her room, sheathing the knife and sitting back down on the floor.

Alright, let's test for an Archon Star. She began to gather power in her finger, just as she'd done before. As she did so, she made sure to pull from her gate, not from the reserves in her body.

It felt painfully slow—glacially so. *What's happening?* At this rate, it would take her days to do what she had been accomplishing in earlier attempts. She examined the flows within herself, finding that her power was being tapped to empower her myriad inscriptions. That wasn't new—she'd noticed it when empowering the cargo-slots that morning—but there were now more than ever, and they were essentially all active, even if not all currently working.

She didn't even bother making the Archon Star spell-form because she could tell that she just didn't have the available power flow. *I could pull from my reserves. That should make an effective star.* But the goal wasn't to make more stars like she had. She wanted to make a full-powered star, and her reserves were not sufficient for that task.

I could direct the entirety of my flow into the star. But that would cause her inscriptions to drain her reserves. It wouldn't be a quick drain, but neither was the making of a star.

Growling, she released what little power she had gathered back into the natural flows within herself. She needed to increase her power accumulation rate. *Okay. My soul is exercised, so I should be able to stretch it now.* She smiled determinedly to herself. *Yes, because my soul is a muscle and must conform to all I think I know about strengthening those.*

She shook her head, closing her eyes. *It's worth a shot or at least a look.*

She turned her magesight inward, focusing on her gate. To the best of her knowledge, that was the approximate location of the physical manifestation of her soul. *How have I never done this before?*

Distractions fell away as she narrowed her intent on the keystone inscription, surrounding her gate, and slowly, she moved inward, doing her utmost to examine the source of her magic.

* * *

Tala found herself bodyless, her perspective floating in a clearing within a wooded valley. Before her towered a colossal mountain.

She knew that she was still sitting on the floor of her room, but the experience *felt* real.

Within her vision, she found herself inexorably drawn forward, towards the base of the nearby mountain.

The trees were old-growth and lusciously beautiful. Their dark green canopy created a stunning, swaying green tint to the light.

The undergrowth was sparse, and she didn't see any animals.

After a short minute of movement, Tala came out of the forest and saw the base of the largest mountain, rising as a cliff from the valley floor. Set in the base of the cliff was a deep, wide pool. Set deep within that pool was what looked like a huge vault door, which currently hung open.

From the opening, water gushed forth, filling the pool from within and causing it to spill out into the valley, nurturing the growth therein.

Why is there a door? I never want it closed... The door was thrown wide, but even so, its mere presence seemed to restrict the flow somewhat.

Investigate first, Tala. She looked to the bubbling stream of water and followed it through the valley, away from the mountain and the pool.

Within this vision, the water was fast flowing, and it quickly split into countless streams, each splitting further until the main trunk of the waterway was minuscule. The side paths continued to diverge and diminish until they simply ended, the liquid absorbed fully into the fertile ground.

She returned to the central flow and followed it to the other end of the valley. There, the barest hint of a waterfall trickled out into the world outside.

"Fair enough, I suppose. That's what I already understood." She almost laughed. *Of course my mental map of my magic is going to follow my understanding of such. Did you expect differently, Tala?*

With a simple thought, she was back at the pool and the vault door.

Her presence dipped into the pool, and she felt the buzz of energy from the liquid around her. *My reservoir of power.*

She approached the door, examining it for a long moment.

"So, this is dumb and unneeded." She examined the hinges, and to her surprise, she found that they seemed to have a simple mechanism to release the heavy contraption of metal to allow it to fall away. *Well, I was just going to look, but this seems designed to detach.*

"No, Tala. That would be foolish. Don't go messing around with your power."

It's right there! It's designed for me to do this.

"Why? Why would it be designed to allow such?"

Because I want it to be...

"Exactly. So, is this wise?"

Yes.

"Why?"

Because our magic functions based on our understanding, and that mechanism is a representation of my understanding. Therefore, it will function as I believe that it will.

There was actually some logic to that. Tala groaned. "Fine. Fair enough."

Besides, if it fails and I die, I'm done. Debt gone; problems solved.

She decided it was best not to follow that train of thought.

Strangely, she had the odd sensation that she actually had this type of conversation with herself quite often but usually didn't pay this close attention.

She gave a mental shrug and reached forward and activated the mechanism.

The hinges popped open, the force of the water knocking the door away. It instantly vanished, dissolving as if it had never been.

The newly freed portion of the opening into the mountain allowed for a marginal increase of flow into her reservoir.

Tala began to scream.

*   *   *

Tala found herself writhing on her back, pain lancing outward from all across her keystone inscription. Heat like a bonfire radiated from her skin, and a deep tearing sensation caused her vision to fuzz. She was utterly unable to make a sound or even draw breath. *I thought I was screaming?* That must have just been an inner manifestation.

Even so, she soon heard the sound of running feet.

Lyn burst into the room, Terry beside her.

The other woman dropped to her knees beside Tala, wiping something away from the latter's mouth. "Tala! What's going on? Talk to me!" She turned Tala's head to the side, but Tala already knew she wouldn't vomit despite the agony.

Tala met Lyn's gaze but couldn't speak. Instead, she arched and clawed towards her own back.

Seeming to understand something from the flailing, Lyn forced Tala to sit up, having to leverage her up from above her head, then push her forward into a slumped, seated position from behind. She then stripped off Tala's top. The elk leather seemed to know that Tala wanted it away because it came off without difficulty. Tala didn't know if Lyn even undid the ties first.

Lyn gasped. "Tala, what's going on? Your keystone… Parts of it look like they're melting." As if in response to Lyn's words, Tala heard liquid dripping onto the floor, along with a strange hissing. "Tala, you're bleeding and leaking metal. It's hot enough to boil the blood." Lyn was surprisingly calm, all things considered. "What do I do?"

Tala could feel her inscriptions working, already healing her skin and the deeper tissue as well, even as new portions were burned open, more metal expelled. *Why is it getting through the defenses?* She could feel the active defensive scripts on her back. It didn't do anything to prevent what was occurring. She finally managed to pull in a breath and gasped out. "Holly."

Lyn nodded and tried to stand, carrying Tala.

She failed.

Lyn struggled to lower Tala back to the floor, on her side this time, then ran towards the door. She hesitated in the doorway, looking back at Tala. "I'll be as fast as I can."

Tala couldn't muster a reply from where she lay.

A moment later, Lyn was gone, and Tala was alone in her agony.

Well, not completely alone. Terry came over to hunker down next to her face. Somehow, he looked concerned. *How can I interpret emotions on an avian face?* Well, she could, so now was hardly the time to analyze it.

She felt unable to move, barely able to think. It was as if something was digging into her back, paralyzing her, locking her in place.

Over the next half-hour, the pain moved across her keystone in waves, the damage always healing shortly after the bits of metal were expelled.

At long last, Tala groaned, able to move once more. She rolled onto her stomach, putting her tear-covered face to the floor. The stone was cold on the bare skin of her chest and abdomen, erratically interspersed with the wetness of drying blood and oddly smooth lumpiness of now cooled bits of metal.

A few minutes later, she heard the front door open, and Holly and Lyn came in with quick steps.

They hesitated in the doorway, and there was a long pause before the two women stepped in. One—Lyn, if Tala had to guess—waited just inside Tala's room, the other circled her on the floor.

Like a vulture. Tala didn't feel like lifting her head.

"Child. What have you done to your keystone?" She continued to circle. "It looks like all portions for closing your gate have been removed."

Lyn, who was near the door, took in a sharp breath.

Holly grunted. "Those portions weren't really needed for her, anyway, but I'd planned on simply letting them fade. What did you do?" she repeated.

Tala groaned, again. Her head was turned to the side now, but her hair covered her face. She spoke through that impediment. "I was examining my gate with my magesight, and I noticed that the ability to close it off was restricting the flow. So, I took the door off its hinges."

Holly laughed mirthlessly. "Mistress Tala. Magic works on intent and ability. In effect, you caused your body and magic to reject that portion of the inscription. Your power and flesh then worked to remove it, so it could no longer act upon you."

Tala grunted. "There was an obvious mechanism for removing the door. Why would it be there if I wasn't supposed to or it would be harmful?"

"Did you want it removed?"

Tala grunted. *Oh...* "Is this unusual?"

"No, it is quite common in those who haven't gone through academy training, especially if their inscriber doesn't ensure compatibility before laying the spell-forms. It *is* unusual for a fully trained Mage to be foolish enough, however."

She groaned, again. "Yay, me."

"You are lucky that you aren't a Material Creator. When they have a reaction like this..." She sighed. "The regeneration scripts have kept you whole, and your inscriptions seem to have kept their other functions intact. In this case, I will say don't worry. I could tell if they were otherwise broken. As usual, you've done something that would have seriously injured almost anyone else I've ever worked with."

Tala grunted. "Yay, me..."

Millennial Mage, 3 - Binding

"The process seems complete. Get yourself cleaned up, put on a shirt, and then we'll talk about *exactly* what happened. Yes?"

"Yes, Mistress Holly." She spoke into the floor and her own hair.

Holly didn't respond. Instead, she walked from the room, drawing Lyn after her.

Lyn spoke over her shoulder. "I'll get the bath heating, Tala."

Tala grunted her thanks.

The door was pulled closed, and she slowly pushed herself up.

Her front was liberally speckled with dried blood, and bits of metal were held to her skin by the crusty red adhesive. She sighed, brushing it off. The sensation was oddly satisfying. As she moved, she felt similarly encrusted portions on her back. *Probably more, there…*

She heard the water running in the bath room across the hall. It cut off shortly after.

So, not a full bath, just enough for me to get cleaned up. That made sense, she supposed.

She gathered up her elk skin tunic and crossed the empty hall. The small amount of water in the tub was already warmed by the small fire beneath.

Chapter: 7
Already Lost to the World

Tala came out of her quick wash in less than five minutes. The small amount of water had heated quickly, so she'd put out the fire before she'd even gotten into the tub.

She took a moment to clean up the blood from her floor and gather the bits of gold, putting them in a small cloth and storing it within Kit. *I'll have to get them changed back into currency… Or maybe Holly can use them?*

Now clean once more, dry, and fully dressed, Tala sat in the living room with Lyn and Holly.

The two women listened intently as Tala told them what had led up to her body's rejection of a portion of her inscriptions, and they both sat in thought for long minutes after she had finished.

Finally, Tala was sick of the silence. "Well?"

Holly looked up to her. "Well, what?"

"Did I break something? Should I avoid looking at my gate with my magesight? What?"

Holly sighed. "Technically, you broke a portion of your keystone, and it was expelled, but I think you knew that. Otherwise, from what I could see, you seem to have left everything else intact and functional. I did already tell you that."

"Why didn't my defensive scripts prevent me from bleeding or my skin from breaking open?"

"Simple answer? Because those defensive measures function by keeping your body working normally. Your body's expulsion of a foreign, unwanted material was a normal function—or as close to it as could be. So your magics had nothing to work against."

"So… I'm not protected against my own body killing me?"

Holly shrugged. "I don't actually know. I'm not sure what extent would have been allowed, but I doubt that you could have actually died."

Tala grunted and then pulled out the bits of gold. "Can you use these?"

Holly took the cloth in which Tala presented them, looking at the red-stained pieces. She sighed. "I'll clean them and weigh them. I'll give you a fair price, tomorrow afternoon."

Tala smiled. "Works for me."

Lyn looked up then, clearly a bit stressed. "I need to know: Why are you doing experiments here? It's really unpleasant to continually find you in some form of distress…" She sighed. "Don't misunderstand me, I'm glad that I was here, and that I could help, but…" She glanced away.

"I'm sorry, Lyn. I don't really have another place to practice, yet. I think I'll have one, starting tomorrow, but"—she frowned—"where do Mages go to practice, generally?"

The two other women looked at each other, then back to Tala, speaking in seemingly unplanned unison. "The Wilds."

They both smiled slightly. Tala grunted. "Fair, I suppose… I'd rather not have to walk out beyond the city every day just to practice…"

Holly's smile grew. "Honestly, it depends on what you want to practice. Healers, regardless of quadrant, have plenty of places they can practice, and so do most Material Mages, either Creators or Guides. Mostly, though?" She shrugged. "It's on missions. Inscriptions are too expensive to burn through for practice alone."

"I'm not using my inscriptions to practice."

"And the best Mages do likewise, but in the Wilds."

Tala sighed. "Fair enough. I might have a place I can go. It's one of the Guardsman's Guild training grounds." She then frowned. *Speaking of the guards...* "Mistress Holly, how do the guards use magic?"

Holly took a moment, seeming to consider before she answered. "All creatures, humans included, use magic almost constantly. It helps the being accomplish their goals and augments their physicality—if just slightly." Holly was nodding to herself. "As the magic acts, it flows through the flesh and leaves an impression. With enough repetition, that impression becomes a pathway through which magic flows more easily. If the being, in this case a human, knows what they are trying to do, that satisfies the requirement for a mental construct. Thus, they have a form, a mental construct, and their own power."

"The requirements to work magic."

"Precisely."

"But they aren't inscribed."

"They don't need to be. They aren't doing anything unnatural, so the body can be the template for the working. There would be no way for one of them to, say, manifest a gravity manipulation; there simply isn't any basis within the human body to even begin to create those spell-forms."

"So, without inscriptions, we can't do anything unnatural?"

Holly hesitated, then shook her head, sighing. "There are records of ancient warriors, burning themselves over and over again, very precisely and under incredibly controlled conditions, to imprint the pathways for heat and fire within themselves. From what I've gathered, it was only possible with healers nearby, whether herbal, alchemical, or magical. It wasn't often successful, and it usually resulted in horrible disfigurement." She smiled ruefully. "Inscriptions bypass that need. It's expensive and has to be maintained and refreshed regularly, but it works exactly as intended."

Like Emi. Her body's natural magical pathways perfectly mirrored the magic of her inscriptions. Tala's eyes widened in realization. "Then, wouldn't the inscriptions become unnecessary in time?"

Holly shrugged. "Yes, and no. As the pathways settle into the body, that allows the power to flow more efficiently, thus the effects created can be greater. Eventually, the inscriptions wouldn't be needed, but without them, the potency of the spell-forms would radically decrease. Few are willing to make that trade-off, especially since most who are Mages for that long have the available funds to spend on inscriptions, and it does help." She smiled. "Also, Mages are prone to change their inscriptions fairly often. That is a flexibility afforded to us by inscriptions. Without the consistency and long-term application of specific magics, the body cannot form sufficient natural pathways for the magic to function bio-magically, without inscription."

That's why she wanted to get me transitioned over and settled on my new schema so quickly. "Is there any way to speed up the process?"

"Of course. Spell-forms that are always active 'set' faster. Otherwise, using them as often as possible builds the paths."

"But Mages don't really practice in that way."

"It is quite expensive."

After a moment, Tala nodded. "That's why you wanted my scripts to be always active?"

"One reason, yes. Your scripts lend themselves to being active at all times, as well."

"Well… thank you?"

Holly smiled. "We'll get you all sorted. I'm happy to help. You are a very interesting specimen, and I expect to have learned a lot from you before we're through. Especially after you become an Archon."

Lyn sighed, interjecting for the first time in a little while. "I knew it. This has something to do with that stupid spell-form, too, doesn't it?"

Holly glanced to the woman. "What do you mean?"

Lyn shrugged. "My master, before I left her charge, showed me the spell-form for an Archon Star. She said I should work my way through her practice exercises until I could create a stable star within a material. She said a lot more, but it always seemed pretty useless to me."

Holly blinked owlishly at the Mage. "You… Your master recommended you for the path of Archon, and you haven't pursued making an Archon Star."

"Didn't seem useful."

"Are you aware that that's how you become an Archon?"

"Of course. I'm not an idiot. If I became an Archon, I'd have to be moved to upper logistical positions. I like my work as I am."

Holly's eye twitched. "You don't have to accept further positions if you don't want to. You won't receive an Archon's pay, in all likelihood, but that doesn't seem to bother you."

"But what's the point?"

Holly opened her mouth and closed it several times. Finally, she rubbed her forehead with one palm. "To improve! To get better. To—" She cut herself off and groaned. "There is *so* much that cannot be even attempted until you are an Archon. Please, for the love of all that shines, work on your star, Mistress Lyn."

Lyn let out a weary sigh. "Fine, if you think it's so important."

"It is." Holly rubbed her temples. "How many worthy Mages haven't ascended because they saw no point?" She let out a low growl. "The current policies are maddening."

Tala quirked a smile. "So… why do they exist?"

Holly smiled sadly. "Because it is better to lose out on a few potential Archons than to have hundreds of perfectly adequate Mages kill themselves attempting to ascend."

Lyn cleared her throat. "So… no. Then, I'm not doing it."

Holly practically ground her teeth. "If your master thought enough of you that she taught you about Archon Stars, then you are capable, and the danger is minuscule."

"But it still exists?"

Holly threw up her hands. "You could choke and die on a grape. Yes, there is still danger. What are you, thirteen?"

"I'm thirty-six."

Holly gave Lyn an incredibly patronizing look.

Tala frowned. "Wait… you're thirty-six?"

"Yes? How old did you think I was?" Lyn had a quizzical look on her face.

Tala shrunk down in her seat, just a bit. "Like… twenty-five?"

Lyn barked a laugh, and Holly snorted in amusement. "Well, I suppose I should be flattered? My mother looked twenty at fifty, and she wasn't even a Mage, so I suppose I shouldn't be surprised…"

She's thirty-six? Tala didn't really know how to handle that. *She could almost be my mother…*

Holly closed her eyes for a long moment, breathing deeply. "As entertaining as this has been, I need to go. I'm in the middle of quite a few things." She looked to Tala. "I'm glad you didn't die. Work towards your star." She turned to Lyn. "You won't die from this. Work towards your star." She narrowed her eyes, looking back and forth between the two women until they both nodded, Tala easily, Lyn reluctantly. "Good." She stood. "Goodbye."

Without another word, the woman departed.

"Well... that was something." Tala smiled at Lyn. "So, thirty-six?"

"As far as I know. I am flattered that you thought me so much younger than I am."

Tala dropped her gaze, a bit uncertain about where to take the conversation. *Archon Stars. That should be safe.* "Do you know what material you're going to use?"

Lyn frowned. "You, too?" Her frown faded to a look of defeat. "Fine... my understanding is that diamond is an easy medium, and I can probably get one fairly inexpensively." She glanced Tala's way. "Do you need one, too? Or are you using a different material?"

Tala looked away, clearing her throat. "A different material."

"Care to share?"

She hesitated, looking back. "Promise you won't try it? Or tell anyone else?"

Lyn shifted forward, a half-smile tugging at her lips. "Now I have to know. I won't tell, and I won't try it. I'm barely willing to try the easiest method I know of. Knowing you, you're doing something truly insane."

Tala quirked a smile at that. "You aren't wrong." She pulled out her iron vial, feeling the faint connection with the star inside. "Here. Be careful when you open it."

Lyn frowned but took the vial. She spun the cap free and stared inside. "Tala..."

"Yes?"

"That looks like blood."

"That's because it *is* blood."

"It's not dried. How did you keep it from drying?" She looked up but didn't leave space for Tala to answer. "Am I to understand that your intention is to make an Archon Star in blood?"

Tala nodded, opening her mouth, but Lyn kept talking.

"I was right. You're insane. Tala, that isn't possible. My master said that Archon Stars have to have a solid, dense medium."

"Use your magesight."

Lyn frowned but complied. "Did you modify the blood? Give it a structure that could…" She blinked in obvious confusion. "Tala?"

"Yes?"

"What is this?"

"A weak Archon Star."

Lyn's head snapped up. "This is an Archon Star."

"A weak one, yes. That's what I said."

"And you've already made it."

"You can see that I have."

"So, why aren't you an Archon?" She shook her head. "What am I saying…? You shouldn't be anywhere near becoming an Archon."

"It's too weak. I could probably force my way into being recognized, though I have no idea about the specifics of that, but it would hurt my position among other Archons… somehow. I need to make a stronger one, first." She shrugged. "Well, that's what I've been told… several times."

"Does Holly know about this?" She held the vial up, after placing the cap back on securely.

"She does. She is one of those who advised I work on making a stronger one."

"That's why she wants you to work on your star…" She was shaking her head. "You're insane."

"I didn't do it on purpose." Tala felt a bit petulant. *But it's true!*

Lyn laughed. "Of course you didn't."

Tala briefly explained how she'd come to form her first star.

After the tale, Lyn was smiling. "That is very you, Tala."

"I try?"

They both grinned at that. "Well, at least my life won't ever be boring with you around."

"So… you need to practice, and I need to do some experimenting… Can I do it here?"

Lyn gave her a long look. "If I say 'no,' you're going to go find an alley or someplace to do it in, anyway, aren't you?"

"Probably."

She groaned. "Fine. My master left me a set of exercises to work up to the creation of an Archon Star. I suppose I'll focus on those."

Tala perked up at that. "Oh?"

Lyn smiled, slightly. "More interesting than experimenting?"

"My experiments were attempting to pin down such exercises." *In a really, really roundabout way…*

"Well, let me get my old notebook and see what we can do."

*   *   *

Three hours later, Tala wasn't sweating, but she felt like she should be. The exercise was rigorous.

They had begun simply, the instructions short: draw all the power within her reserves away from her gate, creating a void around it. It was simple in concept but truly straining in practice.

Tala had an advantage at first, given her practice drawing her power away from the healing scripts in her finger, along with pulling back the endingberry power any time she needed to enact a transaction.

Lyn, being an Immaterial Creator, had a harder time manipulating her own internal magic in general, but she was quickly able to pick up the technique.

The result was amazing. The deficit in magic just around the gate caused a cavalcade of power to flow through, seemingly in an attempt to even out the levels. During that time, Tala estimated that her power flow was easily quadrupled, but she couldn't maintain it for more than a minute, at least not at first.

Lyn's master had said that the final stage of the exercise, which she should work towards, was to hold a small void of power around her gate at all times.

It was a daunting goal.

Lyn had managed three minutes on her first attempt, once she'd been able to manipulate her power enough to attempt it at all.

Was that because she's older? Less power-dense? Tala didn't know, and it didn't really matter.

They had spent the three hours tackling this single exercise. In the end, Tala could hold the void for ten minutes, Lyn for fifteen. It was growing late, and they were both mentally exhausted.

"That was nice." Tala smiled. "I'm not used to working beside someone else. Not on the same thing, at least."

Lyn smiled in return. "Yeah. I think I liked that quite a bit."

The house felt uniquely saturated in power. As neither of them had directed their increased flows of power into anything, it had simply flowed outward, dispersing into the air.

Tala could see a slow drain, pulling the power from the air and down into the ground. *Feeding the city.* Similarly, the items she carried seemed to be drinking in the magic from around them, at least those she could see.

"We've raised the power levels to near those around Alefast."

"Oh?" Lyn's magesight activated, and a wide grin spread across her face. "So we have."

"I should probably find something to do with the excess…"

Lyn rolled her eyes. "You don't need to be perfectly efficient, Tala."

"True, but if there's something easy that I can do?"

Lyn smiled, pulling out her notebook. "Well, the second step will likely solve that. I can tell you now?"

"Sure."

"At the moment, we are simply allowing the increased flow to fill us, the excess flowing away on its own."

Tala nodded.

"The next step is to control the increased inflow of power, splitting it in two. We are to divert the amount we usually use into our body and its inscriptions and send the rest outward."

"But… that's what we're doing already?"

Lyn shook her head. "Right now, we are allowing a river to flow into a leaky cup. Sure, most overflows, but what this is saying is that we want to direct a small portion of the river into the cup, just enough to maintain its level, and have the rest bypass the cup entirely."

Tala found herself nodding again. "And that excess can be directed into anything. This second step just lets it dissipate into the surrounding air, but I'd bet the third has us put it into something? A magic-bound item or…?"

Lyn looked back at her notes but was already nodding. "Precisely that. She recommended that once that was mastered, I should split the power into thirds." She met Tala's gaze, a serious expression apparent on her features.

"Don't rush this, Tala. We are nowhere near mastering even the first step. My master said I could move through the steps of this exercise when I believed I was ready, but I still want to be cautious." She closed the notebook. "She did say that the second, different exercise shouldn't be attempted until I could maintain the void every waking moment." She gave Tala a stern look. "That means I won't be letting you know what it is until then."

Tala chuckled. "Fair enough. But you should probably get a magic-bound item, so we aren't walking around dumping power into the city's air."

Lyn smiled at that. "That's probably true. I don't want the city watch to get irritated at unexpected fluctuations in the power matrices."

"We could take a trip back to Alefast, to get you an artifact."

She shook her head. "No, a simple item is better for me. I know I'll have to keep getting it re-inscribed, but I'll find something reasonable."

"As you wish. Oh! You could get an incorporator."

Lyn gave her a long look, then rolled her eyes. "I'll consider an incorporator, and I'll go with you to Alefast, but only after we're Archons. Not immediately, mind you, but sometime after."

"Deal!" Tala smiled at her friend, then let out a weary sigh. "But now, we should sleep."

"To sleep we go."

Tala hesitated, realizing something. "Did you get dinner?"

Lyn hesitated, too, then snorted a laugh. "I didn't." She looked to the window, seeing that full dark had fallen. "I don't really want to go out, either. I'll be fine."

Tala waved that away. "My treat. I'll go get something for us and be right back." *A new exercise deserves celebration. I'm not starting my budget until tomorrow anyway.*

"Well, if you insist. I'll take it as an apology for earlier, and I did want to read another chapter or two…" Lyn patted a book, which sat beside her chair.

"Great! I'll be back shortly." *Apology? Oh… for breaking myself, a little, in her house… Sure. That, too.*

Lyn was already opening the volume, eyes flicking over the page to find her place. "Take your time." Her voice was a half-mutter.

Already lost to the world. "Terry?"

The bird appeared on her shoulder. She watched him for a moment, noticing his deep, long breaths. The power in the air was still dissipating into the ground and her magic items. To her surprise, there was a flow towards Terry as well, and not just into his collar. He seemed to be reveling in the ambient power.

"Does that feed you, too?"

Lyn glanced up, having been temporarily pulled back out of her book. Terry didn't seem to mind, or he didn't notice. The bird bobbed contentedly, his eyes half-closed.

"Well, glad to assist, I suppose. Is there a danger of you becoming magic-bound to us?" As soon as she said it, she realized that it was a silly question. "No… you can't be magic-bound to more than one source."

Lyn cleared her throat. "Once undirected power leaves a Mage, it quickly loses the unique signature of the source and disperses into ambient magic."

"Huh. Good to know."

Lyn was already back to her reading.

"Well, see you soon!"

She grunted, waving absently without looking up. "Be safe."

Chapter: 8
Group Breakfast Deal

Lyn stared down at the food log before her. "What even is this?" She picked it up, examining it from all sides. "Can a single person eat it?" She was bouncing it up and down slightly, seeming to be testing its heft.

Tala quirked a smile. "Well, I ate two for dinner."

Lyn gave her a flat look. "Can a *normal* person eat this?"

Tala scoffed. "I'm hurt, Lyn."

"No, you're not."

"Fair enough."

Lyn hesitated. "Wait, Tala... *This* is dinner. Are you telling me that you already ate two of these, earlier this evening?"

"That may or may not be the case."

She sighed, rolling her eyes. "Fine, keep your secrets." She lifted the log a bit, returning to the earlier topic. "So... what's it called?"

"Right! It's called a 'Little Caravan.' I guess because it carries so much amazingness in one package? I think that one is a standard meal. Oh, this particular variant is called the 'Little Cheesy Caravan,' likely because it's double-wrapped, with a layer of melted cheese between the wrappings. I just call it a food log."

"I think I like 'Little Cheesy Caravan' more."

"Food log is shorter."

Lyn gave Tala a long-suffering look, eventually shaking her head slightly and returning her attention to the food log.

"Well, here it goes." Lyn lifted the food log up and took a bite. Her eyes opened wide. "This is amazing! What's the name of the restaurant?"

"Anachronistic Delights."

Lyn clucked her tongue consideringly. "Interesting name."

Tala shrugged. "Probably means something to the owner."

Lyn took another bite and let out a contented sigh, speaking around the food. "Meh, who cares; this is amazing."

"So you said." Tala grinned and tore into her own food log. *Money well spent.* This time, she'd gotten extra of the thick, green, veggie sauce. It added an additional robust, creamy flavor to the already incredible medley.

The two ate in companionable silence.

Tala let her mind wander as she ate. The magic that she and Lyn had pumped into the air within the home had already faded. *The city's collectors are quite efficient.* The exercise that they'd been doing was fascinating in concept. It didn't open her gate any wider, at least not directly, but it greatly increased the amount of power coming through. If she was right in her estimation, that increased flow was causing the gate to widen as a secondary effect. But it didn't seem to be a quick process.

Still, quadrupling my accumulation rate, even if just for short bursts, is amazing. This is definitely worth pursuing.

Continuing to eat, she focused within herself and created the void around her gate, pulling her magic back with an effort of will. The power flow instantly increased. With Lyn's earlier words in mind, Tala attempted to take a more active role in the distribution of that power. She split roughly a fourth off, allowing it to flow into her body and scripts as usual, and the rest, she pulled away.

Where to put this? Her hands were full of the food log, so she couldn't easily direct it into any of her items. She really did feel like sending it into the air was a waste.

Flow! The knife was connected to her soul, so she didn't need any sort of physical contact with the weapon to send it power. It didn't need the power, of course, but every bit that she actively put in would increase the strength of their bond and deepen the well that the tool could draw upon. *I'm sure there's a limit or a threshold, but I'm not there, yet.*

She directed three-quarters of her increased draw into the knife. It absorbed the magic like deep, desert sands taking in water.

As Tala focused, she realized that a quarter of the power was more, if just barely, than her body and active scripts needed, combined, as they were both benefiting from that portion of the influx. She did her utmost to carefully adjust the amounts until only the needed amount went to her physical form. *There.* It was not easy to maintain such a precise balance, but it was becoming easier by the moment.

Lyn shuddered slightly, opening her eyes and focusing on Tala. "What are you doing?"

"Hmm?"

"What are you doing, Tala?"

"Oh, I'm just practicing."

Lyn sighed. "Can't you just enjoy the meal?"

"I'm doing both." Tala took another big bite, relishing the harmonizing flavors.

Lyn shook her head, taking a last bite and setting fully half the food log back on the plate before her. "I'm full."

Tala ate the last bite of her own, leaving her hands empty as she savored the mouthful before swallowing. "Really?"

"This is much too much food for me." Lyn hesitated, looking to Tala's empty plate. "Do you… want the rest?"

Tala brightened. "Are you sure?"

Lyn pushed the plate across the table, pulling out her book again. "Enjoy. I bet this would be a pain to reheat. I can get another tomorrow."

Tala picked up the food, happily. "They do sell smaller versions." She pondered for a moment. "Even Littler Caravans?" She shook her head. "No, this was called the Biggest Little Cheesy Caravan. I'm sure they have a medium Little Caravan… or something like that."

"That makes no sense."

Tala shrugged. "I didn't make up the names."

Lyn sighed, leaning back, hands coming to rest on her stomach. "That was quite good. Thank you, Tala."

Tala smiled around a new mouthful.

"So, I suppose I should be doing the exercise every time I think of it, too?"

Tala nodded, mouth still full.

"Very well…"

Tala saw a flood of power immediately begin to radiate from the other Mage. Tala swallowed. "We really should get you a magic-bound item or an innocuous incorporator."

Lyn sighed but didn't stop. "I'll look into it tomorrow."

Tala smiled and took another bite, all the while maintaining both the void around her gate and the two flows of power into her body and knife. It did feel odd, keeping a portion of her self bereft of power, but she was getting used to it. Thankfully, the magic void was not at a surface level, so she wasn't creating a vulnerability in her defenses. It wasn't at a physical level at all. Her gate was *deeper*, somehow, than the flesh it connected with.

Tala had just finished her food—or rather the second half of Lyn's food—and Lyn was still going strong with her practice, when Tala had to release her hold on the power within herself, slowing the accumulation of power. She stood, stretching.

"Lyn?"

The woman looked up from her book and smiled. "Yes?"

"I'm supposed to ask you to schedule my meeting with a senior guild official."

Lyn's smile moved towards a smirk. "I *thought* I saw you drop by the guild." She nodded. "Sure. I'll do the scheduling tomorrow."

"Great. When should I show up?"

Lyn gave her a long look. "I'll know... tomorrow."

"Oh... right." Tala glanced away, feeling a bit foolish. *Of course, she wouldn't know now...* "Good night, Lyn."

"Good night, Tala. Sleep well."

"You, too."

* * *

Tala woke early, as usual. She smiled up at her plain ceiling, stretching under her blanket. *Good morning!* She felt fantastic.

After she'd filled the tub and started the fire beneath it to heat the water, she returned to her room for her morning routine.

She moved through her physical exercises, doing her utmost to maintain the void around her gate throughout. She kept the excess power streaming into Flow. *Waste not...*

The split concentration made it even harder for her to balance through the complex movements, but she was beginning to get the hang of her strengthened body. As such, she only fell a few times.

She also did her utmost to keep her breathing in the correct patterns, along with maintaining the other things Adam had taught her.

Millennial Mage, 3 - Binding

It was a fairly complicated conglomeration of things to focus on, and she had no doubt that she'd have been unable to even attempt it if not for her enhancements.

Her stretching and physical exercise complete, Tala stripped down and headed for her bath. *I'll get the hot water incorporator today. That will remove the need for the fire.*

She put out that fire before climbing into the tub.

Tala had to release the void and rest for a few minutes before she returned to that exercise. It certainly felt like she could hold for a bit longer each time, and the instructions given to Lyn by her master had indicated that this exercise was tailored to be safe. Once she *felt* recovered from it, she *was* recovered. There was no danger of injury due to repetitive strain over a short timeframe, just so long as she followed the instructions.

Thank all for that.

She finished up and allowed the water to drain away. A few minutes later, clean, dry, dressed, and refreshed, Tala came out into the empty living room. *Lyn's still asleep?*

She glanced at a window and saw it was still dark out. *What time is it?*

Tala had simply gotten up when she'd awoken. She felt rested, but she really didn't know how long she'd slept. She'd always trusted her body to wake once it had the rest it needed. *Maybe, I should get a clock... or a pocket watch?* Those could be incredibly expensive; the mundane ones were almost as much as their magical counterparts if she remembered correctly.

She sighed. *Yet more things to eat up my funds...* Her stomach made a resonant, forlorn, gurgling wail, and Tala found herself grinning. "Alright, alright. I'll go find something to eat."

She looked around. Terry was nowhere to be seen, so she returned to her room.

There he was, curled up on her pillow. *Huh...* She renewed her internal void and sat, considering. *Should I let him sleep and just read until he wakes up?* That probably wasn't necessary; he did seem to sleep a lot during the day.

"Terry?"

One of the avian eyes popped open, regarding her.

"I'm leaving."

He groaned with a deep, trilling sound but was instantly on her shoulder, eyes closed once more.

"Well, that works, I suppose." She stood and departed. *If he's actually sleeping, how does he stay balanced?* It was a question for another time.

The streets were still dark as she strode through Bandfast. *Let's see... I remember seeing a clock tower around here somewhere...*

She did, indeed, find the tower in question shortly after. *Seven past four in the morning.* It wasn't as early as she had feared, thankfully, but it was still too early to reliably find food. She groaned in irritation, pulling out a hunk of jerky to chew on in the meantime.

She flicked a bit to the side, and Terry caught it without seeming to move. Only the slow grinding of some inner parts of his beak and lack of meat hitting the ground indicated that he'd taken the bite.

Tala found a park near a breakfast place, the latter of which was still closed. She sat on a deceptively comfortable bench and pulled out one of Holly's books. *It should open in an hour or two. I can wait.*

She spent the time reading the book and practicing the maintenance of the void. Her enhanced vision made reading with less-than-optimal light no issue, and she was able to practice the void at the same time.

After what seemed like a surprisingly short period, Tala was pulled from her tasks by the sound of a lock grating within a door. She looked up and saw lights on within the eatery, a worker unlocking the front door. *Magic lights, eh?* They did provide a much more consistent, reliable illumination. Even a copper-inscribed item could provide days of light, if done properly, with the added benefit of being able to be turned off. *Yeah, if I had a business, I'd invest in such lights.* They were likely hooked into the city grid for power. *Cheaper than using harvests.*

More importantly, however, the place was open now. *Hey! Very nice.*

She could still see the clock tower. *Six in the morning already?*

The two hours had passed without leaving much of an impression. *Still, I finished another set of reviews.*

In fact, she was well into the third set of topics she'd decided to tackle.

In addition, if her estimates were right, she could now hold the void for nearly twenty minutes, even while splitting the power between her physical self and Flow. That thought made her think back. *Ahh, right. I'm in the middle of my sixth cycle of the exercise, aren't I?*

She closed the book, tucked it into Kit, and stood. "Breakfast time."

She was the first customer through the door, but as she entered, she saw other people moving about on the street outside. She likely wouldn't be alone in the restaurant for long.

"Hello! Welcome, and good morning. What can I get for you?"

Tala looked over the menu. *I need to get some jugs to buy coffee in bulk...* "Morning to you. I think a couple—no, four—breakfast sandwiches and the largest coffee you have."

The young man hesitated. "Well, we sometimes sell coffee by the gallon, when a foreman wants to treat their workers or for similar situations. Are you looking for that amount?"

She found herself grinning, almost uncontrollably. "Oh, yes. How much would that be?"

"A silver, if you don't have a container. Half that, with one, assuming it's clean and easily usable." His eyes flicked to Terry, and he smiled. "That's a beautiful bird. Does it have a name?"

"Thank you, his name is Terry." She smiled in return. "As to the order, I can keep the container in the first case? Then use it as my container to get the cheaper rate later on?"

"Of course." He looked back to Terry. "Good morning, Terry."

Terry cracked an eye and let out a little, drowsy chirp.

"He's pretty neat."

"I like him." She patted the supposedly sleeping bird. "How much for the sandwiches?"

"Twelve copper." He hesitated. "But, if you want, we can do a group breakfast deal." His smile shifted back towards one of professionalism, rather than friendly interest.

"Oh?"

"It's six sandwiches and a container of coffee for one and a half silver ounces."

Tala frowned, her coffee-less brain doing quick math. *That's almost a quarter ounce, silver, in savings.* "That's fantastic! I'll do that." She hesitated. "Why the deal?"

The young man shrugged. "A few other eateries have started opening as early as we do, some earlier, and the boss wants to keep our customers loyal, at least those who buy a lot." He quirked a wry smile.

She shrugged. "Makes sense, I suppose. Thank you. Is that deal available with the discount, if I bring back the container?"

Millennial Mage, 3 - Binding

The worker smiled. "If it's clean, empty, and usable, as I said before? Then, yes, that would drop the deal price by a half silver. I'll get that started for you."

She glanced to his name tag, then back up to grin at him. "Bnar, I think I'm going to become a regular whenever I'm in town."

The young man was surprisingly quick at his job, and she left in less than ten minutes, a cloth sack containing the sandwiches and an earthenware jug full of coffee both safely tucked away in Kit.

She'd been right, and quite a few customers had come in after her, but Bnar was already handling them quickly, efficiently, and professionally. *I don't think I could do that job.* She pulled out one of the sandwiches, taking a large bite.

It was a heavy, whole-grain bread with a sausage patty, fried eggs, chopped bacon, and a savory yellow sauce that tied it all together. *Oh... my... I'm so glad that I found this place.* It was quite good, to say the least.

She ate the sandwiches as she walked towards the work yard, only pausing to take deep swigs from the jug of coffee. Each of the six masterpieces was varied, and the eatery's menu indicated at least two dozen more combinations to try. She'd liked the first one the most, so far, but she appreciated the variety more than she likely would have liked six sandwiches of the same type. *I never considered the downside to eating so much. I'm going to have to be careful to avoid becoming sick of certain foods.*

She was just licking her fingers clean of the red sauce from the last treat when she arrived. Tala was quite glad to have eaten and to be arriving at her first destination so early. *I'm getting into a good pattern.* She grinned. The sun still wasn't up, on this autumn morning, and she was well into her tasks for the day.

True, she'd paid a bit more for breakfast than she'd planned, but it should mean less expensive breakfasts going forward. *And I got the jug I'd been hoping for, so...* She shrugged. *My budget can be flexible.*

There were a couple of guards patrolling, but the work yard was otherwise empty of people, and the guards didn't give her more than a cursory glance and slight bow. Her cargo-slots stood to one side, and she saw other groupings of cargo-slots and some of cargo wagons, which she assumed were for other Mages to empower for their own ventures. *Were there others before?* Probably. She thought back and realized that, yes, there had often been other cargo items in the work yards she'd empowered cargo-slots in. *Never really paid much attention, I suppose.*

The guards moved on as she walked towards her task. *I guess I look like I belong?* She had no idea how they assessed possible threats. *They could probably tell I'm a Mage.* Their bows lent weight to that assumption. *Dealing with a Mage is likely above their pay grade.*

Tala shrugged and smiled, a thought coming to her as she refocused on her purpose. *I can divert into the cargo-slots.*

She walked to the start of the line, right hand outstretched. Her gate was gushing into the magic-starved void that she currently maintained around it.

It was a mild additional effort to interpose the mental construct and funnel the power through it as she touched the first charging panel, but it seemed to work well enough.

Every indicating symbol flared to life instantly, glowing fiercely in the early-morning dark.

It was too much power.

She snatched her hand back, allowing the void within her to fill, her eyes widening. *Rusting, really?*

Surprised, she thought back, remembering that she'd been able to charge the cargo-slots the day before in mere seconds by shunting her full flow into each. *Right.*

Thankfully, she was able to see the cargo-slot bleeding off the excess power.

Then, she remembered the first time she'd empowered cargo-slots of this type. *Didn't it take nearly a minute? There's no way I've increased my flowrate by sixty times since then...*

That had been before she was using the mental construct. *Wow, those really do make a difference. Hmmm... I think it took around ten seconds per indicator when I began using the mental construct.*

More than anything, that spoke to the benefit of well-formed mental models for what she was doing. *And my mental model has only gotten better since then.*

Tala forced herself to focus back on the present. She rebuilt the void, splitting the power further and sending a bit more than half of the power into Flow, just less than a quarter into her own body, and about a quarter into each cargo-slot as she tapped down the line. *That should be just more than I used yesterday.*

Each cargo-slot's three indicating symbols pulsed to full brightness after the touch, the influx of power, and a couple of seconds. It wasn't instantaneous, but it didn't need to be. A smile grew, spreading across her face with every success.

She reached the end of the line, charging the last cargo-slot and almost laughing in delight. *Yes!*

Even so, she felt her grip on the power slipping and allowed the void around her gate to fill in, the flow of power drastically slowing. *Good to know, splitting the flow further requires much more attention and lowers the time I can hold the void.*

She felt a bit of a headache, but a swig of coffee seemed to help.

Splitting it three ways had lowered her time to just more than a minute. Her smile didn't fade, however. *So, I can increase the difficulty by splitting the flow further, eh?*

She stretched her arms upward, arching back and feeling her muscles respond happily to the motion. *Well, I'm way too early to go to the training yard for the class...* But maybe they'd let her use a space until they needed her? It was worth asking. *Maybe the Constructionists are open?* It *was* after seven in the morning. *I'll drop through there first.*

That decided, she turned and strode towards the Constructionist Guild building that she'd visited the day before, Terry happily sleeping on her shoulder.

Chapter: 9
Mana

The Constructionist Guild was open—or so it seemed.

Tala noted that the entrance didn't actually have doors on it. *I guess they never close?* That seemed a bit odd, but Tala guessed that Mages, especially Archons, likely kept odd hours.

As she strode inside, she again felt the magic in the surrounding stone scan her and project an infrared pulse, at least to her magesight.

It was nearly a minute before an attendant came out, looking a little bleary-eyed. "Mistress? How can we help you?" She was inscribed but not a Mage. *An assistant?*

Tala frowned. "Did I wake you? I'm sorry, the entrance was open so—"

The attendant held up her hand, clearly stifling a yawn. "It is more than fine. We wish to be available to our customers whenever they need us."

"Oh… okay." *Well, I'm here already, and she's already awake.* "I came to see if my incorporators were ready. I commissioned two yesterday."

The young woman pulled out a slate from behind a nearby desk. "Name, please?"

"Tala."

She waited for a moment longer. "Full name, please."

"Don't have a last name."

"Oh!" She colored slightly. "My apologies, Mistress Tala." She began working on the slate. A moment later, she brightened. "Here you are. Yes, they are complete. I can see you've already paid, so let me go grab those, and we can confirm receipt." She left the room for a moment. Returning, she handed a small wooden box to Tala with a small bow, her slate now tucked under the other arm.

Tala took the box and opened it; the lid was attached with small brass hinges that moved smoothly and silently. Sitting in the cushioned interior were two obviously magical devices.

They mirrored each other, and the other incorporator she had, in only a single respect: There was a circular opening in the center, just large enough for her two thumbs to go through together.

The one on the right was a white material, seeming softer than metal but still somewhat glossy. When she picked it up, it was lighter than she'd expected. Around the central circle, dull blades, or fins, radiated a short distance outward to an outer ring, all of the same material. Those blades, however, were very nearly black, and they held the same gloss as the white rings, which bordered them.

The young woman was smiling. "That is the one for hot air. Care to test it? You can point it however you desire as the air isn't hot enough to permanently damage anything in here."

Tala nodded, pointing the device at her other hand, which still held the box. She funneled some power into the device, but nothing happened. She sighed. *Right, incorporators take a* lot *of power.* She created the void around her gate, splitting the flow and sending just more than three-quarters of the power into the incorporator.

Hot air flooded out of the device. The assistant had been correct; it wasn't burning hot, but it would quickly become uncomfortable.

It was a strange thing, the sound of rushing air was the only indication that something was happening. "Seems to work." She looked up and saw the other woman's eyes were wide. "What is it?"

The assistant cleared her throat. "That is a much greater flow than I've seen produced. If I may ask, Mistress, how much power did you funnel? Did I misread the customer beacon? You aren't an Archon, are you?" She frowned, looking at her slate. "No… you're not listed as one."

Tala opened her mouth to answer but realized that she didn't have a way to answer. "Huh… You know, I don't have any way to convey it." She placed the incorporator back in the box.

The woman cocked her head to one side. "What do you mean?" Then, she seemed to understand. "You're not familiar with the theories of the rigorous documentation of magic. That is understandable, I suppose. Most Mages who join our ranks from the academy are missing that knowledge." The look on her face made it clear how she felt about *that*.

"I guess not." Tala felt a bit foolish. *Weight has pounds, distance has miles, how do I not know a unit to measure magic with?* It was a colossal oversight. *This seems like the exact type of thing the Academy should have taught us.*

"If you will allow, I can get a device with which you can measure your output."

Tala hesitated. "I'm not really looking to spend more…"

"Oh! My apologies. This would be for you to use in my presence. I'm sure we do have an extra if you wish to purchase one, but that was not my intention. Honestly, I want to satisfy my own curiosity."

Tala shrugged. "Oh, sure then." After an instantaneous pause, she asked, "I'm sorry, I didn't catch your name."

The woman looked down at her own chest, then back up. "Oh! I completely forgot my name tag. Apologies, Mistress, I am Anan."

"A pleasure to meet you, Anan."

"Likewise, Mistress Tala." Anan bowed slightly before leaving again. She was only gone for a brief moment, returning with a flat, round disk of a material that resembled dark steel. "We can test the other incorporator after if that is acceptable to you."

Tala nodded, smiling as she held out her hand. "So, I just send power into it like a magic item I'm charging or empowering?"

"Precisely." Anan put the device into Tala's hand.

"Won't that bond it to me?"

"That is an excellent question. This device does not use the power that it is given by a Mage, it simply analyzes it. Therefore, no bond is created. You don't need more than an instantaneous pulse of power for it to register. It will only register to the first decimal place."

"Huh, good to know." Tala glanced down at the disk. "Here goes." She still had the void around her gate, and she had been channeling the excess into Flow. She took that portion and sent it to the disk in her hand. The metal lit up, and Tala immediately moved the stream back to Flow. "Fourteen point three."

Anan was nodding. "As I suspected. That is quite impressive, Mistress."

"What does it mean?"

"Well, one mana per second is the standard amount of power produced by an average human."

"And mana is a unit of magic power, then."

"If I remember right, it stands for: Magic Accumulated Naturally, Average. One mana is defined as the amount of power an average, non-Mage human produces through their gate every second, averaged over time."

"I suppose that makes sense." Tala blinked, thinking through the meaning of what Anan had said. "Wait… So, I'm producing more than fourteen times what a standard human does?"

Anan shrugged. "Probably more, actually. I doubt you funneled all your influx into the device."

She's right about that. Wait, that means that my active scripts currently use magic at around four or five times what a normal person's gate produces? Holly truly was insane. "I guess I didn't actually have a reference." Surreptitiously, she let the void drop and channeled all her standard flow into the medallion for a brief instant. *Four point six.* She smiled. *Not terrible at all.*

"Ah, of course. We usually test incorporators at three or four mana per second. From what I understand, the head researchers for new designs often stress-test their prototypes at around a hundred MPS, but they're all Archons, and I've never seen it myself."

Tala found herself desperately wanting one of these measurement devices. *No, Tala. You'll just start obsessing over numbers...* She still wanted it. She reinstated the void and briefly pushed all the power at the medallion, letting her body draw from her reserves. *Eighteen point five.* So, just more than quadruple the flowrate.

Anan grinned. "I can see that look in your eyes. You want one." Her gaze flicked to the medallion, which Tala still held. "I also see that you're already testing it out."

"I do, and I am, but I shouldn't."

The assistant's grin widened. "That is surprisingly wise. My understanding is that the Archons, here, forbid their Mages and Magelings from using these for anything other than required tasks. Apparently, it can cause odd developments within magic users who use them too often. I don't think it's a side effect of the device, but apparently, such Mages soon have their heads filled with numbers and become obsessed with exactly how much power goes into each script activation, how much they hold, and things like that."

Tala could see that being quite appealing, actually. "And that's bad?"

Anan shrugged. "I wouldn't know, myself, but the Archons seem to believe so." She seemed to ponder. "I believe what was conveyed was something to the effect of: 'Magic isn't numbers, withdrawals, and deposits. Your mental constructs and proper inscriptions are more important than any number. Attaching numbers too closely to various magical effects can taint, and even weaken, the mental constructs for their spell-forms.'"

Tala found herself nodding. "I suppose that makes sense. The three points on the triangle and all that."

Anan gave her a puzzled look but then just shrugged again. "Such are the things of Mages."

Tala paused, then decided to go for it. "If I may ask, why aren't you a Mage?"

The other woman smiled slightly. "I didn't have the funds to attend the academy, and I didn't want to take on debt. I'm learning, though, and my supervisor thinks I'm nearly ready for a keystone inscription." She looked down, clearly a bit embarrassed by the fact. "It's not the same as a formal education, but I think I prefer learning on the job." She looked back to Tala, her eyes twinkling just a bit. "Besides, I'm being paid to learn now, instead of the other way around."

"Huh. I wish I could have done that."

Anan glanced to the side, seeming a bit out of her element once more. She brought the subject back to the matter at hand. "Well, do you wish to verify the other incorporator?" She held out her hand.

Tala placed the measurement medallion onto Anan's palm, the number immediately vanishing as it changed hands.

Tala's attention returned to the wooden box in her other hand and the second incorporator.

She opened the lid, focusing on the device. This one was a twisting copper ring, and even though it didn't look at all like one, it somehow evoked the idea of a copper kettle.

Odd.

As she looked closer, Tala noticed that the cross-section of the twisting shape was a triangle. There were four and a third twists around the circuit of the device, and Tala couldn't see a seam anywhere. It was slightly warm to the touch, whereas the other had just felt room temperature.

"That one could damage some things in here. Would you mind pointing it at that corner?"

Tala looked over and saw a small grate set in the floor of the front corner of the room. "Oh! Sure." She took a few steps that way, orienting the ring to point at the drain. She again directed the excess power from her void-surrounded gate through the lensing device. A healthy flow of steaming water streamed out. It was just more than the rate from the cold tap in Lyn's bath room, if Tala was estimating correctly. "Very good. This will do nicely."

She allowed the stream to end, moving the power back towards Flow. *Ha! Flow gets the flow.*

She hadn't aimed perfectly, and the corner was now liberally splattered with droplets of water. "Can you hold this?" She held out the box containing the hot air incorporator towards Anan.

Anan accepted it.

Tala re-empowered the hot water incorporator, then carefully touched the water streaming forth with her other hand. It was a bit too hot to comfortably leave her finger in it. "Yes, this will do nicely, indeed. Thank you."

Anan bowed slightly, handing the box back.

Tala placed the incorporator back in and closed the lid. "How long will the water last?"

Anan pulled out her slate and manipulated it, reading from the surface. "That one is particularly stable. For quantities of less than five hundred gallons, stored together, the water should remain material for at least an hour."

Easy baths, here I come! "Wonderful. How do you need me to confirm receipt of the items?" Tala slipped the box into Kit.

"Just certify here." Anan held out the slate, a sharp spike of stone rising from one corner. The magic for the morphing of the material was faint but still registered to Tala's magesight. *Fascinating devices.*

Tala glanced at the contents of the slate. They were simple: she was just acknowledging that she had received the goods that she had already paid for. She allowed her finger to prick on the stone and marked the slate. As usual, the blood faded instantly, the spike of stone retracting. *That must be an expensive feature.*

"Is there anything else I can do for you this morning, Mistress?"

"No, thank you, Anan. I appreciate your assistance."

"We are here to serve. Take care."

"Take care, and good luck!"

"Thank you, you as well."

"Thank you." Tala departed without another word.

Once she was outside, Tala glanced at Terry. "You were quiet, and she didn't seem to care much about you being there."

Terry shifted slightly but didn't respond.

She shrugged. "Either way." She turned and headed towards the training yard. It was going to be a wonderful day.

As she walked, she recreated the void and split her flow two ways: body and a magic item. She quickly recharged Kit, then her clothing, then the hammer, and finally, Terry's collar before redirecting the excess power fully into Flow once more.

There we go. Terry had shifted irritably when she'd placed her hand on his neck, but he remained dedicated to his sleep.

If she remembered right, she hadn't gotten to the training yard until close to nine in the morning the day before. So, she was still close to an hour ahead of schedule. *I could go and check in, see about a place to train?* That could be valuable. At the moment, she was just wandering, her void in place and power strengthening her bond with Flow.

I could try another Archon Star… If she could maintain the spell-form while resting between periods of void-enhanced power accumulation, she might be able to do it. She started trying to do math in her head, but she didn't have solid numbers. Something told her that was a good thing; she had to trust her instincts, trust her power.

I think I could match the stronger star I have in less than two stints with the void. She stopped walking as she came to that conclusion. She'd taken four hours to make that star, and now she was estimating that she could make it in half an hour? *Give or take.*

Even taking into account the void's effectiveness, that meant that she'd nearly doubled her base flowrate. *Just as Rane said. It lessened a bit but not nearly all the way back to how it was before.*

A nearly manic grin spread across her face. *No wonder Holly was unimpressed with my gate when she first checked me. I must have barely been above a non-Mage.* She almost laughed. *I might have even been worse than a mundane for all I know. Now, though.* Her face hurt from her massive smile. *Now, I'm making real progress.*

She knew that she wouldn't keep doubling her output—that would be insane to expect—but she could likely keep the pace with linear growth. *If I can add roughly three mana to my base accumulation rate every two weeks or so.*

Millennial Mage, 3 - Binding

She shook her head. *No, I'm not going to obsess over the numbers. I will progress and enjoy every step.*

She nodded to herself, still insanely pleased. *So, am I going to make another Archon Star?* She didn't really have a use for such if she was being honest, and it wouldn't be better practice than anything else she was doing. *No. I'll keep my current work.*

She paused. *If I can maintain it between cycles, I could make a star in a few hours...* That... that might just be worth it. *Become an Archon this afternoon?* She snorted. She doubted it was as simple as: 'Here's the star!' ... 'You're an Archon.'

I'll ask Holly this afternoon. She hesitated, the thought of more inscriptions putting a bit of a damper on her enthusiasm. *That will take more power to maintain...* Knowing Holly, it might perfectly use up all her standard flow of power.

That would make a lot of sense, actually. Her inscriptions seemed to take a bit more power when more was available, but not a whole lot. *Likely, they would take more if they're put under stress.* It was fair to assume that healing a broken bone or deep laceration would take more power than when the scripts were idle.

She supposed that she could make a bunch of little stars and combine them into one of enough power to be seen as acceptable, but somehow, that felt like cheating: like she wouldn't actually be earning the title. *If I want to take shortcuts, I can just force my way in with my current stars.*

She kept deflecting her mind away from obsessing over the numbers she'd just learned. The more she thought about it, the more keeping the separation made sense. *The better a mental construct is, the less magic will be needed, and the more effective a spell effect will be. If I got it locked in my head that this effect took this much mana, then that would permeate the mental construct and keep me from ever improving in that facet.* She shook her head. It was a subtle trap, and if Anan hadn't explained the basics, Tala could easily have fallen for it.

These thoughts were all well and good, but she still hadn't decided where to head. *No reason to go anywhere else. To the training yard!*

It was a pleasant walk, and she soon arrived to find the training yard in a very similar state to the day before. She had no idea if the same people were there or doing the same activities, but the general sense of the place was the same.

She smiled. *Maybe this place will work for me.* She definitely liked the overall atmosphere.

She'd had to allow the void to vanish once more, resting while she walked, before resuming the exercise just as she arrived.

Just like the day before, when she stepped from the street into the training yard itself, someone immediately stopped what they'd been doing and approached her.

"Mistress, can I be of assistance?"

Prompt bunch. "I'm to meet Guardsman Adam, to assist with a class today, and I hope to utilize a training space until then."

The guardswoman seemed a bit taken aback. "Oh, umm. Let me go see what I can find out for you."

"Thank you."

The woman gave a slight bow and departed.

Tala used the time, while waiting for the guardswoman to return, to take in those practicing around her. Thankfully, the wait wasn't long.

"Mistress Tala?"

"That's me."

The woman nodded. "You can proceed to that building, there. An officer will meet you, just inside."

"Thank you."

Millennial Mage, 3 - Binding

"Happy to assist." The woman returned to her stretching, and Tala set off across the yard.

Chapter: 10
That Has Merit

Tala reached the indicated building at the edge of the Guardsmen's training yard and was met in the entrance as soon as she'd stepped inside.

By the insignia, the woman who met Tala was a sergeant, though Tala had never met her. "Sergeant."

"Mistress Tala. Welcome. I found you on the approved access list, but there wasn't much beyond that. I was told you wish to use our training yard?" The sergeant eyed Terry with a mixture of interest and caution but seemed to have decided not to comment.

"Or another space if that is preferred. I will be here many mornings to assist with one of the classes, and it would be convenient if I could train around those times, or if I have need of a space at other intervals."

She nodded. "Understandable. However, our facilities are generally only used by those in, or directly benefiting, the Guardsman's Guild. I can check with the teacher of the class to see if your training, here, would qualify."

"That could work. I'm really not sure what he'll say."

"Very good, Mistress. Please wait here."

"Certainly."

Tala considered what she would do to train if they gave her a space. *I guess it depends on what the space will bear.* She smiled, thinking about the class of people coming up with tests for her abilities. *What madness am I about to be subjected to?*

Millennial Mage, 3 - Binding

The sergeant returned a few minutes later. "Mistress?"
"Mmm? Yes?"
"There is a courtyard set aside for today, and if I understand correctly, it has been reserved for your use, in conjunction with the class, going forward."
"Oh! Thank you."
"Right this way."
They walked through clean, sparsely decorated corridors until they came to a place where the current corridor was open on one side. The hallway surrounded a fairly large courtyard, providing a covered walkway all the way around with a few diverging paths going perpendicularly off the sides.

The open space was hard-packed sand, without any other feature.

The sergeant gestured to the space. "Have at it, ma'am."

Tala grinned. "I'll try not to damage it too much."

The guardswoman snorted. "Kind of you. Is there anything else I can do to assist?"

"I think I'll be fine. Thank you."

With a slight bow, the other woman departed.

Tala walked out onto the sand, her feet barely scuffing it. Even so, she felt like it was at least a few feet deep. *Just not used very often?* It didn't really matter.

The sand was cool and rough on the soles of her feet, in a smooth sort of way, some getting between her toes. *Yeah, Tala, it's smoothly rough.* She didn't have a lot of experience with sand, but the description seemed to fit.

Terry vanished from her shoulder, appearing on the roof nearby, already basking in the early morning sun. *You do you, little guy.*

She sat, cross-legged, in the center. Having just come from the Constructionist Guild, she had the incorporators on her mind. As such, she pulled out the three she possessed: cold water, hot water, and hot air. *Huh, should*

I have gotten a cold air one for completeness and to cool off with on hot days? Winter was almost upon them, though. *Maybe, in the spring.*

She regarded the devices. *Splitting the flow of power increases difficulty.* She grinned. With effort, she divided her natural influx of power into the three incorporators, as well as her own body and Flow.

Her reserves began to decline but not rapidly. She did have *vast* magic density, after all.

It was a tricky thing, splitting the magic five ways, but she was able to get a handle on it after a minute or so.

Once she had the pathways locked in place, she created the void around her gate.

A headache began building almost instantly as she strove to hold the six distinct mental tasks in place. But it worked.

The incorporators, which had been dormant, given the pathetic amount that had been funneled their way, suddenly activated. Two were held in her right hand, not overlapping, and the third in her left.

Cold water and hot air trickled out on one side, and hot water dribbled onto the sand on the other.

It was a lackluster amount, but she was doing it.

She clenched her jaw, forcing the division of power, and the void, into existence by sheer force of will.

She held it for ten seconds.

Twenty.

Twenty-five.

Her concentration slipped.

Her vision fuzzed, and her head rang as if someone had struck her with a hammer.

Tala groaned, flopping backwards onto the hard sand.

The pain passed quickly, relatively speaking. She'd only held the full complexity for less than half a minute.

Millennial Mage, 3 - Binding

If her estimate was correct, she took less than three minutes to recover her mental coherence.

Okay. Not bad. She considered how to proceed.

She could repeat the performance, in theory stretching herself and improving, but that felt like a half measure. *I need to rethink this.*

At the most basic level, she was creating a suction force, pulling power through her gate. Then, she was directing that power down four equal channels and one which was smaller that went to her body.

She frowned. Something about that seemed inefficient. *What if...*

She sat the cold incorporator aside and focused. *Simple first.*

She recalled how it had felt to empower each of these less than an hour before.

She had felt the flow, felt the power.

She held one incorporator in each hand and created mental channels for the power, making the channels large enough for the amount of power that she'd used earlier. Knowing of nothing else to demarcate the paths since she wasn't working with power, she opened the paths as voids. In so doing, she made them ready for the power rather than letting the power's flow create the needed channel.

The newly created, internal canals led to the two incorporators. Those pathways were utterly devoid of power, empty and hungry. They didn't move through her flesh, to interfere with her inscriptions; instead, they existed on some deeper level. *The domain of magic and the soul?* Her body and soul were separate, so it made sense that her body would be mostly devoid in that aspect.

She stretched her mind and connected the channels to her gate.

Power erupted outward, the void of the channels sucking magic through in a relative torrent.

Hot water and wind shot out of the two incorporators, much greater than the most recent display but not quite what she'd managed, individually, at the guild.

The power channels weren't full, and the remaining emptiness was a constant pull on her gate, the magic moving too quickly to spread out and equilibrate within the paths.

She gasped, panting as the power blasted through her.

Her output was not doubled from that of her simple void, but her straining mind would have guessed that *each* void-channel was pulling at least one and a half times her normal rate. *Fifty percent increase.* That was less than the void, alone, but she felt like if she could create more such channels, each would be able to sustain the same flow.

If I can create four of them, I'll be sustaining six times my passive rate.

She released the mentally constructed channels, and the power tapered off.

She rolled to the side, up onto her hands and knees, and retched. Her whole body wanted her to vomit, but her inscriptions effectively countered the urge.

Tala kept her breakfast down.

She groaned. *Effective, but awful.*

She snorted out a rueful laugh. *Awfully effective.*

She looked at her third incorporator, at Flow, and finally down at herself. *So, I can practice with up to five channels, eh?* The one to her body would be smaller, but that was likely safer in any case.

Her smile was somewhere between a grimace of anticipated pain and a grin of inevitable victory. The result was overtly manic.

"Let's get to work."

* * *

Millennial Mage, 3 - Binding

Tala was unsure how much time had passed when the sound of many feet became evident, the murmur of voices accompanying the rumble.

She released the sucking void channels, and the three incorporators ceased their output.

Opening her eyes, she realized that she was coated in sweat. No one was in sight, yet. *Maybe I do need the cold air incorporator sooner than spring...*

She quickly tucked the two hot incorporators away and created two void-channels—one to her body and one to the brass incorporator. She fought through a growing headache to maintain the constructions.

She stood, dousing herself with cold water and washing away the sweat and sand in a quick moment, at least as best as she could without soap. That device went into Kit as well, and she pulled the artifact comb through her hair, drying and detangling it with a few quick strokes.

How echo-prone are the halls, that they still haven't arrived yet? She quickly worked her hair into a braid with dexterous fingers flying over her scalp. The action tugged pleasantly at her head, lessening the pain.

Her elk leathers were clean, dry, and fresh—as always. She gave them a pulse of power via a void-channel, topping them off in thanks. It only made her a little dizzy. *These are becoming so easy to create. If only the headache would stay down...*

She tied off her braid just as the first person came into view. It was the older gentleman, the instructor for the class that she'd met the previous day. *I don't know that I ever got his name...* Rane was beside him, and they were speaking amicably.

The rest of the class followed after.

They continued along the hallway, spreading out on the covered walkway, as the instructor, Rane, and Adam came down on the sand.

Rane looked around quizzically. "What happened here? I didn't think you used any creation scripts."

Tala looked around and saw that she had disturbed the sand quite a bit.

Aside from the puddles currently around her feet, there were ripples and waves in the sand where water, or something like it, had clearly disrupted the smooth surface, though the culprit was mostly gone now.

Tala knew that much of the water had discorporated, so she wasn't quite sure how it would appear to others.

She looked back to Rane and shrugged. "Practicing. You are right, though: No creation scripts."

He just grunted.

"So, I didn't know you were going to be here."

"And miss this?" He grinned. "This is going to be interesting."

Adam smiled and gave her a slight bow but didn't say anything.

The instructor cleared his throat. "Mistress Tala, are you ready?"

She turned to him, smiling. "I think I am, though I've no idea what you all have planned." She waved at those waiting to the side. "Good morning."

A hodgepodge of responses came back.

"So, let's get started. What do you have for me?"

The first test was one of basic strength. They asked her to do push-ups, but she responded by balancing on just her hands and doing push-ups. Without falling, she then shifted into a handstand and did some more push-ups from that position. It was a tricky thing to balance, especially on the stone steps, leading down to the sand, but she'd been practicing. She was *not* confident enough to do them on the sand, itself.

She finished with an explosive last push, doing a half-turn and landing cleanly on her feet.

The class took a minute or two to rework their tests after that. They decided that her basic strength and balance were as she'd promised.

As such, they decided to trust claims about her own endurance, after she assured them that it was high. The other option was to take much of their time to prove it, and that sounded boring to everyone. They went with option A. Thus, they determined that she wouldn't have to take risks to end engagements quickly.

They tested her reaction speed, her perception, her vertical leap, and a dozen other aspects. They quizzed her on what her abilities could do, and when she didn't have an answer, they brought forth tests.

The most painful such test was slamming her arm with a sledgehammer and increasing force until it broke—her forearm, that is. It turned out that her bones were close to four times as strong as normal, just like her muscles. *I'm glad I'm not full of endingberry power...* It had been wise to let it dissipate and not renew it for her stay in Bandfast.

The fracture they were able to eventually cause realigned and healed completely in less than a minute, which was a good test of her regenerative abilities.

As the bone had pulled back together, Tala had felt the odd sensation that, if she poured power into the requisite scripts, she could force the limb to heal faster. She didn't do so, as the point of these tests was to establish baselines.

When they began discussing what it would take to cut her, she protested. "Why do you need all this to create a fighting style? Some, I understand, but these?"

The participants looked around at each other, no one, in particular, wanting to answer. Finally, a singularly brave individual stepped forward. "The main reasons are to help determine what you need to block versus avoid."

Tala snorted. "That's easy. Avoid everything."

The woman shook her head. "That would work if your goal was only survival and departure, but you said you wanted to fight, to defend others."

Tala hesitated.

"To fight, you have to be able to strike back, and that is easiest if you can block or otherwise create openings." The speaker looked a bit awkward. "That's pretty basic to any fighting style, Mistress. We can focus purely on dodging, and if you're right about your endurance, you could probably win isolated encounters via attrition, but you'd be worthless in defending someone else, and you'd fail horribly against groups, especially if they were at all intelligent. Wasn't that one of your core goals?"

Tala nodded, frowning.

"Then, against groups, you need to be able to finish individual encounters quickly before you can be swarmed, assuming you can't just shrug off all comers. In either case, you need to know what damage you can take, of what types, and how to use that to create openings to take down your opponents. Any blow that you could have taken, which you dodge instead, is an attack that you could have made but didn't."

A man stepped forward. "Dodging is wonderful, but it's a response. If you only respond, you let your enemy control the fight."

Tala sighed, glancing at Rane. He was grinning happily. *He's loving this...* He nodded, adding his thoughts, "They're right, of course."

She rolled her eyes. "Fine, fine. But why jumping? I'm glad to know I have an impressive vertical leap, but even I know that you usually want to keep your feet on the ground if you can." She did not think back to the arcanous birds, snatching her and carrying her through the air. *Nope. Not thinking about that.*

Every one of the students turned to regard a younger woman near the back. She shuffled her feet, glancing down before sighing and stepping forward. "That is the objection they had…"

Tala cocked an eyebrow. "So?" It was a bit funny that Tala had thought of her as younger. The other woman was likely at least three or four years Tala's senior. *Maybe more, given how badly I misjudged Lyn…*

"Well, it comes down to one thing: Can you increase the effect of gravity on yourself? I mean acceleration, not just weight."

Tala opened her mouth to say 'No' but hesitated. "Technically? Yes. Why?"

The other woman grinned wickedly. "I knew it. The reason that leaps and acrobatics are so dangerous is that everything behaves the same once airborne. If you slow and fall twice as fast as your enemies think you will, then their instincts will be on your side, and they'll struggle to compensate. Opponents don't consider how fast you'll fall—it's a known quantity on an instinctual level. They won't even consider it. If you are affected by gravity more strongly, that would open a whole host of options to you that anyone else would be foolish to try."

Tala considered that for a long moment. "It would lower my capacity, make me slower."

"At first, probably, but you're faster than normal, now, and your body should adjust."

Tala found herself nodding. "That has merit."

The student beamed. "Thank you, Mistress." She looked around at her fellows happily, standing a bit straighter.

"Well, then…" She looked at the device they'd brought out, returning to the topic of her 'cut-ability.' It had a blade and a very precisely controlled actuator. "Let's see how hard it is to cut me…" She sighed. *It's going to be a long morning.*

* * *

The sun was past high noon when the testing was finally completed.

Tala had been broken, stabbed, sliced, punctured, burned, and corroded. She'd balanced and snatched, leapt and pushed. Truthfully, she'd lost track of all they'd had her do, even with her improved memory. *That really shouldn't be possible…*

"Alright, then. So… you have what you need?"

The students looked around at each other, nodding enthusiastically.

The instructor gave a bow. "Yes, I believe we do. Thank you." When he straightened, he smiled. "We will have the foundations completed in a day or so, but it would help if you can get the gravity modifications in place so that we can understand their extent. Much will be the same as for any human-shaped fighter, but we will be able to fine-tune it as your skill advances."

Tala sighed and nodded. She suspected that she already had the inscriptions to enact the gravity alteration, but she wanted Holly's input, and she thought an additional set for her feet would be useful as well. *I don't want to be breaking everything I walk on…* "I should be able to have that by tomorrow. Expect a fourfold increase in my acceleration due to gravity if I'm able to get it to work."

"We can find you, here, then? I took the liberty of reserving this training yard for your use for the time being."

"Thank you, that was incredibly kind. Yes, I should be here tomorrow morning. But we've set the day after as the start of true training and work on the fighting style, correct?"

The clarification was acknowledged, and the class thanked her and departed, talking animatedly amongst themselves.

Adam walked over to her. "You're progressing quickly."

She shrugged. "It's nice to be fully inscribed, finally." She hesitated. "Well, nearly so."

Rane approached. "I still can't believe that you were walking around with an incomplete set."

"I'm not blessed with boundless money."

Rane twitched at that but didn't comment further.

Adam cleared his throat. "Well, I'll be your opponent for most sparring for the class in the coming days. I do hope for a bit of a challenge." He smirked.

Tala rolled her eyes but found herself smiling. "I'll do my best. I'll try not to hurt you too badly."

He laughed. "Thank you. My wife would be cross if I died. We'll have a healer on hand if we're to fight, though."

She looked around. "Right. You have access to those… Why not have one now? I was certainly injured a lot today."

"You said you could heal. We believed you."

"Still, it might have been nice…"

"While we work with many healers, they aren't an unlimited resource."

"Fair enough."

Adam glanced to Rane, then back to her. "Well, I'll leave you to it. I'll be excited to see what's changed tomorrow." He bowed slightly to her and to Rane, then departed.

Rane cleared his throat. "So… you still available for lunch?"

She quirked a smile. "Sure. You paying?"

"Sure."

"Then let's get to it." *The poor boy doesn't know what he's signed up for.* She'd try to take it easy, but she was *hungry* after all that they'd put her through and all that her healing inscriptions had needed to repair.

"After you, Mistress Tala."

"Thank you, Master Rane." As they began walking, and after Terry flickered to her shoulder, she glanced towards Rane. "Did you have any place in particular, in mind?"

"Well, I'm not from around here, so my knowledge is limited, but I tried a place yesterday that had *fantastic* noodles. They had them available with all sorts of toppings and sauces. We could go there."

"Master Rane?"

"Hmm?"

"That sounds wonderful."

Chapter: 11
A Hodgepodge Foundation

Tala was decided: Rane knew his food, and she was quite happy with the noodle place he'd led them to.

To her surprise, Rane hadn't objected to her order. He'd insisted that she get whatever she wished, and he'd cover it. He'd remained adamant, even after she'd asserted that he didn't have to pay for her full order—or any of it, really.

Thankfully, the place was inexpensive, so her meal, enough food to feed a normal household, had only cost around three silver.

Now their food had arrived, and Tala was doing her best not to gorge… at least, not too quickly. Terry had briefly sampled each type of food that they'd ordered, but in the end, he was content with bits of jerky.

She had a plate of ridged, tube-like noodles with a red, beef sauce. A serving bowl beside that held long, thin, round noodles, covered with a form of mild pesto and chicken. A second plate contained small, curved tube-noodles with a spicy, orange sauce, mixed with quite flavorful pork. The final dish, a cast-iron skillet hot off the stove, held wide, flat noodles, which had been caramelized with the sauce within the skillet. That one tasted salty with a very subtle sweetness and a chargrilled flavor. It was served with beef strips and a medley of vegetables.

Rane had ordered a large salad, with a small plate of noodles, dressed with strips of chicken and a white sauce.

Bless the man, he looked on with a mixture of awe and horror as she began to eat the entirety of her order. Tala took small bites, of course, even if they were rapid. *Cleanliness and all that.*

"How are you planning on keeping all that down?"

Tala swallowed the current mouthful. "Digestive inscriptions. I need a lot of energy for my inscriptions to have their full effectiveness. So we modified my systems to allow for high intake. At the moment, it's more 'requiring' than 'allowing,' but even so."

He nodded, slightly. "A downside of being a guide, rather than a creator, I suppose." He thought for a moment. "So, your storage systems are inscribed, too?" He nodded more completely. "That's right. I remember you saying something about this to the class yesterday." Rane quirked a smile. "I'd love to be able to eat anything I want, but it isn't worth the modifications my inscriptions would constantly need."

"Mistress Holly took care of that, too. I won't change size unless I deeply deplete my reserves, in which case I'll shrink."

He grunted. "So you said. Must be nice."

"Except on the coin pouch."

Rane grinned. "Hence accepting my invitation."

She paused, another bite halfway to her mouth. "I would have come even if you weren't paying."

His hand came to his chest, a look of false afront painting his features. "I've been robbed! I could have had your company for free?"

Tala laughed, feeling the tension bleeding away from the situation. True, he'd insisted upon paying despite her earlier inquiries, but for some reason, she hadn't really believed he was genuine until then. "Thank you, again, by the way."

He waved dismissively. "Think nothing of it. I'm glad to have some of your time."

She snorted a laugh around the current mouthful, chewing carefully and swallowing. "My schedule does seem to fill up, doesn't it?"

"You seem like you don't take much time off."

She shrugged. "Too much to do."

"Well, we can focus on eating, so long as we can talk after? I did have a purpose for asking you to meet."

She smiled. "Sure. I want to do some practice, but aside from that, my only obligation is with my inscriber later this afternoon."

He nodded, bringing a forkful of salad up for a bite.

* * *

Their food consumed, the staff thanked, and the restaurant left behind, Tala and Rane walked side-by-side through the city.

"So, how have you been liking Bandfast so far?"

Rane smiled, looking up to the sky. "There are so many people. Honestly, it's a bit overwhelming." He chuckled, ruefully. "And, it's only been... what? Less than two days?"

"I can imagine, and just about, yeah. Alefast is minuscule compared to here, and you spent a good deal of time in the Wilds, right?"

"True enough."

"So..." *What do I even talk about? Why am I here?* "How are you progressing on your star?"

He glanced her way. "You really don't take a break, do you?"

Great question, Tala. Nicely done... She shrugged. "I'm behind in so many areas, and I want to catch up."

"I suppose that's fair." He sighed, eyes returning to their path forward. "Good, I think. Master Grediv gave me several different paths towards making an Archon Star. Well, they're helpful in general but specifically useful for making Archon Star creation easier. I read through them and chose the one that seemed best suited to me, to my methodologies, and to my way of thinking."

"Oh?"

His eyes flicked to her, then away. "Trying to steal my family's secrets?" But he was grinning.

"I'm already well down the path towards making a full-powered Archon Star."

"'Well down the path.'" He shook his head. "I bet you've spent less than a day on your chosen path." He snorted. "Most Mages don't even have the luxury of a path at all."

She opened her mouth to object, then closed it into a pouting frown. *He's right...* That didn't make it better. Probably made it worse if she was being honest. "Fine, but I'm not trying to steal your techniques."

He grinned. "I know, I know." He let out a breath. "There's honestly nothing very secret involved. I'm just not used to Mages being as direct as you are."

"So...?"

He laughed. "I chose a method that lined up with my magics. As power comes through my gate, I pull it along faster, which causes the magic to flow quicker. It was called the 'Way of the Rapids' in my notes."

"That... Huh. I wouldn't have thought that would work, but it seems almost like what I'm doing."

"Which is?"

"Creating a void around my gate that sucks power through."

He blinked and stared at her for a long moment. Finally, he barked a laugh. "If I'm pulling a string through the mud, you're moving all the mud away, so the string moves on its own. That sounds annoyingly difficult."

Tala quirked a smile. "A bit, but the results are extraordinary."

"Oh?"

"I get a four-fold increase with the most basic form, and a variation I've discovered seems to yield an additional bump." *And that was just when I was working with the two incorporators in my first attempt.* She hadn't analyzed her current ability fully.

He was frowning again. "Four-fold? Additional? You aren't obsessing over the numbers, are you?"

"No? I did come across the term 'mana' as a unit for measuring magical power."

"Came across?" He hesitated, then nodded. "Right, you're Academy-trained." He sighed, shaking his head. "It's easiest to keep Mages out of their own way if they don't have hard numbers to put to their abilities. It's possible, but not 'efficient.'" He made air quotes as he said the last word.

"It does seem that a lot was hidden from me, or at least not mentioned, at the academy."

"They aim to make as many passable Mages as possible. They aren't concerned with helping the good ones be great." After a moment's pause, he continued, "Well, that's what Master Grediv said their intention was at the founding. Now? I fear the instructors actually believe they're teaching a fully realized, deeply applicable curriculum."

So, he does have some knowledge of the academy. Tala snorted a short laugh. "Seems a waste."

"Meh. Most students get snatched up by good masters after graduation, and the deficit is corrected. I think I can understand the methodology, even if I don't like it." He chuckled. "Not like I have a better way to do it."

"Fair enough." She thought about it. "Yeah, I'm glad I'm not in charge of teaching the next generation."

"So, back to the stars: I have heard of the technique you're using or at least something like it."

"Let me guess: Way of the Void?"

He laughed. "Precisely."

Of course, it is. "What were some of the others?"

He gave her a look.

Tala held up her hands in surrender. "Just the names?"

Rane sighed. "Way of Compression, Way of the Breath, Way of the Vortex, Way of the Channel, and Way of Denial of the Existence of Intervening Space."

Tala blinked a few times. "You made that last one up, didn't you."

He shook his head. "Nope. Apparently, Way of Denial is something else, but Master Grediv thinks *that* path is for 'those without a firm concept of reality.' Which fits, I suppose, given the name."

She grinned. "I suppose so, yeah." She considered the names. "You know, I think I'm doing something like Way of the Channel, if the name is any indication." *Could I build the channels without making them void?* She briefly tried and found that her power flow did, indeed, increase, if just marginally. "Huh. It seems so."

Rane stopped walking. "Did you just try out a new methodology for power manipulation, after intuiting how from the name?"

"Long question, but… yes?"

He just stared at her.

"What?"

"You're…" He shook his head, looking embarrassed. He turned and started walking.

"What?"

He just shook his head again.

She walked quickly to catch up and fall into step beside him. "What, Master Rane?"

He sighed. "You're something special, Mistress Tala." Then, he barked a laugh. "And you are just insane enough to try things most people actively avoid, as well as just clever and skilled enough not to kill yourself."

"Surviving is all about mitigating the risks. Hence my inscriptions." She grinned. "Wait until I try combining all the methodologies you mentioned."

Rane looked her way, suddenly serious. "No, Mistress Tala. Please. Perfect what you are currently doing before you add in more. My understanding is that most Archons do combine many of these but *after* they are Archons. You can kill yourself, or at least do serious damage if you try to force too many changes at once."

She opened her mouth to argue, but he cut her off.

"Please? If you're getting good results, perfect what you have, then add more. Don't make a hodgepodge foundation that can't support you later."

That's a fair point... She sighed. "Very well."

They walked in silence for a long while, not going anywhere in particular.

Finally, Tala glanced towards Rane. "So, what did you want to talk about?"

He straightened, clearly having thought about what he wanted to say. "Well, I was curious when you were planning on venturing out once more." He didn't look at her.

"Not quite sure, yet. Why?"

"I don't know many people, and I'd really rather not go off on my own just yet."

Tala quirked another smile. "So, you want to come with me?"

He shrugged. "If you've no objection."

"Mistress Lyn said that once I'm an Archon, I should be able to renegotiate and be both Dimensional Mage and Mage Protector for a caravan."

He frowned. "Why after?"

"Because the services I can offer will have materially changed."

"And they haven't already?"

Tala opened her mouth to say 'no' but stopped. "Huh… Have they?"

"From what I saw and heard? Yes. You shouldn't be the sole protector for a caravan, but then few should. Plus, I'd be there, too."

She found herself nodding. "My new cargo-slots should be done by the end of the week. They'll allow for a two-wagon caravan."

Rane perked up. "Oh? Just the cargo and chuck wagons?"

"Precisely."

"Could go faster, then. It's always a delicate balance between size and speed. A single rider can go as fast as they like, in general, but as soon as there are two, there is an argument for caution."

"I was wondering about that. Why are caravans so slow?"

Rane smiled. "You know, a master would have told you that."

"Sure, probably, but now you can." She gave him an expectant look.

Rane shook his head, but his smile never faltered. "Fine, fine. You'd be surprised how many things have perception based on movement but on a grand scale. I'll give an easy, well-known example: the tralvoldoc can detect anything outside a city that's moving faster than a quick walk, up to a hundred miles away, but they usually don't care if the combined mass in motion is less than a reasonable herd." After a moment, he added, "Or a few wagons."

"Tralvoldoc?"

"They look like a huge pile of vines, roots, and tentacles. They can teleport miles at a time. Supposedly, they appear above their prey and drop on top of them to cover and consume."

"How huge are we talking about?"

Rane looked around, then pointed at a nearby park. It filled most of the city block. "Mature ones are easily about that big, piled twenty or thirty feet high."

"Arcanous or magical?"

"I think arcanous? Plant-origin. I've never seen one myself."

Tala stared. "That… sounds unpleasant to deal with. A bit scary actually."

He huffed a laugh. "Not really. People have escaped from those fairly often. It's the ones we don't know of that scare me. Caravans go slow to avoid notice." He shrugged. "A two-wagon caravan could go faster, by a bit, than a wagon train of a normal size."

"And thus, my question is answered." She shuddered slightly. She would likely survive under such a pile of hostile limbs, at least at first, but whether that would be preferable or not, she had no idea.

Rane cleared his throat. "But, back to my inquiry?"

She smiled. "It has merit. I'd prefer to travel with you as a co-protector than a stranger."

He smiled in return. "Well, then, might be worth asking your handler to investigate your fitness for that duty. Yeah?"

"It might be worth it, indeed. I can probably discuss it with the senior official when I have that meeting."

"Meeting?"

"Oh… right…" She sighed. "I need to meet with a guild higher-up before I can take another contract."

Rane quirked a smile. "Makes sense. You didn't exactly act as a typical Dimensional Mage on your last trip."

"Yeah, not sure what the result will be." Tala turned back towards the park. There were several groups of children playing, adults watching from the sides or from various benches. She smiled. She used to love playing with her siblings and the other neighborhood kids in their local park. She shook her head to clear it, returning her focus to the present. "I'll talk to Lyn this evening, see if she thinks bringing that up in the meeting makes sense. I can tell you what she says tomorrow?"

"Where can I find you? We aren't needed for the class tomorrow."

"I'll be in the training yard, nonetheless. Look for me there. I probably won't have an answer 'til tomorrow evening, at the earliest, but we can still discuss it."

"That sounds like a good plan." He looked around and let out a long, contented breath. "I suppose I'll let you get to your training. I've my own tasks to accomplish today."

Tala grinned, waving goodbye. "Take care, Master Rane."

He waved back as he strode away down a side street. "See you soon, Mistress Tala."

She stayed and watched the families playing for a few minutes before turning back towards the training yard. "Ready to bask on the roof again, Terry?" She flicked a piece of jerky for him.

He didn't respond, happily remaining on her shoulder despite the piece of meat vanishing.

"Glad to hear."

He opened an eye to regard her for a moment, then closed it again, clearly not minding her oddities.

* * *

Early afternoon had passed, and Tala now sat in the shade, near one side of the training courtyard that was set aside for her.

She closed the final volume of Holly's books. She hadn't come close to reading them in their entirety, but she had filled in her knowledge gaps sufficiently to ensure all the scripts would function properly. *I can expand that base of understanding over time.*

She looked back to her incorporators, sitting in her lap.

Her head hurt from the mental strain of manifesting the void channels, though her improvement was obvious. She could now power active scripts, feeding her body the power it needed, and then divide the remaining power among the three incorporators and Flow, each device producing at roughly three-quarters of the rate she'd managed individually, that morning in the Constructionist Guildhall.

The exercise had stretched her gate to the point that she'd bet her unaided power accumulation rate was at least a couple of mana higher. The rate enhancement, now that she was using the channels along with the void, was almost double that of the void alone.

And it felt like someone was driving a chisel through her left temple.

She'd been able to hold the most recent stint for five minutes.

With my inscriptions, I should not even be able to have a headache. What is going on here?

Her needed breaks had been getting longer and longer. This last one had been a full ten minutes, and the headache wasn't gone yet. *Maybe… I might be pushing too hard.*

Lyn's master had told the Mage that she could push with these exercises without hurting herself.

But that was an easier version, and they were talking to Lyn, who is cautious by nature…

She flopped backwards to lie flat on the sand. *A nap sounds really, really nice.*

She was thirsty, too.

I need to rest my eyes. Yeah… just for a minute or two. But first, a drink.

Tala tucked the other incorporators into Kit, verified that Flow was on her belt, and sat back up to be able to drink more easily from the cool water incorporator.

Come on, Tala. Power it up. She hazily moved to do so and realized that she'd created the same five channels that she'd been using all afternoon. She groaned but was too out of it to stop now. She connected the smallest one to her body and inscriptions and then just shunted the rest to the incorporator. *There, now I'm not just dumping power into the air.*

She activated the channels, connected their voided paths to her gate, and brought the incorporator up to her mouth.

As she did so, her sluggish mind caught up to her actions, and her eyes widened.

Water rocketed out, not fast or hard enough to harm even a regular person, but still vastly more than anyone would want shooting into their mouth.

The flow of power immediately cut off, Tala choking, gagging, and retching up the fluid that had invaded her lungs. *Idiot!* She spat, coughing uncontrollably.

She hacked into the sand, her whole body convulsing.

Finally, the last bit of water came back out of her, and she was able to draw a full breath.

Her lungs felt… heavy. Like she was beside the ocean on a particularly humid day, after sprinting down from the Academy.

"That. Was. Awful." She spat again, uselessly.

She noticed Terry standing beside her as she knelt on the sand, her hands holding her up. He was regarding her with an odd expression.

"What?"

He tilted his head back and forth regarding her intently, then vanished.

"Yeah… Not dead this time, either." She groaned, thinking back over the idiocy she'd just performed; she hesitated. *I connected four channels to a single destination, a single outlet.* Her fuzzy mind was having a difficult time tracking through all the implications, though her headache was a *bit* better.

Unless she was lying to herself.

There is no way it's worse now.

"If I could maintain that, funneling into an Archon Star spell-form…" Her headache flared, and she groaned again, flopping over onto her side on a patch of dry sand.

After a long break, she very carefully, finally, got her drink from the incorporator. She used the absolute minimum amount of power possible to activate it.

Minutes more passed. "If I could maintain that four-pronged approach, I could make a full Archon Star in a few hours." She couldn't maintain it, obviously, but she was close to enacting the technique half of the time if she alternated.

No. That wasn't true. It was much closer to one-third of the time.

Well, fine… I should be able to do that after a rest, though. If she could hold the form while resting her mind, she just might be able to make it work.

I should ask Holly… Her eyes flicked to the sky. *Regarding Holly…* It was time to return to the inscriber. *Duty calls.*

Chapter: 12
Fleeing the Madness of Reality

Tala moved through the city in a bit of a haze, Terry on her shoulder.

If she was being honest, she didn't really register anything at all until she was standing in Holly's personal workshop, looking at the auto-inscriber.

She tilted her head to the side, regarding the machine. "Is that bigger?"

Holly was frowning in her direction. "Are you alright, Mistress Tala?"

Tala shifted her gaze to the small, older Mage. "Yes? Why?"

"I just told you that I've been adding to the device, increasing the surface area it can cover."

"Oh... I guess I wasn't listening."

Holly was frowning. "But you should have memory of hearing it, regardless." The inscriptions for magesight lit up on the inscriber's face. Holly blinked in surprise. "What have you been doing to yourself? Do you have a constant funnel of power into your soul-bound weapon?"

Tala looked down at Flow. "Yeah, I had some excess, and it seemed a waste to just dump it into the air." *Wait... I was directing the power into Flow from my Way. When did I start feeding it at all times?* It made sense, given that she'd increased her passive power accumulation rate. *The excess has to go somewhere, after all.* As she examined herself, she realized that she'd only directed most of the excess into Flow. She still allowed the incoming power to push at her body, stretching her power density ever so slightly before that minuscule overage seeped out.

"What have you been doing to increase your influx so much?"

She shrugged. "Exercises to move towards creating a full Archon Star." She gave a quick description, a bit surprised at her own eloquence.

"You are using a technique you came up with yourself." Holly's voice was monotone.

"Well. No? It's just the Way of the Void."

"But you aren't following the instructions you were given for such."

"No? This created better results."

Holly's fingertips massaged her face as the Mage let out a frustrated growl. "Do you grab the heaviest weights available for every exercise?"

Wow, she's really confident that she won't accidentally activate her inscriptions with cross-over... "I do mostly body-weight exercise, but after these enhancements?" Tala patted her rather average-looking bicep, through the leather. "Yeah, probably."

Holly huffed a breath. "Fine, bad example." She seemed to be considering. "Now that I think about it, I doubt I can come up with a suitable one." She gave Tala a critical look. "You're a bit insane when it comes to training." She brightened. "Ah! Have you ever juggled?"

"No?"

"Then, if you were going to learn, would you simply pick up as many knives as you could hold and start throwing them up?"

"Well, I've no idea, but that sounds like a bad idea." After a moment's hesitation, she shrugged. "I don't suppose I could get hurt by the knives, so maybe?"

Holly's lips pressed together in irritation, her eyes widening just slightly. *That kind of makes her look a bit manic...*

Tala held up her hands. "But I see your point!"

Holly seemed to calm herself. "Rusting right, you understand my point." She took another breath, calming further. "The different 'Ways' have been developed over... well, I'm not sure how long we humans have been working on them. The point is, they are tried and tested, proven to be effective, efficient means of progressing. Making up your own would be like..." She seemed at a loss for a good comparison, once again.

"Like making an Archon Star in a new substance?"

"Exactly!" Holly snapped, pointing at Tala and visibly brightening. Then, she stopped, eyes narrowing and smile fading. "No. No, you can't use that fluke to justify your insanity."

Tala was grinning broadly but held up her hands in surrender. "Fine, I'll exercise caution."

The inscriber rolled her eyes and sighed exaggeratedly. "Which means you won't change anything, but you'll *consider* being less rash." She shook her head.

"Anyway. I have a couple things to discuss with you."

"Besides burning yourself alive from the inside out with magical power?"

"Yes, besides that." She smiled again. "I want to activate my crush attack, on myself, but I don't want it to scale up."

Holly didn't blink at the idea, just nodding. "That's simple. You know the inscriptions that are responsible for recursion. Keep power out of those to alter the activation as desired."

"Yes, I *think* I do, but I don't want to kill myself through arrogance."

Holly gave her a flat look.

"This is totally different. Gravity is serious business." After a pause, Tala giggled. "It has gravitas."

Holly cocked her head, frowning. "Are you alright?"

"Yes, yes. You're just taking this so seriously."

"Magic isn't serious?"

Tala opened her mouth to respond, but Holly waved her off.

The inscriber sighed. "Fine, fine. I am actually glad that you asked. So, here, let's verify."

"You… aren't going to ask why?"

"It's obvious. You can take the increased weight, and the benefits in training alone would be monumental. I imagine you have other, less reasonable thoughts as to why you should do it, but my sanity begs me not to ask."

Tala wasn't quite sure how to take that.

"We'll need to use the inscriptions I recommended for your feet earlier."

"The ones to distribute my weight more widely?"

"Yes. I was concerned that, given your increasing mass, that would be needed to prevent you from causing damage as you walked. If we're going to be amplifying your interactions with gravity, too? I think we should give your feet at least a one-foot-radius pressure distribution each. That should keep you in the range of pressure that a normal person exerts as they walk. You'll still have the weight, but it should keep you from sinking into softer materials."

"That should work, yeah." *And because it's affecting my foot directly, and the ground only indirectly, my iron salve shouldn't interfere.*

"We should give the same to your palms."

"Why?"

"You do push-ups and similar exercises, yes?"

"Oh! Right. That makes sense." She didn't want her hands sinking into the ground either.

"For your reference, once your bones are completely restructured, and your reserves are as full as is reasonable, you should be around two hundred and eighty pounds. Add in a quadrupling of your gravitational constant, and you'll break the scale at well over a thousand pounds. It is going to be inconvenient."

Tala frowned. "I supposed I could just set a mental condition to allow the change to be shrugged off when I needed to."

Holly hesitated. "That is possible, but I'd recommend against it. You will have to move almost entirely differently. Your body will need to adjust. Your mind more so, and switching back and forth will be an unneeded, extra strain."

Tala sighed. "Fair enough."

"Now, let's get your inscriptions finished and these new ones added."

"Don't you need to work up a schema?"

Holly gave her a knowing smile. "Your inscriptions are being used to test my invention, dear girl. I've worked up a thousand versions of dozens of possibilities for you. Those we are to add just need to be flagged as good to go."

"Fair enough. I've finished my topical review for the remaining inscriptions." Tala had also already read about, and understood, the surface area increasing enhancements, so that shouldn't be a problem.

"I assumed so. This will be our last session… for now. You'll get all the remaining scripts." She hesitated. "I trust you noticed the section for your eyes?"

Tala sighed and nodded. "Yes. Having them pop within my head was unpleasant enough that I'll not fight you on it. They are only protective and regenerative, so I won't have to adjust to new stimuli." She shrugged. *Should be worth it, especially with the auto-inscriber in place of her jabbing my eyes with a needle, over and over, manually…*

"Good to hear. After this is finished, you and I can ensure you don't turn yourself to jelly as you increase your weight."

Tala nodded. "That's the idea." Her focus had pushed the fuzziness aside for much of the conversation, but she still felt like she was thinking through a cloud. *That doesn't really make sense.*

As she allowed the auto-inscriber to be positioned on her, this time completely encompassing her torso, neck, and head, Tala allowed her mind to fall back into the comfortable absence of thought.

*   *   *

"Mistress Tala?" Motion before her eyes pulled at Tala's attention. "Tala!"

Tala started, looking around.

Holly's hand was dropping away from in front of Tala's face.

"Hmm? What's going on?" The auto-inscriber was tucked off to the side.

"We're done." After a moment, Holly added, "We've been done for nearly five minutes, but you've just been standing there."

"Oh, I'm sorry. So, shall we do my feet and hands, then?"

Holly gave her a concerned look. "No. We're done. All inscriptions are complete."

Really? Good. "Great. So, let's do the gravity work."

Holly glanced towards the wall in front of Tala, then back to her. "Are you sure you're alright?"

Tala looked to where Holly had glanced and saw an expanded version of her crushing script, the portions she needed to keep power from emphasized. "Ah, yes! Thank you." She shook her head. "I've just got a lot on my mind."

"So, it seems. Maybe—"

Tala brought up her right hand, fingers and thumb pulled in tight. Her index and middle fingers pointed towards the ceiling, and her ring and pinkie fingers were bent down. She focused her magesight inward, ensuring that she thought of herself in her entirety. *No repeat of the midnight fox incident.*

Crush. As power leapt through the activating scripts, she held it back from the recurring functions. She almost staggered as she was suddenly *much* heavier, but then the power faded from her spell-form, and the danger was past, leaving her with quadruple her previous weight. "There."

Holly sighed. "Maybe it would have been wise to wait."

She fought to stay upright. Her heart was laboring against vastly heavier blood. *That's what kills most.* Her heart, however, was enhanced and was able to beat more forcefully than others. Her entire vascular system was reinforced, so it could take the strain of high blood pressure. All of her tissue was or else she'd likely pop her own organs. "You know"—she found the act of talking much more difficult than before, too, yet still, she persevered—"if I do get cut, I'll be a fountain." She kept herself from giggling.

Holly shook her head. "At least that shows some deeper-level thinking. But, no, you won't. Remember? Parts of the inscriptions on your blood system was to redirect kinetic energy. Unless you will it, you'll never bleed more than a trickle." She hesitated.

Right! She shouldn't have forgotten that. Tala frowned, even that felt odd, the world pulling on her face differently than she was used to. "I feel a little funny." She took a step, feeling like someone was clutching her leg. *Or that my leg is now much, much heavier.*

"You don't look so good." Holly was frowning with obvious concern. "Why don't you lie down?"

Millennial Mage, 3 - Binding

Tala shook her head, feeling momentarily dizzy as her inner ears struggled to understand what was going on. She groaned and sat down. Well, she tried to. The chair, which she'd used in the past, creaked then splintered, dumping her unceremoniously onto the ground.

Holly was at her side in a moment. "Deep breaths, Mistress Tala. Focus on acclimating."

Tala nodded, again feeling like the world was spinning without her. She didn't vomit—her inscriptions wouldn't allow it.

As she examined herself with her magesight, Tala realized that she was still funneling power into Flow, strengthening the knife and her bond to it. *Interesting. That's become an unconscious thing.*

As she focused on the knife, she got the sudden feeling that it, and their bond, was approaching a threshold of power. Her steady stream was minuscule, but the barrier was close.

I wonder what that is? Her unfocused mind did some rough calculations, and she spoke without thought. "Huh, I think my bond with the knife is almost powerful enough to match a true Archon Star."

Holly pulled back, eyes wide. Her mouth opened, but Tala never got to hear what she was about to say.

The threshold was reached, the link between herself and the knife pulsed, and the world went white, her mind fleeing the madness of reality into the comfortable nothingness of sleep.

*　*　*

Tala woke slowly, staring at the ceiling in her room, in Lyn's house. *What?*

The ceiling seemed too far away. It felt like someone had strapped weights to her body, but she was still able to move. A small fuzzy warmth was tucked against her bare feet.

Strangely, she felt incredible. Her mind was clear, and she didn't feel tired in the slightest.

She lifted her arm to free her eyes from the sleep that had gathered during the night. There was a lot.

I don't remember going to bed... With more effort than she'd recently required, she sat up and looked around.

She was on the floor, on her bedroll. The bed that she had been using was gone, along with the chair for the desk, leaving the room feeling strangely empty.

Terry was curled up near where her feet had been.

Tala was dressed in her elk leather clothing still, but they felt weak, like they were starving.

Oh, no! She reached inside herself for power to dump into the item and found that only about three-quarters of her inflow was going to her body and the active inscriptions therein. The rest was going into Flow, just as she'd directed so often of late.

Quickly, Tala moved that excess of power into the outfit, funneling it into Kit next as soon as the elk leather was full. Thankfully, the dimensional bag was still functional.

She noted that each item filled as fast as any time previous despite the inscriptions that Holly had added in their most recent session. *Even when I was using the void.* True, she was doing them one at a time, but even so. *I guess my gate has expanded?* She really didn't want to put numbers to it, but she couldn't help the mathematical portion of her thoughts from spitting out. *I'd bet my base rate is around eight mana per second.* The finalization of her spell-forms had increased their running magical draw.

As she thought about it: if the void channels still had the same multiplicative effect, she'd be able to make a top-rate Archon Star in just over two hours. *Around one, if I'm happy with lesser results.* True, that was only if she could maintain the void channels for the entire time and didn't give her active inscriptions anything, but it was still a mind-bending realization.

She reached out and refilled Terry's collar as well, causing the bird to stir. He stood, regarding her quizzically. *Does he look stressed?*

A smile tugged at her lips, and she got him some jerky, which he ate slowly, watching her critically the entire time. "What's—" She stopped, her voice sounding like a croak.

Water. She got her brass incorporator out and very carefully took a drink. That triggered her thirst, and she spent a little while drinking as much as she could. Her stomach was utterly empty.

Finally, she felt like she'd drunk enough. "What's going on?" Her voice was a whisper, but at least it was no longer a rasp.

Terry just looked at her. If he'd had eyebrows, she suspected one would have been raised.

"Right, too complicated."

Her hair was still braided, but there were a *lot* of strands that had come loose. *I did that at the guardsman's training yard, right?* Even with her mind clear, her memories were fuzzy. *That can't be good...*

Her every movement felt heavy, and it clicked in her mind that she'd enacted the weight increase that she'd discussed with the class of guards.

Well, I survived that, then. But how had she gotten here?

She stretched, lightly, trying not to move too much. As she did so, she assessed her state. *Hungry but not starving. No broken... anything, no bleeding. No concussion. Blade's sharp—* She hesitated at that. *My blade is sharp?* She held out her hand, and with a flicker of movement, Flow was in her grasp. The weapon had come to her more quickly than ever before. *No, that isn't right. It moved where I wanted. It was already with me.* The blade reshaped into a sword and back just as quickly, though it still took virtually all her incoming power to enact the change. *Something's different.* She narrowed her eyes, examining the weapon.

She heard footsteps in the hall, and a voice carried through the door. "Thank you for dropping by to get me. Just let me check in on her, and we can leave."

Tala sheathed the knife as Lyn pushed the door open and froze. *I'll examine it later.*

"Tala?"

Tala cocked her head. "Lyn."

A startled exclamation came from outside, and Rane poked his head around the doorframe, looking past Lyn. "Mistress Tala. You're awake!"

Tala frowned. "That's what you do after you sleep." She wetted her lips. "What happened?"

Rane looked lost, but Lyn sighed. "You lost consciousness at Mistress Holly's workshop."

"And? That's happened before."

"You overtaxed your mind, your will, and likely your soul, too. Mistress Holly said that your soul-bond to that knife reached a cusp of true strength, and it became too much for your weary self to take." She shrugged, looking uncertain. "Your mind began to fray, and so, it retreated into unconsciousness."

"How did you get me back here? Where's my bed?"

Lyn opened her mouth, but Rane cleared his throat, answering the question. "When you weren't at the training yard, I tracked you down to Mistress Holly's shop." He smiled, holding back a chuckle. "They couldn't move you, and Mistress Holly was getting very cross at your presence in her personal workroom. Apparently, the doorways were too small for any heavy lifting machinery, and she wasn't willing to commission something special just to move you." He cleared his throat. "I suspect that she could have solved the problem, but likely, she wanted to keep an eye on you. After there was someone else around to do it, though?" He shrugged. "She was content to pass off that responsibility. I can impart kinetic energy, and that depends on mass, not weight, so we were able to get you here… if a bit unconventionally." He looked a bit embarrassed by that.

"I won't ask." She got a mental image of herself suddenly flying in a chosen direction, flopping through a hallway or down a road.

"I think that's for the best." Rane cleared his throat. "When we got here, I gave you enough energy to lift up onto the bed. The bed immediately broke under you. The wood of the structure shredded the mattress. After that, we cleared out the broken pieces and got your bedroll set up."

Tala frowned. "How did you get my bedroll?"

He shrugged. "It just sort of flopped out of your pouch." He scratched the back of his head. "We took out the chair, too, just to be safe."

She looked down. "Thanks, Kit." She patted the dimensional storage.

The pouch did not respond.

Tala sighed, returning her attention to the two people in her doorway. "Alright, so… what? I was unconscious for a day?" She glanced at the window, her heavy movements still feeling odd. *The light is right for afternoon.* She turned back. They were sharing a look. "What? Losing a day is rusting awful, but if I work hard enough, I'll recover the lost time."

It was Lyn's turn to speak, apparently, as she cleared her throat. "It's been four days since you fell unconscious, Tala. You've been here for three."

Tala's mouth opened, but she couldn't form a response.

"A healer friend came by and said you were alive, and your soul was still in your body, but he couldn't tell me when you'd wake up."

Four days... That is so much time I've missed. Wait... Does that mean they had to get me to the privy somehow? *No.* She shook her head. *The digestive inscriptions ensure I use all parts of anything I ingest, even recycling what would normally be expelled.* That was a relief. Even trying to imagine them handling that was... humiliating.

"The wainwrights were a bit irritated that you couldn't come by to test the cargo-slots that they made for you, but it hasn't become a true problem, yet. The guardsman class has the first version of your fighting style ready, but they were able to shift their schedule around to work with Master Rane until you recovered."

Rane cleared his throat. "Mistress Holly is *livid*, by the way. She insisted that I tell you that as soon as you woke up." He looked a bit embarrassed as he added. "And she wanted me to say: 'I told you so.' From her, of course."

Tala snorted a laugh. "Sounds like her."

"Also, the bits of gold that came from your keystone?" He looked incredibly confused by his own question.

"Yeah?"

He grunted. "I'll ask later, I suppose. Well, she said those were now payment for the inconvenience you caused her."

Tala sighed. "I suppose that's better than I deserve..." Then, the seriousness of the lost time settled back down on her. She took a deep breath and let it out quickly. "Well, rust. Thank you, both, for the help, for getting me back here. Seems that you all might have been right: Slow and steady would have been better."

Lyn's eyes narrowed. "Might? No, Tala. We *were* right. It is better. I can hold the void for more than five hours, now. How's your progress?"

Tala groaned. "Low blow, but fine. I won't push *quite* so fast."

Lyn opened her mouth, but Rane put a hand on her shoulder. She glanced at him and closed it.

"Take the win, Mistress Lyn."

Tala looked back and forth. *Had they met before?* Her mind was still a bit fuzzy. She shrugged. "Well. Time's wasting." *I have four days of meal budgets to spend.* She found herself smiling. *I can get at least one good thing out of this debacle.* "I need to eat."

Chapter: 13
She's a Scary Lady

Tala finished eating her fourth Cheesy Little Caravan—to Rane and Lyn's increasingly awed concern.

"How are you not distended?" Rane hesitated as Tala's eyebrows rose, and Lyn gave him a horrified look. "What? I know you're inscribed, but how does it fit? That's way more than you ate at the noodle place."

Tala looked down at her stomach, not a bulge in sight. "Stronger muscles? But, that's a rude question, Master Rane." She was kneeling beside the table as she'd almost broken the chair when they'd first arrived. Thankfully, she'd been tentative in her sitting and had immediately risen when the exterior-grade chair had started groaning.

Rane had also eaten one, and Lyn had gotten the smallest Little Caravan that this place sold—she'd still had trouble finishing it. Rane rolled his eyes, wiping his mouth. "For some people, I'm sure it is rude, but you'll never get fat, so"—he shrugged—"normal rules hardly apply."

Tala snorted a chuckle, taking a long drink from the restaurant-provided earthen mug. *I should get one of these to make drinking easier. No need to shoot water straight into my mouth...* But it was probably an unneeded expense. *Only a few copper?* Budget tight now, live large later.

"So... how are any of my items still functional? True, they were starving, but four days should have utterly drained them."

Lyn quirked a smile, speaking a bit slower than usual, likely due to her full stomach. "I practiced the void beside you."

Tala nodded. "Raising the ambient magic in the room. Clever. And thank you. I cannot tell you how much it would have been rusting awful to lose Kit and Terry here?" She patted the bird on the head and flicked a bit of jerky randomly away for him. "If his collar had lost all power, he'd have been obliterated by the city's magics."

Terry was giving her a hard look, even while he consumed the jerky.

Lyn nodded. "It was rough on Terry. He kept going to the edge of acceptable range and squawking in irritation. I think his collar was glowing red more than not for the first day you were back home."

Tala met Terry's gaze. "I'm sorry, Terry. You were stuck. If you fled, you'd be struck down. If you stayed, your collar could have run dry, then you'd be struck down."

Terry let out a low, irritable chirp.

"I'll try not to be incapacitated again."

He repeated his chirp.

"Agreed."

Rane and Lyn shared a look. "Can she understand him?"

Lyn shook her head. "I'd think not, but with her? Who knows."

Tala ignored them. "So, I need to drop through the work yard? For my custom cargo-slots?"

Lyn glanced her way. "No, they're at their guildhall." She hesitated, then amended, "Well, likely in their private work yard in the back."

"And where would I find that?"

"I'll take you." She glanced to Rane, then back. "Master Rane tells me that you agreed to work with him on your next assignment?"

"Yeah, seems like a good idea."

"I agree. I think getting you back out of the city will help get you out of your own head and slow your pace to one of reasonable progress."

"And get me paid."

Lyn gave a half-smile. "True enough. I'll need to see the custom cargo-slots for myself, so I can confirm their use for an out-and-back run. Any preferences I should know about?"

Tala shrugged. "Leave in a week? Depending on when my guild meeting is."

Lyn narrowed her eyes menacingly. "Why then?"

"I promised Adam that I'd work with the guardsman class. I need to give them at least some time."

She seemed a bit mollified at that. "Fine. I'll see what I can do. This will be a longer haul, in all likelihood." Lyn sighed. "Speaking of your meeting with a senior guild member, Master Rane took the last few days to collect written statements on your behalf. He and I were just heading to the Caravanner's Guild to file that paperwork when you woke up."

He was grinning. "We can drop by on the way to the wainwrights."

Tala rocked back a little bit in shock. "That must have been a lot of work, Master Rane."

He shrugged. "I have very little to do while in the city, and like I said, I want to go on the next venture in your company. Can't do that if they hamstring you for a time."

She didn't know what to say. "Well… thank you. I deeply appreciate that."

"Not all the statements were favorable, but that's likely better. The group will be accepted more readily if it at least has the appearance of balance." Lyn smiled at Tala. "I've been officially told to not interfere or influence the meeting in any official capacity. I'll still be your appointed point of contact, but as we're sharing a residence, I'm no longer considered neutral enough to represent the guild or comment on proceedings."

"Fair enough. When will I be meeting them?"

"I had you scheduled for two days ago, but with you unconscious, I asked them to bump it back." Lyn thought about it. "I was actually going to ask for another extension when we dropped off this paperwork at the guildhall, but now I don't have to."

"Oh? When is the meeting?"

"Late this afternoon. We'll come back to the guild after we test your cargo-slots."

Tala swallowed involuntarily. *Today?* Should she ask for a delay? *No, Tala. Get it over and done with.* She nodded, mostly to herself. "It sounds like we have a plan for the rest of today then. We should be off."

* * *

The stop through the Caravanner's Guildhall had been uneventful, and Lyn had confirmed Tala's appointment for later that same afternoon. It was also confirmed that Tala would have to attend alone, though Terry should be allowed.

As they walked, Tala had found her newer method of movement critical. By keeping her center of gravity so carefully controlled, she kept her steps from thundering against the ground. The few steps she took without that care caused tremors to reverberate through everything around her. If she was right in her guess, she was effectively close to nine hundred pounds at that moment. Her reserves were still vastly below what they could and should be, so she expected her weight to rise.

During their meal, she'd almost flipped their sturdy table by resting her arms on it too aggressively. As a result of that, and other incidents, she was being more careful than ever with her movements.

From the Caravanner's Guildhall, the three went straight to the Wainwrights, where Master Himmal was called out to meet them.

"Mistress Tala! I'm so glad to see you well. Your handler was unwilling to explain why you were unavailable."

Tala smiled back, a bit self-consciously. "Master Himmal, always a pleasure. It seems I was pushing too fast and rendered myself insensate for a few days."

The man blinked a few times, processing what she'd said. After a moment, his face blossomed with power as his magesight came to bear. He took a step back. "Well"—he swallowed—"you're lacking whatever barrier you had in place before." When his gaze met hers, his eyes narrowed. "Your magesight is always on?" He started laughing. "That's amazing! How are you not braindead?"

Tala quirked a smile. "That is the question."

"So, that is why you asked for the visible indication lights to be removed. You don't need them at all." He was nodding as he examined her visible lines.

He can likely see something *radiating out through my clothing but likely no specifics.*

"Your lines are the most intricate and delicate I've ever seen. Where did you find an inscriber with the patience and precision to do this work?" He hesitated. "I apologize, I'm forgetting myself and being rude."

Tala waved him off. "You're fine to ask and to use your magesight. Mistress Holly has some new methods."

He nodded to himself. "It's been a decade or so. About time she shook the world once again." He gave a little chuckle. His voice suddenly lost its mirth, and he was staring at her knife. "Mistress Tala. What have you done?"

Millennial Mage, 3 - Binding

Tala place a hand on Flow. "I soul-bound a knife. Apparently, it was a poor choice of timing."

He was frowning at her. "You can create Archon Stars, then? But no one explained that you shouldn't bind the knife first? Why haven't you been guided to make another?" He smiled then, though his confusion and concern were still evident. "I am glad you found your way to that spell-form. Please let me know when you are up for consideration, and I'll happily give my hearty backing to the proposal."

"That is very kind of you. As to your questions, I'll just say that this"—she patted the knife—"this was a bit of an accident and an exception, though I should be able to form a star soon." *Maybe tomorrow.* She nodded to herself. After a moment, she shrugged. *Why not tell him?* "I'm going to be making an attempt tomorrow, as I have obligations the day after." Rane had agreed to go speak with the guardsman instructor and schedule the restarting of her participation two mornings hence. He'd go to do that directly after this visit with the Wainwright's Guild.

"I see…" Master Himmal seemed to be contemplating. "Ambitious to attempt a star with such a short time available, without a"—he stopped, cleared his throat, and changed what he'd been about to say—"but it should be educational, one way or another." He smiled. "Do you have a quiet space to work? One should not be interrupted during an attempt."

Tala glanced to Lyn, thinking to check with the woman about making the attempt at home, but she found Lyn glaring fiercely. Tala took an involuntary step back. It wasn't a careful step, as she'd become in the habit of making. Instead, it was a quick, heavy footfall that caused a tremor to ripple through the ground. "Lyn"—Tala held up her hands—"what's wrong?"

Lyn thrust her finger at Tala. "You. You are *supposed* to be taking a break, going easy. Now, you're planning on making a star?"

Tala glanced to Master Himmal for support, but she found the Mage wide-eyed, mouth agape, staring at her. "Mistress Tala... why are you shaking the ground with a step? I didn't feel any magic in that vein radiating from you, but the result was obvious."

Great, two issues to address...

Tala addressed Master Himmal first, simply stating that her effective weight was now around a thousand pounds.

He seemed to take it in stride. "We'll reinforce the carrier wagon for your cargo-slots then. I presume your preference is still to ride atop that wagon—as you did on your recent journey?"

"It is. At least during the day."

"Is your mass increased or just your weight?"

"Just my weight." She frowned. "Does it matter?"

He smiled. "Of course. With just your weight increased, we'll have to reinforce vertically but not horizontally, at least not to the same extent. In addition, there shouldn't be extra strain on the oxen or harnesses as they won't be overcoming vastly increased inertia."

That made some sense. She hadn't really thought about the logistics of having increased weight but not increased inertia. *Hard to lift me, but not hard to push me? I suppose I'll have more friction against the ground, due to the higher weight...* It was something else to contemplate. *Maybe, this wasn't such a good idea...* In either case, she'd give it a good effort, at the very least.

He nodded. "Neither would be insurmountable, but this is the easier to work with. It will increase the cost, even so." He quirked a smile. "The bonus from the Caravanner's Guild for especially large storage capacity will be tapped to pay for the difference."

Tala sighed. "Fair enough."

Lyn cleared her throat, possibly even more irritated as she'd had to wait. "So? What do you have to say for yourself?"

"I'll be taking it easy, not stopping, Lyn."

Master Himmal quirked an eyebrow at the lack of a title but didn't comment. *I guess he didn't notice the first time.* Rane either didn't notice or didn't care.

"You nearly killed yourself. Please. *Please.* Don't succeed?"

Tala gave a tired smile. "I won't lock myself away. I know that my mistake cost me days of progress and nearly killed me. Even though it didn't, it could have damaged me enough to halt my growth entirely."

Master Himmal cleared his throat. "Yes, that is not something you should do."

She gave him an apologetic look. "I am doing my best to be careful."

He grunted. "Make your star. Get yourself raised to Archon, and much will be made clearer." He looked to Lyn, smiling slightly. "Truthfully, that is one of the safest things our young Mage, here, can do."

Rane nodded. "Besides, I don't want to rise to Archon alone."

Everyone turned to regard him, and he grinned widely. "I finished my star yesterday."

Tala looked around but didn't see any such thing on his person. "Oh?"

"It's in a little iron box. I figured if you were going to be done soon, we could go through the rigmarole together." He shrugged. "Paperwork and bureaucracy are always better with friends."

Tala snorted. "You say the nicest things." Then, she frowned. "That was fast, though…"

He shrugged again. "Master Grediv has been pushing me to make one for years, and though I refused to let him give me the spell-form, or to start training on the Ways, he still managed to trick me into preparing. The small shifts I was able to make, based on his letter, pushed me over the edge." He was grinning.

Master Himmal cleared his throat. "As wonderful as this is"—he looked to Rane—"and it is wonderful; congratulations, Master Rane"—he looked back to Tala—"shall we test your cargo-slots?"

"That is a fantastic idea." She smiled at him. Tala reached out and patted Rane's shoulder as they walked after the elder Mage. "Good job, by the way." She smiled. "It sounds like I still need to catch up."

He grinned back. "You'll be there sooner than you know."

Lyn rolled her eyes. "You two are ridiculous."

Rane glanced her way. "You're one to talk. Didn't you say you were going to be making an attempt soon?"

Tala looked to her friend. "Lyn? Do you think five hours with your void will be sufficient?

She shrugged. "Maybe? From my master's instructions, I'll be close. I think I can maintain the spell-form through a rest as well." She smiled. "I'm not looking to make a splash." She chuckled lightly. "I just want Mistress Holly off my back."

Tala nodded at that. "She's a scary lady."

The group came out into sunlight, and Tala beheld the new creation.

Her eyes widened. "Beautiful."

The cargo-slots were a dark, almost black wood with a unified matte finish over the entire surface. The handles for doors were black iron, lacquered to prevent rust or irritation for Mages. The rivers, streams, and swirls that composed the spell-lines were polished, almost red, gold.

"Is that an alloy?"

Master Himmal seemed quite pleased with the product. "Proprietary information, my good Mage."

Lyn was already walking around the constructs.

Tala walked up and examined the descriptive inscriptions. "These are four times the size of my last voyages' cargo-slots." *Without a mental construct, this size took me twelve minutes in my initial testing.*

"Precisely so. Though, with your increased capacity, we added several features we can only implement on occasion."

"Oh?"

"First of all, they are almost weightless when active. The cargo-slots themselves have their mass negated to the point that they react as if they were roughly thirty pounds apiece. We got much of the power for that by negating the indication lights." He gave a small smile as he continued. "Mass isolation is in effect, of course, so anything inside will have a perfectly smooth ride, and we have built the accouterments to make one a dedicated, high-value passenger transport, another a combination of venture resources and guard barracks, and two more into standard passenger carriers—as needed. We can even fit in Mages' quarters into the barracks cargo-slot—again, as needed." He was smiling happily. "With the specialized wagon to carry all the cargo-slots, I see no need for any other wagon on any caravan route, save the chuckwagon." He nodded definitively, clearly proud of the work.

"So, there are fourteen?"

"The classic ten for a caravan load, then four for the purposes of personnel."

She grinned. "Well, let's see what I can do then." She walked forward and placed her hand against the activation point of the detailed, stunningly beautiful spell-lines. To reach it, she had to step up onto a stepstool already in place, the plate, itself, being on the top of the slot.

"Why is the activation conjunction on the top, by the way?"

"So that you can recharge them all from the wagon's roof, even while the sides of most are covered by those in use for personnel and passengers."

She nodded. That made a good amount of sense.

Tala turned back to the cargo-slot before her and carefully built the mental construct of what her power would do. *Out, not up. More symmetrical than oblong.* She imagined exactly how the power would flow through the script and what it would do to the dimensionality of the space between the front and back panels.

It was similar, but not identical, to the cargo-slots that she had been empowering.

She moved to create void channels, connecting to the inputs of the construct, but then she glanced to Lyn.

Lyn had a suspicious frown on her face.

Tala sighed. *Fine.* She simply channeled her excess power accumulation through the mental construct and into the device, empowering it.

It felt painfully slow. Roughly twenty seconds later, the first indicator blossomed to her magesight.

"Remarkable improvement." Master Himmal was talking to himself.

Tala fought not to roll her eyes. *If I used my void-channels, I'd have it filled in two or three seconds.* She *might* have been correct, but she'd not attempted to hold a mental construct with multiple through lines before. This was safer. This was wiser.

It took her right around a minute to fully empower the cargo-slot. A twelfth of her previous attempt at a like-sized dimensional empowerment, and this endeavor hadn't touched her reserves. She was utterly fresh, in mind, will, and power. *How inefficient was I being, without a mental construct?* It was a humbling thought. *How inefficient am I still being?*

Tala stretched back, then twisted, cracking her back. "Well, that wasn't bad at all." She grinned. "Thirteen more to go."

Master Himmal cleared his throat. "Well, no. Not right now."

She looked at him. "Oh… right. I don't have a contract, currently."

He smiled and nodded. "Exactly." He opened the door, and they all walked inside, examining the cavernous space.

To Tala's surprise, it wasn't dark within. It wasn't bright, by any means, but the sides and top of the space were mildly translucent, allowing in the sun from outside. "How does that work?" She pointed at the closest side wall.

"The sunlight that strikes that side of the device is allowed through and distributed evenly across the entirety of the expanded space."

"Huh… that actually makes sense."

Lyn was frowning. "No, it doesn't."

Tala waved her away. "It does to me, and that's what matters here."

Lyn sighed but didn't comment further.

After they verified correct and complete empowerment, the four of them left the enlarged space, closing the door behind them.

Master Himmal reached out and tapped a portion of the script, sending power with an intricately constructed form into the point. The cargo-slot flared with power for a brief moment, and the magic bled away.

Tala looked between Master Himmal and the construct several times. Finally, she managed to stammer out. "But… that was gold!"

He was smiling mischievously. "Are you sure?" he replied, but then he turned away before she could respond.

Lyn cleared her throat. "Secrets aside, Master Himmal, I'm not sure I can sign off on a spell-form that can be powered down. That would obliterate cargo and passenger alike."

He waved her off. "It cannot be powered down if anything remains inside. Had we tracked too much dirt and dust in, I'd have had to order a cleaning crew to scrub the place before it could be deactivated. I assure you that it is perfectly safe."

She gave him a hard look.

He sighed. "The Wainwrights will send a letter of assurance to the Caravanners as soon as you leave. We fully certify this design."

Lyn nodded, satisfied. "Very well, then." She looked to Tala. "I'm happy. You?"

Tala nodded, smiling broadly. "Oh, yes. This is going to be amazing."

They all bid Master Himmal a good day and departed. Tala and Lyn set off towards the Caravanner's main guildhall, while Rane made his way to talk with the Guardsmen. Tala's primary tasks for the afternoon were almost complete.

I just have to talk with a senior guild official, which will likely include a renegotiation of my contract. No big deal. It wasn't like much was on the line.

Tala shifted uncomfortably as she walked.

Lyn, who was coming to the guildhall but not the negotiation, noticed. "Everything okay?"

Tala grunted. "It seems silly that so much could hang on a single conversation."

Lyn smiled. "It's why I have a job."

Tala snorted. "Do you know who I'll be meeting with? Any tips?"

Millennial Mage, 3 - Binding

"No, and yes. Know what you're worth, and know what you're saving the guild. The bonus for the custom cargo-slots is negotiated with, and goes through, the Wainwrights, so don't bring it up. It shouldn't factor into your discussion, from either side. They are going to be upset by your… extra-curricular dangers. After all, you *did* act recklessly quite a few times, but you also didn't fail in your duties. Try to keep that in mind—both facets of it. Don't let them push you around." She shrugged. "Also, stop getting in so much danger. I don't want you to die."

Tala smiled, gratefully. "I'll do my best." She thought for a moment, then addressed a different aspect of the topic at hand. "So, don't bring up the savings from the reduced wagons?"

"Oh, you should definitely do that, just not the fact that custom cargo-slots have been made for you. Your pay should go up for reducing the needed peripheries but should *not* go up because you can facilitate a larger cargo-load. Does that make sense?"

Tala was nodding. "I think so. I need to negotiate for my rate as a Mage Protector as well, right?"

Lyn looked hesitant. "No? Those rates are set per danger thwarted, with some modifications based on the specific route. It would be appropriate to note that by reducing the need for another Mage, you further reduce the peripheral requirements, though."

"Got it." She sighed. *I hate money…* No, that wasn't right. *I hate dealing with money…* Again, that didn't seem *quite* true. *I hate having to make decisions that will greatly affect how much money I have?* That seemed right.

"You seem lost in thought."

Tala sighed. "Just deciding what, exactly, I hate about this."

Lyn huffed a laugh. "Seems about right."

Tala grinned. "Any generic advice?"

"They won't kick you out, though they may offer to let you end your contract. If they can't give you the amount you're asking for, they will simply let their offer rest. Unless you are truly unprofessional in this meeting, they won't forcibly eject you from the guild."

"That's good, at least."

"That doesn't mean you can simply say, 'Give me your best offer,' and expect such. You'll probably still have a job, regardless, but you want to be paid as much as possible."

"Don't we all."

Lyn grinned. "I'm quite satisfied with where I'm at."

Tala rolled her eyes. "So I've heard."

"You want as much freedom as possible in contract choices, but they are going to want to restrict you, somehow, to keep your... more dangerous actions in check. Consider the wisdom of letting them."

Tala almost objected, but the more she thought about it, the more she realized that Lyn was right. *Maybe I could use a steadying influence...* Rane would not be a good source for that, even if she were willing to accept such advice from him. *I'll hear them out.*

Lyn seemed to be contemplating something. After a moment, she shrugged as if to herself. "Do something to take the official off their guard. Disarm them and put them on the back foot but not with anything overt."

Tala frowned. "How am I supposed to do that?"

"Be you? You really are quite odd, and most people don't know quite what to do with you."

"So... your advice is to be me?"

"Precisely, that's why I wasn't sure if I should say anything."

"Alright then..."

Shortly thereafter, they arrived back at the guildhall, and Lyn bid Tala goodbye. She had work to do. "I'll see you tonight, if not before. Good luck!"

Chapter: 14
Watching for a Trap

Tala waved goodbye to Lyn over her shoulder as she walked through the Caravanner's Guild headquarters and to a nearby receptionist. "Hello."

"Greetings, Mistress."

"I'm Mage Tala, here to see a guild official?"

The assistant looked down at his notes, flipping through a book, hunting for her name. "Ah! Here you are. Yes, right this way."

He came out from behind the counter and led her down a side hallway. "Will your bird be with you?" The assistant wasn't inscribed, and he was young, obviously in his middle teens.

She nodded, patting Terry's head as he slept on her shoulder. "Yes, he is an arcanous animal, on a training collar."

The teen nodded, seeming satisfied. "Very well. Can I get you anything to drink?"

"Some coffee would be lovely if you have it."

He gave a nod. "Certainly."

Tala was grateful that Lyn had thought to ask for a first-floor meeting room. Tala would *not* have started out on the right foot if that foot was through the floor. Thankfully, the floors down here were solid stone, some set in place, some poured.

She was led to a closed door. "Your appointment should be along shortly. Feel free to wait where you feel most comfortable. I'll return in a moment with your coffee."

"Thank you."

He gave a small bow and departed.

Tala pushed open the door and walked into a simple, small room. Two chairs sat facing each other across an appropriately sized table. A pitcher of water and two empty cups already sat in the middle of that flat, wooden surface. A window looked out on the street, slightly below. The street outside sloped just enough to put this window above eye level for the passersby, giving the room a good view and light while maintaining a modicum of privacy.

Tala moved over and examined the chairs. They were identical and seemed ill-suited to bearing her new weight. *Great.*

She briefly considered undoing her increased weight but shook her head. *No, I need to give this a good try, at the very least.*

She moved one chair away, tucking it into a corner, but remained standing. *I don't want to be kneeling when they arrive.*

Terry immediately flickered over to the chair, curling up and continuing his rest.

As Tala was taking in the room, she allowed her mind to wander, really for the first time since she'd woken up. *I am much, much heavier now.* All of her was heavier. Her heart didn't *feel* like it was straining too hard, but she supposed that it had had four days to acclimatize to the changes. All her involuntary systems had.

She glanced down and quirked a smile. *Holly's inscriptions really are excellent. Even at four times the weight, I still don't need a corset.*

The assistant returned, pushing the door open with his back. Tala's head whipped up. *That would have been embarrassing... Yes, come in and see me staring at my own chest. Real professional, Tala.*

He carefully held a large mug of steaming coffee. Tala's eyes narrowed. *They have a coffee incorporator, too. I just know it.* That really didn't make sense as a non-inscribed assistant couldn't use an incorporator. *Even an inscribed one, without a keystone, shouldn't be able to...*

He turned around and extended the mug to her. "Mistress, your coffee."

She accepted the beverage. "Thank you."

He bowed, smiling. "Is there anything else I can get for you?"

Tala almost asked for more coffee but held herself back. It was late afternoon, after all, and after sleeping for four days, she might have an issue falling asleep that night as it was. "No. Thank you."

"Very good, Mistress. The Exchequer will be with you shortly." He bowed, again, and left, closing the door behind himself.

Tala looked down at the earthenware mug. *Nicely fired.* She examined the vessel more closely, letting the coffee inside cool just a bit. *Nicely glazed, too.*

A light knock came on the door.

Tala looked up, distractedly. "Yes?"

The door opened just a crack. "Mistress Tala?"

"Yes."

It was pushed open, fully. "I'm Senior Exchequer Mrac." He was a middle-aged man, with wings of gray in his otherwise brown hair and a clean-shaven face. Surprisingly, he was not a Mage.

Tala stepped forward, offering her hand after moving her coffee to the other. "Good to meet you, Mrac."

He took the offered hand and smiled. "Shall we get started?"

She nodded.

Mrac walked over and sat in the single chair still at the table. Tala knelt beside the table, where the other chair had been. This placed her head a little lower than his.

He frowned, cocking his head to the side. "Is everything alright? Was something the matter with the chair?" He glanced over, seeming to notice Terry for the first time. "Do we need to get another?"

Tala looked away, feeling a bit embarrassed. "Well, I'm quite a bit heavier than usual. I don't believe standard chairs would hold me, so this seemed a good solution."

He seemed taken aback by that. "Well, I'm so sorry that we don't have the proper accommodations for your"—he seemed to be searching for the right word—"particular circumstance."

Tala smiled in what she hoped was a disarming way, turning back. "It's understandable."

Mrac cleared his throat, looking down at the notes on his slate.

Tala took a drink of her coffee. *Very nice.* Sadly, it tasted a bit different from that offered at the Constructionist's Guild. *Not an incorporator, then.* She hesitated. *Not the same type of incorporator, at least.*

"Yes, here we are."

Tala returned her attention to the man. *Wait… he seems a bit off guard… Lyn was right! I did it without even trying.* She smiled.

"Let me begin with a question: Do you know what most Dimensional Mages do in their caravan, after charging the dimensional scripts each day?"

Odd question to begin with… Tala shrugged. "No, I don't."

"Nothing."

She blinked at him. "What?"

"They do nothing. They stay in their wagon. They read; they eat; they work on little projects; they exercise. They do pretty much whatever they want, but in their wagon."

"That doesn't sound like nothing."

He cocked an eyebrow. "From the perspective of the caravan, they do nothing."

"Ah..." Tala took another drink. "Alright."

"Do you know what you did?"

"That sounds like a rhetorical question."

He quirked a smile at that. "True enough." He glanced down and began reading from his notes. "On your very first day, you left the safety of the caravan to harvest from a felled arcanous beast."

The blade-wing? "I was with guards the whole time."

His eyebrow rose as his gaze lifted. "That is noted, yes." He looked back down at his notes. "You slept on top of hostile flora, causing a stir but no real inconvenience."

"It bled. Shouldn't that make it fauna?"

He glanced up at her. "Was it blood or a type of sap?"

"I..." She didn't know. "Not sure."

"Hardly important, I suppose, in the grand scheme of things. Do you wish me to change the classification in your file?"

"Would it matter?"

"If it is classified as a true threat, the First Driver will be penalized for leading the caravan so near it, unawares, and the Mage Protectors would be entitled to a bounty for its demise. Traditionally, much of that would be given to you, but that is not required.

Den would be penalized? "No, I think it should stand as it is."

"Very well." He straightened a bit. "You again left the safety of the caravan, walking behind the last wagon, thus exposing yourself to the attacks of a terror bird, which you fended off. Such a threat would likely have attacked someone, but you did put yourself into a vulnerable position."

When she didn't comment, he proceeded.

"You left the protection of the caravan to approach an obviously magical, dangerous tree, though under the approval of a Mage Protector. It is also noted that you did not engage with the tree, itself, simply harvesting a fallen branch."

"That's true."

"You engaged in a verbal contract with one of our passengers to procure an arcanous harvest while still on a job for our guild. You then left the safety of the caravan, again, to engage a thunder bull on your own."

"I won."

"That is not in dispute." He looked back to his notes. "Depending on which Mage Protector's reports I reference, you either caused a magical beast to attack or lured one to do so at a more auspicious time. Both reports agree that when that midnight fox threatened the safety of the caravan, and at the behest of a Mage Protector, you slew said beast."

She looked down, still feeling a bit of awkward shame at how that had transpired.

"Then, you arrived in Alefast." He looked up, and she met his gaze. "Should we cover the trip back, or have we thoroughly established that you did very much more than 'nothing?'"

"I will agree that my actions are atypical for a Mage in my position."

Mrac relaxed just slightly. "Good. That makes this all much easier. I assume that you do not wish to be confined to a wagon, except for each morning, when you recharge the cargo-slots that are in your care?"

"That would not be ideal, no."

"Understandable." He gave a small smile. "Now, I've reviewed your file, and I agree that the services you can and do offer our guild are greater than taken into account in your first contract negotiation."

Tala rocked back slightly, a bit thrown at the change in tone. "Thank you?"

"My understanding is that you wish authorization to have the dual role of Mage Protector as well?" He had an almost eager glint in his eye.

"That is correct." *What's he getting at...?*

His smile blossomed wider. "I can sign off on that immediately. From the testimony, here"—he indicated his slate—"you did not exhaust yourself when you empowered the cargo-slots, and as previously mentioned, you even assisted in the defense of your caravans, without that being a portion of your role."

"Thank you; that is accurate." *What is happening here?* She felt like she should be watching for a trap.

He nodded, making a mark on the slate. "Rates for Mage Protectors are not open for negotiation. I trust that is acceptable?"

"It is," she answered hesitantly. *What is going on?*

"Good. As you are a new Mage Protector, we will be assigning a senior Mage to oversee your activities and duties, outside your role as Dimensional Mage."

There it is. "Wait, so I'm to have a minder?"

Mrac shrugged. "If you see it that way. We see it as a guide for a new role to prevent misunderstandings or missteps."

Would that really be such a bad thing? Lyn said I should consider their suggestion. It would be like a master but without as much... servitude... and with better pay. "That... could work, I suppose."

"Good." He seemed to relax more fully. "Now, as to your rate as a Dimensional Mage. Why do you feel that five and one-half ounces, gold, is insufficient for your service? That is a higher starting rate than any other indentured I could find in our records."

Tala nodded, falling back on what she and Lyn had discussed. This was an expected topic. *Deal with the rest later.* "I can understand your reluctance, but with all due respect, my benefit outweighs the cost, significantly, as you have already agreed."

"Oh? I simply agreed that what you offer is more than was considered in your first negotiation. I did not state that it merited an increase above your already high wage."

That caused Tala to pause. *Interesting.* She hadn't expected that. She gestured at the slate. "I'm sure that indicates that my original contract did not include a requirement or expectation for the use of cargo-slots as opposed to wagons. That distinction, alone, saves the need for dozens of oxen, many drivers and wagons, and the additional peripheries that would be required to support such an increase to the caravan size."

"True." He looked down, marking the slate. "But it does state that you will empower the largest dimensional storage that you can, and that we require, for each venture."

Good point... "It should note that I have forgone a private wagon, saving that expense, as well as that of a driver and servant for such."

"It does." He didn't look up. "That will not continue, however."

"What?"

His gaze lifted. "Were you, as an asset of the caravan, safe without a secure place to sleep?"

Tala opened her mouth, then closed it. After a moment's pause, she answered, "Yes. I am very well protected against physical harm—maybe uniquely so."

"I did review the summary of your capabilities. They are impressive and go a long way from moving your actions from foolishly suicidal to merely inconsiderate."

"Inconsiderate?" *Suicidal? Is that really how my actions looked?* Was that really an incorrect assessment? *This is hardly the time to consider that…*

"Yes. What would have happened if you'd been killed, carried off, or rendered unable to function?"

Tala found herself nodding. "The caravan cargo would have been lost…"

"And how many people's livelihoods would that have impacted?"

Tala didn't know. *At least the guards and protectors.* "Forty on the way out, and close to a hundred on the way back?"

"For those *directly* impacted, that guess is close enough, but you are forgetting those around the trip itself. Those who would be paid to unload it, and those who are expecting the materials or mail carried within. Caravans are lost, and mitigations are always put in place so no one would be destitute, but it would have been a blow to hundreds of people, hundreds of families." He took a deep breath before continuing. "Can you not see how it's a bit inconsiderate to put yourself on the line when a mistake would drastically harm so many? I would have chalked it up to Mage arrogance, but you genuinely don't seem to have considered all the implications. That is why I call it inconsiderate."

Tala sank down a bit, thinking over what he had said. *I did consider them… but mostly after the fact.* She had *tried* to be more careful, but that had mainly meant not doing the *same* dangerous things again. *I really didn't ever change my overarching outlook on my own actions…* "I suppose… but if I shouldn't have been doing those things, why didn't the guards try to stop me?"

Millennial Mage, 3 - Binding

Mrac looked genuinely confused. "I don't understand the question."

"Why didn't the guards prevent me from taking such risks if it was really so important to avoid them?" Tala grimaced slightly. *Wow, I sound petulant, even to my own ears...*

"In the hierarchy of the caravan, you outranked them." He shrugged. "A Mage Protector could have stopped you, technically speaking, but from the reports, you weren't exactly willing to listen to them. They did what they could to mitigate your dangerous behavior. Even so, each has already received... feedback on their performance." He glanced down at his notes once more. "It seems that one of the guards did begin to train you in the area of combat and self-defense. That was a wise way of helping ensure the safety of one he couldn't control."

Adam's agreement to instruct her suddenly took on a new light. *Was that really why he agreed?*

"But we have lost the thread. We are not willing to allow you to sleep outside going forward. The loss of your person would constitute a full loss of the caravan, especially now that there would not be ancillary wagons available for the most critical cargo, let alone passengers. The guards are not in a place to mitigate the danger of that with you sleeping so exposed."

"If it is as you say, why would you allow me to be a Mage Protector?"

"Your particular... survivability seems to lend itself to best effect when you enter encounters deliberately. We, therefore, would prefer that all your encounters be deliberate. In addition, as a Mage Protector, you can be ordered away from encounters in which you would have a low likelihood of survival."

That makes a sort of sense, I suppose. "In that vein, then, my work as a Mage Protector will remove one further private wagon from every caravan I accompany. The new cargo-slots, which I can empower, will allow for a two-wagon caravan, almost regardless of the number of goods needed. Just one cargo wagon and the chuckwagon."

"I see that in an addendum, here. One of our other Senior Exchequers, along with the Wainwright's Guild, have testified that such is the case. The issue with your point is that, with this increased space, your being a Mage Protector does not reduce the wagon count. The Mage you replace would simply have their sleeping quarters within your larger dimensional spaces." He looked down, flicking one hand to the side, dismissing the idea. He was frowning. "With all this in account, what do you request as payment?"

"Firstly, I do not want a restriction on the routes I can take. Even on the shortest, my empowering will greatly reduce the cost of the caravan. Added to the reductions in cost I allow, the smaller caravan should be able to go more quickly, thus increasing the efficiency of the trips as well."

Mrac shrugged. "Possibly, but we pay by the trip, not the day, and if you arrive before the destination city is expecting you, you will still have to wait until your pre-set departure date to leave."

"But, that preset date could be moved, beforehand. Preset earlier, if you will."

"Possible in some cases, but not all. In many instances, that could cause logistical issues. In others, the journey is too variable to cut it that close. We do have other Mages with your abilities, Mistress Tala. You are especially useful, not uniquely so."

Tala opened her mouth to argue, but he held up his hand.

"Your point, while not perfectly correct, is valid enough. So, my question?"

"Twelve gold ounces per trip, with no renegotiation required once I attain Archon. At that time, I will be granted seventeen ounces gold, per trip."

Millennial Mage, 3 - Binding

Mrac just stared at her.

She took a long drink of coffee.

He looked down at his notes, then back up at her.

She poured herself a cup of water. "Want one?"

He shook his head. "No, thank you." He looked down to his notes, seeming to do calculations.

She drank her water.

Finally, he cleared his throat, meeting her gaze once more. "Let me understand. You think you are worth more than double your initial already high wage, and you want nearly an additional fifty percent beyond even that, once you've gained the title of Archon?"

"That's correct."

"Seven ounces gold. Ten, once you have the title."

Tala grinned. *I have him.* "I'm removing the need for more than *twelve* wagons and accompanying personnel. Even on larger trips, like the return voyage from Alefast that I just did, the caravan will not require more wagons. Without those additional wagons, additional guards and Mage Protectors won't be needed. At the least, that's saving the guild more than eighteen gold per trip. I'm offering you a bargain."

He frowned. "Not wholly accurate, but I understand where you are coming from. What do you think you will offer, as Archon, to justify the second bump?"

"An Archon Protector is more valuable."

He shook his head. "Protector rates are not up for negotiation. We are discussing your value as a Dimensional Mage."

"Why were you willing to raise my pay from seven to ten, in your offer, once I was an Archon?"

He quirked a smile. "I was simply matching your proposal's format."

She shrugged. "Very well. Seventeen ounces, now, and I won't renegotiate once I attain Archon."

His left eye twitched. "That is not—" He stopped himself, his hand rubbing his left temple.

"Or, I am willing to set my rate lower and only invoke higher pay once I have become a more valuable indenture."

He was shaking his head. "If higher pay, alone, is what you seek, the local city lord has heard of your... tendencies and abilities. He offered to buy out your contract, that you may join his personal guard."

Tala stiffened.

"Such can obviously not be done without your permission, but given your proclivities, maybe you would prefer that line of work?"

She swallowed, involuntarily. "What would that entail?"

Mrac sighed. "I am obligated to inform you of the terms since you asked." His gaze made his irritation clear. "You would receive five ounces gold, per week, plus half your inscription costs would be covered. You would be forbidden from leaving the city for the duration of the ten-year contract, save at the behest of your lord, and your terms would be locked as stated, regardless of your advancement."

That was, at once, an amazing and a horrible deal. She almost started listing out the pros and cons in her head, but then shook it instead. *No. It is too restrictive. Too long-lasting. Too much like true slavery, if gilded prettily.* "Thank you, but I will pass."

He nodded, clucking his tongue and looking down. "At the moment, you are contracted for five years—or thirty trips. You have, remaining: four years, eleven months, and two days—or twenty-eight trips."

"That sounds right."

"The highest I can reasonably go is ten ounces, then twelve when you're an Archon. But I can only justify that if you up your contract."

Millennial Mage, 3 - Binding

Tala hesitated. "Oh? What are you asking?"

"A flat ten years, minimum of eight city-to-city ventures per year, and you must remain under the senior Mage Protector's authority on every trip until they deem you otherwise ready. We would, of course, also remove the renegotiation clause going forward."

He's expecting my worth to go up. So, accepting a slightly higher valuation now to lock me in later. Ten years. That was a long, long time. "Fifty trips, same minimum number per year." *If I pushed, I might be able to do that in two years...* It would probably take longer.

"I don't like the time requirement removed…"

He knows I'll be more useful as time goes on, and he doesn't want me blasting through my required trips before that utility comes into full effect.

"Ten years, seven trips per year."

She shook her head. "Sixty trips total."

He did not look happy.

She softened her tone and leaned in, just a bit. "Listen. If I blast through sixty trips in two or three years, you've still saved the guild dozens, if not hundreds, of ounces gold by my reducing the peripheral expenses on those ventures."

He sighed, doing some work on his slate. Finally, when she didn't say anything else, he looked up. "Seventy trips."

"Total. So sixty-eight remaining." She shifted on her knees, and he glanced from her to the chair in the corner.

Mrac huffed a laugh. "Fine. You are authorized to work as a Mage Protector, in addition to working as a Dimensional Mage, for any given caravan. You have no restriction on which routes you can take; however, every trip you take will be under the authority of a senior Mage Protector that *we* choose until they deem otherwise. Your rate will be ten ounces gold, per leg, going up to twelve ounces once you are a fully recognized Archon. This rate is not up for renegotiation. You will have a space to sleep within a wagon for each voyage, and you will use it. No servant will be provided. You will receive food, as a regular member of a caravan, and no other benefits. You will complete sixty-eight further trips in the capacity of Dimensional Mage, at these rates, at a pace of at least eight per year. Then, and only then, your indenture will be concluded. Are we agreed?" He seemed to be marking down all his points on the slate as he went. After he finished, he looked up at her.

"And, as a signing bonus for this new contract..." She trailed off as he gave her a flat, unamused look. She grinned, nodding. "Very well. We are agreed."

He passed the slate to her, and she verified all that he had stated.

"Looks good." She retracted power from her defensive scripts, pricked her finger, confirmed the contract, and handed it back. *Scripts are working great; I didn't fountain blood from my finger with my increased blood pressure.* She got a brief mental picture of accidentally spraying the room with a geyser of red, but before the impression fully formed within her mind, she shook herself to drive the visual away.

Mrac was focused on the slate and didn't seem to notice the movement. The device became green for a long moment, then faded to blank. "Thank you, Mistress Tala." He stood, offering her his hand in farewell.

She stood and took it. "Thank you, Mrac. It's been a pleasure."

Chapter: 15
About Time You Finished

Tala stopped by to say goodbye to Lyn on her way out of the Caravanner's main office. The other woman seemed surprised, for some reason, but otherwise, she didn't comment, except to say, "I'll see you at home."

It was late afternoon, and the sun had already set, though light still clung to the sky to highlight the clouds overhead, and periodic lights on the main streets provided easy illumination.

Tala knew it was cold. Even Terry seemed to snuggle closer into her neck as she stepped outside, but to her, it just felt wonderful.

There was an especially lovely park on the way, and Tala left the road to walk through it, across the grass. *Still green? I wonder what that takes…*

After she was a ways out onto the lawn, she had a realization. *I hope I'm not crushing the grass as I walk.* She looked behind herself and found that there didn't seem any permanent damage, marking her path. She looked down and took a moment to analyze what she saw.

In a circle around each bare foot, the grass was pressed flat as if under the boot of a giant. Tala couldn't help but grin. *I was wondering how it would look. Nice!*

She could see the telltale threads of magic across her sole, increasing the surface area of her feet. She could also feel the power in the gold inscriptions enacting that spell-form.

Millennial Mage, 3 - Binding

The manifestation is obviously beyond my foot, but the magic, itself, is contained there.

Magic was amazing.

She shifted up onto the balls of her feet, and the circle of compressed grass moved forward just a bit but didn't reduce in size. *Exactly as expected.* It was an elegant solution.

A great solution to a problem I've created. She shook her head. *I need to give it a solid try.*

So long as what she stood on could bear her weight, it shouldn't be damaged. If she'd done the math right, once she reached her maximum weight, anything she stood upon would experience the same pressure that it would under a normal person. *Weight could still be an issue but shouldn't be terrible. If a floor can hold four to eight people, standing in a huddle, it* should *be able to hold me.*

It wasn't a perfect analogy, but it was close enough.

She bent down and placed a palm down flat on the lawn.

An identically sized circle of grass depressed as she shifted her weight onto that hand. The active spell-forms on her hand were shaped differently from those on her feet, due to the difference in the form of the limbs, but they had identical functions.

I wonder what would happen if I slap someone... She grinned.

Now, she kind of wanted to slap someone. *No, bad Tala.*

It was time to get home.

*　　*　　*

Tala sat cross-legged on the floor of the sitting room.

She was just finishing the last vestiges of a miniature vat of custard. She'd scraped the last out with her finger, which she'd then licked clean.

Lyn walked in, stopping when she saw her housemate. "What did you eat this time?"

Tala pointed at four different bowls, each in turn. "Beef stew, bean porridge, chicken chowder, and butter-cream custard."

Lyn shook her head. "Each of those bowls looks sufficiently large to hold enough food for a family."

Tala grinned. "That's why they're called 'family size.'"

Lyn snorted. "Fair enough. How was the meeting?"

"You didn't just look up the results?"

"I thought it better to hear from you."

Tala shrugged at that. "I think I did pretty well. I'm going to have someone watching over my shoulder, but I think I can probably learn from them, so it's probably for the best."

"That's... surprisingly mature of you?"

"No need to sound surprised."

"You aren't exactly the... wisest person I know."

"I follow wisdom when it really matters."

Lyn opened her mouth to respond, then paused. "I think that might actually be true, at least from your perspective."

"Of course, that's why I said it."

Lyn sighed. "So, you have a minder. Did you get a pay increase along with that restriction?"

"I didn't get my initial ask, but I didn't expect to."

"Oh? So, you did get a bump. How much did you get?"

"Ten ounces but upped to twelve as soon as I'm raised to Archon."

Lyn blinked at her, then she started laughing.

Tala was grinning, but slowly, that expression faded.

Lyn sat down in a nearby chair, shaking her head. "You robbed each other."

Tala frowned. "What do you mean?"

"I looked at your file before the meeting. I saw what he was authorized to give you. I also saw a note added by someone else." Lyn had a small, knowing smile on her face. "Someone who didn't know you very well."

"Oh?"

"The addendum was a notification that you were newly graduated, and while your ability was acceptable, impressive even, we should not expect further advancement for quite some time."

Tala tilted her head. "So…?"

Lyn grinned widely. "He was authorized to give you up to eleven ounces per trip."

Tala cursed. "That slippery—"

Lyn held up a hand. "No, Tala. You don't understand. He was specifically forbidden from giving you more."

"He didn't."

Lyn cocked an eyebrow.

"Well, he hasn't yet."

"And aren't you planning on making an attempt at Archon tomorrow?"

Tala opened her mouth, closed it, then barked a laugh. "Oh!" She laughed again. "So, he thinks he saved an ounce, or I could have gotten one more ounce from him, but as soon as I succeed, I'll have violated my maximum, by what he was told."

"Precisely. If you'd actually gotten eleven ounces gold, per trip, they would not have renegotiated any time soon." She was shaking her head. "Somehow, you got more than you should have by accepting less than you had to."

Tala gave a seated bow. "Breaking the system, one decision at a time."

"That does seem to be the way you work, doesn't it?"

Tala sighed, leaning back and bracing herself up on her palms. "So, when are you making your own attempt?"

"I took tomorrow off. I'll see what I can do with the five hours in which I can maintain my void."

"So, didn't your master tell you not to move on until you could hold that constantly?"

"Yes, and no. She said that I shouldn't move on down the Way of the Void until then. He actually left tips and tricks to allow for the creation of a star much sooner than that." She smiled fondly. "Everything I can see seems to indicate that our learning and improvement will be opened to new horizons by becoming Archons."

"And you didn't want to do it."

Lyn gave Tala a flat look. "I still don't really want to do it. I'm not driven to be the 'best Mage I can be'—unlike some people. I'm looking on the bright side, but I am content where I am."

"Oh?"

Lyn shifted slightly. "Mostly."

Tala just smiled.

"Fine! I've been feeling a bit stifled. I like my work, but I feel like I'm in a rut. Every day is the same." She gave a half-smile. "Well, it was until you arrived. That's probably why I took such an interest in you; you were odd from the start."

"Glad to help."

Lyn rolled her eyes. "Anyway. Mistress Holly is right. It's time for me to move on with my magic." She let out a sigh. "I was going to fight to keep my position, but who knows? Maybe, those I can move into will be more fun." She did not sound convinced.

Tala shrugged. "Sounds complicated." She pushed herself up. "I was just heading to sleep. See you in the morning?"

Lyn looked a bit surprised. "Oh? I just got home."

Tala hesitated. *Does she want something from me?*

Lyn shifted again. "Could we… just talk for a bit? I feel like all I do all day is have quick touchpoints with people. I'd like to just talk…"

Huh… why not? She settled back down. "Sure. What do you want to talk about?"

The next couple of hours passed simply, the two friends discussing small things, lacking significance and without import.

Somehow, Tala loved it. She didn't particularly enjoy the topics—they were fleeting and largely meaningless—and she didn't enjoy the passage of time—after all, she had *so* much that she wanted to accomplish. No, what she relished was the friendship; something her younger self just might have killed to have. *You're not alone anymore, Tala.*

* * *

Tala woke early the next morning, feeling refreshed despite the short night of sleep. She knew that Lyn would likely sleep quite a bit later than she herself had. So, Tala got to work on her morning routine.

Stretching, exercise, soul-work, and a bath. Every step was odd.

For the stretching and exercise, Tala's new weight added strain and subtly changed her balance. Every bodyweight exercise, as stood to reason, was much more difficult, and the motions were ever so slightly off. *Just as easy to move, harder to hold up.* It was a strange balance.

As she thought about it, she was glad that they'd reinforced all of her tissues, or else her eyelids might not have been able to open or close against the increased force, and all her soft tissue would likely be sagging toward the floor in a truly horrifying manner.

No one likes baggy cheeks.

Her hair was more like her clothing than a part of her. Her years without it and her own internal thinking had caused it to be exempt from the gravity working. *Good thing, too, or I'd have the ugliest, flattest hair in the world.*

Not that she cared, of course. Not one bit.

True to Holly's prediction, Tala was now well past Grediv's requirements for another soul-bond. Tala honored Holly's advice and didn't even consider bonding something new.

Not one moment's consideration.

She didn't stare longingly at Kit, wondering what she could accomplish with a soul-bond to the dimensional storage.

Nope.

The pouch was just as excited about the prospect as expected, meaning it did not respond.

The bath creaked ever so slightly when she climbed in, but thankfully, since it had been overbuilt with a couple hundred gallons of water in mind, it bore her well enough.

It was still well before dawn when Tala finished her in-house tasks, and it was time for food. She used a measured pace and, thus, arrived at the breakfast eatery just as it opened. She purchased the group-meal, breakfast deal, this time with her coffee jug ready to hand.

The café was so close to Lyn's house that she'd almost decided to go home to eat. Even so, she'd ended up sitting on the grass in a nearby park, under the slowly growing light of dawn, eating her breakfast.

She almost felt at a loss as to what she should do while eating. The basic reviews of the texts from Holly were, obviously, finished, though she'd likely need to delve more deeply, to continue to strengthen her understanding of the workings inscribed throughout her body.

She didn't have a current research project, and she wasn't willing to start a new one, given that her task for the day would be all-consuming.

I could start making the star?

That had merit, but she didn't want to divide her attention.

Ah! Right. She took the time to charge her magic-bound items while she ate. She didn't use a void or channels. She simply allowed her excess to flow into each, in turn, before returning it to the constant filling of Flow.

Unlike the day before, she took the time to really examine the items, and her connection to them, as she topped off their reserves.

There were some marked changes. First, as she noticed the previous afternoon, she was able to fill each of the items as quickly as before, but without the need for her void-channels. If she had to bet, Kit took around a quarter of the power that the cargo-slots did, though it obviously used the power differently. She suspected that her mental construct for Kit was less precise than that for the cargo-slots, so it was likely that Kit should require even less power.

The elk leathers took half of what Kit did.

Her comb, as usual, needed nothing.

Terry's collar took more than Kit, though she suspected that was mostly because the power wasn't really going to be doing anything specific, so she had no mental construct for it.

The hammer…

The hammer!

She reached into Kit, pulled out the tool, and found it… mundane. *No! Rust me to slag…* It was utterly without magic—aside from that which was naturally found in all matter.

That was a blow.

Tala looked at Kit. "You were starving despite Lyn's attempts, eh? I imagine dumping the hammer out to pull from the same ambient magic might have starved you all."

The pouch did not respond.

Well, that's rusting stupid… Could she re-empower it? Worth investigating, but from what she understood so far, the answer was no. The magic was sustained almost in parallel to physical reality, and with the collapse of the spell-forms, there was nothing to re-empower. The spell-forms were gone.

She felt the absence of her hammer keenly. It had helped her survive the raven-ines and the terror birds. It had had the potential to be an asset to her for the rest of her hopefully long life. *I hate that I lost that tool...* She shook off the loss. *Not the time for self-pity, Tala.*

She sighed, turning her attention to the other change that had stood out before her; she could influence the flow of power within Flow.

The knife still kept itself topped off, connected directly to her soul as it was, but now, she could shift that power around within the weapon. She could feel the inscription-like place where she could activate Flow's change into a sword. She could also shift the cutting and resilience spell-forms and power, just like with her own body—better and more easily, in fact.

She would bet that, if she wished, she could even invert the power, weakening the blade to the point of falling apart.

She never would, of course, but it was fascinating to see the alteration of her control over the power. She couldn't deactivate any of the spell-workings, of course, but she could fiddle. *Yeah... not doing that now. Let's not muck with my soul, eh, Tala?*

But the greatest change with Flow was that Tala could pull power *out* of Flow and back into her gate or keystone, then from there out into her body. And Flow's well of power was *deep*.

Could I pull from Flow to make my Archon Star? Intuition told her she could, but it would be a *very* bad idea, at least after a point. *There seems to be a level of power required for this new stage of connection. If I drain Flow below that, I might shatter the connection.*

That didn't feel perfectly correct, more like the bond would be strained—*and* might *break under that strain.*

In either case, it wasn't a good plan.

Though, I could dump into Flow for days, then pull it all out at once, down to that threshold, to make a star. That… that could work beautifully. *I'll keep that in mind if required, but today, I do it the right way.*

She also had no idea if she could actually handle all that power at once.

She licked the remains of the last breakfast sandwich from her fingers and sighed, contentedly. *That was good.* She drained the last of the coffee in one long pull and stood, pushing up off the grass.

To her amusement, she noticed that her backside had actually left quite a depression in the ground where she'd sat. *I'll need to be more careful about where I sit.*

But that was for later.

Now?

Now, it was time to forge a star.

*   *   *

Tala was irritated.

She held the slowly building spell-form of the Archon Star in her left ring finger. She was alternating between holding void-channels and resting.

When she forged the void-channels, she maintained a smaller one for her body and four funneling directly into the growing spell-form.

As she rested, she pushed the comparative trickle of excess into the spell-form to maintain its growth and keep it from solidifying.

At the start, she could only maintain the void-channels for ten minutes at a time.

True, that was a marked improvement from her earlier attempts, but it was still paltry compared to Lyn's supposed five hours.

I must get better.

Her recovery time had improved as well, however, so each rest had started out taking around five minutes.

Thus, she was averaging around four times her usual power accumulation rate, mostly directed towards the star.

That great progress wasn't what frustrated her.

No. She was irritated because she'd been at this for *hours,* and she was starting to slip. Her slips were minuscule, like an alchemist *almost* cutting a finger or nearly adding the wrong ingredient; not fatal, but not great.

Sometime after the first hour, Lyn had joined her, sitting on the floor across from her, holding a small, roughly spherical diamond between her palms.

That was over two hours earlier.

Tala was currently resting and used her freed mental space to glance at Lyn.

Her void is constant, consistent, and strong. Tala, herself, was improving. If she had to guess, she'd say she was holding the void-channels for nearly twenty minutes now, and her required resting time had only increased marginally. *I'm getting better.*

Still, Lyn was doing it and doing it well—no sign of slipping in evidence.

Tala frowned as she looked more closely at the diamond in Lyn's hand. Power was pouring into it, but a lot was flowing off of and around the surface, dissipating into the room.

Her mental construct of the Archon Star isn't perfect? Or there is some loss through the change of medium...? It was most likely both.

Millennial Mage, 3 - Binding

It was almost as if Lyn was simply throwing the power at the gem, trying to alter it so it would take the proper form on its own.

But that would be madness. This is really hard, even while I'm controlling the power directly...

She looked down at her own hand, inside of which her own Archon Star blazed with vastly more power than Lyn's partially constructed one. *I'm not seeing the same inefficiency.*

As she thought about it, that made sense; she was an Immaterial Guide, and magic was immaterial, especially within her own body. She had nearly perfect control over her own internal power. So, even if Lyn could have been working within herself, she wouldn't have the same advantages that Tala was experiencing.

Tala had also created quite a few stars by this point, and her mental construct was likely much more refined than Lyn's. *This is going to be easier for me than her. It is easier for me in basically every conceivable way.*

While they each had advantages, Lyn's mainly being her better, longer-lasting void, Tala decided she liked her own more.

Yes, I like having all but one advantage. Massive insight, Tala.

As rested as she was going to be and ready to dive back in, Tala closed her eyes and reforged her void-channels. *Another round!*

To her surprise, as she precisely guided her power into the spell-form, she could feel it coming to a tipping point. *Just like Flow.* If she had to guess, she was about to cross the lower limit of a true Archon Star.

As she guided her magic, the spell-form *ticked* over the hurdle and began drinking in power much more easily. In fact, Tala suddenly had to fight the spell-form on several fronts.

First, it seemed to want to draw all the power out of her, to drain her dry as some of her earliest versions had before she'd gained greater control.

Second, it was trying to move on its own.

The Archon Star *wanted* to move up the flows of power, towards her core. Tala felt silly, anthropomorphizing the spell-form that way, but it was an accurate description of how it felt.

Similarly, she *knew* that that was not a good idea. Something deep within her rebelled at the idea of the Archon Star reaching her gate.

So, she fought the star, even as she continued to drown it in magic, using the pressure of inflowing power to assist in pushing the spell-form back.

The void-channels were now simpler to maintain as if they were naturally meant to be there, but Tala was now working harder than ever. As the star grew in power, it also grew in strength.

Somehow, Tala knew. *This is a fight for dominance like no other Mage has to face.* She snorted a rueful laugh. *This might even be why they don't suggest Archon Stars be forged within a Mage's flesh.* She didn't know what would happen if she failed. She simply did not know enough. Even so, she *knew* that she, as she was, would cease.

Somehow.

And so, she fought.

She considered allowing her accomplishment to be enough. She almost stopped, realizing that she had a fully powered star—if in the lower reaches of acceptable power. *No.*

The channels were locked open, now, and while she could cut them off if needed, they were trivial to maintain. *Like adding one to Flow, since its change.*

Tala gritted her teeth and turned her entire focus inward.

Millennial Mage, 3 - Binding

*   *   *

More than an hour later, Tala was gasping for breath, her breathing pattern forgotten.

She was coated in sweat, more so than she had been in her memory. *Academy calisthenics have nothing on this.*

Her lungs burned, her every muscle quivered, and her inscriptions weren't helping. The strain was beyond physical, and that was all those spell-forms could address.

Her star was complete.

Not only had she hit the level Grediv had recommended, but she, in her near-infinite stubbornness, had gone beyond that, and the spell-form was no longer taking in power.

The Archon Star sat on the cusp of… something. She had no idea what.

All she could interpret was that no further power could be incorporated into the form, and she had to *get it out, now*!

Her camp knife, not Flow, came up in a shaking hand, while her left hovered over the prepared iron vial.

Okay, Tala. Just a moment more. You're almost there.

She pulled her power back from the ring finger's defensive forms.

The tip of the blade pushed into the skin, her shaking making a far larger cut than she had intended.

No blood came out.

What the rust?

The Archon Star did not *want* to leave.

Tala growled, pushing with all she had.

The star wouldn't leave.

Rust you, you stupid, slagging spell-form! She jerked her defensive power back further and cut off her fingertip at the knuckle.

Tala almost lost the fight with the Archon Star, then.

First, the intensity of the pain was staggering, given the totality of her focus on the digit.

Second, she was utterly unprepared for what she saw.

The fingertip fell away, leaving a golden mesh of spell-lines hanging in mid-air, connected back to the stump. *The spell-lines stayed, even while the flesh fell away?*

Power was flowing through them, locking them in place, even if she was forbidding their enactment. *Can't turn off gold lines...*

In the center of it all floated the Archon Star, seeming somehow outside the physical space her finger had occupied.

Each beat of her heart caused blood to flow through where her vascular system should have been and where the spell-lines meant to augment it still were.

The Archon Star was perfectly spherical and ruby in color, set within an impossibly intricate weaving of gold.

Well... rust. What am I supposed to do, now?

As if in response, the star seemed to flex, pulling on its connection with her, to call itself to her as she might have pulled Flow into her hand.

She opposed it with her will, and the strength of her soul alone, but she was *tired.*

Bless you, Grediv, for insisting that I strengthen my soul.

She had no idea if she was screaming in agony and determination or if she was utterly silent. She couldn't spare any of her focus from the internal battle to register either sound or the lack thereof.

Slowly, inexorably, she drove the star through the netting of gold, pushing the lines apart, only for them to snap back into shape right afterwards. Those spell-forms seemed tied to, and maintained by, the flow of magic, which again, was deeper than physical.

Millennial Mage, 3 - Binding

She didn't know if she waged her war for a bare instant or for hours, but finally, the Archon Star moved free, and the conflict was done.

The drip of power-saturated blood rocketed downward, into the iron vial, still enough a part of her that its gravity remained enhanced.

There was a last, sucking attempt to drain her dry, but Tala slapped it aside with contempt.

Then, the knife dropped and the iron cap firmly in place over the vial, Tala allowed her inscriptions to act.

Her finger blossomed outward: flesh and bone, nerve and sinew, drawn into being through the working of her spell-lines, the material and energy for their construction instantly moved from her body's stores.

It didn't take a lot, all things considered; a fingertip really wasn't that massive, and it was over in an instant.

"Take that, you rusting star!" she tried to yell at the vial, but her throat was utterly parched, and it came out as an unintelligible croak. *What possesses people to make these?* She didn't know if she trusted the star outside of its vial. *Good thing I don't need to take it out...*

In that instant of relief, she saw that the windows of their home were dark, and Lyn was sitting in a chair nearby, regarding her critically.

"Well. About time you finished, Tala."

Chapter: 16
A Taste of Human Blood

Tala stared at her friend, still in a bit of a daze.

Lyn seemed to be examining the floor in front of Tala. "I hope you know, I'm pretty sure we can't clean that."

Tala looked down and saw an irregular circle of blood around the stub of her finger. *Just the blood that had been in that piece of digit when it was cut free.*

The rest had been kept in her body. Tala groaned. The slight tang of copper was in the air, along with something that seemed to tingle her nose unpleasantly. *Did she try to use a harsh cleaner on it?* That didn't make sense. Lyn wouldn't have left the finger bit in the middle if she was trying to clean up the blood.

She seems... too unemotional? Lyn was still sitting back, stoically regarding Tala and the mess she'd made. "If we can't, you're buying me a new rug."

Tala swallowed, licking her dried lips. The rug looked well made. *That could be expensive...*

Lyn sighed, handing her a cup that was full of clear, cool water.

Tala took it reflexively, drinking feverishly. Before she was really aware, she'd downed the whole thing. She pulled it back from her lips, letting out a satisfied gasp, pulling air back in with a great gulp. She'd been drinking so fast, she hadn't kept breathing. After that, she felt recovered enough to speak. She smiled up at Lyn. "You seem to be handling this well." She gestured towards the fingertip.

"Oh?" Lyn looked anything but pleased, even as she refilled Tala's cup with a pitcher. "Well, I had a bit of time after I came out of my own meditation to startle, scream, puke, clean that up, and critically examine my housemate."

Oh! It's vomit. I'm smelling the lingering scent of vomit. "It was that bad?" Tala swept her gaze over the area near where Lyn had been sitting. She could see a slightly discolored portion of rug. Normal people wouldn't be able to see it, but Tala could without difficulty. *That was a lot of puke.*

Lyn glared. "I came out of my meditative state, having successfully forged my star, only to find you holding a bloody knife, unblinking eyes locked on the magical matrix that remained behind after you *cut off your own finger.*"

Tala didn't meet her gaze, instead looking down at her hands, which still held the iron vial. "Just the tip." She was not petulant. She didn't feel petulant. *Not one bit.* Besides, Lyn wasn't her mother.

Out of the corner of her eye, Tala saw Lyn cock an angry eyebrow and intensify her glare. "You cut off your own finger. In my house." Her lips were compressed into a hard line.

Tala swallowed to clear her once-again-dry throat, took another drink when that didn't help, and looked up at Lyn. "I'm sorry?" *Is that what she wants? It's not like I enjoyed cutting off my finger.*

"You rusting well better be." Lyn folded her arms over her chest, leaning back with a huff. She'd crossed her legs as well. "You know. At first, I thought you were just ignorant. Then, I thought, 'You know, she's a bit reckless.' But that's not it, is it?"

Tala leaned back a bit, just blinking at her friend.

"No. You genuinely don't care if you die, do you?"

"Of course I do. Why else would I focus so much on my protections?"

"Oh, you *consciously* want to survive, but that's the only part of you that seems to."

"It was just a fingertip, Lyn."

"Oh? And when you broke your brain and were unconscious for four days?"

"Well, I was—"

"What about when you decided to modify your Gate with your will, ignoring *fundamental* lessons that I *know* you were taught."

"Wait a moment, that was—"

"And, let's not mention all the stunts you pulled on your caravan journey. Do you have any idea how bad that looked for me?"

"I did my job."

Lyn leaned forward, dropping her hands to her own knees. "Are. You. Serious."

Tala pushed back a little farther.

"You should be dead. If some part of yourself wasn't as obsessed with survival as the rest was in trying to kill you, you'd be dead a dozen times over."

"I… I don't know if I followed that."

Lyn just glared. After a long moment, the older woman took a long breath and exhaled in something that reminded Tala of a silent scream. She composed herself. "Stop being reckless, please. Please."

Tala did not trust herself to respond verbally. So, instead, she just nodded.

The exchange seemed to have woken Terry from where he'd been sleeping in the corner. He rose to his feet and shook himself, his feathers adding a comforting rustling sound to the otherwise tense silence. Tala smiled at the bird. "Terry?"

His eyes were fixed on the bit of finger.

Millennial Mage, 3 - Binding

Lyn shifted, now more uncomfortable than angry, the avian having successfully distracted the older Mage. "He's been staring at that, whenever he wasn't sleeping, since I finished. Likely before that, too."

"But he didn't eat it." *Huh, the bird has some restraint.*

"He looks like he wants to…"

Should I let him? Tala did have to do something with the fraction of a digit. *But, is that a bad precedent?* She groaned. *I really don't care enough, right now. He seems to really want it.* "Go ahead."

Terry flickered, and the finger was gone. The bird shook himself happily and blinked to her shoulder, where he settled down, seemingly asleep once more.

Lyn closed her eyes, turning her face away and looking a bit green. "Gross." It was barely above a whisper as if she were afraid talking normally would bring up more bile.

Tala cleared her throat. *Distract her; she's vulnerable to cementing the topic change.* "Sooooo… you finished forging your star?" She smiled hopefully.

Lyn's eyes opened, then narrowed. "We'll come back to this; don't think you're off the hook." Even so, she took a deep breath, then smiled. "But, yes!" She pulled out her small diamond sphere, which positively blazed with power to Tala's magesight. "What do you think?"

I think it's less than half the strength of the one I made. "That looks awesome."

Lyn's shoulders sagged, just slightly. "…You think it's weak."

Tala sat up straighter, eyes widening. "What? No. It's great!"

Lyn rolled her own eyes and sighed. "Don't patronize me, Mage. I know I made a bottom-of-the-ladder Archon Star, but I rusting made one. I made one in *five hours*." There was fire in her eyes. Not literal fire, though Tala didn't doubt that Lyn could manifest thermal energy within those orbs to create such. *Probably a bad idea, though.*

"Yes, obviously. That is impressive, beyond what all but the best Mages, your age, could produce." *Well, without a Way, at least.*

"Now you're just being insulting." Before Tala could say anything further, Lyn shook her head. "Doesn't matter, Tala. I know what *I've* made." She held out her hand. "Let's see it."

"Hmmm?" Tala turned a bit away, giving a half-smile.

"Don't be coy. Give me the vial. I want to see what sort of abomination you created for your star. I couldn't get a good look at it while it was still in what remained of your finger. My magesight isn't precise enough." Lyn shook her hand slightly to add emphasis.

Tala grinned, holding out the iron vessel for Lyn's inspection.

Lyn took the vial, activating her magesight as she unscrewed the cap. She looked in and instantly re-covered it. "That's… blinding."

"Does your magesight not adjust?"

"Yes, Tala, of course it does. That is required." Her tone was long-suffering, and her look was one of weariness.

"Fine, fine." Tala waved her off.

Lyn shook her head, carefully re-opening the vial. Once her magesight had had time to adjust, she simply stared down into the opening.

"Sooooo?" Tala was quite curious what her friend thought.

Lyn sighed. "Well, this city's going to have two new Archons, alright." She capped the vessel and tossed it back.

"Three." Tala held up her left hand with three fingers raised, while her other tucked the vial away into Kit. "Master Rane said he was ready, too."

Millennial Mage, 3 - Binding

"Right! He said he was going to get us registered for evaluation and elevation." Lyn smiled contentedly.

"What? When?" *I don't remember him coming in...* She didn't remember Lyn vomiting, either, but even so.

"He was here like an hour ago. He saw my star and stared for a long time at the... mess that was your finger, at that time. Then, he said he would get it sorted."

Tala grunted. "Well, that's kind of him. He coming back?"

Lyn shrugged. "Probably."

Tala pursed her lips and frowned.

Lyn gave her a searching look, then burst out laughing.

"What?"

She kept laughing.

"Come on, Lyn. What?"

Lyn reined in her mirth. "I can see your mind working, little Tala." She snorted another laugh.

"Oh?"

"You are trying to decide if it's rude to get food without him, and if it is, if being rude would be worth it."

Tala blinked in surprise. *That is... surprisingly accurate.* "Huh."

"The answer is yes, it would be rude, and no, it wouldn't be worth it."

She groaned. "But I missed lunch."

"And he's been *insanely* helpful. Don't be utter pyrite."

Tala growled irritably. "Fine. We'll wait." She did her best to keep topics frivolous until then.

Thankfully, they didn't have to wait long before a quick, firm knock on the front door preceded Rane's entrance. "Hello?"

"Come on in, Master Rane." Lyn's tone was welcoming, and she stood to greet their guest.

Tala reached a hand up towards her friend. "Help me up."

Lyn gave Tala a bemused look. "Not mentally recovered?"

What? Tala hesitated. *Oh...* She felt a bit foolish. "Right." She leveraged herself up, careful not to hit any furniture. *This is a bit inconvenient.* She really needed to remember that she was heavier than she had been—and by quite a lot.

"You could release that… I'm really not sure why you would want it constantly maintained."

Tala shrugged. "I'm going to give it a good try. I'll consider removing it later."

Before Lyn could respond, Rane came in and broke into a broad grin. "You're cognizant again!" He glanced to Lyn. "Did you wipe her face? The drool is gone."

Tala colored, swiping her lower jaw with her sleeve, even though that was obviously not needed. *I was drooling?*

Lyn cleared her throat. "That is hardly relevant. Well?"

Rane grinned. "I got us all registered. Mistress Lyn, you will be seen mid-morning tomorrow." He held out a small piece of thick paper. "That contains the details of the location and exact time." He then glanced towards Tala. "We're scheduled for later in the day, after our morning with the Guardsmen's Guild."

Tala gave a slight bow. "Thank you, Master Rane. I trust you know the details?"

He shrugged. "Yes, but I should give you this anyway. I go just before you, so you might not want to arrive early just to wait around."

"Either way." She took the proffered informational card. It was a thick, cream-colored paper with a somehow-metallic black ink.

Rane cleared his throat. "They asked that I pass a single instruction along."

Lyn and Tala turned their full attention to him, each lowering the card they'd been examining.

"We are not to discuss the process of forming our stars, or anything around such, until after our evaluation."

Tala shrugged. "Fine by me." *We'll be better served by eating.*

Lyn frowned. "Why not?"

"No idea, but they were quite insistent."

Tala waved dismissively. "We'll have plenty of time to talk about it tomorrow. Right now, we're all hungry, yes?" She looked to each of the others, and they nodded in turn. "So... food?"

Rane chuckled. "Yes, food."

* * *

More than two hours later, they were each finishing up their dinners. Rane had insisted on paying, in celebration of the two women's accomplishment, and the two hadn't protested the kindness. Rane had even bought a whole roast chicken for Terry.

Terry had accepted the offering with stoic consumption.

They'd all stared on in fascination as the obviously-too-small Terry had swallowed the chicken whole. The other two had refrained from commenting, but they'd seemed to keep a closer eye on the bird after that.

Tala knelt beside the table, content, Terry seemingly asleep on her shoulder. Rane and Lyn did not give her grief about her inability to use a chair, though they both let it be known that they thought it a bit silly.

Lyn, now finished, acted a bit overfull, leaning back as if to take pressure off her stomach.

Their table was outside, set a bit apart from other groups, which had come and gone through the evening. There was a chill to the air, but the patio had several regularly spaced, cast-iron woodstoves, which more than took the edge off the cold.

The stoves were mundane, seemingly completely devoid of magic save the standard traces found in all things. They seemed to have been designed for incredibly efficient use of fuel, and towards that end, Tala had only seen a single one require more wood, and the attendant had only added a single, medium-sized chuck. *It's fascinating what can be done, even without magic.*

The meal had been extravagant. Roast turkey, with the skin crisped *just right,* and honey-glazed ham that fell off the bone came together, served with a thick, smooth, brown gravy.

Steamed peas and carrots were seasoned to perfection; dinner rolls that were light, fluffy, and hot from the oven; and mashed yams that seemed too thick and creamy to be real were all coated by exactly the right amount of butter in accompaniment to the meats.

There had been some sort of casserole made up of alternating apple and sweet potato slices, marinated and baked covered in a brown sugar brandy sauce.

The final side had been some sort of twice-baked cornbread. Apparently, in times past, it would have been cooked inside a turkey or chicken, but these days it was made on its own. *Oh, by the stars, stuffing is the best thing I've ever eaten.* She especially enjoyed it smothered with gravy.

Tala wasn't sure if her new favoritism would hold up after she ate her next meal, but she didn't really care. The celebratory feast had been perfect.

Rane wiped his mouth with his napkin, sighed happily, and cleared his throat. "So, it seems we are, all three of us, quite special Mages."

Lyn grinned, swallowing her last bite of dinner roll with butter. "Don't you forget it."

Tala cocked her head, though, a bit confused. "Oh?" *I know we're all a bit young, supposedly, but that's not that special. Is it?*

Rane nodded as if happy to explain. "Even among those who can create an Archon Star, most don't understand the form well enough for any sort of efficiency. Without a well-established Way, and a good mental construct, even a top-tier Mage can take more than two days to make a barely acceptable star, and most Mages aren't top tier."

Tala frowned. "But why would a top-tier Mage lack those things?" *That makes no sense.*

Rane shrugged. "Many of us are stubborn." His smile shifted to one that was a bit self-conscious. "I, for one, wanted to do it on my own. Only you, Master Trent, and Master Grediv's persistence convinced me of my folly. And hear me when I say that Master Grediv was not one to allow too much self-assurance."

Lyn sighed wistfully, nodding. "My master had to practically strong-arm me into taking the notes on Ways and the Archon Star spell-form. I'd assumed that I'd just figure it out if I ever needed or wanted to. And even with the notes in my possession, I didn't even consider using them until you and Mistress Holly… encouraged me to."

Tala grunted. "That seems pretty foolish." When both her table companions looked at her oddly, she raised both hands. "No offense!"

Rane snorted, and Lyn barked a laugh, shaking her head.

"I'm sorry… I didn't mean that how it came out."

Rane ruefully. "I know that feeling."

Lyn sighed in mock resignation, shaking her head again. "In any case, despite the best intentions of masters for their Magelings, most end up going it alone and without true guidance, thus taking much longer to create inferior products."

Tala's eyes were twinkling, but she didn't say anything, and she did her best not to smile.

Lyn glared. "I'm not just talking about power level, Tala. Mine is no ignorant Mage's construct."

Tala did smile, then, but refrained from commenting, her mind already contemplating something else. She tried to imagine making an Archon Star without the void-channels, or even the void, and shook her head. "Doing it the 'standard' way… That would have taken me *ages*." She smiled at Lyn. "Thank you, again, for sharing your master's wisdom."

She shrugged, her irritated expression fading into an easy smile. "From what I understand, books detailing the Ways will be freely available to us after our raising. I just gave you the insight a bit early." She winked.

"Precisely." Tala beamed. "And thank you, Master Rane."

"Oh? What for?" Rane had jumped a bit at being suddenly addressed. *Had he been falling asleep?* He did look quite drowsy, eyes half-closed, a happy little smile pulling at his lips.

"Food"—she gestured at the empty plates stacked before her—"scheduling our evaluations, discussing the Ways with me, and for waiting for us to be ready to be raised alongside you."

He gave a small smile, clearly pleased with himself. "Well, I'm glad to have been of help."

Lyn added her own thanks, and Terry woke briefly to thrum a happy chirp as well.

"Well, you are all most welcome." He was sitting a little straighter now. Clearly, he was still tired, but he was contented, nonetheless.

Tala stretched, twisting first one way, then the other. Terry ignored the movement. "We should get some sleep. It's a big day tomorrow, and today's been full." She hesitated, a thought coming to her from the depths of her never-ending to-do list. "Though... I think I'd like to swing back through the Constructionists' Guild again on the way home."

Rane stood. "As fascinating as I'm sure that will be, I should get some sleep." He yawned, and Tala noticed, once again, that he *looked* weary. His eyes weren't quite as bright as they usually were, and his face seemed a bit less animated. His shoulders rounded a bit, and his posture suffered now, even if just barely.

Tala gave him a comforting smile. "I hope you sleep well. I'll see you tomorrow?"

"Bright and early." He smiled through his tiredness. "Good night, Mistress Lyn, Mistress Tala."

Terry lifted his head, looking at Rane.

Rane noticed and gave a half-bow, conveying the utmost seriousness. "Good night, master Terry."

Terry shimmied, scrunching lower as he tucked his head down. He let out a happily dismissive squawk and feigned sleep once more.

Rane whispered, clearly hoping Tala would hear. "Every day, he proves that he's more intelligent than I'd have guessed, by a long shot. Please be careful? Once beasts like that get a taste of human blood, it's hard to rein them in."

Tala chuckled nervously, looking away. "Yeah... of course." Blessedly, Lyn didn't comment, though she just might not have heard. Tala cleared her throat and plastered on a smile once more. "Good night, Master Rane."

Lyn sighed, shaking her head and not looking at Tala. "Good night, Master Rane."

Rust, she did hear that...

Rane left without a backward glance, though he did give an offhanded wave as he left the restaurant's patio.

Lyn wiped her mouth one last time as she stood. "Shall we go?"

"Do you want to come with me?" Tala stood as well, not disturbing Terry with the careful movement.

"It isn't too far out of the way, and I'm curious what you're going to do this time."

Tala smiled, feeling genuine affection for the older woman. "I'll be glad to have you along then."

Chapter: 17
Wish Me Luck?

Tala, Lyn, and Terry walked the darkened streets.

It wasn't too late, so they were far from alone as they made their way through the cool, nighttime streets. They moved slowly, lethargic from their feast, and high off their recent accomplishments.

The two Mages chatted about small things, shortly coming to the topic of relationships.

Apparently, several eligible men had been attempting to woo Lyn, but she'd turned down all comers. "I just don't need that sort of complication in my life, you know?"

Tala shrugged. She knew that she, herself, was pretty at the very least, but she'd been an outsider since before her thirteenth birthday. *Since I started using the iron salve at the Academy.*

She shook her head, returning her thoughts to the present and the fact that she really couldn't relate to Lyn's troubles of having men throwing themselves at her. Despite that, Tala inquired politely and made appropriately interested noises to prompt Lyn to go on.

Thus, the walk was filled with pleasant, inane conversation, and Tala was content.

The Constructionists' Guildhall was open, as expected, and Tala felt and noticed the same scanning and magical notifications upon entering. They were duplicated for Lyn, as well.

An attendant came out in short order, giving a bow. "Mistresses." He straightened, warily eyeing Terry before turning his gaze to meet that of the Mages. "How can I be of service?"

Lyn looked to Tala expectantly, and Tala smiled. "I would like a cold air incorporator and a timekeeper." She hesitated. "Well, I want to get the price of the second. The first is thirty ounces silver, yes?"

The attendant smiled and pulled out a slate. "Let me check. One moment, please."

"Certainly."

Lyn was frowning. "Why do you want those things?"

Tala shrugged. "I'm tired of not knowing what time it is, and incorporators are dead useful."

"They are incredibly inefficient. Why not get something that removes thermal energy from what it targets? That would be *so* much more efficient than a cool air incorporator. You *are* an Immaterial Guide, though I don't recall you being familiar with thermal energy; there shouldn't be that much of an efficiency issue, either way, if you decided to power it yourself instead of buying harvests to power it."

She wasn't wrong. The new set of inscriptions she'd received from Holly tested the width of Tala's abilities as an Immaterial Guide. While she'd picked up enough of the basics to use all her inscriptions, her lack of true, deep knowledge was harming her efficiency. It was one of the many deficiencies she needed to correct to reach her full potential.

The attendant cleared his throat. "She is correct, Mistress. Should I look for such an item, instead?"

Tala waved him off. "No, no." She thought for a moment. "But if you have incorporators for lightning, acid, or coffee, I'd be interested in those as well."

He blinked at her. "Coffee?"

She narrowed her eyes. "I know you have one."

He cleared his throat and looked back down to his slate, not engaging.

I know you have one.

Lyn placed a hand on Tala's arm. "You haven't really addressed my question."

Tala gave the young man a last, probing glare before turning to her friend. "No re-inscription cost. I don't have to keep them topped off or find power sources. They are also incredibly useful for training my Ways. I just think that Mages undervalue these things." She smiled.

The attendant cleared his throat. "We do have several schemata for cold air incorporators. Were you looking for a specific temperature?"

Tala shrugged. "As cold as you have, assuming they are the same cost."

"They are, and you were correct. Thirty ounces silver." He made a note on the stone in his hand. "We do have a few for mild acids available, but any of the stronger ones are restricted. They require Archon authorization for purchase."

Tala gave Lyn a meaningful look, trying to convey: *See? If they weren't useful, no one would care.*

Lyn quirked a mirthful smile but didn't comment.

"Mistress?"

Tala turned back to him. "I'm not interested in mild acids. I'll return in a day or two to order a sufficiently strong one."

The attendant seemed a bit uncomfortable. "Apologies, Mistress, but the rule isn't mine. An Archon's approval will still be required."

Tala nodded. "As you say."

He shrugged, clearly still confused, but returning his eyes to the slate, nonetheless. "As to a lightning incorporator, we do have one, but there is a note attached, as well as an Archon approval requirement."

Tala cocked her head. "The note?"

"This says a minimum of one hundred mana per second is required to incorporate even a mild shock through the only currently successful schema. It is marked as a high Fused or Refined item."

Tala slumped, disappointed. "Ah… well, that's not very useful."

"I can add a note that you'd be interested in more potent or efficient versions if such are ever successfully created. I believe that such are a current topic of research for a couple of our Archons in Surehaven."

She perked up. "That would be wonderful."

He took down her specific information, including how best to contact her.

"Alright then. So, how are we looking on a timekeeper?"

He nodded, smiling. "I have several available: From one that simply displays the month, day, and year with discoloration to one with glowing symbols displaying the time down to the millisecond. There are obviously many in between those."

Tala blinked at that. *Who would need such a thing?* "I'd probably be happy with something accurate to the quarter-hour?" She barked a laugh. "Slag, I'd be happy with accuracy to the hour."

He nodded, looking at his slate and manipulating it until he found what he needed. "What I have of that type is a potentially magic-bound item, requiring re-inscription every week to three months, depending on the mage empowering it."

That is not ideal. She sighed. "How much?"

"Two ounces gold for the device, but once purchased, re-inscription is ten ounces silver."

Tala's eyes widened. *Yeah, no.* She sighed, shaking her head. "Thank you for looking. That is more than it's worth to me." She hesitated, then asked, "Why does it need to be inscribed so often?" She hesitated, considering. "And why does it have to be magic-bound?"

"Both excellent questions, and they, happily, have the same answer: we've not found an easily compatible power source." He gave an apologetic half-smile. "Time magic hasn't been found to exist on its own, and untyped power does not efficiently convert to work with time scripts."

Tala just stared at him. "Time scripts."

"Yes."

"As in time magic."

"That's right."

Time is immaterial. Could I study these scripts and translate them into a potential inscription? She almost laughed at that. *Yay! I can have an inscription that tells time.* "Why use such an esoteric power, then? That seems… odd."

He frowned. "How so, Mistress?"

"Why not make something that functioned like a clock or a pocket watch."

He began nodding. "You mean something with a regular cadence inbuilt? It is possible to use such for the regular measuring of time. Some of those have even been constructed." He lifted the slate up, slightly, indicating the very device he held. "These are actually built on a similar platform, but believe it or not, those using time scripts are actually less expensive, both initially and overall. We do have mechanical watches as well, though."

"Oh?" *Those slates are ridiculously expensive. Maybe the mundane way is better?*

"Yes. We—here at the Constructionists' Guild—pride ourselves on pursuing all avenues of creation."

Millennial Mage, 3 - Binding

"How much would a pocket watch be?" *I could keep it in Kit, make sure it isn't broken?* She had a thought; Kit could manipulate dimensionality within itself. *Could Kit wind a watch if it was placed inside?*

"Ten gold, plus or minus an ounce, depending on materials and embellishments. We request a month to properly craft each custom order."

"Oh…" She sighed. "Thank you. I suppose I'll just have to make do." *Or I can find some craftsman who will sell me a less-precise timekeeper. That should cost less.*

"Understandable." He gave a polite smile, then returned to business. "I do have one of the freezing air incorporators in stock if you'd like it now?"

She nodded. "That would be wonderful. Thank you." She hesitated. "Wait a moment."

"Yes, Mistress?"

"You never gave me an answer on the coffee incorporator." Tala's eyes narrowed. *What are you hiding?*

Lyn cleared her throat, placing a hand on Tala's arm. "Apologies. She's had a stressful day."

The young man bowed and left to get the item she'd requested.

"What was that about?" Tala turned on her friend.

"I could ask you the same question."

Tala gazed suspiciously after the departed attendant. "Someone has to have made one. I just know it." *No inter-guild pressure would prevent me from making one… if I could.*

"Then why hide it? If they actually had such a device, they would sell *so* many."

"I don't know. I haven't figured that out yet."

Lyn shook her head, seemingly deciding it wasn't worth engaging any further on the topic.

Five minutes later, Tala had paid and departed with Lyn and Terry in tow.

The new incorporator was fascinating, and she turned it over in her fingers, examining it more closely.

Like the other incorporators, there was a simple opening in the center, just large enough for her two thumbs to go through together. This particular one looked to be made of perfectly clear glass, though it felt like metal to her fingers; she couldn't have said why, though. The cross-section of the circle moved through various shapes in seemingly random order, the ridges coming together and diverging at irregular intervals.

She tested it, and true-to-order, air came out that was *almost* cold enough to make her hand hurt when she put her fingers in the flow. *Well, it would have almost hurt before my inscriptions.* Now, it wasn't even uncomfortable despite the chill already in the air.

She funneled power into the device, sending a stream of cold wind at Lyn.

The woman scrunched her face in a mockingly-outraged grimace. "Stop that!"

Tala grinned and tucked the incorporator away. "Fine."

Lyn shook her head. "You seem so childlike at times. The simplest workings of power are enough to fascinate you."

"Am I supposed to be insulted by that? Magic is *awesome!*"

She grinned. "No, I don't think I meant it negatively. It's refreshing to work with someone who still finds joy in such things."

Tala chuckled. "Glad to help, I suppose."

They fell back into casual conversation as they returned home, together.

* * *

Tala woke the next morning, content.

She stretched and exercised, still acclimating to her increased weight.

After her soul-work, she moved into the bathroom where she used a full seven void-channels to fill the tub. One, as always, kept her body supplied with the ongoing power requirements for her active spell-forms. Four of the remaining went to her hot water incorporator, two to the cold, leaving the water quite hot but no longer near boiling.

It took less than a minute to fully fill the tub, so that didn't stretch her capacity, but instead of disabling the void-channels, she moved them to Flow and her magic-bound items, while she pulled out her two air incorporators.

Her items filled to capacity, she moved the channels to dump into the air incorporators. *Let's see how long I can hold this.*

So, she stood there, over her bath, fully clothed.

Well... slag. She did *not* want to just stand there for close to twenty minutes. *Ideally longer.* Her bath would cool, maybe even begin to dissipate. *Probably not that. I think I have at least an hour.*

She looked around at what she had with her, and her eyes fell on Flow. *I wonder...*

She shifted the path of the void-channel for one of the two incorporators from her left hand to her right, while she, likewise, moved the incorporator itself. That way, she could continue to funnel power to them both with her right hand, each sending a steady stream of air upward. She then drew Flow with her left and laid it on the shelf, placing the two rings atop it.

Now, how do I... Thinking back to how she'd shifted from her left to her right hand, she made a similar mental movement, but this time, it was from her right hand to Flow.

The channels moved easily, now moving through the ethereal connection she had to the knife, rather than down her physical arm.

Hesitantly, she pulled her hand back, continuing the flood of power, now using her soul-bond to Flow as a conduit.

It worked! Tala gave a little hop of glee and immediately had to reach out and steady the incorporators, her landing having shaken the room. *Don't forget, Tala. You are quite… weighty now.* She snorted at that.

With air, hot and cold, still flowing from the devices, Tala undressed and took her hair out of its standard, utilitarian braid.

The power still flowed without pause.

She bathed, keeping a portion of her mind locked on her seven channels.

The magic never wavered.

Her bath done, and her body clean, she retrieved her comb from Kit.

Quick strokes with the comb left her hair water and tangle free, and she took the hot air incorporator from Flow, moving the requisite void-channels back to her right hand. *There is an odd strain when I shift the course of void-channels.*

She dried herself with the hot air, switching hands, and paths for the power, as often as reasonable.

Shortly after she was fully dry, she reached her limit and had to allow the void-channels to collapse. *Nearly half an hour. Nice!* And that was with the added strain of shifting routes. The previous day's efforts had paid dividends. *I wish I could spend that much time every day, working on improvement.*

Shortly thereafter, dressed in elk leathers and with her hair back in its simple, strong braid, Tala left the bathroom.

Lyn was waiting in the sitting room. "Finally!"

Tala stopped, surprised. "You're awake?"

"Of course I am! My Archon evaluation is first thing this morning."

Tala's eyes widened. "Oh! I'm so sorry."

Lyn waved her off as she carried a pile of things into the bath room. "What's done is done."

Tala frowned. "Wait… Wasn't it scheduled for mid-morning?"

"Mid-morning is effectively first thing. Mind grabbing me breakfast?"

Tala laughed, grinning. "Sure, that's fair."

Lyn smiled as she closed the door.

"Well, it seems I've got to get breakfast." She shook her head. "Terry!"

The bird flickered into being, already seemingly asleep on her shoulder.

"You know, I'm aware that you are awake."

He didn't respond.

She shrugged. "Either way."

*   *   *

Tala returned as quickly as she was able with two breakfast deals. *That place really does have good prices.*

She'd had to purchase a second jug for the extra coffee, but that wasn't a huge loss. At least, that was what she told herself.

Two and a half silver. She still had budget to use, due to her four days of unconsciousness, not to mention Rane's generosity. *Lyn will have one, at most two, sandwiches and some coffee, leaving me with at least ten sandwiches and close to two gallons of coffee.* All in all, a good use of funds.

Thankfully, Tala returned before Lyn finished in the bath, even if not by much.

The older Mage came out in a robe of thick, fluffy, towel-like material and joined Tala at the table. Tala, of course, had to kneel beside the surface instead of using the chair, which undoubtedly would've failed to hold her.

"These look amazing!" Lyn looked through the various sandwiches and chose the one that looked best to her.

Tala poured her friend a mug of coffee from one jug before drinking straight from the other. "Hope you like it."

Lyn took her time eating her one sandwich, though she was steady in her pace, only pausing to drink from her mug.

In that same time, Tala devoured eight of the things and finished a gallon of coffee.

"That can't be healthy for you." Lyn pointed at the now-empty coffee jug.

"Oh?"

"The caffeine alone has to be tweaking your brain to no end."

Tala shrugged. "Not really? I think I mainly have issues if I don't drink it."

Lyn gave her a flat look. "You know, that's a pretty clear indicator of a serious, physiological addiction."

"Then I'm addicted to sleep, food, water, and air."

"And coffee."

Tala waved her off. "Do you want another sandwich?"

Lyn gave the remaining three a long look, then shook her head. "They're great, but I'm quite full. Thank you."

Tala shrugged. "Fair enough." She took another and began quickly eating it.

Lyn shook her head. "Well, I've got to get going. Wish me luck?"

Tala shook her head in turn, giving a half-smile. "Nope. You don't need it."

"As kind as that sounds, in theory, I'd still appreciate the more standard gesture."

She grinned. "Very well. Best of luck, Mistress Lyn. May the next time we meet, you be known as Mistress Lyn Clerkson, Diamond Archon."

Lyn winked. "You better believe it." Without another word, she headed for the door, waving goodbye over her shoulder before she closed it behind herself.

Tala sighed, sinking down until she was sitting on her heels, kneeling beside the table. "Well, Terry, it's going to be a busy day."

Terry gave her a one-eyed stare.

She laughed and tossed an especially large chunk of jerky for him. He snapped it up without appearing to move. The jerky had vanished from the air at least six feet from him. "You're a wonder."

He didn't deign to react.

She ate the remaining food and downed the rest of the coffee with alacrity before rising and heading towards the door. "Alright! Time to go learn a new way of fighting."

Chapter: 18
The Real Work

Tala ground her teeth as she circled Adam on the sand of the training courtyard.

Every step compressed a circle of sand but not markedly; there was enough surface area that she still got good purchase. Arguably, she had a better footing now than before the increase to her weight and footing surface area.

Again and again, she threw herself at the guardsman: punches and kicks, elbows, and even headbutts were launched as sweat poured from her.

He was too skilled to allow virtually any of her hits to land.

He ducked and wove around each strike, occasionally reaching out to subtly alter the incoming trajectory of her movements.

Then, like clockwork, after she'd failed with ten attacks, he would lash out, decisively ending the exchange.

If she was quick enough, she would block the attack and lose her momentum, allowing him to step away. If she missed the timing or lost count of her own attacks, he would disable her, if briefly, by taking her footing or striking her head to daze her momentarily.

It was infuriating.

After each exchange, the watching students would analyze how she had failed, while the instructor and Adam, himself, offered advice on how, exactly, she could correct the errors and perfect her fighting techniques.

Millennial Mage, 3 - Binding

"Keep your elbows tighter to your sides."

"Your attacks should stay ahead of your body's movement, don't let them trail."

"Your footing telegraphed your attack; shift like this, instead."

"An elbow strike would have been better there."

"You aren't utilizing your unique strengths with that strike. However, if you change it like this…"

"You should have thrown a hook, instead of a jab, with the previous sequence in mind and how it opened his defenses."

"You allowed yourself to forget about defense."

Oh, how she hated it.

As credit to their advice, and her own resolve to improve, she got closer to landing blows and got hit less as time went on, but it had yet to be as gloriously in her favor as their first exchange.

* * *

When Tala and Adam had first faced off, they bowed in turn.

"Ready, Guardsman?" She wore her elk leathers, as immaculately clean and pristine as ever.

Adam wore a loose-fitting set of workout clothes, light and unrestricting, while being well-fitted enough to reduce the potential for handholds if he were to grapple. "Ready, Mistress."

Tala didn't hesitate after his acknowledgment, launching herself across the short space, her speed clearly surprising the large, lean man. Sand sprayed behind her in large plumes as she'd required *incredible* force to move as quickly as she'd wanted.

She didn't attempt subtlety, throwing a haymaker-style punch.

Adam raised an arm almost disdainfully to block, though he shifted his body and weight to ensure he was grounded and braced against the blow.

He compressed his lips, seemingly in irritation; he'd taught her better than to throw such an easily predicted attack. *Perfect.*

His perfect form hadn't been enough.

Tala was small, comparatively speaking, and so the blow shouldn't have been a question of strength and proper form. Any such contest would heavily favor him over her because she was lighter.

Only, she wasn't.

Her forearm connected with his, and she powered through, trusting her fully grounded weight to lock her in place.

His form had been perfect, and his blocking arm hadn't collapsed despite the tremendous strength behind her blow. Instead, his unshifting body had been driven up and backward. After he'd lifted free of the sand, his shoulder gave way with a sickening *pop* as the joint left its socket.

Adam had grunted in surprised pain before he landed once more, sliding back but maintaining his feet as his left arm dropped, useless, to his side.

The Mage healer they'd had ready to hand took only a moment to fully restore the joint.

Adam had bowed and smiled. "Very well then. Let us truly begin."

* * *

Now, Tala was paying for her earlier arrogance. *He's proving to me, and everyone, that skill trumps weight and strength. At least in what amounts to a point match…*

Millennial Mage, 3 - Binding

Each exchange took less than a minute, even with the feedback, and they paused for water after every ten bouts or so.

Two hours passed with little variation, and Tala, along with most of those watching, decided that the extra weight was more useful in grounding her and adding to her footing than in any sort of acrobatics. *Might change my mind as I gain competence, though.*

Finally, Tala decided a change was in order.

She stored her cool water incorporator, turning to face Adam once more. "Enough. We fight until one of us is truly disabled."

He hesitated, then nodded. "Or to surrender."

She nodded in turn.

"Begin."

They closed the distance, moving together with smooth, even steps.

Tala's quick jab was hooked and jerked downward, Adam's backfist using her resistance to gain a burst of speed and power.

His knuckles caught her nose with a blow that would have shattered the feature on anyone else.

It tingled, forcing her to blink rapidly.

She threw a knee to his gut, and he rolled around it, delivering a hammering blow to her raised hip. She felt the joint shift, threatening to pop free.

It didn't.

She drove her elbow down as she dropped much faster than any other person could, due to her increased gravity.

With that third strike, finally, she caught him by surprise, once again.

She clipped his knee, sending a wet *crack* across the sand.

He didn't stop, though she could see pain in his eyes, held in check by a fiery determination, her enhanced perception presenting his expression to her as if on a canvas.

His chest flexed, bulging beneath his loose shirt, and his two palms thundered, one against each of her ears. Her vision fuzzed for just an instant. It hadn't been sound, not really, so her dampening scripts had done little to soften the impact.

For that instant, she had to rely on feel and animalistic instinct, through incredible disorientation.

They exchanged a dozen blows and counterstrikes.

If Tala had been uninscribed, she would have ended up with broken ribs, ruptured kidneys, shattered joints, and blinded eyes.

But she was a Mage.

There was no question of who was more skilled. Adam attacked her with near-perfect impunity, but impunity wasn't the same as invulnerability.

When her vision finally refocused, her mind clearing, Adam was gasping and standing on his one good leg, his right arm broken in two places. He also had a broken rib to go with his arm and knee, and one eye was squeezed shut against rapid swelling.

Tala *ached,* but nothing was broken; nothing was out of place; nothing was truly wrong.

Adam spat out a wad of blood and spit, then nodded. "I yield."

The healer rushed forward, restoring him quickly. Tala took a moment to appreciate the work of the Material Guide. Their scripts were efficient, effective, and precise, restoring the target to full health, using the patient's own internal maps as a template and guide.

Simply perfect. Her healing, when she used it, influenced the processes magically. The material and energy still had to be supplied in mostly mundane fashions. *If I were to try to heal someone else, they'd be malnourished and skeletal.* Probably an overstatement but in the vein of the truth. *Plus, I'd have to get entirely different inscriptions…* So, no healing others.

But she wasn't here to admire the elegance of another Mage's work or lament an area she'd never excel in.

Tala looked around at those watching. Silence reigned among the onlookers until Adam was back at one hundred percent.

The healer retreated, and Adam cleared his throat. "So, who has a comment?"

No one spoke out, but the students were glancing to each other, the air beginning to fill with mutterings.

Adam grinned. "To her, I would like to say that I, for one, am impressed. She has been listening to every bit of advice we gave. To you all"—he gestured to the watching students and teachers—"I say: any mundane warrior would be a fool to engage a Mage in open combat, this is known. Their methods are usually less up close and personal than this, but they are also usually more definitive as well. Would you rather face her or a Mage that could simply incinerate you at a hundred yards?"

There were more mutterings at that.

"Exactly. She is effective as she is now, but she is still a child when compared to the offensive abilities of most Mages. Now, what advice can we give her to correct that imbalance?"

Rane grinned from his chair off to one side, giving Tala a happy nod but keeping his thoughts otherwise to himself.

And thus, the real work began.

* * *

The sun was straight overhead, and Tala was feeling desperately hungry by the time they called an end to the morning's training.

Adam had received healing more than a dozen times, and after the first two true bouts, the most senior guardsmen had joined him to fight her two-on-one, then three-on-one.

All the while, dozens upon dozens of eyes had scrutinized Tala's every move.

With every angle watched by someone, and a truly impressive staff of advisors, Tala had made incredible progress. Her increasing number of opponents stood as obvious testimony to that, as did her slowly decreasing time to total disablement of those opponents.

Make no mistake, Adam and his compatriots were still *vastly* more skilled than she was, and if she had lacked her inscriptions, she would have lost, quickly, to any one of them. *Or if they used inscribed weapons.*

Still, she was quite happy with the morning's progress. *Good training.*

It was amazing what could be accomplished when injuries weren't a real concern. In that light, she was more than a little impressed by Adam and his fellow guardsmen and women. No matter how hurt they had been while sparring with her, they had never hesitated or flinched in their exchanges. They had never even let a single injury take them out of the fight, likely using the opportunity to train themselves in fighting under those particular conditions. *True masters, it seems.*

Terry had watched from the nearby roof, basking in the sunlight. Even so, he'd seemed much more intent on her activities than usual. *I wonder what he's contemplating.*

Rane walked out onto the sand. "Thank you, all. I think Mistress Tala should grab some lunch, as she has a rather important meeting early this afternoon."

After the collective responses settled down, Rane continued, "Tomorrow, I will be joining those opposing the Mistress, which should allow for increased scrutiny of her fighting techniques as well as allow you to finish your evaluation of my fighting style and abilities."

Sounds and utterances of agreement came back towards them in an incomprehensible wave.

Rane leaned in close to Tala and whispered, "There is a set of private baths in that building there." He indicated with a bob of his head. "I suggest you clean up, then get lunch and head to your evaluation."

Tala nodded. "Thank you." *Lunch sounds so, so fantastic.* "Care to join me?"

He froze, rapidly turning a bright shade of red.

She frowned. *Why would...? OH!* She colored slightly as well. "For lunch, Master Rane. Would you like to join me for lunch?"

He cleared his throat. "Um… well. I'd love to, but I need to get to my own evaluation."

"Fair enough. Good luck."

He quirked a happy smile, the color starting to fade from his features. "Thank you."

They bid each other goodbye, along with the guards—students, instructors, and combatants.

The healer, just as all morning, didn't converse with anyone, simply departing when the need for their services was clearly over.

Tala did take advantage of the baths, though she didn't use their tub or water.

She stripped down in the private room, then blasted herself with hot water, quickly removing the residue of the morning's sweat and sand. She marveled at how she was able to bear the otherwise scalding water. She could probably cook herself, in time, but she wasn't submerged, so it was just unpleasantly hot when used like this.

Terry waited outside, basking in the sun.

Dressed and dry, hair combed and re-braided, Tala left the Guardsmen's complex behind and hunted down some lunch, Terry on her shoulder once again. *With me—as he should be.*

She chose a new place this time around.

Her lunch was beer-battered, deep-fried chicken with a side of likewise battered and deep-fried vegetables, ranging from mushrooms and zucchini to potatoes and squash. It all came with a staggering variety of available sauces.

To her delight, it was 'all you can eat.'

To the relief of the owners, she did not, in fact, follow that allowance.

No need to put them out of business.

Even so, she suspected that she'd eaten as much as any two other patrons she observed, and some of them were *very* enthusiastic diners.

She did not let Terry have any, giving him some jerky instead.

He hadn't been too disappointed. *I might have to start letting him try more varieties of human food.* It bore considering.

The restaurant staff tried to charge her ninety-nine and nine-tenths ounces copper, but she just gave them a silver and refused the remainder. *Stupidly specific prices.*

Thus fed, she headed towards the Archon facility, located within the innermost circle of the city. It was just barely two hours after she'd left the sandy courtyard, and Terry was on her shoulder once more.

When she arrived outside the indicated building, she was at once confused and impressed.

The building, itself, was situated near the bottom of a small hill, clearly extending back into it. Even so, it looked small, seeming barely bigger than a single-family home. *I suppose it doesn't have to be that big, but I expected more.* It also looked decidedly ordinary. *If you don't know it's here, you'll never find it.* She grinned. *Unless you have magesight like mine.*

Millennial Mage, 3 - Binding

To her magesight, the protections were staggering. Not only were the city's standard defenses thicker and more powerfully concentrated around it, but there were many more, cunningly buried in the construction of the building. *They would need Material Guides to re-inscribe the portions imbedded in the walls.*

She swept her gaze across the surrounding area and noticed with shock that the increased defenses encompassed the entire hill. Moreover, though the powerful thrumming of the city's magic made seeing anything specific below ground difficult, she thought she saw the complex, augmented wards extending far below ground. *Fascinating. This is probably the best-defended place in the city.*

As Tala walked forward, she was subjected to more bits of scanning magic than she could count. Many were similar to the one in the Constructionist's Guildhall, examining her magic and inscriptions, but others seemed to be checking her physical form. She even thought that she felt a few focus on her gate: her soul.

It was a bit disconcerting, but nothing hostile was triggered, so she continued forward at a steady pace.

As it turned out, the entire structure visible from the street was solid stone, with no rooms or open spaces to be found. Behind a set of heavy doors, there was only a straight passage, leading from the entrance deeper in.

Once she was well inside the little hill, she came out into a lushly appointed entry foyer. There were thick rugs on the plain stone floors. Heavy tapestries hung on the walls to dampen sound and add warmth to the room. Where the ceiling of the passage had been an unremarkable eight feet, this room expanded upward to at least ten, and that ceiling was textured and oddly shaped.

Tala blinked, taking in the ceiling as a whole. *It's a map. It's a map of the known world.* The detail was staggering, and she quickly realized that the few lights that were in the ceiling itself were each located to indicate the placement of humanity's cities. *Fourteen. So, they marked where one is currently being built, too.* Additionally, there was a hole where a fifteenth would go, but there was no light yet.

There was nowhere to sit, as this was obviously not meant as more than a front entry.

Three other hallways led off from the entry. Like the entrance, each hallway was centered their respective wall

In the center of the room stood a round counter. Four people sat behind the counter, each seeming to be working on something out of Tala's sight.

They were inscribed but not Mages, their spell-lines focused around their eyes and ears. *Are those forms of blinding and deafness?* There were conditions woven in that were far too complex for her to parse at a glance, but she guessed that they were prevented from seeing or hearing information not allowed to them. *I can't even imagine how it determines that. Maybe it's something that Archons can activate at need?*

That was a horrible thought. *I don't ever want someone else activating scripts on my body...* But now wasn't a good time to contemplate that.

The closest, a woman, glanced up at Tala's entrance and smiled a greeting. The expression seemed to be genuine and not simply an affectation for her role as a greeter. "Welcome! Are you Mistress Tala?"

Tala was still looking around but decided she should probably give the woman her attention. "I am."

The attendant nodded, looking down. "Your brother should be finished within the hour, and I'll escort you in, shortly thereafter."

"My... brother?" She had a moment of panic. *Which one? How is he here? What is going on?*

"Yes, the two of you signed up together. 'Mistress Tala and Master Rane Gredial.'"

"Oh!" She felt tremendous relief. "No. He's not my brother."

The attendant's eyes widened, and she visibly paled. "Oh, no! I'm so sorry, Mistress. Your *husband* should be out soon."

Tala blinked at that. "What? No… No! Master Rane is *not* my husband."

The woman seemed completely baffled, now. "Then… I'm so sorry. I don't understand."

Tala cleared her throat. "I don't have a last name."

"Oh!" The woman straightened. "That makes sense. I should have thought of that… It's unusual but not unknown. My deepest apologies for the misunderstandings."

Tala, herself, was now quite flustered. "It's… It's fine." She swallowed. *That's embarrassing.* The other three attendants weren't looking her way, but their body language suggested they were hiding smiles of amusement.

The attendant swallowed. "Well… can I get you any refreshment while you wait? After I get that, if desired, I will lead you to a seating area where you should be more comfortable."

Tala nodded, rubbing one temple against a newly budding headache. "Coffee, please. As much as you can bring me."

The woman smiled. "Certainly." She turned, ostensibly to come out from behind the counter and go and get the beverage.

Tala held up a hand. "Wait."

The attendant paused.

"I'm afraid that you heard me ask for a large mug of coffee."

She nodded hesitantly.

"What I want is for you to bring me as much coffee as you can. I can provide two one-gallon jugs if that would be useful."

The young woman swallowed, again, seeming quite taken aback. "I'll... I'll see what I can do."

That will have to be good enough. "Thank you."

Chapter: 19
What the Rust?

Tala waited.

The attendant, against all odds, came through, and Tala ended up consuming close to three gallons of coffee. She had no idea how the attendant kept procuring the stuff, but it was there, so Tala drank it.

Terry slept.

Kit hung.

Flow rested in its sheath.

Tala was bored.

She didn't know exactly what to expect when her time for evaluation finally arrived. They were going to examine her star, that much was obvious, but she didn't know why that took a special meeting or in-person evaluation.

Tala would have trained her void-channels, but she didn't know what would be expected of her, and it would be horrible luck if she mentally exhausted herself right before she was expected to perform in some sort of rigorous test. It was wiser to wait.

Should I have applied my iron salve?

No, she didn't need to defend herself from magical effects… she hoped. She snorted at that. "Yeah, Tala. The Archons are going to attack you, and you *would* have won if only you'd had your iron salve." She shook her head at the thought.

Millennial Mage, 3 - Binding

She had examined the waiting room and found it extravagant. *I suppose it's meant to impress Archons-to-be or other visitors?* If so, it did its job well.

It was sparsely furnished. Tastefully so. The ceiling was lower than the entry hall, giving a more comfortable feel to the space. The walls held a few, expansive masterpieces, each depicting landscapes in intricate detail. When she'd looked closer, she'd discovered that, even to her improved perception, it was hard to notice every detail, though the works weren't crowded or cluttered in the least.

Each was done in a different medium: one with oils, one with watercolor, one a simple charcoal piece, and so on. She could have spent long minutes simply basking in each one, under other circumstances, but she was feeling a bit too nervous to truly appreciate them at that moment.

She was contemplating the wisdom of taking out a book, to try to distract herself, when the attendant returned, hands empty of coffee. "Mistress Tala?"

Tala stood. "Ready?"

She nodded. "Yes. Right this way."

Tala hadn't seen Rane come out, but she supposed there were multiple exits. *There might even be multiple evaluation rooms...* Though, the attendant had stated that she would go in after Rane was finished, so the evaluations were likely to be held in the same location. *Or at least with the same evaluators.*

The hallways they walked through were simple, if well kept, starkly in contrast to the lavish entry hall and waiting room. Smooth, polished, unadorned stone made up walls, ceiling, and floor.

The attendant's steps echoed through the corridor, but Tala's careful footfalls made hardly a sound.

Finally, the attendant stopped outside a simple, heavy wooden door. "Here you are, Mistress. Best of luck to you." She pointed to a small, padded basket, resting by the dark wooden entrance. "Your arcanous companion will have to wait here."

Terry chirped in irritation, but before Tala could comment, he was already seemingly asleep in the provided bed.

The attendant smiled, bowed, and walked away, the echoes of her steps fading surprisingly quickly. *There are dampening inscriptions set behind the surface of the stone.* The expense of keeping those properly inscribed must have been staggering.

Focus. Tala took a deep breath and knocked.

"Come." The reply came almost instantly, and the voice was oddly familiar.

She pushed open the door and found a large chamber beyond. Three sides held tables, with just enough space beyond them for people to move and sit comfortably, with a walkway behind those left clear, near the walls.

The tables were long and thin, allowing for each side of the room to hold some twelve people. *Archons,* Tala realized. *Thirty-six seated Archons.*

Quite a few other people stood behind those seated.

While everyone she could see had spell-lines, she couldn't see magic around any of them, save two.

Lyn and Rane stood side by side, off to her right. They gave subdued waves and smiles when she met their gazes.

Rane looked exhausted, seemingly requiring the wall he was leaning against to stay upright. Lyn looked a little better, but mostly like she'd also been wrung out, with a bit more time to recover than Rane.

A new hue, underlying their magic, pulsed in prominence to her magesight. *Red.* It was a deep red, barely into the front edge of the spectrum counted for that color. They were Archons in truth.

She grinned back, waving slightly.

Millennial Mage, 3 - Binding

An older man cleared his throat, and Tala turned, regarding the central table.

To her surprise, she recognized several other people in the room. Holly sat on one end of that centermost table, smiling in her direction but not otherwise acknowledging her. Master Himmal sat on the other end and gave her a slight nod when their eyes locked. She couldn't see him with her magesight, just like most of the others, but his invisibility seemed... different somehow. *Is he using an item to blend in with his fellows?* His Archon's mark blazed on the necklace at his chest.

Now that she looked more closely, about half of the Archons present had such marks. Some wore them as a ring, others as a necklace like Master Himmal, and still others had them tucked into pockets or pinned to their clothing as broaches. *Master Grediv seemed to regard them as a crutch. So, are those the least among the Archons?* She didn't like putting Master Himmal in that camp, but he, himself, had told her that he was crippled, magically speaking.

She frowned, considering.

The throat was cleared again, drawing her attention to the main table once more. The center of that table was dominated by a petite woman. She was likely just taller than Tala, herself, though it was hard to tell while the woman sat. She looked close to the same age as Lyn, but Tala had no doubt that she was much older. *Not that I guessed Lyn's age right...* In fact, almost everyone looked on the near side of fifty, with Master Himmal being the most notable exception.

To the woman's right sat Grediv, and it had been his voice that had called Tala in and that she had thought she recognized. *I knew it.*

He gave her a nod, similar to Master Himmal's.

She didn't know the man to the woman's other side.

The small woman straightened her back and lifted her chin, ever so slightly. "Mistress Tala, you stand before members of the local council of Archons and those Archons who wished to participate in, or observe, these proceedings." Her voice was clear and powerful.

Tala gave a slight bow. She was unsure what she should say, so she held her tongue. *You grow in wisdom, Tala.*

The Archon quirked a smile. "I am Mistress Elnea, Onyx Archon and current leader of the Archons here in Bandfast." The woman's mage robes were a deep black, with polished, black buttons as fasteners for their quick releases. *Likely onyx.* It would be on brand.

Tala glanced briefly to Grediv and noticed that his clothes today were sapphire blue. *Maybe it's tradition to model your outfit after your medium?* "Greetings, Onyx Archon Elnea. It is my honor to be here today."

Elnea's smile widened a fraction. "It is. Never have we entertained the elevation of one so fresh from the academy."

Tala had nothing productive to say in response, so she simply waited.

Elnea's smile grew marginally further. "To business." Her voice shifted to one holding deep authority and following ceremony. "Who here stands for this Mage's elevation?"

Master Himmal stood first, followed by Holly, then Grediv.

Elnea nodded. "Who stands against?"

The three Archons in favor sat and every other Archon at the three tables stood, save Elnea.

Tala's eyes widened. *What the rust?* She opened her mouth to interject… something, but Grediv gave her a stern, warning look. *Good thing he's sitting right next to Elnea.* She closed her mouth.

Elnea, for her part, saw Tala's reaction and glanced to Grediv before rolling her eyes.

The Archons returned to their seats.

Elnea's voice resounded through the room. "As there is no consensus, we must see the evidence for your elevation." She pointed to the end of the left-hand table. "Please present your star to Mistress Sonfia."

Tala walked to the middle-aged-looking woman and held out the capped iron vial containing her Archon Star.

Sonfia took it, a puzzled look on her face. "What is this, child?"

"My star is within, Mistress."

She cocked an eyebrow. "You are aware that stars do not lose power if uncontained, yes?"

"Of course."

"Well, it is out of your storage item, so the containment shouldn't be necessary, and I don't really want to touch that. It is iron, yes?"

"Yes, Mistress."

"Then—"

Grediv's voice cut through the room. "Just open it, Fia. You'll understand soon enough, and the iron won't bite you."

Sonfia gave Grediv a searching look, then sighed. "Very well."

Tala walked back to her place near the center of the room and waited.

Sonfia uncapped the vial and looked inside. "I don't understand."

Grediv simply grinned.

"Mistress Tala. What medium is this?" Sonfia lifted the iron vial up slightly.

Tala cleared her throat, suddenly a bit self-conscious. "Blood, Mistress Sonfia."

The room exploded with mutters and sounds of surprise.

"Silence." Elnea didn't shout or pound the table, but her voice cut through the noise, nonetheless. "Please examine the star and pass it on. We can question the applicant once everyone has taken their turn to examine the star."

Sonfia frowned but nodded, looking into the vial for a long count of ten. Finally, she passed it to the man on her left.

Silence filled the room as each seated Archon got a chance to see Tala's star. Most seemed torn between not wanting to touch the vial longer than required and wanting more time to stare at what she'd brought them. *Maybe I should have put it in a glass vial, instead?*

Master Himmal shook his head while he examined the Archon Star, smiling to himself.

Elnea took nearly a minute for her own examination, no expression obvious on her features. She did swirl the iron vial, though, which only a few did.

Grediv only briefly glanced in, grinned broadly to Tala, and handed it off.

Holly passed it on, taking less time to look inside as it passed than Grediv had.

The other Archons reacted with mixtures of skepticism, wonder, and bemusement.

Finally, it got to the far end of the right table, and Tala retrieved it.

Elnea called for those 'for' and 'against' Tala's elevation, again. The Archons were now split fairly evenly: twenty for, sixteen against.

"Those who oppose may now inquire to satisfy their objections."

Several moved to stand, but an older man was the quickest to rise, the others deferring once he was up.

"Mistress Tala, how did you keep the blood stable in order to imbue it with your power in the required form? Is it from some arcane or magical creature? Is it alchemically treated?"

Elnea cleared her throat. "One question, please."

The man spread his hands, palm down, and nodded. "Apologies." He returned his gaze to Mistress Tala. "What is the nature of the blood, such that it allowed this feat?"

Tala quirked a smile. *That was a clever way to combine the questions.* "It is my blood, untreated and unaltered. I have never attempted to use any other medium, so I cannot comment on how it differs."

The man hesitated, then nodded, taking his seat.

So, each objector is allowed a single question? Maybe if they object again, they'll be allowed another.

A woman stood next. "Mistress Tala, what influence did Master Grediv have over the creation of this star? I cannot think his recent theories on liquid-medium stars are unrelated."

Tala glanced to Grediv, but he simply shrugged, seemingly braced for... something. Tala shrugged as well, turning back to the current asker. "I met Master Grediv in Alefast, just under two weeks ago. At that time, he saw an earlier version of this." She held up her iron vial to indicate the star inside. "He examined it, then advised that I make a stronger one before going for evaluation."

Many hard eyes turned towards Grediv, then.

Grediv sighed, clearly irately resigned, something about his reaction conveying that he'd expected this.

Elnea looked to him as well. "Master Grediv, care to explain yourself? A Mage's first Archon Star is the means by which they are measured. Though that not being her first explains why it is at peak power."

Grediv waved his hand dismissively. "The star she presented me at the time was insufficient for her elevation. I recommended that she create one of sufficient power.

That,"—he pointed towards Tala—"I was not expecting her to come back with that."

Elnea nodded. "That is the nature of her bond to the knife then, yes?"

"Yes, Mistress." Tala nodded, drawing the Archon's attention to her.

Elnea frowned. "This is most unusual. You should have been evaluated based on the first star you created."

Tala cleared her throat. "With all due respect, that is impossible. The first star I created was absorbed into the second and third, which I forged. That combination is what Master Grediv examined."

There was a long minute of stunned silence.

Tala turned to look at Grediv as he chuckled, breaking the uncomfortable pause. "Now you understand. Stars in a liquid medium might be able to meld."

Several other Archons began speaking at once, but Elnea held up a hand to forestall them. "Mistresses, Masters, please. There are times to discuss theory and debate findings. This is not among them."

The group quieted, if reluctantly.

"Now, Mistress Tala. Do you affirm and attest that that is the first Archon Star you have created, which fell within the qualifying range?" She pointed towards Tala's hand, which still held the iron vial.

There were mutters at that, some of which Tala caught. "Rusting stupid question; Archon Stars can't be stabilized outside of the qualifying range."

Tala kept from smiling… barely. "To my knowledge, based on what Archons have told me, yes."

Another of the objectors stood for their question. "How can we possibly believe your claims?"

Tala opened her mouth to answer, then hesitated. *Wait…* She smiled, widely, as she remembered something. She stuck her hand into Kit and took out another vial, containing one of her earlier stars—the one that she'd shown Holly. "This is one of the earlier created stars." She walked forward and handed it to the objector. "Please feel free to examine it."

The objector opened this second iron vial and stared into it, clearly stunned by what she found. "Not possible."

Elnea cleared her throat. "Would you object to allowing the council to examine that one as well, Mistress Tala?"

Tala shrugged. "I see no reason against it."

Thus, another space of time passed as each seated Archon took their turn with her weaker star.

Once that was complete, the mood had shifted drastically. Each of the Archons seemed deep in thought, some almost excited, others seeming disturbed.

Tala received the vial back, and Elnea called for another vote, and the results were thirty to six.

"Who taught you this spell-form?"

"No one. It seemed a logical progression after having my blood tested for power density."

There were mutters at that. From the mutters, the Archons took meaning from her answer that she, herself, did not understand. *Who cares if I came up with it on my own?*

Another of the objectors stood in a rush. "Blood for power density tests is empowered within the body."

Tala frowned. It hadn't been a question, but she felt the weight of the collected gazes upon her. "Yes…?"

Another stood. "Are you trying to tell us that you made that star *within* your own body?"

How did they think I did it? Bleed myself then try to dump power in? Would that work? *Probably not.* "Umm… yes?"

There were waves of mutters and exclamations at that. Even Grediv, Holly, and Master Himmal seemed startled to learn that.

I didn't know it was that big of a deal. If their reactions were any indication, it was not only a critical piece of information, but it also made many of them nervous.

No one else stood immediately, so Elnea called for another vote.

Only ten stood in favor of her elevation.

Tala frowned. *What?*

Only one stood against it.

What does that even mean?

That single Archon stood. "Are you human?"

"Yes." She was frowning. "What kind of question is that? You should all be able to see my gate. Are there other options?"

Only silence came back to her, though she did see several small distortions of power, which made her think that some of the Archons had briefly activated their magesight to examine her.

Grediv stood. "May I speak in favor?"

Elnea waited a moment, then nodded when no one spoke against the request.

"Mistress Tala is an unusual Mage. No one denies that, but she has cleared every requirement for advancement and has done so spectacularly. You might be uncomfortable at some of what she has done, and at the specter of what she will certainly do in the future, but is that a reason to deny her elevation? To keep her from joining us, when we are ever in need of Archons? If you have true objections, then object! Air them before this council and let wisdom guide this decision. If she is"—his eyes flicked to her, then away—"the worst of what could be will be proven one way or another soon enough."

What does that mean? Tala was frowning.

Another Archon spoke. "This isn't even your city, Master Grediv. Go home, and let us handle this."

There were several murmurs in response, but Tala couldn't determine whether they were supportive or not.

Grediv laughed. "I say: foreign wisdom is better than home-grown folly."

A ripple of laughter moved through the room, then, and that seemed to break the tension that had been growing.

Grediv took his seat, and Elnea called for another vote.

Thirty-five in favor, one against.

The single opposing Archon stood. It was the man who had told Grediv to leave. "Why should we allow your elevation to Archon?"

Tala thought for a long moment, a thousand rash responses whipping through her head, each being discarded. Finally, she shrugged. "I'll get there, one way or another. I would prefer the guidance of my predecessors, and the wisdom they gained along the way, but I will forge my own path if I must. More importantly: I qualify to be raised. The question isn't 'why should you allow it?' It's 'what reason could you have to oppose?'"

The Archon gave her a searching, thoughtful look, then nodded. He turned to regard Elnea. "I withdraw my opposition and stand in favor." He then, ironically, sat.

Elnea stood. "We, as representatives of the Archon Council of Bandfast, are united." She looked directly at Tala. "Mistress Tala. Swallow your Archon Star and join us."

Tala blinked back at her. *What?*

Her mind immediately began frantically scouring through various possibilities. *I had to fight for control, against my star... Have all these people succumbed? Did the stars win and take over? Am I surrounded by Mages who are no longer quite human?*

She glanced to Lyn and Rane. *And they got them, too?*

Because of her. Lyn had only made her star because Tala had brought Holly's attention down on Lyn.

Tala looked to the Archons around her, none showing any visible reaction, though she thought she could feel some undercurrents of magic building.

Something is wrong.

She took a step back, drawing Flow and preparing to flee. "Yeah… No. Rust that."

Chapter: 20
False Choices

Power exploded from several distinct points around Tala, various workings lashing out towards her, and she reacted on instinct, not waiting until she determined what they were intended to do. *Too coordinated. They were expecting me to resist.* If that was true, they'd underestimated her. Most of the Archons were simply watching, seeming almost curious.

She channeled power into Flow. The blade swept outward, becoming the wire-thin outline of a sword, surrounding a field of throbbing heat. That transformation took place even as she swung, slicing the first working to come within reach, and ending it before it could affect her.

She dodged, ducked, dipped, dived, and... wove through the magics sent her way. She cursed her lack of iron salve, even as Flow split the few incoming magics that she couldn't avoid and would otherwise have struck her. The blade sheared through spell-workings like Terry through a pack of murderous woodsmen, leaving the incomplete magic to spark and fizzle out without taking effect.

Terry.

"Terry!"

Thankfully, they hadn't thrown anything but spell-forms her way. She didn't know how she'd handle lightning or fire, created first, then flung at her. *I'll just have to trust in my defensive inscriptions.* They weren't designed to fight Mages, though, let alone Archons.

She kicked backwards, driving downward to use her weight along with her strength to shatter open the door behind her... or she tried. It was somehow *incredibly* reinforced. The resulting *boom* shook the walls, causing dust and debris to fill the air. *They built this place to contain Mages.*

It didn't matter though; her voice had reached him.

Terry appeared on her shoulder.

"Bigger, defend me!"

He flickered and was suddenly next to her, already the size of a horse, crouched low. He screeched forth a bellow of challenge, his razor talons sinking into the stone below them with ease.

There was a collective hitch from everyone in the room at Terry's appearance and enlargement. Silence briefly settled, and several watching Archons let out overlapping curses, which blended together to Tala's battle-deafened ears.

Terry settled down, ready to spring, then called again, low and thrumming, but he didn't attack.

He glanced to Tala as if in question.

He agreed to not kill anyone without explicit consent from me. Tala found herself smiling despite the situation at large. *That's some impressive restraint, Terry.*

From the side of the room, Rane was laughing, and Tala heard him talking to himself. "I *knew it*. I knew that bird was more than it appeared."

She glanced his way and saw Lyn smiling back at her. *They're taking this well, but I supposed if they've already been co-opted, they wouldn't be bothered.*

Tala allowed Flow to shrink so that she wasn't wasting power, but she didn't lower it.

Elnea cleared her throat. "Well, this is unfortunate."

"You think?" Tala tsked. "So, what is this? You force Mages to give in to their Archon Star, replacing their soul with an arcane construction? Is that the purpose?"

Elnea blinked at her. "No, child. We verify that the Mage to be elevated hasn't *already* been subverted. Being subverted before this evaluation is rare, but it does happen."

Tala hesitated. "You told me to swallow my star."

"And you will, eventually, but every Mage, when they first make a true star, must fight for dominance. We do not allow Mages to discuss their forging process, to keep that a secret. If the Mage does not balk at ingesting the star, then we can gather that they have fallen to it or, more likely, another earlier. There are tests to verify, of course, but they are *quite* invasive and not advisable, except at great need."

"So, you allow Mages to experience the temptation blind?"

"Did you want to swallow it?"

She hesitated. "...No?"

"That gut instinct is what is required. Forewarning actually lowers the number of Mages who succeed. If we'd told you not to swallow your star before you came here, even if we'd explained why, is there a chance you'd have done it anyway?"

Yeah... I'm not answering that. What Elnea was saying made a sort of sense. *It also seems a bit too convenient.* Tala narrowed her eyes. "So what now?"

"Well, generally we would have restrained you, then released you to show our good faith before explaining all of this." She glared at Grediv, then Holly. "We were warned that that might be difficult, but when we confirmed that your defensive layer was absent, it still seemed a reasonable course."

Terry began pacing back and forth in front of Tala, between her and Elnea. The terror bird had shrunk to the size of an incredibly large dog, so as to not block Tala's line of sight. He seemed no less protective, however.

"Your companion also complicates things, as I doubt we could safely restrain both of you without at least someone being injured, and we are not willing to risk that."

Tala felt another smile tugging at her lips but restrained it. *That's right, Terry's a rusting monster.* My *rusting monster.* "So, again I ask: What now?"

Elnea sighed. "You do not make things easy, do you?"

Tala quirked a smile, then. "So people keep telling me." She sheathed Flow, and Terry, noticing the action, flickered to sit on her shoulder, small once more.

"That terror bird is ancient, Mistress Tala. I don't know what binds him to you, but be careful."

Tala snorted. "Says the woman in charge of a room full of Mages who just attacked me."

Elnea seemed to realize something. "Were any of the spell-forms directed at you harmful?"

Tala thought back. *No. They had all been for restraint.* "No, but if your goal was to co-opt me, you'd want me alive."

The Archon sighed. "To become an Archon in truth, you must soul-bond your own body."

Tala blinked, considering. *That… that makes sense.* It was laughably obvious now that she thought about it. At the moment, she was technically magic-bound to her body. *Huh, Flow is more me than I am… or than my flesh and bones are… That's weird.* It also lined up with how using the weapon had felt. "How do you prevent the star from taking over?"

"By not allowing the star through your gate. The danger isn't it bonding with your body. The danger is with the star interacting with your soul, supplanting it. Like switching which end of a line is the fixed anchor."

That… also made a sort of sense. She didn't know how or why it made sense, but it just… did. "Alright."

Elnea sighed, seeming to relax a little. "We've a spell-form, which defends your gate, while you soul-bond your body. In your case, it will be powered by four Archons because your Archon Star is as powerful as they can get. Usually, they are much weaker, and therefore, they are obviously subservient to the soul that forged them. After they are used, the Mage then increases the bond's strength to that upper limit before proceeding to the next steps. You… you forged a star that has more power at its immediate disposal than your own soul. If it wielded that power against you, you would fall to it, rather than it to you—as it should."

That made sense, too, in a way. "That's why you were hesitant after learning I'd made my star within my own body."

Elnea nodded. "Precisely. That harkens back to a time when most Archons fell—before we learned to forge them outside ourselves. If it reassures you any, you are welcome to examine the spell-form before we enact it."

Tala almost nodded, then her gaze flicked to Holly. *Much of my understanding comes from, or is augmented by, my magesight, which she inscribed. Can I trust it? Has she been setting me up?* Tala groaned, rubbing her face with one hand. *If I believe that, I'm already dead. I could never get re-inscribed, and I'd have to leave, immediately, never to return.* She groaned, again. "Fine. Let's do this."

* * *

A short time later, Tala stood in the middle of an intricately inlaid spell-form of intertwining gold lines, both across the surface of the floor and going down into it.

She had examined the working to the best of her ability, which was sorely lacking given the complexity before her. From what she could tell, it was a simple spell of augmentation. It would add the collective power of those empowering the spell-form to her own actions. *Not exactly a defense of my gate, but I suppose if I am working to defend such, the effect would be the same.*

In truth, most of the complexity of the spell-forms were workings of purification, to prevent the Archons assisting her from tainting the bond with the signature of their power. In the end, if she understood correctly, it would be like the ambient magic of the Wilds working at her behest.

I could do a lot of fun things with this... If she had the proper inscriptions to take advantage of it.

She sighed. Terry was crouched on the floor beside Rane and Lyn, watching her closely, now the size of a medium-sized dog.

Tala dropped to a cross-legged position, turning her gaze inward.

As she looked through her body, she searched for the small void that she now knew would be there, among her natural magical pathways.

There.

In the center of her sternum, there was a distortion as if there was a depth to that point that went beyond the physical; there was even a depth beyond the layer of and for magic throughout the rest of her. As she probed it with her magesight, she found an almost identical void to the one she'd found in Flow and the other artifacts.

It somehow didn't disrupt or displace the inscriptions that now filled most of her being. Again, it was *elsewhere* while still being there.

"Found it."

The four Archons who would assist her were Grediv, Holly, Elnea, and the male Archon who had been the last to oppose her elevation. *An honor or a punishment?*

She understood why Master Himmal couldn't help; his power was broken, uneven, and not reliable. Still, she felt a bit saddened by that. He had been kind to her, though they didn't know each other that well.

The other Archons watched this ceremonial binding.

Elnea nodded. "Let us begin." She and the other three settled into their circles, stretching out their hands and pouring their power into the compound spell-form.

The lines were slow to come to life; the glow flowed outward, following various splitting paths in no pattern that Tala could discern, but soon, the entirety was powered.

Tala gasped.

She *felt* their power in a very abstract way, like a parent helping her do a chore that was beyond her ability. It didn't force her to do anything. *Hey, I wasn't deceived.* At least, not yet.

She already held the vial containing her most powerful star. She was about to drink it but hesitated. *No. That's wrong.*

She drew Flow.

Tala focused, pulling her defensive power away from her chest. With a quick motion, guided by instincts she didn't exactly understand, she drew Flow in a hard line down the center of her chest, splitting her tunic, skin, and bone in a clean line, not going deep enough to near her heart.

She almost blacked out from the pain, but the reinforcing power of the Archons helped her cling to consciousness as she sheathed the knife.

Several of the observing Archons gasped, but no one moved to interfere.

Tala dumped her Archon Star out of the vial and *pulled.*

Millennial Mage, 3 - Binding

Just as she had called Flow to her hand so many times, she pulled the star into her chest and straight into the void that awaited it.

As the spell-form entered her flesh, it took on a life of its own, attempting to divert from her desired path for it, but she clamped down, feeling the weight of the four Archons' power added to her own. The star didn't so much as tremble from side to side on its short flight.

With a deep thrum, the star vanished into the void that was ready for it, and Tala's entire being shattered.

She lost control of her power, and her chest sealed instantly, her clothing closing just after her skin.

Her body's natural magic subtly shifted to incorporate her Archon Star. Physically, she felt minor blemishes and scars smooth over. Her flesh moved around her inscriptions. The magical spell-forms were immune to the changes around them, but they stayed enmeshed with their designated portion of her form, nonetheless.

Something within her eyes changed, but she couldn't see herself to determine what it had been. Her nails blackened, but she recoiled at that. *No.*

The force of her will, still supported, reversed that change, and she suddenly felt something *click* within her mind.

Her vision went white as a torrent of magic slammed into the Archon Star and through it, into her body.

* * *

She was suddenly outside herself, without form, looking into a white void. It wasn't bright; it wasn't dim; it simply was, and it was white.

It was familiar in its strangeness. *This is like when I modified Flow.*

As expected, a manifestation of herself appeared for her scrutiny.

She stood, a vision of terrible beauty. Her skin was the red of wet blood, her eyes black, her hair silver-gold. Her best features were all accentuated to an inhuman degree, and her inscriptions rested upon her like the mantle of an empress.

Flow rested at her hip, and it resonated with this form, ready to strike down all who opposed her.

And, within her, she could feel that she had been lost.

Making another bid to win, eh? Just in a different way?

This one was a lie. She couldn't choose this and still be herself.

The next hundred versions of herself that flew through her mind varied in any number of ways, but none of them were *her*.

She felt a force, with four blending components, helping to guide her through the hordes of false choices, itself guided by her desire to find herself.

Finally, she came to three manifestations that were *her*.

All retained her stature and general features. One had hair as red as new-shed blood. One's hair was such a dark red that it was almost indistinguishable from black. The final retained her natural, deep, dark-brown hair.

Their eyes all had irises of ruby red. *That's what I felt. I suppose that change happened before I took control.*

She could tell that each option was different in half-a-hundred little ways, but the hair was a good overall indicator.

I can change a little or a lot. She somehow knew that this wasn't the end. She would have chances to make more subtle changes as she continued to advance.

She might have laughed if she'd had lungs or a mouth with which to do so. *I could change myself as I wished, now. Break bones and force them to heal back in different configurations. I could make my face look like anything I want.* But she liked her face. It wasn't perfect, but it was *hers.*

Similarly, the changes she saw open before her were… odd, and she somehow knew that the less she felt like herself, the harder she would find the next steps.

She chose the version of herself with the fewest changes. The only stark alteration was her eyes, and those, somehow, seemed proper if a bit brighter than she expected. *For some reason.*

As she made her choice, she felt the rightness of it. She had forced her body to mold to her *self,* instead of allowing her body and the Archon Star to alter that self.

Hah, another false choice? How did most people pass this? Those other options had been pretty tempting. *Maybe it's because of how powerful my star was?* She hadn't seen any physical changes in Lyn or Rane. *Not that I really examined them that closely…*

Power fragmented through her, body and soul; her very self, that which she had defended and chosen above all else, felt as if it was being scraped raw.

*   *   *

Her vision splintered back into normal sight, and she found herself sitting cross-legged on the smooth floor of the same room.

All traces of the spell-forms were gone, and Elnea stood over her, hand outstretched. "Rise, Mistress Tala, Blood Archon. First of your title."

Tala swayed, the now-familiar feeling of soul-deep tiredness washing over her. It was actually pretty bearable since she was used to using Flow to work that part of her. As she shifted, moving to take the offered hand, she almost gasped. Her whole body felt alive, more *her* than ever before. *Like Flow does.*

It was as if she'd been wearing a suit of heavy armor, using gloves to feel about in the dark, and all that had fallen away, leaving her free to experience the world, truly, for the first time.

There weren't more sensations, nor were they really stronger. The only descriptor she could apply was that everything felt more *real*.

Tala finally grasped Elnea's hand, but she remembered to not actually use it to stand. *I don't want to fling the poor woman across the room. That would be embarrassing.* Tala nodded her thanks. *I really do need to seriously consider how useful the extra weight really is...*

"Let what was witnessed here stand testament to the wisdom of our ways. She is mighty without question, but still, without our added strength, she may have followed a false path. The victory is hers, and part of that was her acceptance of assistance."

Tala quirked a smile, whispering for only the woman to hear, "Cementing your power?"

Elnea gave her a quick glance, then responded in a low voice that somehow didn't seem to carry at all. "Cementing the value of this council in their minds. Archons like their freedom. It is good to remind them of the value of working together, even if only to raise up the next generation."

Tala smiled in truth and gave a bow over their still-clasped hands. "Thank you, Mistress Elnea." She spoke loudly enough for all to hear. They released each other's grasps.

Tala heard several people comment on her eyes, likely those with better vision, enhanced or natural. Elnea headed off any issue. "Her star fought well, seeking to oust or bend her eternal soul. That fight left obvious signs, just as many of you bear more discreet marks." She gave a half-bow to Tala. "Welcome, Mistress Tala, to the rank of Archon."

A single, all-pervasive cheer echoed from every Archon present—more like a shout of triumph than a crowd's adulation. Tala scanned those around her.

Grediv looked quite smug, clearly pleased with himself about something, and Tala thought she caught hints of quiet comments. Apparently, she'd weathered the bond better than anyone had expected, save Grediv apparently.

That's why Lyn and Rane looked so exhausted, she realized.

She looked to them, seeing happiness in their expressions, and smiled in return.

Tala was about to turn away, to walk towards her fellow new Archons, when Elnea raised her right hand as high as she could reach, palm facing forward. Her left was tucked in front of her chest in what Tala recognized as a knife-hand shape, though it wasn't to attack. Instead, that hand looked as if it was resting on an invisible surface, bisecting the woman.

Magic swirled around the Archon, clearly designed to be showy, both to normal vision and magesight.

The upraised hand glowed for a moment with a deep, red light. It wasn't Elnea's aura but light visible to Tala's normal vision. The woman's voice lanced out, easily reaching everyone present, and if Tala read the magic correctly, her voice would be carried… somewhere else, as well. *To other Archon councils?*

"Archons of Humanity, today, Bandfast welcomes its third new Archon, first of her title: Mistress Tala, Blood Archon." Elnea clenched the upper hand into a fist, and a final burst of magic washed over the room and to the other destinations. Tala received, into her own mind, a picture of herself.

She stood straight despite being below average in height. She was trim and fit, finding a comfortable middle ground between childishly slim and bulky.

Her hair was pulled into an ordered braid, artfully woven from near her left temple, across the back of her head to where it blossomed from the base of her skull, near her right shoulder, hanging in front of that side of her chest. *And dark brown.* Tala felt immensely proud of retaining her natural hair color, though she couldn't have said exactly why.

Her eyes were now, by far, her most striking feature. They were as brilliant and pure a red as they could possibly be without actually glowing.

Her face was angular without being sharp, and soft without being round. She'd always thought of herself as pretty, rather than beautiful, and this image bore that out. With the addition of her new eye color, however, she was certainly striking.

She had a decidedly hourglass figure and was curvy without it being inconvenient, but she didn't focus on that.

She was clad in her perfectly fitted elk leathers, her near-white tunic and thunder-cloud gray pants setting off her skin's natural tone. Kit and Flow hung from her black belt, one comfortably resting on each hip.

Oh, I could have—and probably should have—worn one of the formal outfits that Merilin made for me. It was too late for that, by far.

Her bare feet were obvious below the cuffs of her pants, but they were just as obviously intentionally bare.

On all her exposed skin—feet, hands, neck, and head—there was a sheen of gold over her natural skin color. The spell-forms were *far* too delicate to be distinguished. Instead, the appearance was almost like a fine mesh of metal had been pulled tight and flawlessly shaped to her every contour. Even her eyes had veils of gold, highlighting their ruby irises.

The look of delicate, precious-metal work, combined with the positively gem-like nature of her eyes, caused her to almost look like a jeweler's masterwork.

Throughout the manifestation, power was in evidence. Her aura was distinctly red, and that gave her a thought. *Are my eyes red to match my aura, or is it a coincidence?* While they were probably red because of the blood medium for the Archon Star, only time would tell.

On a more ephemeral level, the woman that she, and everyone else, beheld had a weight of confidence and *action* as if she knew where she was going, and may the stars above help any who got in her way.

Tala's eyes widened at the brief image, her jaw going slack in shock. *Is that really how I look to others? I wish I had that much confidence…*

She didn't know how to feel, if she was being honest. The impression passed in a heartbeat, but the memory, crystal clear, lingered in her mind.

Elnea grinned, lowering her arm, her magic worked, her job done. "Welcome, Mistress Tala, one of us in truth."

Chapter: 21
Plentiful and Free

Tala gave a slight bow, once more, but this time, it was to give her a moment to think. When she straightened, she was still no closer to having a coherent response. She was still feeling quite overwrought by all that had happened.

Elnea's grin shifted to a more companionable smile. "It can be overwhelming, so many things changing at once, then to see yourself as others do?" She shook her head. "You are holding up surprisingly well." She leaned closer and spoke in a conspiratorial whisper, "I wept at my raising."

Terry appeared on Tala's shoulder, giving Elnea a pointed, hostile look before he settled down and closed his eyes in mock sleep. The Archon pulled back, though seemingly not in fear.

Lyn and Rane were working their way towards her, but Grediv reached Tala and Elnea first. "Mistress Elnea! You cannot dominate the time of this guest of honor as well."

Elnea gave Grediv a long-suffering look. "I tolerated your intrusions because your... pupil was being evaluated as well, but you did *not* tell me you had such a strong hand in this one's advancements."

Grediv shrugged. "I've told all I did. I gave her access to no forbidden knowledge. I didn't even inform her about the Ways. That would have been a breach for any Archon who wasn't her master." He gave Tala a subtle wink. "The only contribution I claim is doing my utmost to prevent her from killing herself or becoming a lich."

Tala cleared her throat. "Okay. I'm an Archon, now. Explain how I could have become a lich."

Elnea gave Grediv an irritated look.

"I don't want to become one; I want to avoid it."

Grediv grinned. "The biggest danger of that passed with your elevation to Archon. Mages, in general, are in danger of all sorts of horrors, mostly volitional until their body is bound to their soul…" Elnea was giving him a *very* unkind glare, so he tapered off. "But you can read about those in the library, if you so wish. Or purchase the volumes yourself, but I imagine someone will be kind enough to gift you the basic texts." He gave her another, less subtle wink.

Tala smiled in return. Grediv had, in fact, given her such a set, though most of the volumes were sealed against her until she was of sufficient stature to warrant the information. *I wonder if I'll be able to read all of them now or just some?* She was excited to check, but it was hardly the time.

Elnea cleared her throat. "Certain information remains restricted by level of advancement."

Tala sighed. "Do I, at least, get to know how I am supposed to advance?"

"Of course."

Tala blinked at that, surprised. "Really?"

"Absolutely. Moving from being a Bound to a Fused is a simple matter of fusing your body and soul together, inseparably. To be clear, you are not making them one; that is impossible as they are now."

That's not foreshadowing or anything. "Okay, that explains the name. How do I do that?"

Elnea smiled broadly. "*That* you must learn for yourself."

Tala returned a flat look. *Seriously, woman?*

Grediv interjected. "You, Mistress Tala, have a leg up on most new Bound. What you've accomplished with"—Elnea was glaring at him once more, so he seemed to change what he'd been about to say—"your items, proves you've some insight."

My items, eh? She contemplated that, glancing down at herself. Then, she started to smile. *Right! I fused my elk leathers into a single item. It's probably something like that.* "I see. Thank you, Master Grediv." She hesitated. "Wait... you never told me how one becomes a lich?"

Elnea shook her head. "Too late, it seems; your fellow new Archons are here."

Rane and Lyn finally got close to her through the now milling and conversing crowd. This seemed to be as much a social event for Archons as for the raising of new members.

Tala glared at Elnea, but then something moving around the perimeter of the room caught her attention.

Are those trays of food? It appeared that servants had come in while Tala was distracted, filling the three large tables with a banquet's worth of food.

"Tala!" Lyn wrapped Tala in a fierce embrace. "I knew you'd be fine."

Elnea gave them an odd look, likely from Lyn's lack of an honorific.

"Lyn. Or should I say Mistress Lyn Clerkson, Diamond Archon?"

Elnea looked back and forth between them, then shook her head in resigned exasperation.

Lyn grinned. "You could but don't. That's a mouthful."

Tala laughed.

Rane hung back, just a bit, until Tala turned towards him. At that point, he smiled, gave a bow, and extended his hand. "Congratulations, Mistress Tala." *Something looks different about him...*

Tala reached towards him, taking his offered hand. "Thank you, and congratulations to you, too, Master Rane Gredial, Sapphire Archon."

He rolled his eyes. "None of that, Mistress."

It's his scars. His scars are faded, somehow. She decided not to point it out, for now. It wasn't a huge change, but it was noticeable. She put on a mock-serious tone. "As you wish, Master."

Lyn snorted a laugh. "Come on! This banquet is for all of us. Apparently, they didn't want to bring out all this food for any one of us, alone."

Tala glanced towards Elnea and Grediv, but they seemed to be having a heated argument, though Tala couldn't hear even a flicker of sound from it. From the brief glimpses Tala had gotten of the woman's power and spell-lines, Elnea was a Material Guide, specializing in sound. *Rare specialty.* That didn't explain the mental image of Tala, which had been projected, but Tala supposed every Mage did have their secrets.

She shrugged, returning her attention to her companions. "Food sounds great." She hesitated then, turning back to fully face Lyn. "I am so, so sorry about the finger, Lyn. I was going to explain, but other things kept coming up, then Master Rane said we couldn't talk about our star formation." She gave a pained smile. "I had to get it out, and cutting off the fingertip was the only thing I could think to do."

The woman gave her a long look, then sighed. "That does explain it." Lyn nodded once. "You're still buying me a new rug, though."

"...I suppose that's fair..." Her nose caught a whiff of the dishes now laid out around the room. "Now, let's get to the food. I'm *starving.*"

The other two grinned jovially, clearly not surprised by the revelation.

As they moved towards the food, many gave them hearty congratulations. Though, all tallied, many more intercepted the other two, individually, than Tala, herself.

For Tala, some asked if she'd be interested in collaborations or other opportunities. All of those, she gave noncommittal answers, which amounted to: 'Too much going on right now. Reach out later, please?'

Everyone seemed to take that well, even seeming to have expected something of the sort.

She didn't listen closely enough to know exactly what was said to the other two, but from context, and what she did catch, it all seemed to be in the same vein.

When Tala finally broke through the crowd, she gaped at the sheer quantity and variety of food. *And everything is finger or bite-sized.*

One whole table, the one they'd reached first, was covered in little sandwiches. The type of bread varied, as did the fillings and addenda, which made the permutations staggering. *And there seemed to be hundreds of each available.*

In contrast to the ocean of food, the plates were barely bigger than her hand, spread wide. *What the slag is this?* She took a small stack.

As they filled their laughably small plates with food, Rane leaned over. "I can't believe you were ready to fight off a room full of Archons."

She quirked a smile his way. "Did you bow to their command?" She was currently balancing one fully mounded plate, while preparing the second for cargo.

"Well, no, but my protests were verbal."

Lyn leaned around the big man. "He demanded his 'master' intervene. He said that he would be a fool to obey such a command."

Tala hesitated. "Oh… that idea never crossed my mind."

Rane grinned, and Lyn rolled her eyes before remarking, "Of course, it didn't, Tala. You are a woman of action—however ill-advised."

"Yeah, yeah." They reached the end of the first table, Tala straining her dexterity to the limit with four fully loaded plates in each hand. Then, she beheld the central table.

Instead of sitting on beds of ice, like those used to help keep the little sandwiches cool, these trays were heavy metal, over burners of some kind, clearly meant to keep this food hot. The first item available looked like bacon but much thicker and not fully crisped. The little sign near the sizzling platter said it was pork belly.

Oh, I need some of you. She was frowning down at the food, including the plates in her hands, then smiled. *Right!* With deft movements, she set her plates down, opened Kit wide, and lowered the full dishes into the pouch, one after another. "There." Just as quickly, she overfilled another plate with the pork belly and slipped it into Kit as well. She looked up to see Lyn and Rane giving her odd looks. "What?"

Lyn looked at the pouch, then back up at Tala. "Won't that get everything in there greasy and covered in crumbs and sauce?"

Rane took a more direct approach. "Isn't it a bit rude to pack out food?"

Tala shook her head. "No, Kit manages the separation of items perfectly, and no, it isn't rude. This food is for *us*. I'm not going to say 'no' to that. Besides, I'll still probably eat most of it here. I just don't want to have to take dozens of trips to the serving table. *That* would be rude." She thought for a moment. "Hmm… how long will this go on?"

It was Rane who responded. "You just want to know how long you'll have access to this food."

Tala opened her mouth to object, then stopped. "Yeah, that's true. So?"

Rane sighed. "Likely a couple hours. I think there's some sort of closing... something to wrap up the event after socializing."

She nodded, smiling towards the two other new Archons. "Alright then. It would be a shame if we didn't get all we could out of *our* banquet."

Rane and Lyn looked at each other, then shrugged. Lyn gave a little laugh, and Rane snorted a chuckle. "Sounds fair." Thus, the three began to work over the tables in earnest, piling plates high with food before passing them to Tala and, through her, to Kit.

Every so often, one or more of them had to pause their great work to talk to Archons who approached; they were the guests of honor, after all. Even so, it didn't really take from their newfound mission.

Lyn grinned with what seemed to be barely contained glee the first time she saw a servant refresh one of the platters of food. The supply might just be functionally infinite.

No one noticed, seemed to mind, or cared enough to say anything.

As it turned out, Rane had been correct, and the festivities lasted for two hours—or as close as Tala could reckon.

Tala was not a social person, and in the end, the food, as plentiful and free as it was, was not worth enduring more socializing.

After only half an hour, Tala had tried to slip out for the first time, but each time she'd tried, there were suddenly a lot more people interested in talking with her, and in truth, she was still not quite desperate enough to be as rude as would have been required to break free.

Millennial Mage, 3 - Binding

Thus, she inevitably drifted back to the food. *At least there's coffee.*

She'd filled both her coffee jugs, immediately, and was nursing a tankard of the stuff. The tankard had been taken from the side table where kegs of beer and ale were tapped.

The attendant in charge of coffee now visibly twitched whenever Tala walked by, and if Tala was being honest, she moved through that part of the room more often than strictly necessary.

Maturity is a process, not a destination, after all.

Near the beginning of the time, Master Himmal had approached Tala for a quick conversation.

"Congratulations, Mistress Tala. I am so glad that we of the Wainwrights' Guild get to work so closely with you."

Tala smiled, bowing to the much older-looking man. *And he's probably much older than he appears, too.* "Thank you, Master Himmal, and thank you for your support and encouragement."

He waved her off with a smile. "Think nothing of it. I did want to let you know that we've finished modifying the main wagon for your increased weight, not that I understand the purpose of that. There should be no issue with you riding on the roof or sleeping within your portion of the designated cargo-slot."

"Thank you, I appreciate that." She hesitated. "You know, there's something that I've been meaning to ask but keep forgetting."

"Oh?"

"Why not simply give the wagons a higher power storage capacity so that you only needed Dimensional Mages at the start of each journey?"

He thought for a moment, then nodded. "What do you know of the Arcane Chaos Theory?"

"I would say that I know nothing but the name."

He smiled at that. "That makes sense. Few outside of the unified Constructionist Guilds need to know of it. The underpinning is this: the more power contained in a reservoir, the less stable it is. This is actually the basis on which we know that a Mage's power, drawn through their gate, is not finite."

"Really? Did anyone ever believe that?"

"Oh, yes. It used to be a popular theory that we each only had so much power. So, if you drew more deeply, you were shortening your own life."

"But that's nonsense."

He shrugged. "I'll make no play at justifying the debunked theories of our ancestors. But it applies here, too. If we were to double the power capacity of the cargo-slots, we would get at most another hour out of the spell-form. Triple? Maybe another half-hour beyond that."

"So, why aren't bigger cargo-slots out of power much faster?"

He smiled. "Ahh, that is an excellent question. Simple: magic applied only dissipates as it's used, and the reservoir's rate of decay is directly correlated with the spell it is meant to supply."

She blinked and shook her head, trying to process that. "Wait, so if I'm understanding correctly, then no spell-form could last longer than a day or so."

"Without an external source of power, yes." He shrugged. "It is a fundamental truth behind magic. Any item that doesn't need such regular influx is simply getting its power in some other way. As an example, harvests, used as a power source, are not reservoirs and don't suffer from this limit as a result. Well, they don't suffer in the same way."

Tala opened her mouth, but Master Himmal held up a hand.

"We are delving at a very surface level into deep theory, and if we continue, I fear I will need to dominate your entire afternoon, and still, we'll have barely begun. If you wish to learn more about crafting theory, I am happy to take the time, but not here, not now." He smiled.

Tala hesitantly nodded, then smiled. "Thank you. I just might take you up on that."

"I hope that you do." He patted her shoulder, the one opposite where Terry rested. "I'll not take more of your time, but it was a pleasure to see you, Mistress."

"And you, Master Himmal."

As he turned to go, he hesitated, leaning back towards her and speaking in a conspiratorial whisper. "You know, if you ask one of the staff members, they'll make up carry-out containers of any food you'd like to request."

Tala's eyes widened, but Master Himmal left before she could respond, a small smile obvious on his face. *That's genius!*

She immediately sought out staff members. First, she asked what would be done with the leftover food, when the event ended, and she was horrified to learn that it would most likely be thrown out. *Madness, utter madness!*

She put an end to that immediately, requesting that they pack it all up for her to take. The poor young woman that she'd accosted didn't really know how to process the request, but after they'd found a more senior staff member, Tala was assured that no edible food would be thrown away. *It rusting better not be.*

Lyn and Rane worked the room much more readily than she did. As much as their initial enthusiasm for raiding the food table had delighted Tala, she'd known it wouldn't last, not in the face of so many people focusing in on the three of them.

In Lyn's case, Tala had expected the networking, glad-handing, and jovial relationship building. *She is basically a recruiter and face for the Caravanners, after all.*

Rane's acumen, however, was startling. True, most of the positive interactions that Tala witnessed from afar seemed to stem from him almost visibly restraining himself from speaking, but it still seemed unexpectedly successful. Several of the Archons who came up to him were younger-looking women. *All gorgeous, of course.* If his blushing countenance was any indication, they seemed to be asking him to break his word… or something, Tala had no idea, and they never seemed to talk to Rane, while she was within earshot. Even so, the interactions never seemed to go anywhere.

As she thought about the afternoon in general, she realized that Rane, in his words, was often similar to her in her actions. The restraint he was demonstrating bore contemplation. *Maybe I could be a little less rash in my actions?*

She thought about it for a full thirty seconds. *Nah. I'll get good progress, or I'll die.* Still, she would continue to avoid things she knew, for a fact, were deadly. *At least those that would be deadly to me.*

Even so, she knew that she would try to contemplate her actions and their repercussions more deeply. *At least more than I have previously.*

If she kept that up, every day, she just might make significant improvement. *One can hope.*

She startled her current accoster by pulling a fully loaded plate out of her belt pouch and beginning to eat. *I'm running low.*

"So… as I was saying, if you'd be willing to allow a detailed examination of your blood, along with one of your Archon Stars…"

Millennial Mage, 3 - Binding

The conversations, well-wishes, and opportunities were decidedly blurring together.

"Congratulations!"

"I can't believe you drew a soul-bound weapon. Fantastic!"

"Once your current contracts run out, we'd love to have you…"

"Your talents are wasted with the Caravanner's Guild. Let me buy out your indenture. You'd be much better served…"

"Your companion is unlike any terror bird I've come across. Would you be willing to…"

Tala was not interested in joining someone else's research, nor subjecting herself or Terry to such. She was happy with her current contract and the terms. The work would be lucrative and leave time for her to pursue her own projects on the trips, even if the role as Mage Protector would take more effort than she'd put forward before. *Plus, I've seen three cities and the Academy. I want to see the others, and my work in the caravans will allow that.*

After almost two hours, she was about to bolt for it, rust manners, when Holly found her.

"Blood Archon, eh?"

Tala turned at the familiar voice and smiled. "Yes, Mistress Holly. I hope I still managed to surprise you despite your earlier exposure to my form of Archon Star."

Holly gave a nod and smiled. "Decidedly. I do almost wish I could have seen you continue to resist the entirety of the council, attending here." She sighed, dejectedly. "It would have been a wonderful look into what those inscriptions are truly capable of."

Tala cleared her throat. "Well, I, for one, am glad that you aren't all inhuman monsters, bent on subjugating anyone of potential power."

Holly hesitated, then shrugged. "Fair enough."

Tala rolled her eyes but huffed a laugh. "Thank you, again."

"Hmm?"

"You have elevated my inscriptions to a level that I feel reasonably in my element here, among so many magical power-houses."

Holly snorted. "Dear, aside from the two Head Archons, most of us are weaker members of the local council. Those of real weight don't concern themselves with new Archons." She leaned in, whispering conspiratorially, "And, if we're being honest, the really powerful ones don't have interest in dealing with the others at all, so the Heads aren't the best, either."

"Ouch, but I suppose that's fair."

Holly patted her arm. "You'll get there, dear. Just keep from killing yourself, and you'll do fine." She turned, her mind clearly already elsewhere. "Now, where did I see those raspberry mousse cups?"

Wait, there's dessert, too? How had she missed the presence of a dessert table? That was unacceptable. *I'm getting distracted by unimportant things.*

Chapter: 22
The Crux of the Matter at Hand

Tala was again trying to decide how to depart from the increasingly straining event when Elnea drew the focus back to herself. "Attention! We all have things to be about, so we will now perform the final steps of the elevation." She motioned to the three new Archons, drawing them to her from where they'd dispersed through the room.

Tala had just finished adding desserts to her food reserves in preparation for departure. Thus, she came from a side table, tucked in one corner.

Lyn had been discussing the choice of diamond as a medium with several other Diamond Archons in another corner.

Rane had been receiving some pointed words from his former master, though Tala didn't know what about. *Why do all the interesting conversations happen outside of my hearing?* It could be that they weren't actually that interesting, and the myth that she made of them in her mind vastly outstripped reality, but she doubted it.

The three smiled at each other before taking their places, standing before Elnea, and the Archon motioned three assistants forward. "This officially confirms your elevation and your Bound nature. Once you confirm, your records within the archives will be altered to reflect your rank."

They each pricked their chosen finger and confirmed the document as presented. Tala and Lyn read it first. Thankfully, it was short. Rane simply shrugged and confirmed the slate. *Some people like to live dangerously, I guess.*

Once all three stone devices had briefly colored green, Elnea continued. "In your time as Mages, you have had many teachers, and you will have many more. At this time, it is my honor to become one of them, if only for a simple thing."

The three glanced at each other briefly before returning their eyes to the Archon before them.

Well then, time to learn something new. Tala couldn't help but grin.

"Now, you each have an aura, which amounts to your soul attempting to influence the world around you. At your current strength, it will be mildly uncomfortable to non-Mages, but as you advance, it will become damaging and eventually lethal. Because of this, it is forbidden to have an unrestrained aura in public."

An Archon in a back corner decided to add his opinion, "And it's rusting rude!"

Elnea quirked a smile. "It is somewhat like neglecting hygiene, in how it impacts those around you, yes. Though *that* is hardly ever lethal." A few Archons chuckled. Then, her smile faded, her tone becoming serious once more. "The aura is the result of your body now being, in effect, a soul-bound item. Your gate is now *yours* and yours alone, bound almost unbreakably to your soul."

That surprised Tala. *Isn't all power coming through my gate mine? Wait… aren't my gate and my soul the same thing?* But no silent pause was given for question or comment.

"You no longer naturally project excess magic outward as untainted power to disperse into the air. All magic coming from you is now *yours*. That is the nature of an aura."

Wait, you said it was our soul attempting to affect the world around us. Now it's excess magic? Tala focused inward and saw that, true to Elnea's words, her excess power was now diffusing out from her in a way that looked reminiscent of a teabag in hot water. *Huh...* She focused, turning the power back at her skin. Her aura was still there but only barely visible to her incredibly sensitive magesight. *So my soul is still trying to extend, but the power is a medium for greater effect?* That seemed to fit.

Her efforts to restrain her power were effective; she was an Immaterial Guide, after all. Thus, she immediately had a feeling of building pressure. Her body was already at capacity, and she was preventing the outflow.

She grimaced, and Elnea stopped mid-sentence. She'd been saying something else, but Tala had stopped paying attention.

Elnea sighed, and her inclusion of Tala's name in her next statement caused it to register. "Or, as Mistress Tala is currently demonstrating, you could simply force the power to remain within your body, over and above the normal levels. That will not, actually, restrain your aura effectively, however. Nor is it precisely safe."

There was a wave of power through the room as most present activated their magesight. Tala was only able to easily detect it because so many activated their inscriptions at once, though no individual spell-form was discernible.

Tala was focused elsewhere, however. *My aura seems pretty restrained to me, Archon.*

That said, the contained power couldn't be static. She could not allow her reserves to be the placid reservoir they had been up until now. *But what do I do with it?* That was a laughably simple question. She shunted the entirety of the excess into her items, in turn, and finally to Flow. *Huh, Kit is much lower on power than I'd have expected.* It had been straining to accommodate the food she'd been shoveling in.

Millennial Mage, 3 - Binding

It apparently takes quite a bit of power to reshape dimensionality within the pouch in order to accommodate a few plates of food? She absentmindedly patted Kit after the pouch was refilled.

Kit did not respond.

Her focus back on her internal power, there was a difference between what she was doing and what she had been doing up until now. Mainly, she was preventing even the barest hints of power from leaving her form to go anywhere except her strictly maintained outlets. It was exhausting.

Elnea shifted, straightening her robes irritably. "Mistress Tala."

Tala met her gaze, without really giving the woman her attention.

"If you insist on trying that now, you should know: power isn't water."

Tala blinked at that, then frowned. *What?* True to the woman's words, Tala had been visualizing her power as water. *The Academy ensures that every Mage sees it as such. What madness is she spouting?* A thousand features of water flickered through her mind, far fewer than a Material Mage would have considered, and that likely helped her narrow it down.

She quirked a smile. *Didn't Rane mention a Way of Compression or some such? Water is incompressible.* Power isn't water. *I can compress my power.* Of course she could. She knew that. *So, why have I never compressed my reserve?* Hadn't she? Her power density was incredibly high. *The natural density... density isn't really the right word, though, is it? Holly was referring to my total amount of power, not how compact that power was within me.* Related, sure, but not the same.

She had to be careful. She didn't want to increase her inflow, not at the moment. So, she bent her will, bearing down on her power, which she still kept trapped within herself, compressing it into a hollow sphere around her gate, in alignment with the placement of her keystone. The concentration around her gate, itself, remained the same, so as to not create a suction or a blockage.

Instantly, the difficulty of keeping the power within her body dropped off considerably. All the power was contained in that sphere, only flowing outwards as the keystone directed, following her spell-lines, instead of saturating them. *They are aqueducts in the desert now, instead of underwater pipelines.*

To her surprise, the power didn't fight her in the least, at least not directly. *Like crumpling up a tablecloth.*

That thought made her hitch, and instead of simply compressing it into shape, she *folded* her power, compressing it in carefully regulated layers.

It wasn't hard, just like tossing a ball into the air wasn't hard.

It was hard because juggling was hard, and she was mentally juggling more magic than she could quickly quantify. She began to feel a building headache.

Tala groaned. The whole process had taken less than ten seconds, and even newly complete, it was already becoming increasingly difficult to maintain. It was easier than simply holding the power in by leaps and bounds, but not easy by any means.

Mutters rolled through the room. Grediv snorted in disgust before barking a laugh. "One bit of advice, that's all she needed. She didn't even need a demonstration. I don't even see how your advice applied to her aura."

Elnea shook her head. "Look closer, Master Grediv. She is channeling her excess into her items, specifically the soul-bound weapon."

Tala spoke as evenly as she could despite her distraction and straining. "Is that not correct?"

Millennial Mage, 3 - Binding

"It is a crutch. For the few Archons who cannot master the true technique, we suggest soul-bonding an item for such a purpose, or we create an item that effectively soaks up their power, reducing their aura down to a harmless state. They are then required to bond with that, so as to make the patch permanent." She gave Tala a serious look. "They never advance after that point."

That explains those with Archon marks… those here really are the 'lesser' Archons… It was an incredibly uncharitable thought, and she threw it aside. Tala found herself frowning. "My aura is still there, diminished, not restrained."

"Precisely." Elnea gave a slight smile. "What you are doing is moving towards an advanced power flow in the vein of Ways. They are too numerous to cover, and each is relatively easy to enact briefly but hard to hold. However, they are not the intended topic I am discussing here."

Tala let out a relieved breath, her concentration on the internal technique breaking, her power reserves, and flow, returning to normal, though the excess was still mostly directed into Flow, now that her other items had refilled.

Elnea nodded. "Now, as I was saying: Right now, the three of your souls are like toddlers, spinning around without a care to what their arms hit, what damage they can do. Pull yourselves in. Restrain your inner toddlers." A ripple of laughter moved through the room again, and Tala found herself smiling along with the levity.

Okay… how?

Grediv cleared his throat. "Like your knife, Mistress Tala. Master Rane, Mistress Lyn, observe her."

My knife? Tala looked down at the weapon, feeling the connection, knowing it would come as she called. *Ahh!* She *pulled* on her aura, not the knife. She lifted her arm and watched as, to her magesight, the red withdrew inward, fading entirely behind the power in her spell-lines.

Before, she'd been running circles around a tarp, frantically sweeping water back towards the middle. Now, she picked up the edges. *So, so much easier.* The effect was almost identical to her first attempt but was accomplished with an absolutely trivial amount of effort.

Lyn smiled briefly, and her aura shimmered, pulling inward just slightly before it washed back out. She clutched her abdomen. "Ow." She groaned. "Oh, that's… that's like writing a thousand contracts after a month away from work."

Tala grinned. "Turns out that your soul is a bit like a muscle."

Lyn sighed. "More training to do, I suppose." For some reason, she sounded resigned.

I must be misunderstanding.

Rane, for his part, had closed his eyes. His aura was moving inwards in slow, steady pulses. As a result, it was smaller every time he exhaled, having shrunk on each inhale.

Tala checked her own aura, verifying it hadn't crept outward once again. It hadn't.

She could hold this indefinitely. Her daily soul-work with Flow showed its value. *Just as Grediv said it would.*

Still, she wasn't in the clear yet. *It'll take a bit before I can keep it contained in my sleep, too.*

"Even once I have this down, I could slip. No one is perfect. How can it be safe for us to be around other people?"

"It isn't, not as you are."

There was a long pause. When no further answer was forthcoming, Tala's eyes widened. "So… All of you, all of us, are walking disasters. One moment of lapse, and our aura can level a city block?"

Grediv helpfully interjected. "Just the creatures within a certain radius. Buildings would be fine." After a moment, he shrugged. "Would mainly hurt mundanes and non-arcane animals, and even then, you would need a fully realized, Paragon soul before it would be instantly lethal to any but the weakest…" His voice tapered off as he noticed the other Head Archon.

Elnea, once again, was giving Grediv a supremely irritated look. "Master Grediv, you are not Head Archon, here."

"Apologies, Mistress." He raised his hands, stepping a bit farther back.

Elnea tsked, turning back towards them. "As you guessed, Mistress Tala, this is incredibly important. This is also one more reason we so closely guard the process for elevation to Archon, but it isn't as dire as you assume"—she glared towards Grediv—"or as Master Grediv implies. Your aura, as we said, will cause discomfort, not injury. By the time that it is dangerous to others, the restraint will be second nature, and you will have to force your aura to expand outward, should that ever be desired." Elnea added one final point. "It does get harder with advancement, but if that ever becomes a problem, there are solutions."

The Archon marks. Most probably didn't fail and stop as Bound. That made so much more sense.

Tala frowned, remembering Holly. *Wait, I saw Holly's aura…* Rane spoke before she could, however. "I'm sure I've seen Archon auras before. I wasn't struck down, hurt, or made wildly uncomfortable."

Lyn nodded. She often worked near Archons, herself.

Master Himmal's aura is sometimes visible, and I never got any discomfort from him.

Elnea gave a weary smile. "You can have a scent without your smell overpowering those around you." When they didn't respond in understanding, she sighed and explained. "Withdrawing or weakening your aura to the point that it doesn't automatically affect those around you is much easier than eliminating it entirely. Some like to 'relax' and let their aura free on occasion, while keeping the harmful nature at bay. Others are unable to fully restrain it, to the same result. That is still often seen as rude or lesser, however, at least when others are around."

Tala grunted. That made a sort of sense.

"Now, to complete the lesson." She gave them each a firm glance. "Before you are Bound, your body is not you, not really. So, the power it used was not yours. The power you gave it became your body's power—again, not yours. Your body was magic-bound to your soul, unable to receive power from anyone or anything else, but it wasn't *you*. Can you take power from one magic-bound item and give it to another?"

Tala had no idea, she'd never tried, but Lyn shook her head.

"Why not?"

Lyn nodded, seeming to ponder. "Because the power now belongs to that item, not to me. I cannot take it and give it to another."

"Precisely."

Lyn smiled and then continued, "So, all power that came from our gate, except that specifically directed into other bound items, flowed into our body, into three categories. First, the human body uses magic for basic functions; though very little naturally, the amount it uses increases as our power density increases. Second, our inscriptions; that's self-evident. Finally, our reserves, also known as our magic, or power, density. The power within our reserves wasn't really claimed by our magic-bound body, but it wasn't 'clean' either. Is that right?"

Elnea gave a proud smile. "Exactly. Well-reasoned, Mistress Lyn." After a moment's consideration, she nodded. "It is best to consider your reserves before the rank of Archon as a rusty, placid tank. If you were careful, you could draw from it without pulling tainted power; you have each likely empowered something using a bit from your reserves, but you couldn't drain it, completely, to do a working outside of your physical body. Now, as Archons, you taint the entire tank. No power in your reservoir is unclaimed by your body, but that isn't an issue for empowering things bound to you anymore."

Tala's head was hurting, again. "So… it's possible to pull from a magic-bound item's reserves? If you're careful?"

"Yes, but no."

Tala waited.

Elnea sighed. "While you can, in theory, do as you ask, you do not actually have the authority or sway over the power within, say, your dimensional storage. Were that item sapient, *it* could theoretically direct some of its reserves into other items, but they would more likely magic-bind to it, than to you, and would likely reject the power if you had already bonded them." She waved away Tala's further questions. "We are delving *deep* into empowerment theory and have, once again, lost the thread."

Rane made a triumphant sound, both because he'd finally pulled his aura fully inside himself and because he seemed to have realized something. "So, our soul-bound body effectively gives our excess power to the air around us, binding that air to us in turn?"

Elnea hesitated, seemingly taken aback by the radical change in subject. "That—"

Grediv cut across her. "Yes, lad. That is precisely right. Archons, when not using proper soul and aura control, effectively constantly magic-bind the air around themselves, making that air a reserve with no outlet, so it dissipates. Now, if done properly—"

Tala's eyes widened at the implications, even as Elnea shot a peeved look towards Grediv, cutting across him. "Yes, Master Grediv, but as you well know, that is not usually explained until new Archons have mastered basic aura control completely."

He shrugged. "He guessed it. I'm not going to lie to the lad. Were you?"

Her glare sharpened but then faded, and she let out a tired sigh. "I suppose not." She clicked her tongue, still clearly irritated. "But, Master Grediv, you will be silent for the remainder of this portion of the proceedings, no matter how short that may be."

Tala thought she caught the hints of power across the spell-lines on the woman's left forearm before a spell-form flashed into existence, fully manifested around Grediv. *Sound isolation. No sound can exit that field.*

The Head Archon of Alefast gave a disgruntled glare towards his Bandfast counterpart but didn't act to counter the magic.

"Now, we have gotten away from the crux of the matter at hand... again." Many of the surrounding Archons chuckled. "Like anything else, you will need to practice the aura restraint technique until you can perform it even in your sleep."

Just like the Ways... Tala realized that this was quite obviously a complement to the Ways she'd learned of. *Another thing to practice, another way to improve.* She almost snickered to herself. *Hah, another 'Way' to improve.* She was hilarious.

"Many new Archons take a sabbatical or otherwise go into seclusion to master their aura. The quickest on record needed only a day. The longest? A month. No one has failed as a Bound in a *very* long time." Her smile held a motherly cast. "You will find this is much easier to maintain than a Way, and you should find this meshes well with whatever Ways you choose to pursue, once you delve more deeply into those."

Tala didn't know enough, or have enough experience, to tell the truth of that assurance, but she decided to accept it as it seemed. She still effortlessly maintained her aura contraction, her soul strong, steady, and used to her 'self'-control.

She glanced around and noticed that the tables had been cleared, the room returned to its pre-celebration state. *Quick work.*

A servant, looking clearly very nervous and a bit awkward, took the momentary pause as an opening and approached.

Elena gave the young man a quizzical look. He bowed to her. "May I have a word with Mistress Tala?"

The Archons around the room seemed a bit surprised. Elnea, for her part, sighed. "Very well." She glanced to Tala. "The servants must depart before we conclude."

Tala nodded, turning a questioning look to the young man.

"Yes?" *Get on with it...* This was a bit embarrassing.

"The un-eaten, still edible food has been packed up for you."

Elnea gave Tala a long-suffering look but, again, didn't comment. Tala turned back to the servant, after glancing at the Head Archon. "Thank you. Is there anything else?"

"The thing is…" The servant looked away, clearing his throat and reddening slightly.

Tala cocked her head, frowning. "Yes?"

He refused to meet her eyes, and his response was barely more than a whisper. "We are missing quite a few plates."

Missing plates?… Tala's eyes widened in realization. *Oh… oh slag.*

Chapter: 23
In Ancient Times

Tala stared at the servant for a long moment. "Oh, slag." *The plates... Right...* She looked down at her pouch. "Kit, if you would?" She reached in and immediately felt a few stacks of plates. *...Wow. That's way more than I expected.* She smiled, attempting to hide her embarrassment. "My apologies."

Tala did *not* look at the watching Archons.

Instead, she walked over to the closest table and pulled out a stack of around twenty plates, setting them on the table. She heard a few mutters and some chuckles. She stuck her hand back in.

Yup. She came out with another stack, then another after that, and a fourth... then a fifth. Then, a sixth.

The servant looked on with widening eyes. He reached out and took the top plate from one of the stacks.

"It's... clean?"

"Did you expect me to give you some of the food back?"

Grediv casually flicked outward with his right, pinkie finger, and the sound isolation around him vanished.

Elnea gave him an irritable look but didn't comment. She walked over to Tala since the younger Mage hadn't returned immediately. The Head Archon was frowning. "Are you quite done?" Then, she saw what the servant had. "Did your dimensional storage clean and stack those plates?"

Tala shrugged. "Seems so." She stuck her hand back in and drew out a final stack, only about twelve plates this time. "That should be all of it."

A couple other servants came over, bringing several tall stacks of boxes made of a thin, fast-growing wood. *Not meant for heavy use?* That was an interesting concept. Had she seen other establishments giving out one-use containers? *Maybe...* She hadn't really paid attention as she never really had leftovers.

Several of those watching barked laughs, others rolled their eyes, and the murmur of side conversations grew.

Tala, ignoring the reactions of the Archons, lowered the stacks into Kit, one by one. Each was held together with loops of heavy twine, tied tight. "Thank you. And I apologize about the plates. I really didn't even consider them, and I should have."

The servant who had initially approached her bowed, smiling. "Think nothing of it, Mistress. Mistakes happen."

What a politic answer... I wonder if they really think I was trying to steal more than a hundred little plates... It probably didn't matter.

Elnea cleared her throat. "No, Mistress Tala. I need an answer. Did you stack those plates yourself?" She was frowning. "No, that makes no sense. Why would you clean and stack the plates, then put them back in your pouch?"

Tala shrugged, patting Kit. *Wait...* She looked down at the pouch. *It's really low on power, again.* "Huh." She stuck a finger into the bag and directed a couple of void-channels to dump power into Kit. "There you go, Kit."

The pouch did not respond.

Elnea's eyes widened, and she whispered harshly, "You are speaking to it? You have a *sapient* dimensional storage?"

"No?" Tala looked up at the woman, the servants having already taken their plates and departed.

"Mistress Tala, dimensional storage items control the space within them, and they are *loath* to use more power than necessary." She tsked. "But that's anthropomorphizing them too much. I can see that that is clearly an artifact, not inscribed, but I can't see any magic around it, save through the top… I must know: Is that item containing its own aura, or are you somehow doing that?"

Tala hesitated. *Oh! That's how someone else would make a magic item look mundane. Soul-bind it, then restrain the aura.* Even so, there seemed to be some hidden question behind what the Archon was asking or something she missed. With that in mind, she decided the truth was best. "I have treated the outside to protect it from hostile magic and help contain its power. I also do my utmost to empower it whenever it's not as full as it can be."

Elnea examined her critically for a moment, then grunted. Tension Tala hadn't noticed building around the other woman vanished in an instant. "Well, at least you believe what you are saying." She sighed. "Did no one teach you how to keep magic-bound items?" She waved away her own question as soon as it was uttered. "Of course not, Master Grediv informed me of your unique situation, and that is decidedly something the academy leaves to masters to teach their Magelings." She sighed.

Tala shrugged. "I got the basics. Artifacts, specifically, need empowerment only when outside high magic zones. Seemed dumb to me. If it's hungry, feed it. Right?"

"Feed… you just give it power, right?" Some of the tension had returned.

Tala thought about it. "Well, I am storing a"—she cleared her throat. *She doesn't need specifics*—"a lot of food in there. I can't swear it hasn't consumed some, but why? What am I missing?"

Rane, Lyn, and Grediv had come over to join them, silently listening. The other Archons were largely distracted by each other, though some of the closest did seem to be attempting to listen, and the last of the servants were well and truly gone.

Elnea shook her head. "So long as you aren't feeding it lifeblood, or… other similar things, it should be fine."

Tala swallowed involuntarily. *Like a newly dead Mage?* Well, Kit hadn't eaten him, but still…

Elnea seemed to be contemplating. "You've somehow convinced the natural flows and patterns in that pouch that it will never run out of power, so it uses its reserves with near impunity."

Grediv cleared his throat. "Mistress Tala's many oddities aside, however fascinating and enlightening, there is still something that *must* be conveyed. Yes?"

Elnea nodded distractedly. "Yes, yes"—she met Tala's gaze—"but first, Mistress Tala, I would ask a personal favor of you."

"Oh?"

"When you soul-bond that storage item, would you please allow me to witness the bonding?"

Tala hesitated. *That seems a bit intrusive.*

"I've made a study of artifacts, and I've not seen one act *exactly* like that one does."

She shrugged again. "I suppose."

Elnea gave Tala a last, lingering look, then turned and strode away. "Very well." She led them to the center of the room once again, then clapped her hands, gathering the attention of the Archons. She stood for a moment in solemn silence. "While today is a day for celebration, as we welcome three new members to our fight—"

Wait… what?

She continued, clearly uncaring of Tala's surprise, "—it is also a time for remembrance and for enlightenment."

Tala looked to Lyn and Rane. Lyn looked equally confused. Rane was clearly unsurprised. *Grediv did seem to tell him far more than most Mages get to know.*

"In ancient times, humans were the least among the civilized races. Our bodies were frail, and we couldn't draw in ambient magic nearly as well as those whom we lived among."

Tala opened her mouth to interject, but Elnea gave her a level, silencing look, then simply continued.

"At best, we were savages, worshipping and sacrificing to trees for scraps of power. At worst, we were meat animals or menial slaves, only useful for the tasks beneath even our masters' use of magic."

Every Archon around them lowered their heads at the reflected shame of that earlier time. Then, as if following a script, they all looked up as Elnea continued.

"Then came a time when natural magic began to fade, and we saw our chance. One young man, whose name is lost to antiquity, broke his own soul in twain. While still loosely connected, the part only weakly tethered to reality, to his body, began to generate power, pulling it from the world beyond. He was the first of a new humanity."

Tala glanced to Grediv. *So, breaking my soul wouldn't have been so bad?* She doubted that was the intended lesson from the story.

"Sadly, the breaking of his soul also broke his mind, and while he lived on, he never used his gift. His children, however, born after the great sacrifice, had the gift without the madness. They had the potential to become the first Mages."

There it was. So, no soul-breaking. *Assuming it's true… No.*

"But the other races, those of more power than we, even still, saw the gift to humanity as something to be taken. They twisted those born with a gate, taking the weakest willed and severing them completely from their bodies. Thus, they created fountains of power, stopping the lessening of magic in the world, and even reversing the trend, eventually."

Tala's eyes widened. *The fountain of power I found in the wilds… that used to be a person? I was right?* She immediately thought of her lessons. Modern keystones were designed specifically to help prevent Mages from turning their entire being into an open gate. If they did such, they would utterly obliterate themselves and leave behind a hurricane of power without end. *A fountain of power.*

"For generations, we were bred for our gates, used as cattle, trained towards the singular purpose of our eternal souls rebalancing the world's magic."

There was a moment of silence.

"Then, the first of our great heroes stood up and said, 'No.'" She straightened, smiling. "Akmaneous, Krator, and Synathia discovered spell-lines, though we would hardly call them that were we to see them today. They broke their fellows free and died to give our ancestors time to escape."

Tala remembered those names, parts of those stories. Primordial human power, and those with the strength of character to sacrifice themselves for the good of all. They had died from magic poisoning, imparted by their imperfect power. *So, there are pieces that can be shared with mundanes.*

"We fled into the south, where the lower levels of power meant our pursuers were weakened, but we were hunted, nonetheless. For generations further, we hid among the tribes of non-gated humans, among the tree worshippers of this region, biding our time. Many of us were found, but never all."

A moment of solemnity passed once more.

"Finally, the first builder, Adraman, forged the first city. It drew deeply on the surrounding power, making the region anathema to other races, to those who must draw from their environment for power."

Like artifacts. The other races function like artifacts?

"And there, modern humanity truly begins. Our scripts are not eternal, and the world itself rebels, increasing power in the regions we try to deprive. Arcanes can strike at us, relying on stored power for short raids, but they must always retreat, and no Arcane can enter our cities. Our defenses are impervious to them." She smiled with pride at that. "Even so, any but the most capable, strong-willed Mage is destined to become a fount, should they attempt to rise. We are still under threat from our ancient chains."

Tala's eyes widened at that, and Elnea gave her a comforting smile.

"Yes, that is what you fought against. Ancient magics, ancient chains, set within our ancestors' flesh and passed down through the ages, designed to take control of us, to trick us with false promises of power. If a Mage falls, they are led into the Wilds, their soul enslaved. That is why we no longer place our mediums into our flesh in order to build Archon Stars within ourselves. We must be fully capable, fully ready when the Bond is forged, that we may lock our soul and body together, rather than freeing our gate from our flesh and enslaving our body to deliver it to our oppressors."

Tala couldn't contain herself any longer. "And you didn't feel that merited telling us? Why not tell every Mage? Every person?"

"You could not be told. For any information that came from outside of you would be tainted by doubt. You had to feel it yourself, to know for yourself, in order to overcome."

Just like I've always pushed back against the restrictions put on me. It still felt like a foolish reason. "And if I had failed?"

"We would have escorted you beyond the walls and wept at the falling of one so young."

"That is rusting idiotic."

"Oh? And how did you know the spell-form?" She gestured around her. "How do so many of the most promising know it, without being taught? Something deep within us fights against being taught the form because part of our nature *knows* the danger. Even still, those best suited to becoming springs of power *know* the form in the end. They 'discover' it by accident, research, or luck. They are at once both the most in danger and the most suited to overcome that peril. Some few more are able to overcome and are in less danger, so their masters guide them to the form—despite objections. They have the clearest pathway to power, and humanity needs all the power we can gather. I was one such, as were Mistress Lyn and Master Rane."

Tala didn't know how to feel about that. *Does that mean I'm more powerful? Or that I have more potential? Or that I was suspected to be easier to subvert? Easier to sway and control?* She didn't like the seemingly obvious answer.

"There is not enough time in a year to go through the intricacies of it, but know this: Most Mages would fall, were they to attempt an Archon Bond, and every Mage attempts it, if and when they fully learn the form."

Lyn was nodding, and Tala turned to her, questioningly. Lyn smiled. "As soon as I actually read the notes my master gave me, I felt *compelled* to attempt it. I can't explain it, really. At the time, I just thought I wanted to get it over and done with. But in truth, it was like…" She shook her head. "No. No other drive or urge I've ever experienced was so strong." She met Tala's gaze. "I could not have resisted, once I knew how to do it." She let out a small laugh. "Even after I made the star, I wanted to swallow it. It was the silliest thing; I knew it was a gem and I shouldn't, but I *wanted* to. And the urge to do so grew with every passing hour."

Elnea cleared her throat. "Mistress Tala. I am aware that your circumstances were more unusual, and I, or another, would be happy to discuss that with you at a later time."

Tala gave a half bow. "Thank you, Mistress Elnea. I have only one further question, if I may?"

Elnea sighed but nodded. "Go ahead."

Tala turned towards Holly with a fierce glare. "Mistress Holly. Knowing this, how *dare* you encourage her to read those notes? You were putting her life on the line, for what?"

All eyes shifted to Holly, but the woman seemed utterly unaffected by the attention. "It is always a gamble, and a Mageling's master is always the best person to make the call. Hers gave her the notes, clearly determining that Mistress Lyn was one who should learn and should be able to weather the difficulty. I had no reason to disagree, so I pushed her to honor her master's choice. Evidence suggests that we were both right to do so. It was much better than the alternatives, as her mind and will are stronger now than they might have been later."

Tala did *not* like the answer, but it was at least reasonable. She frowned. *But most Magelings aren't under Archons…*

Elnea cleared her throat. "But the danger *is* real. As Archons, you are now privy to so much more but not everything. You may not share this with non-Archons. You must guide any who discover the form towards the local council for aid."

Tala couldn't help herself. "But what about magelings who aren't under Archons?"

Elnea sighed. "Most magelings aren't under Archons."

"Exactly, that makes no sense. How can a Mage determine if their mageling is ready for something they cannot know about?"

Grediv cleared his throat. "Did you read that book I gave you? 'A Mage's Guide to Their First Mageling: Basics Every Mageling Should be Taught?'"

She frowned. "I've skimmed it."

He snorted. "Of course, you did." He shook his head slightly. "Some of those tests and tidbits direct the Mage to seek an Archon under various circumstances." He shrugged. "That takes care of the lion's share."

That made a sort of sense. She had skipped the regular system, so it was incredibly alien to her. "Fair enough, I suppose."

Elnea cleared her throat, bringing Tala's attention back to her. "Now, that out of the way. You need to know that you are much less useful to any invading arcane. Many of them could still sever the bond you just forged and use you regardless, but not all. Once you're fully Fused, doing so will just kill you and send your soul to the great beyond, so they don't even try. That said, if they sense you, they *will* try to eliminate you, and that is just one more reason to work on your aura shroud."

Elnea took a deep breath, while the three new Archons processed the flood of new information.

She smiled. "Now, Master Grediv has requested the honor of accompanying us as I show you to our local Archons' Library." Elnea gave a sharp look to the Archon, who was hovering just to one side. "While I am tempted to decline, now, I think it wisest to allow such. Our companions, the other Archons, will bid you farewell here."

Tala, Lyn, and Rane looked around, smiling uncertainly. By her fellow's expressions, they were clearly burdened by much of what they had learned but also tentatively excited, likely for the good their elevation could bring.

Elnea straightened, her voice ringing out once more. "For the new Archons!"

A single unified shout of praise sounded back.

"Go in strength."

The other Archons did just that, each giving some form of wave or small bow as they departed en masse.

Tala watched them go, allowing her magesight to attempt to examine each of them. While she couldn't see any of their auras, she did realize one critical thing. *Most of them have no power visible at all.*

As she thought about it, she realized that if holding back her aura's power was easy, and hiding it entirely was harder still, then hiding her aura completely, while allowing all other signs of her power to be visible would be *incredibly* tricky.

That's what Holly is doing, along with several others. A few Archons, scattered through the crowd, looked exactly like any other Mage that Tala had ever seen.

My iron salve made me resemble an inexperienced Archon to those who knew what to look for with their magesight. Well, except her eyes and palms.

She didn't know how to feel about that. She wanted to be the best she could be, but she also knew that, regardless, her iron salve would render her looking like the less-skilled Archons. She frowned at that. *No, Master Grediv hid himself completely from my magesight.*

She was left confused. *Elnea did say that the stronger you are and the higher you climb up the ladder, the harder your aura is to restrain at all...* There was just too much that she didn't know.

When the room had emptied of Archons, save the five who would be remaining, Tala glanced towards Terry. *Oh!* She'd been so distracted that she'd not fed Terry recently.

Millennial Mage, 3 - Binding

Though, if the little flickers of dimensional power she'd picked up from the avian through the banquet were any indication, Terry may have eaten more than even she had. "Terry, you hungry?"

He opened one eye, giving her a condescending look.

She snorted a laugh and flicked out a bit of jerky.

Elnea frowned at that. Her magesight didn't seem to be active, so it had likely appeared to her as if Tala had just thrown a bit of meat under the table. "Are you trying to teach him to fetch? Why would you teach that sort of trick to such an animal?" She seemed genuinely confused.

Tala opened her mouth to reply, but Grediv cleared his throat. "As fascinating as that bird is… we should probably head towards the library."

Elnea rolled her eyes, the last shreds of ceremony falling away. "Very well. This way, please."

They walked out through the seemingly indestructible door.

I bet I could break it with time… and without a room full of hostile Archons to contend with.

They left the not-yet-destroyed door behind them as they moved through the stark, empty passage, back to the entry hall.

Chapter: 24
That's a Bit Embarrassing

Tala and the four other Archons came back out into the entry hall, and Tala waved at her coffee acquirer. *She really came through.* The attendant gave her a hesitant smile and wave. *I suppose I dampened her enthusiasm a bit.*

Elnea led them down another passage. This one had a thick, deep-blue rug running the entire length. Paintings and tapestries hung evenly spaced down either side, most depicting some form of creature. They each seemed a bit embellished, as Tala thought she spotted a thunder bull that was depicted as wreathed in lightning.

Who knows? Maybe if it had seen me coming...

There were obviously magical beings sprinkled among the arcanous if her guesses were right. She saw a midnight fox, and in the company of the other images, it really sank in how minor that being really was. *And it still nearly killed me.*

Creatures of legend looked down on them as they walked down the hall: dragons, griffins, silver wolves, titans, and many more.

Tala tried not to slow, but there was such artistry and detail that it was hard to keep up her pace.

At the end of the wide hall, two heavy, black, wooden doors stood open. They seemed to be bound in silver, with gold inlay in the shape of spell-forms.

Not just in the shape of; those are *spell-forms.* If her magesight was correct, when those doors were closed, an incredibly powerful barrier would be generated, just this side of the entryway. *Assuming it's powered by something.* The magical shield made her think of Alefast's magical defenses but on a much smaller scale. *It's likely connected to the city's power matrix, just like all the lights.*

They took the protection of their library seriously it seemed.

When they passed through that entry, Tala found herself gawking, mouth open in unabashed awe.

Thousands of tomes filled the floor-to-ceiling shelving. Ladders were regularly scattered around the place, all on rails mounted to the shelves. The twenty-foot ceilings allowed for a *lot* of books per shelf.

All the wood was the same black as the doors, all the metal either bright silver or burnished gold.

The space wasn't a rectangle. Instead, it seemed constructed like a hedge-maze to maximize wall space for shelving and nooks for reading and research spaces.

Attendants were moving through the space on silent, slippered feet, and Tala could see several people reading in the few nooks visible from the entrance.

Elnea gestured. "The Bandfast, Archon Library, otherwise known as the Arcanum. Any attendant will assist you in finding whatever you are seeking and ensure the works you peruse are returned to their proper place afterwards." She gave them each a serious look. "Bound are not permitted to remove any tome from the shelves. You *must* go through an attendant. Is that understood?"

Rane, Lyn, and Tala each gave some form of verbal assent.

"Good." She gave a half-smile. "In centuries past, we would simply inform new Archons of the library, but so few actually realized the extent of what was available to them that we changed our policy."

Grediv cleared his throat. "You should be aware that Bandfast is known for having the most extensive physical library of the human cities. While it's not the only source of these books, it is an incredibly convenient, central location. As an example of why, I can tell you that the Alefast Archon Council moved all but the most general texts here from our library, in preparation for Alefast's final waning."

Rane was nodding and leaned closer to Lyn and Tala. "Bandfast is the current hub of Archon activity. That is one reason Master Grediv wished me to visit."

Elnea had gestured, calling over four attendants. "I suggest you become familiar with the process, even if you have no immediate subjects for research." One attendant approached each of the other Archons. "I will leave you in their capable hands. Welcome, Archons, to the Bandfast Arcanum." She gave a half-bow and departed.

Tala looked to Lyn and Rane; Grediv had already departed with his attendant. "Meet at Lyn's house tonight?"

They each nodded in agreement and turned towards their individual attendants, separating and moving to places with a bit better sound insulation and privacy.

Tala regarded the magically inert young woman who stood to one side, waiting for her. The young-looking woman wore a simple, clean, undyed linen Mage's robe. Simple leather slippers peeked out from below the garment. Her auburn hair was held up in a simple bun. If she had spell-lines on her visible skin, they were hidden in some manner or blended too seamlessly with her already somewhat silver skin. *Is that natural?*

Though she looked to be just younger than Lyn looked, Tala guessed that the woman was *much* older. *I really should stop thinking I can guess people's ages…*

"You're an Archon."

Millennial Mage, 3 - Binding

The woman quirked a smile. "Yes, Mistress. How can I assist you today?"

"You could wipe me from existence. Why would you assist a new-raised Archon like me?"

She seemed to consider for a moment before her smile became mischievous. "The truth?"

"That would be nice."

"I'm serving the books and knowledge by protecting them from you."

Tala hesitated for a moment, then barked a laugh. She immediately covered her mouth in embarrassment but couldn't help but smile. After a moment, she lowered her hand. "That"—she grinned widely—"that I can believe. I'm Tala."

"A pleasure to meet you, Mistress Tala. I am Ingrit."

"Thank you for your honesty, Mistress Ingrit."

"I am a lover of knowledge. Lies are… distasteful." She scrunched her face exactly as if she'd eaten something unpleasant.

"I couldn't agree more."

Ingrit glanced towards Terry. "Shall your companion wait outside, or can he be trusted not to cause issue?"

Tala looked at Terry. "You going to behave?"

Terry opened his mouth expectantly, and Tala rolled her eyes, tossing a bit of meat to one side.

Ingrit's eyes widened in horror and anger, but as her gaze followed the moving bit of meat, she froze. The jerky was gone. Her eyes narrowed. "I didn't see any movement."

Tala shrugged. "He's quick."

Ingrit opened her mouth, probably to inquire further, but then she paused, shaking her head. "No, we are not here to satisfy my curiosity at this time. How can we assist you, here and now?" She seemed to keep a closer eye on Terry after that, though.

"What services does the Arcanum offer? I can see the books, but I suspect that there is more available than simply an extensive reading collection."

"You are correct, Mistress." Ingrit turned and began walking. Tala followed so as to not be left behind. "On the simple side, we offer assistance in researching any unrestricted topic or outright answering such queries. We do not force our librarians to work on any project, but our interests are varied enough that it is rare for an Archon to wish to research something without at least one of us wanting to assist. More often than not, we have to figure out which of those who are interested will get the honor." Her eyes seemed to sparkle with unspoken mirth.

I'll bet you get any topic you want... That brought to mind a bit of a silly topic, but Tala thought she might as well ask. "What do the cooks have in their chuckwagons?"

Ingrit regarded her for a long moment. Then, she sighed. "Sadly, we are forbidden from investigating that. As part of the inter-Guild agreements, chuckwagons are inviolable, and if any Mage is ever allowed inside, as does happen occasionally, they are not permitted to poke about."

"Inter-Guild agreements?" She thought for a moment, then started to nod. "Right, everything involves at least a couple of guilds. There would have to be ground rules and basic strictures."

Ingrit simply nodded.

Is the Order of the Harvest so widespread that that is a portion of the negotiated secrecy? That was pretty likely if she considered it. *I might actually be able to learn, then...*

Ingrit gave Tala a searching look. "You know something?"

"I think so."

Ingrit shook her head, a half-grimace curling one side of her lips. "I wish I could ask, but as I am a node of the Archive, it would be a violation for me to allow you to tell me, even unprompted." She sighed. "Such follies are sometimes the bedrock of civilization… unfortunately."

Indenture's rusting terrible, alright. "Well, then. Techniques for the fusing of body and soul?"

"That is forbidden material for one of your rank, though I can give you one hint to add to the other you've received."

"Oh?"

"First, new Archons should develop their internal magesight, in order to facilitate progression. Be aware that that is incredibly difficult, given external distractions."

Tala kept her expression neutral. *My iron salve has already helped me there then.*

"Beyond that, the advice Master Grediv gave you should be enough for you to go on."

Tala stopped walking. "How do you know what advice I got?"

Ingrit gave her a puzzled smile, then nodded in understanding. "You weren't aware; all official events that take place within the Archon compound are recorded and filed for transparency and as a record for future generations."

Tala gave her a deeply skeptical look. "You cannot possibly watch everything, and how do *you* know specifically?"

Ingrit gave a wide smile, that same gleeful sparkle back in her almost emerald eyes. "I am not a combatant. My inscriptions bring to my mind any potentially relevant information if that information is present in the Archive and not restricted based on my rank. The massive caloric intake of a new Archon could inform future Mages' inscriptions, depending on how you turn out."

Tala cleared her throat, looking away. "And there's a permanent record of that?"

Ingrit nodded, still smiling.

"That's a bit embarrassing." Then, Tala frowned. "Wait. Does that mean I could learn what was discussed in each conversation in that room?"

"The intention and use of such recordings are not permitted to violate personal privacy." Ingrit cocked an eyebrow, disapprovingly.

Tala shrugged. "Ah... okay. I suppose I appreciate use restrictions, but that still seems pretty creepy."

Ingrit sighed. "You don't have to be here, nor do you have to attend official events. You are welcome to leave and never return, and nothing further will be recorded of your actions."

Tala grunted. "I suppose." She frowned. "So... if you were watching. How would I have done, had the Archons attacked me in earnest?"

Ingrit gave her a long look. Finally, she clicked her tongue. "Nothing I have observed about you implies that you are an idiot."

"Is that supposed to be an answer?"

"If a gathering of Archons had attempted to kill you, how long do you imagine you would have survived?" Her eyes flicked to Terry, then back. "Even with help?"

"Not long?"

"And your powers of deduction are verified. There was absolutely no desire to harm you or your companion, or to have either of you harm others. That, and that alone, allowed the outcome as it stands."

Not really an overt answer, but I suppose it was a bit of a silly question...

The two began walking again. "Now, aside from books, research materials, and research assistance, we offer many other services, including magically sealed rooms for experimentation. We can adjust the magical density in the air, even change out a portion of the air for other materials, as requested."

Tala grinned. "Oh, that's fantastic." *How much do they spend to keep the inscriptions for all this intact?* She had a sudden thought, remembering an oft-asked question, and her smile widened. "Do you happen to know if an incorporator for coffee exists?"

"I'm afraid that what incorporators have or have not been perfected would be proprietary knowledge for the Constructionist's Guild. I can contact a representative if you so desire?" Her inflection on the last framed it as a genuine offer.

Tala sighed. *That would have been too easy.* "No… It's fine." She did a quick check and was happy to note that her aura was still restrained. *The trick is making it reflexive. Right now, I'm still thinking about it.* She smiled. "Well, if you've no objections, I have a few more questions."

"Of course. I will answer if I can."

"Why did the strength of my Archon Star matter? Aren't they just a touch point for my soul?"

Ingrit sighed. "If you wish to tie down a bull, as compared to a dog, do you need a hitch of the same strength?"

"No?"

"Precisely. A weak Archon Star is more like a tether—your soul is connected but not inseparably." She gave Tala a long look. "Yours was at full strength. So, your body and soul are now fully, almost irrevocably bound."

"So… why couldn't I make it stronger?"

"Two reasons: First, the spell-form cannot sustain more power. A free-form, inscription-less working, like an Archon Star, utilizes the inherent properties of magic to remain stable, and too much power would have overcome the other features that allowed for permanency. As to others, whose stars were weaker than yours"—she smiled—"their first task as Archons will be to strengthen the bond, strengthen their soul's attachment to their body so that the two can then be fused. You just have to fuse."

"Which you won't tell me how to do."

"Which I *can't* tell you how to do."

Tala grunted. "Fair, I suppose." She looked up, considering. "Is an unused Archon Star a weakness?" She was thinking of the two she had within Kit.

"I would say more a temptation than a weakness. If you have one, which you have yet to use, it is easy to bond something frivolously, without thought. Whereas, if you forge a star for a specific bond, that takes preparation, intent, and time to enact, allowing you to fully consider the act."

"But they can't be used to harm my soul?"

"No."

Simple enough, I suppose. "Well… can they be unmade?"

Ingrit thought for a moment, seemingly accessing something within the archives. "There is debate on that. The stars, themselves, can be destroyed. Nothing is invincible, but quite a few scholars postulate that the part of your soul, which you extended and attached to the star, remains extended and is simply utilized for the next one you create, making that process easier. If you never make another?" She shrugged. "I have no record of such an occurrence."

"Is there any benefit?"

"To unmaking a star? No. You don't get the power back, and you can't bend that power to anything…" She thought for a long moment. "No, that isn't true. If you unmake a star, the energy is released but not attuned to you. It is not dangerous or damaging, but it will elevate the ambient magic in the area for a time." She quirked a smile. "It is noted that I advise any asking this type of question to not unmake an Archon Star within a city. Such would be inconvenient for power balances within our local spell-forms."

"Noted. Thank you." *Speaking of spell-forms.* "A broader question, how has humanity not run out of metals for inscriptions?"

"I have two questions for you, first."

"Alright." Tala felt a bit taken aback.

"First, do you have any idea how much gold there is in this world, in Zeme?"

Tala shook her head.

"There is a lot. Some…" Her eyes unfocused for a moment, then her gaze returned to Tala. "Some thirty thousand years ago, something destabilized our local system's closest asteroid belt and showered this world with meteors. Those in power at the time were able to mitigate the fall-out, as well as the initial damage, but the result was an *incredible* increase to the precious metal content of Zeme's surface."

There was a lot there that was beyond Tala's knowledge.

"Please understand that I am summarizing and simplifying. No part of what I said is actually, explicitly, exactly true, but it is close enough to answer your question."

"So… we haven't run out because there's just so much?" *That doesn't seem right.*

"Ahh, now for my second question. What happens to the metal in inscriptions when it is used?"

Tala opened her mouth to say, 'It's gone.' But then, she remembered. "'Matter cannot be created or destroyed…'" That was a fundamental tenet of understanding before magic was involved. *Right?*

Ingrit grimaced. "Well, it can, but you're heading towards the correct answer."

Well, obviously Material Mages can create and destroy... "It's... gone?"

"It's temporarily shifted, dimensionally, towards magical power." Ingrit paused for a moment, then tsked. "I cannot give you a sufficient grounding in the theory needed to properly answer this part of the question... You've encountered incorporators, correct?"

"Of course."

"What do they do?"

"They bend power into creating matter, temporarily."

"Exactly!" She hesitated. "Well, not exactly, but close enough. The use of inscriptions does the opposite to precious metals."

"It bends them into"—Tala's eyes widened—"temporary power."

"More or less, yes. Then, they return to their base state."

"So... after I cast, sometime later, a bit of gold just seems to appear where I was standing?"

Ingrit shrugged. "If it wasn't interfered with? Yes. Such is minuscule, only a few atoms at a time, under usual circumstances, but it adds up." She smiled widely. "One of the great innovations were the gathering scripts. Decades before the renewed founding of each city, and as a final script laid at the end of each waning, the Builders layout and activate a network of Material Guiding spell-forms, which draw that metal, while it is in flux, into the ground around cities. Specifically, into where the mining districts will be. It has the added benefit of drawing in surrounding precious metal as well, even drawing it up from the core over time. Thus, we lose very little metal, in the end; we actually gain over each cycle. This city's gathering scripts are only now, finally, nearing the end of their current cycle. They will be refreshed in just less than two centuries when Bandfast's waning is at an end."

"And we empower such scripts around waning cities in preparation for the next time we use that location for a city?"

"Precisely. The ambient magic at the end of a waning is perfect for empowering a surge of effort to draw materials up from lower in the world's structure and to lay the groundwork for a future city." She nodded. "All that is required, then, is to wait for the ambient magic of the area to return to normal, and it is ready for a new city's foundations."

Tala felt like she was a bit inundated with all the information that Ingrit had given her. *So much for a simple question...* She had a thousand more questions, based on what the woman had told her, but she couldn't process it all, not yet. *Simpler questions.* "So… is there a list somewhere of all the metals and alloys, which can be used for inscriptions and spell-forms?"

"Unfortunately, that is proprietary information, locked to the Constructionist and Inscribers Guilds." She gave a small, sad smile.

"Alright, then. I think I have a few simpler questions."

*   *   *

An hour later, she decided to let Ingrit free. Even though the older Archon had shown nothing but kindness and patience, Tala was beginning to feel bad about dominating her time. *I'll be back, though. After I've had time to collect my thoughts and gather better questions.*

Tala now knew the rates for using the various experimentation rooms: expensive; how many of her current inquiries were beyond her current rank for easy answer: most; and which of her remaining inquires she should bring to the Constructionists: the rest.

It was a bit disappointing, if she was honest, but she knew it wasn't really Ingrit's fault.

She'd also gotten a brief tour of the library, which was vastly more extensive than she'd expected. As it turned out, there were nearly thirty million books, two-thirds of those being duplicates, so that the library was never without any given title, even discounting those held magically in the Archive.

It was a staggering number. Ingrit had explained that the works contained were of all sorts, including personal journals dating back to the first city, scholarly works delving into various subjects, and a few fictions, which were determined to contain enough fact or cultural relevance to be meticulously maintained.

To contain all those volumes, the library was an astonishing fifteen stories, each one larger than the one above as they descended into the ground. The lowest level was mostly the experimentation chambers and other similarly dangerous or critical rooms.

In addition to the physical copies of each book, every work was available through the Archive, and as an Archon, Tala could now purchase a slate that would grant access to many of the works. It would be restricted, of course, by her rank and guild affiliation—or lack thereof.

They were too expensive for Tala to contemplate at the moment.

She was too fiscally wise to waste her precious coin on such luxuries at this time.

She didn't give the acquisition of such a second thought.

Nope.

Not at all.

I can't afford it anyway...

On the positive side, there were publicly available slates, which could be rented for a small fee: one ounce silver, per hour. *Small fee. Ha! That's my budget for a meal.*

Tala bid the librarian good day and smiled at the woman's well-wishes in return. She lingered in her walk back down the passage, towards the front hall. She did her best not to gawk, but the creatures depicted were just so fascinating.

As such, it was almost sunset when she finally emerged from the Archon's facility once more. She basked in the cool, autumn breeze and reveled in the sight of the pastel sky.

You did it. You're an Archon. Tala grinned.

Terry stirred in his place on her shoulder, looking up at the sky as well. Tala glanced his way, noticing that he had a bit of a forlorn look. "Missing the Wilds, the open space?"

He gave her a long look, then a small bob of his head.

"Just a bit, eh?"

He bobbed more firmly.

"I can understand that. We'll get back on the road, soon. Lyn's supposed to get us an out-and-back contract in about a week, so we'll be able to stretch our legs."

He bumped her with his head.

Tala grinned back at Terry. "Thank you for backing me up in there." She pulled out a big hunk of pork belly. "I know it's not jerky, but do you want some?"

Terry quickly, and precisely, snatched the meat from her fingers, not even brushing her skin.

"I'd hoped you'd like that. You tried some during the banquet, right?"

He gave her a searching look, then bobbed a nod.

"Good. Want some jerky, too?"

He shifted happily, and she tossed out a chunk. She barely registered the flicker of him claiming it.

"You really are something." *And I really should ask Brand what spice mix he used for this jerky. Terry has a favorite it seems.*

The last couple of days since she woke up had been crazy, and even before she'd worked herself into unconsciousness, she'd barely had a moment's rest. *I've not seen Gretel since I regained consciousness.* Her meat pies would be perfect for dinner. *I should get Rane and Lyn, first. It would be rude to go without them.*

That decided, Tala walked towards Lyn's house, eating what would be a healthy dinner for anyone else from her banquet loot on the way.

Things are looking up. I should be able to pay my debt off without issue and much faster than I'd hoped.

Her debt.

Her first payment.

Her eyes went wide. *Oh,* rust*!*

Chapter: 25
To End a Very Long Day

Tala turned and walked as quickly as she was able, which was surprisingly fast given her increased gravity.

Terry sunk his talons into her shoulder, the points failing to pierce her skin but holding him securely, nonetheless.

I know I saw a Banker's Guild office around here, somewhere...

And there it was: a beautiful, stone building. It was eye-catching without being ostentatious.

If she understood the windows on the outside correctly, it was a single-story structure, but that single story seemed to be nearly twenty-five feet high. Its large entrance opened onto a small park-space. The green area had clearly been designed more for looks and to walk through than for families or children to play in, but that was fine. *I like having greenery around as much as the next person. It doesn't all have to be family focused.*

She walked through the bank's large double doors, closing them softly behind her.

Inside, she was greeted by an environment that struck her as more archival than that of the library she'd just left. The rugs were thicker, seemingly more for sound dampening in the vast space than to make walking or standing comfortable.

Large, unicolor hangings periodically decorated the walls. She hesitated to call them tapestries because they literally were simple lengths of cloth, with no artistry, no embellishments at all.

As she stepped farther in, she felt a small magical probe and heard a distinctive *ding* echo through the far part of the room.

Almost immediately, a gray-haired man bustled out. He was straight-backed, and he held a slate of deep green stone. *That's odd. Aren't most such devices made of as light gray stone as possible?*

He stopped before her and gave a deep bow. "Mistress Archon. Welcome to our humble Guildhall." As he straightened, he glanced at Terry, sitting on her shoulder. "Would you like your companion to await you in a side room?"

"No, thank you. I am Tala."

"Greetings, Mistress Tala. I am Nattinel, one of the senior bursars of this branch of the Banker's Guild. How may I assist you this day?"

"A pleasure to meet you, master Nattinel." He wasn't a Mage or inscribed at all, that she could detect. "I need to make a payment on my debts."

He looked a bit surprised but immediately hid it. "Certainly, Mistress. If you would?" He held out the slate, and a small, gold-outlined square grew into existence, centered near the edge that was towards her. *Expensive.*

Tala didn't see anywhere to prick her finger and frowned.

After a moment's hesitation, Nattinel smiled. "Am I to assume you are a relatively new Archon, Mistress?"

She nodded.

"Completely understandable. Walk with me, and I will explain some things that may be of interest."

He turned, and she took two quick steps so that she could stroll beside him as he led the way off to one side of the spacious room.

"You see, Mages and mundanes must provide blood infused with some of their power signature to authenticate transactions and gain access to records, things of that nature."

Tala nodded. This was known. *Though, I wasn't aware mundanes could do that...* Had she ever seen one confirm a transaction with blood?

"Once the Archive has been updated to recognize an Archon, for reasons unknown to one such as me, they can simply will that authentication to occur with a touch."

"Oh!" That made so much sense. Now that her body was soul-bound, her skin could act as an untainted catalyst for her power signature. *I wonder why blood doesn't taint a Mage's power...* That might be an excellent question for Ingrit. "Thank you."

He led them to a couple of *very* comfortable-looking chairs and gestured to one.

She hesitated, feeling a bit awkward.

"Is something the matter, Mistress? Does the chair dissatisfy you in some way?"

She gave a little chuckle. "Well, you see, I am quite heavy."

He blinked at her, obviously confused.

"If the chair couldn't hold a horse, I probably shouldn't sit in it."

Nattinel gave a slow nod. "Were you not a Mage, I would, of course, allay your fears about being overweight, but I imagine that this is more a matter of magic than a false self-image?"

"You could say that."

He nodded again, more firmly this time. "Very well. We can stand." He again held out the slate to her.

Tala smiled. "Thank you." She reached out, placing her thumb within the square and willing her power out, into the slate for verification.

The entire tablet shifted to blood red, immediately.

Tala startled back, retracting her hand and clearing her throat. "Did I... break it?"

Nattinel simply smiled. "Not at all, Mistress. Tell me, I've never seen this exact reaction before. Was your medium less common than usual? It doesn't look like ruby."

"You could say that." She glanced away.

"It seems I shouldn't inquire further. My apologies." He gave a half-bow, pulling the slate back and looking it over. "Oh! You are quite right. Today is the final day to make a... first?" He looked up at her. "Mistress." He seemed to be fighting within himself about what he should say next. Finally, he gave a quizzical smile. "Did you only graduate from the academy a month ago?"

She nodded.

His surprise was evident. "I know that they are very loose with graduation dates and course work, tailoring to the individual—I have a nephew there right now, myself—but how are you an Archon so soon?" He stopped, seeming to come back to himself. He shook his head slightly and straightened, his mask of professionalism returning. "I apologize, Mistress. I meant no offense, and I should not have asked such a personal question. We are, of course, honored to have one such as you within these walls." He made a vague gesture around himself.

She gave a forced smile, feeling quite self-conscious.

"Would you like to pay the minimum or some other amount?"

"Four ounces gold, please."

"You are aware that that is more than you owe for this payment?"

"I am aware that four is more than the minimum required payment, yes."

He nodded, manipulating the construct. "Would you like that to be a prepayment on the next monthly charge or an up-front amount?"

"Up-front, please." Not that there was much difference... She'd think about it. *Maybe I'll change that.*

More alterations. "Would you like to set up an automatic transfer for all future due dates?"

She blinked at him. "I can do that?" That would probably be interfered with by prepayment.

He smiled, seemingly back in comfortably familiar territory. "Of course! Most people do, as it helps prevent fees and such from negatively impacting you, should life become busy. We can even lock the automatic payment amount for a month prior as soon as it is available. That can further reduce the chances of mistakes."

"Well, I don't think I need that last offering. But the automatic payment sounds reasonable."

He nodded again. "For the minimum amount or some other figure?"

"Let's just do the minimum for now. I can change that later, correct?"

"That is correct, Mistress."

"Then that should be fine. Thank you."

He seemed to make a few more alterations on the red slate, then turned the tablet back around for her confirmation.

She read over the short bits of silvery text and confirmed.

The construct shifted back to green, and Nattinel bowed over it. "Is there anything further that I can assist you with today?"

"No, thank you. I appreciate your kindness, professionalism, and the time that you took to assist me."

He smiled genuinely in response. "It was my pleasure, Mistress. I hope that we see you again, soon."

They each gave a half-bow and parted ways.

Now, home.

Tala stepped outside into the cool evening air and stretched her arms wide. *I did it. I paid off a part of my debt!*

It was just less than a percent of the total amount owed, which was now some four-hundred-eighty-three gold and change, but it was still progress. She couldn't keep a grin off her face.

She walked through the garden-like park, feeling giddy. She knew that she'd been making progress with every silver earned, but to actually pay some of the debt off? It was a heady feeling.

A light sprinkling of snow was just beginning to fall, and she took a moment to breathe deeply and simply enjoy the beauty of the evening.

As she made her way to her and Lyn's house, she watched the city slowly turn white beneath the gathering snow.

The temperature was cool but not cold, and she was reminded that she'd promised herself to get some shoes. While she didn't *need* them, and she definitely preferred to be without, there were situations in which having footwear was just better.

Even so, the snow beneath her toes was pleasantly cool. It reminded her of snowball fights when she was younger.

She felt her grin shift to a sad smile. *What am I going to do about them...?*

She shook off the memory and fell back into quick, happy steps. *Nope! Happy thoughts, Tala.*

When she arrived at the house, Lyn and Rane were waiting.

"There you are, Tala! Did you already eat?"

Tala shook her head. "No, I just needed to make a debt payment."

Rane frowned. "Can't you get that automated?"

"Yes, and I have, now, but I hadn't done that previously."

He shrugged. "Ah, I see."

"So… hungry?"

Lyn nodded. "Gretel's?"

"Definitely."

Rane frowned. "Gretel?"

"You'll see!" *I am soooo hungry.*

It was a short walk to the courtyard, and soon the three new Archons were sitting at one end of a table, near a well-contained bonfire, enjoying the mountain of mini meat pies stacked before them.

Rane had insisted on paying, yet again, and Tala had reciprocated by pulling out food from the earlier banquet to supplement and augment the meat pies.

All three tossed bits of food for Terry at irregular intervals and in random directions. That kept the avian busy and content, while the Mages engaged in small talk.

Lyn had just returned with three tall mugs of hot buttered rum when Rane's eyes widened, and he lightly smacked himself in the forehead. "I haven't checked if I can read any of the books!"

Tala's eyes widened, and she sat up a bit straighter. *That's right! I never checked, either.*

Lyn rolled her eyes and slid a mug in front of each of her companions.

"Oh! Thank you, Lyn."

"Thank you, Mistress Lyn."

She smiled at that. "Try it, then you can tell me what you're talking about."

Tala and Rane complied, both hesitating after their first sip.

Rane immediately took another, longer pull from his massive earthenware mug. "This is fantastic!"

Tala had to agree. It was thick and creamy, sweet and rich, and so alcoholic that she would bet that she'd feel the inscriptions on her liver begin to draw extra power soon. *Well, I'd suspected I'd be less susceptible to toxins, and alcohol is a toxin, after all.* She wasn't sure how she felt about it. *It's not like I enjoyed getting drunk; I just enjoyed the taste, every so often.* That settled it, in her mind. It was a net good.

She grinned. "This really is wonderful. Where did you get it? I haven't seen it available around here before."

Lyn pointed to a cart tucked off to one side, where a massive cauldron sat on a slightly glowing, inscribed metal plate. "He usually has drinks of some kind. I think last time we were here together, he had a spiced mead?" She seemed to consider, then shrugged. "This is one of his specialties, which he only brings out when it's especially cold or when the weather turns." She gestured around them to the newly falling snow.

"Why? This is so amazing!"

Rane grunted, having just taken another long drink. "It is, but I think it'd be too much if I had it too often."

Tala hesitated at that. *He's probably right.* "I suppose…"

Lyn smiled, taking a sip of her own, much smaller mug. "Now, the books?"

"Right!" Tala reached into Kit and pulled out 'Soul Work.'

Lyn leaned forward. "That's a beautifully bound volume. It looks new; did you buy it in Alefast?"

Tala hesitated. "I got it as part of a payment for some work I did around Alefast."

Lyn shrugged. "Pricey payment."

Rane widened the opening around his sword hilt before sticking his hand through the leather circle. As expected, the limb didn't come out the other side. A moment later, he drew it forth once more, holding a worn and beaten leather-bound text. The leather was much thicker than Tala's cover but didn't seem to have a hard surface underneath.

If Tala's book was an academic text on the topic, then Rane's was the travel journal the original researcher had used to compose his ideas. Well, at least if the outsides were anything to go by.

Rane looked back and forth between his copy and Tala's, then he sighed, shaking his head. He muttered under his breath, and Tala grinned when she caught the words, "Master Grediv's playing favorites again…"

Tala did her best to hide her smile as Rane glanced her way, and if he saw her mirth, he didn't seem to mind.

"Well, let's see." He opened the book and stared. "You have to be rusting kidding me."

Tala opened her own book to the first page and stared at the incomprehensible words. "Why…? Oh!" She placed her hand on the book and moved her power outward, giving the warding a good look at her soul.

Rane grunted in realization of what she'd done but seemed to decide on waiting to see her results.

The page shifted under Tala's scrutiny.

> 'Congratulations, New Archon. Your soul is not yet ready for the techniques described in this book.'

Tala seriously considered burning the volume.

"Rust you, too, book."

Lyn cocked an eyebrow but didn't comment.

Rane looked at his own book. "So, you don't need blood?"

Tala grinned. "Not anymore." She then gave a brief explanation, based on what Nattinel had told her.

Lyn was nodding, and Rane smiled. "Very nice. I really didn't like constantly pricking my fingers…" He frowned. "But no luck with the book?"

Tala shook her head and sighed. Terry was once more perched on her shoulder, and he was staring at the book with seeming interest.

Rane placed his hand on his own book, and Tala saw power shift within the big man as he clearly let his magic be felt by the book. It was interesting; his power seemed to move more sluggishly than hers had. *Being a Guide has its benefits.*

That done, Rane stared at something she couldn't see. "Well… that's unhelpfully vague."

"Oh? What did yours say?"

"Let your soul settle before forging ahead."

Tala glowered. "My books are lippy with me. That's actually helpful."

"Oh?"

Lyn was nodding as she set her mug down once more. She leaned forward, speaking quietly, the sound likely drowned out a couple of feet away, given the surrounding murmur of conversation. "Our souls are newly bound to our bodies. I imagine it will take a bit for them to fully adjust. Try again in a day or two? Maybe a week?"

Tala gave her friend a skeptical look. "Do you even know what these are?"

Lyn rolled her eyes. "Books keyed to keep their contents hidden from those not ready to read them."

"Oh… yeah, that's exactly right."

Lyn snorted a chuckle and took another deep drink.

Rane and Tala checked their other books and found similar messages on all those, which had been locked previously. *Okay, alright… I'll be patient.* She looked up at Lyn. "So, how hard is it to crack this kind of protection?"

Lyn grinned. "Depends on who put it in place, but most will erase the contents if breached, even if you vastly overpower the original power source—which I doubt you could do as I've never heard of anyone but older Mages putting these in place. Now, I suspect they were more senior Archons."

Tala wrinkled up her face. "That's pretty irritating."

Lyn nodded. "Oh, decidedly. The librarian I was talking to lamented how much knowledge was lost before it was universally realized that such measures couldn't be breached."

"Lost?"

"Yeah. Apparently, some of the earliest Archons left whole libraries of information keyed to help humanity at various stages of our progress. Some of their successors got greedy and attempted to crack the spell-forms, and the knowledge contained within was lost."

"That's pretty horrible."

"Quite."

Tala placed the last of the other books back in Kit and frowned; 'Soul Work' was still sitting in front of her as she examined it. "How, under the stars, can they stay empowered?"

Rane was the one who answered. "The way Master Grediv talked about them, they are *very* power efficient and are thus maintained even in environments that we can't detect ambient magic at all."

"Like cities?"

"Like cities."

"But what about the metals? Shouldn't they need to be re-inscribed?"

Rane shrugged. "They're designed based on artifacts, incorporators, and the like."

Tala gave him a flat look. "That seems unlikely. If they have trouble coming up with incorporators for specific materials, how can they do it for something as specific and convoluted as a book?"

"Ah. I understand the confusion. No, the magic doesn't create the words, it obfuscates them. Thus, the integral spell-forms only have to be developed or altered depending on the concealment specifications. At least in principle."

That made a sort of sense, Tala supposed.

Terry, for his part, had been staring at 'Soul Work' for a while, now, and he suddenly flickered, appearing standing atop the book.

Tala registered a shift in the bird's internal power, and the wards around the book altered in response.

Tala's eyes widened. In quick movements, Terry flickered off the book, and Tala opened the front cover. She was greeted by an illustration of a terror bird glaring out from the page, clearly conveying disapproval.

Rane leaned over and laughed. "So, this one tailors the warning message to the one who tries to activate it."

Tala sighed. "So, you're saying that I'm responsible for the books' attitude?" She looked at each of her table companions as they just smiled back at her. "I hate you both."

Lyn chuckled, pushing Tala's mug closer to her. "Drink, Tala. This is meant to be a celebration."

Rane wisely did not speak, taking another deep drink from his own vessel.

Tala tucked the book away, then patted Terry's head, where he sat on her shoulder once more. She took up her mug and raised it. "To new beginnings."

"To new beginnings." The three mugs clunked together, and the three new Archons returned to more amicable topics of conversation.

Overall, it was an incredibly pleasant way to end a *very* long day.

Chapter: 26
Progress is Progress

Tala spat out a mouthful of sand, vaulting back to her feet with a motion similar to a pushup. *My first impression was right. I hate this man.*

There had been snow on top of the courtyard's sand earlier that morning, but now there was mostly just wet sand.

Rane was grinning at her, his massive sword held in a high guard. He wasn't even sweating as he stood solidly upon the soft ground, barefoot and just in close-fitting, short pants. His spell-lines were on full display across his toned, tan flesh, ready to render her attacks meaningless… if she could ever land any.

She growled and lunged at him again, her practice sword driving towards his heart.

Force, Rane's sword, came down like an avalanche. His reach was greater than hers, so she wouldn't land her strike before he hit her.

She cursed, raising her weapon to defend herself.

Even though she got her sword up in time to block, it didn't matter. Power flowed through Rane's weapon, and since she used her considerable strength to hold her weapon in place, the marginally reinforced stick shattered.

Rane's strike continued, catching her between her shoulder and neck.

Millennial Mage, 3 - Binding

She was thrown to the ground like a sack of flour, even though Rane clearly pulled his attack after the initial contact. Her defensive scripts were getting a *heavy* testing.

There were collective, audible intakes of breath, but no one gasped or cried out. They'd seen this too many times to react that way any longer.

Adam sighed from where he watched, sitting on one of the surrounding walkways. "Mistress Tala, you cannot block him. That has been made *incredibly* clear. You are wasting practice weapons. Why do you still try to block?"

She swept the sand from her face, once again, rising a bit slower this time. "Better to block than just let myself get hit?"

"Did blocking help?"

"No…" She grunted irritably. "I even angled the blade correctly that time. I know that I did."

Rane nodded, resting Force on his shoulder. "This sword cannot be deflected by a like-powered opponent, and your practice swords are mundane. My sword resists any acting force, except that exerted on the handle."

One of the students called out from the side. "What if she struck at his hands, instead of blocking the blade?"

Adam pointed at the young woman. "That is an excellent suggestion." If Tala read his expression correctly, he'd been waiting for someone to suggest just that.

The sand in Tala's eyes and up her nose made her want to curse him for that. *You could have suggested that yourself earlier.*

"If you cannot dodge, which I'm beginning to wonder about, that would be an excellent thing to attempt."

Tala understood him to be saying, 'You really should have thought of that yourself.'

"Fair enough."

An assistant tossed Tala another wooden sword. She caught it with more practiced ease than she liked. *I've broken* way *too many of these...*

Rane raised his long blade high once more.

The next exchange *finally* lasted more than a couple of movements. Tala's probing strike at Rane's hands forced him to pull his blow, simply knocking hers aside.

She was never able to land a strike, but the change in paradigm kept him from easily putting her down yet again.

Finally, Rane made a mistake. With a great, sweeping movement, he struck upward.

Tala stepped into the blow, dropping her left hand to catch the rising blade, even as her sword-wielding-right lashed out.

Force smacked her left palm so hard it stung despite her inscriptions. She had braced the arm, and so it didn't collapse before the blow. Instead, she was lifted *just slightly* from the ground. *No opposing you with power, just weight, so our ranks don't factor into it.* She grinned, adding more force to her own strike.

Her sword connected with the side of Rane's head... or it should have.

The inscriptions on his head sparked to life, shimmering silver weaving through to activate dull copper, and Rane was suddenly moving along with her strike, the blow not *quite* connecting.

As a result, Rane spun a full circle, feet overhead, seeming to rotate around his abdomen. As he finished the rotation, Force whipped around, sweeping sideways.

Tala *almost* attempted to block the blow but fought down the reaction just in time to duck under it, launching herself forward to tackle Rane.

His scripts activated again, but this time it was to her advantage as they moved him back and away, taking him to the ground just ahead of her. There, she landed on him without having lost momentum from an earlier impact.

She drove the wind from his lungs with her weight as she pinned him in place. If she felt correctly, she might have even cracked a couple of his ribs. *Success!*

In a quick motion, she brought her sword around and rested the 'edge' against his throat, one hand on the handle, one on the back of the blade. She grinned down at him for an instant before Force struck her from the side.

Rane had somehow used the fall to spin the blade around once more.

She was blasted from atop him to drive a furrow through the sand and smash into the stone steps at the edge of the courtyard. *What are these steps even made out of?* She'd hit them often enough that *something* should have broken…

She groaned, staring up at the clear, cold sky. "That's rusting idiotic. I won! If I'd wanted to kill you, you'd be dead."

Rane lifted his feet, then kicked up to a ready stance. He gasped in sudden pain and clutched his abdomen.

How did he do that on sand?

The healer rushed forward and fixed him with a brief touch. Rane nodded his thanks to the healer, then regarded Tala. "Yes, you *could have*, but you didn't."

She frowned. "What?"

"You didn't deliver the strike. You didn't trust my defenses or the waiting healer, so you hesitated."

"I didn't want to crush your throat, Master Rane."

"And if you had?"

She opened her mouth to respond, but then her eyes flicked to the healer, waiting off to one side. *Oh…* She growled, then. "Fine." She stood back to her feet. "Again."

She rushed for him with controlled, precise, thundering steps. *This will take that grin from his face.* She stuck her hand into Kit, grabbing for the repeating hammer... and found nothing.

For the first time in her memory, Kit hadn't offered up what she was reaching for. *Because I lost it. I allowed it to starve.* She slowed, causing Rane to hesitate.

Tala glanced down at Kit. Thinking of the now non-magic hammer. It came into her hand, and she drew it out of her bag.

It was utterly, magically inert. The innate magic in the tool had collapsed when it ran dry.

Tala growled at the loss, then flung the hammer at Rane anyway.

The next two hours were *brutal*. In the end, Tala only won once: right after she threw the hammer, she tackled him again, while he was distracted. She was never able to replicate that initial moment of surprise, even by throwing other things, her practice sword included.

She didn't win again.

Even so, she improved, largely due to the suggestions of those watching the bouts, and in the end, she could hold her own for long stretches before Rane inevitably drove her back into the sand.

They finished out the last hour of the morning with weapons sparring between Tala and Adam, along with several other guards. That, thankfully, she excelled at, though it was similar to her unarmed conflicts with the guards.

They were *much* more skilled but had no way of truly ending the fights, even when they could knock her down; there just weren't enough of them to pin her to the ground. So, she always won by slow, incremental attrition. *Not great for protecting someone else but good practice.*

When high noon arrived, the class was over, and the instructor assigned the students to write up detailed analyses of both Rane and Tala's abilities and fighting styles, as well as how a unit of guards could overcome each of them.

Tala, for her part, immediately went to the compound's baths and did her utmost to clear herself completely of sand. She was mostly successful.

Following yet another vigorous self-scrubbing, she soaked and munched on banquet leftovers pulled from Kit. Her thoughts drifted back through the morning's combat. She felt stronger than ever, and her body was moving *exactly* how she wanted it to, but she still didn't have the experience to 'want' the right movement for efficient victory.

Give it time, Tala. She felt more connected to her inscriptions now that she was an Archon. Her body felt more *her* than ever before, and those magics were an obvious, integral part of her as well.

Rane seems to have gotten a similar benefit. She didn't begrudge him that. She *did* wish that he hadn't been quite so brutal about showing his dominance. *Rusting man. If I could use my sword, things would have been different.*

Still, they'd agreed that her weapon was just too dangerous to use in practice matches.

Adam had been cagey on the subject, but Tala didn't press him. *Not worth alienating my instructor.*

When she was done in the bath, she dressed, clicked her tongue to get Terry's attention from where he was sleeping in the corner of the room, and walked out into the cool, afternoon air.

Okay. I have a few things I need to do before returning home. Let's get to it.

* * *

The rest of the week fell into a pattern for Tala as the day of her next departure drew ever closer.

Lyn had signed Rane and Tala up for a round trip to Makinaven and back, and Tala's 'minder' had agreed to the contracts, though Tala had yet to meet the Mage so assigned. Tala was going to meet her for dinner the night before their departure, so at least she wouldn't be going in totally blind.

The trip to Makinaven was purported to be a bit longer, time-wise, and usually more dangerous than that to either Alefast or Marliweather. This was mainly because nearly two-thirds of the journey went through the old-growth, southern forest, and unlike the trees that sprang up around the waning city of Alefast, these were not mostly clumped together with convenient paths around them.

No. That would be too easy.

In the worst case, they would have to circumnavigate around dense clusters of trees and other obstacles, searching for a path for the caravan, all while keeping it well-defended.

Lovely.

If what Tala had learned was to be believed, the trees were truly massive, but the figures she found seemed too fanciful. She would have to see for herself. *More than four times the height of the defensive towers? Unlikely.*

But that was an issue for later. She'd gotten a general understanding of the dangers, both arcanous creatures and otherwise. She'd trust to her 'minder' to fill in the gaps.

Around sparring for the benefit of up-and-coming Guardsmen, and to improve her own abilities, Tala did a few more minor errands.

She sought out the alchemist she'd worked with before and purchased more bars of iron salve: two ounces silver.

She convinced a blacksmith to make her a steel folding chair, sturdy enough that it could have been a stepstool for a thunder bull, while folding small enough to easily fit into

Millennial Mage, 3 - Binding

Kit: four ounces silver. The result was surprisingly well-contoured and comfortable.

She also bought a pair of thick-soled, simple leather shoes, in case she needed to walk in snow again, which seemed likely: one ounce silver. She did *not* want a repeat of the discomfort and pain she'd experienced after being accosted by the raven-ine. The cobbler seemed to notice her increased weight, likely noticing when he had taken measurements of her foot. He'd hemmed and hawed about it, not wanting to offend, but after coming to an understanding, he'd hesitantly told her that the shoes wouldn't last long under such increased pressure. He didn't know if the pressure distribution scripts would increase their useful life, but he thought it was possible. *Worth paying attention to, at the very least.*

Additionally, she hounded no fewer than six Constructionist Guild assistants, all of whom firmly maintained that there were no available schemata for coffee incorporators of any kind. Boma, likewise, remained cagey. Thankfully, she was allowed to purchase an acid incorporator now that she was an Archon: hydrochloric acid, specifically. Thirty silver ounces.

With the incorporator, she received a 'warning and safety' booklet and a mandatory, hour-long lecture from Boma on the safe and legal uses of the device. Even with her full flow directed through it, using several void-channels, she could only produce a thin trickle of the stuff. *For now.*

Even so, it was a useful tool to have at hand if she found need.

Through some light experimentation, Tala found that she could easily maintain a constant single, small void-channel to her body. However, if she used other void-channels too much, she would have to collapse all of them to properly recover. As such, she often played with her void-channels on the side, while doing her other tasks, but she never pushed too hard. *Moderation, Tala. Slow progress is good progress.*

Given her soul-bound body, she no longer had to actively power her body or her scripts since they had a direct connection to her gate, but she found it helped with efficiency to use a void-channel, nonetheless. The main result was that her keystone was under much less pressure. *Hurrah! That will last longer now.*

Finally, Tala socialized with Lyn daily and Rane, too, often enough. She ate well, using all three silver ounces of her budget on food each day—fifteen ounces silver—along with finishing out the food she'd gotten from the banquet. And the last two days before departure, she charged her custom cargo-slots down at the work yard.

That, all told, filled her days quite nicely.

*   *   *

Tala lunged out of the way of the falling halberd blade, blowing through half a dozen sword strikes as the students strove to overwhelm her.

They didn't even sting, and her increased weight kept the blows from diverting her path too much, her downward pressure giving her surer footing, and she was getting better at posting her feet in opposition to incoming strikes.

She lashed out, breaking limbs with precision, culling their numbers with ease until an enemy thrust went between her knees and tangled her legs, causing her to stumble and fall, even as the weapon bent under the stress.

Immediately, some dropped on her, trying to pin her down, as others grabbed madly at her limbs. Some used their weapons, driven into the soft ground, like pry bars to lock her in place.

One star-cursed student decided the best solution was to jump on her head, driving her face into the coarse sand.

She struggled, but eventually, they got enough weight on her that she simply had no hope of breaking free any longer.

She signaled her defeat, and they let her up.

Adam's voice rang out from where he stood beside the other instructor. "Why were you able to win?"

"She couldn't cut us," one student said in a dejected voice. He gasped as a healer realigned, then healed his broken forearm.

"We took her foundation from her, then took advantage of that," another answered.

Adam nodded. "You are both correct. When facing an opponent like Mistress Tala, containment is the best option, and you are fighting her when she is at a distinct disadvantage." Even so, he smiled. "You did very well. Today is Mistress Tala and Master Rane's last day with us. Tomorrow, we will see how you fare against unfamiliar adversaries. I hope you are up to the challenge."

Tala glanced into the cloudy sky. *Almost noon, then.* This group attack on her had been the last activity of the morning after she'd fought Rane, then a group of senior guards, first armed, then unarmed.

Rane still utterly dominated her when he was armed, though he could never definitively end the fight. Her defenses were simply too good for that. *I can't imagine what he'll be able to do once he soul-bonds that sword.* Even so, she'd learned enough about his defenses that, unarmed, he couldn't hold her at bay, and she cinched victory fairly quickly each time. True, she had to rely on her near immunity to his attacks since he still outclassed her, if not as much as Adam did, but victory was victory.

The only change after a week of intense sparring with the senior guards was that she won more quickly, though still only by slow steps against their overwhelming skill. *Progress is progress.*

Adam cleared his throat, bringing her attention back to the present, and she glanced around. All the students were looking at her, the last of them having already been healed.

She smiled. "Thank you, all, for your help and feedback over these last days."

There were collective nods, 'You're welcomes,' and 'Of courses.'

Adam smiled. "We wanted to thank you, as well. Very few combat-oriented Mages are willing to allow their abilities to be so thoroughly explored and delved for weaknesses. Fewer still will let us test our hypotheses on them directly." His smile widened. "Truly, thank you."

There were a chorus of agreements from the students.

"We wanted to give you a small gift, to say 'thank you for the time.'"

Someone in the crowd shouted out an addition. "And to tempt you back, when you return!" A ripple of laughter moved through the group.

Adam walked forward and held out a simple sheath. It was sized for a dagger and appeared to be incredibly intricately worked from myriad materials.

It was sized for Flow.

Tala took it, a slight frown creasing her forehead.

"Many magical weapons are too dangerous to train with, and as such, their wielders suffer from a lack of practice. To correct that, the Constructionists have long made a study of methods to render them safe for training bouts. I am no Mage, but it was explained to me as a lensing item that would allow you to better train with your particular bound weapon."

Tala almost dropped the training tool in shock. Her eyes widened as she looked up at him. "Adam… this is perfect."

Millennial Mage, 3 - Binding

He nodded, and the watching students laughed. One in about the middle of the bunch commented, "If you use that, you won't break us as easily."

Nervous chuckles followed that pronouncement.

"This must have been quite expensive." At least a half ounce, gold, if her estimation was correct. *Those that I remember were just a bit more expensive than incorporators.* At the most basic level, it was just an advanced incorporator.

"In your training, you broke *dozens* of training swords." His grin removed most of the reprimand. "This was the only smart choice we could make if we're to ever have you back. Especially if you work with us long term, as some few Mages do. I just wish they could have had it completed more quickly."

"Of course... Sorry about all the weaponry."

He waved that away. "It was expected." After a moment, he chuckled. "Between you and Master Rane, it was more extreme than anticipated, but that's why that makes sense." He nodded towards the item.

She pulled Flow from her belt, momentarily keeping it in the simple leather sheath she'd had it in since Alefast. That sheath came off and went into Kit, and she placed Flow into the new item. The sheath reacted to the movements of power around and through Flow, and it subtly shifted shape so that it was a perfect fit. The effect was to make Flow simply appear to have a bit of a heftier, and duller, blade. Even the clasp to place the sheath on her belt was designed for holding Flow in the sheath when it wasn't on her belt. *Very streamlined.*

She tested the design, clasping it to her belt easily; she removed it with equal ease. With a quick motion, she twisted the fastener to lock Flow in. *Simple.*

She took a slow breath. *Here it goes.*

She pushed her power into Flow, down the sword path. The blade extended until it was fully in its sword form.

The sheath expanded likewise, thinning out and clinging more tightly to the blade underneath. As Tala expected, the burden of power required to maintain this shape was increased, probably because the sheath was utilizing some of the magic in the weapon for its own transformation. *Good, the training version should be harder to use.*

She tapped her open left palm with the edge of the sheath and felt a *whoomph* of impact like her hand had been struck with a particularly heavy pillow. Tala grinned, allowing Flow to contract.

She met Adam's gaze and nodded before sweeping her eyes across the assembled crowd. "Thank you, all. Truly."

She took another half-hour or so to speak with those who wanted to wish her well and bid them all a final goodbye. After that, she bathed and applied her iron salve. *I've been without this defense for too long.*

Now that she wasn't going to be rolling around in the sand every day, she wanted the protection it provided.

That done and verified, she dressed and headed off to lunch.

Brand and his wife greeted her warmly as she entered their restaurant, and she spent the meal chatting with them—as she had several other times, earlier in the week. Sadly, Brand wasn't going to be a cook on her next expedition, but he assured her that the head chef for the trip was competent, and he'd warned her about Tala's dietary needs.

She left them with one last goodbye and a promise to visit again once she returned.

The snow on the ground was cool to her feet but not unpleasantly so. It was a light dusting across most of the city—a beautiful highlight rather than an inconvenience.

Millennial Mage, 3 - Binding

If she'd been planning on being out in it for longer than a short walk, she'd have slipped on her shoes, but for the short trip, it seemed unnecessary. *No need to get soft.*

The beginnings of winter had settled in, in truth, and snow was a near-constant feature of the city.

She loved it.

Growing up, she'd enjoyed playing in it with her siblings and the neighborhood children. Even at the academy, snow had entranced her, though she'd enjoyed it alone there.

She almost dropped through the Caravanner's Guild lounge, but she didn't like the attention she got there. Mrac had apparently received a mild reprimand for allowing her to get a higher pay than he was authorized to grant now that she was an Archon. Because of that, the whole Guild learned how much she was going to be making per trip.

It was apparently far from the highest wage per trip, but it was more than any other Dimensional Mage got with so little on-the-job experience.

Some were impressed at what she'd managed to wrangle from the guild, and a few were ambivalent, but many were quite irritated that she was to earn more than they were. All in all, she found it better to avoid them… for now. *Maybe things will calm down after another few weeks.*

She would enjoy dropping back through, maybe getting to know some others in her profession. *Yeah, when I come back.*

But that wasn't for now. Now, she wanted to ask a few questions of the librarians. *I wonder if Ingrit's available.*

Chapter: 27
More Questions

Tala was pleased to find out that not only was Ingrit available, but she was also the one to greet Tala when she entered.

"Mistress Tala, welcome back."

"Mistress Ingrit, I'm glad to be back."

"I assume that you have more questions?"

"Oh, yes."

Ingrit let out a bell-like laugh, smiling as she did so. "Well, then, right this way. We can sit in an alcove."

The Archon led Tala to a small, secluded table with a cushioned seat on either side. Tala looked at the seating warily.

"It will hold you, Mistress. We are aware of your increased weight." After a moment's hesitation, she continued. "We would love to learn if that is beneficial at all. There is quite a bit of debate on the merits of the idea." She gave an apologetic smile. "Though, I will say, most think you are causing yourself quite a bit of inconvenience, for little to no gain."

Tala shrugged. "I'll let you know when I figure it out." She sat, Ingrit settling across from her.

"Very well." The other woman seemed to consider the matter closed. "One moment, please." She placed her hand on the edge of the alcove, and Tala watched her feed power into a hidden script.

Copper?

It seemed to seal off their seating area, preventing others from listening in. "What do you wish to ask?"

"I assume you can discern the... protection I now have on my skin?"

Ingrit's face *almost* showed a hint of power before she nodded. "Yes." She frowned for a moment. "Iron, with some sort of emulsifying agent to help it bind both to the medium of application and to your skin?"

"Yes." Tala cocked her head, frowning in confusion. "What?" Tala found herself blinking, trying to process what Ingrit had said. *There is no way she was able to tell that just by looking at me.* "How could you possibly know that with that level of specificity?"

"If I was to say it was due to the exact way power reflects and refracts around you, would you believe it?"

Tala frowned. "That's pretty hard to believe."

Ingrit hesitated a moment, seeming to consider. "Would you believe it's obvious by the color of your skin?"

Tala almost laughed, given the twinkle of mirth she noticed in Ingrit's eyes. "No."

"Would you believe I'm a very good guesser?"

Tala did laugh then. "Well, not now, I wouldn't."

Ingrit grinned. "Well, my perception helps, but there was a recipe logged by a local alchemist, which stated that it was for 'unknown purposes.' The uses of that would theoretically match close enough to the effect I see around you."

Tala grunted, still smiling. "Fair enough, I suppose." *They really do get records of virtually everything...* "Wait. Why wasn't it restricted to the Alchemist Guild or some such?"

"He noted that he came to the exact formula due to a Mage working outside of guild affiliation. Thus, it wasn't theirs to claim."

"Ahh." *Huh, surprisingly honest.* Not that she'd expected anything else. Even so, it was nice. *Well, he's secured a loyal customer.* That was probably part of the purpose.

"So, what's the question?"

"Oh! So, Master Grediv was able to see through the iron on my skin. How?"

"Well, as it is a mundane effect, I think I understand what you mean. If you were using an inscription, I would have to study that to provide the answer."

Tala nodded. *That makes sense.*

"So, most magic is like a child's ball. Your iron, as it is currently applied, acts like hog-wire."

"Hog wire?"

"A fencing made out of steel wire, arranged in a grid with moderately-sized holes."

"Oh! Alright; I think I've seen that."

"Good. So, what happens if you throw a leather ball against such a fence?"

"It bounces off."

"Exactly."

Tala hesitated. When nothing further was stated, she cocked an eyebrow. "So?"

"I'm not a book, Mistress. You should do some intuiting yourself." The glint of mirth was back in the other woman's eyes.

"Fine… So, was Master Grediv forcing his magesight through the fence?"

"Precisely."

"But it didn't feel the same as when others have seemingly been able to see through it."

"So?"

Tala sighed. "So, their magic is finer? It fits through the fence?"

"Very good."

Tala grimaced. "Is the patronization necessary?"

"No, but your reactions make it entertaining. I'm not required to be here, after all. I have to make my own fun." Ingrit winked.

Tala snorted a laugh. "Well, I guess… thank you?"

"You are most welcome."

"So, does that mean that some magics could pass through those defenses?"

"Absolutely, and obviously so. Any Refined, and many Fused, will be able to brute force their way through—if they know they need to. You should get some forewarning because of that, though. A Paragon, such as Master Grediv, will be able to power through as a matter of course. Above Paragon? They could easily push through that defense as if it weren't there, assuming they target you directly, even if they aren't aware of the iron before they act. They might even be able to burn it away entirely. Keep in mind I'm speaking of blunt spell-workings. I wouldn't let anyone try to heal you through that iron unless they are at least Ascending."

I suppose that makes sense. "And, what about finesse?"

Ingrit thought for a long moment. "A Fused who specializes in fine workings will be able to get through that defense one time in ten? If they know it's there, that ratio might go up. It is an impediment, which is why Master Grediv likely had to force his way through. Also, he's not seen the need to update his magesight recently. The time of reduced efficiency just isn't worth the marginal improvement to him."

"Improvement? So, we have to redo our inscriptions fundamentally as we advance?"

"Hmmm? Oh! No. His magesight is simply an older generation of the form, and we've made fairly significant advancements in that particular working since he last modified his inscriptions."

"Ahh, okay." *Speaking of Grediv...* She pulled out one of the books the Archon had given her. It was still locked against her. *For some reason...* "How can I implement wards such as this? I'm learning a lot of... sensitive things, and I like to take notes." *Speaking of which...* She pulled out a notebook as well and began writing down the highlights of the answers she'd already gotten.

Ingrit took the book and opened it. "Yes, this should be locked information for you." She nodded. "It is sufficiently guarded that I won't be required to confiscate it." Ingrit passed the book back.

Tala's eye twitched even as she tucked the volume away. *Right... don't let my guard down too much.*

"To enact these yourself, you must be a Paragon."

"...Why?"

"I am sorry, Mistress Tala, but I cannot tell you how."

"Oh, I understand that. I want to know why. Why do you have to be a Paragon to enact these?"

Ingrit hesitated, seemingly contemplating. "I think I can share a piece of that." She nodded, smiling. "A Paragon's soul is utterly cleansed of impurities, allowing for a much better connection both with the realms beyond, thus the incoming power, and with this world, through their likewise pure body. That increased connection is required for workings such as this."

"...I didn't understand that at all."

"And yet, that is all I can say."

"Very well... Is there something similar I can do?"

"Of course!"

Tala leaned forward, smiling expectantly.

"If you use an Archive-linked slate, you can lock your notes to you and you alone. Though, we would appreciate a death clause, which would allow us access in the event of your passing."

"Oh..." That was disappointingly simple. *And expensive.* Then, she processed the last sentence. "A death clause?"

"Oh, yes. It is incredibly irritating when a brilliant researcher has their notes locked because they 'aren't quite ready, yet.' Then, they do their 'final' experiment and die, their life's work forever lost." She shook her head, sadly.

Tala straightened. *Brilliant researcher, eh?* That was quite a kind thing to say.

"One day, you might have one or two interesting things to contribute, and we'd prefer that you already had good habits in place."

Tala deflated. *And good feeling gone.* Terry shifted on Tala's shoulder, and Ingrit's eyes flicked to him briefly. *Well, that's as good a transition as any.* "Has anyone ever made an arcanous animal into a familiar?"

Terry's eyes opened, and he regarded Tala for a breath before turning to look at Ingrit.

Ingrit regarded them for a long moment before shaking her head. "First off... please don't. Not right now."

"Why?"

Ingrit looked vaguely uncomfortable as she shifted in her seat, a slight grimace on her face. Finally, she sighed. "I'm not really permitted to comment on the wisdom of soul-bonds."

"But you just did."

"And I shouldn't have..."

"Alright then... So, an answer to my question?"

"Yes. Many have tried." She was giving Tala a very disapproving look.

"How did it go?"

"In general? Very well."

Tala frowned. "I don't understand..."

"Traditionally, if an Archon desires a familiar, they find a young arcanous creature, ideally less than a year old, and they raise it until they have a strong emotional bond. If that doesn't happen within a year, it's too late."

"And if they bond emotionally?" She tossed a bit of jerky for Terry.

"Then they give the creature an Archon Star."

"So… what's the issue?"

"The issue is that being soul-bound radically changes the development of the animal. Their intelligence is shifted dramatically, as well as their innate capacities for magic. Through the power of the connection, they also become magical creatures in truth." She nodded towards Terry. "His density is already high enough that he *should* have transitioned into a magical beast. I have no idea how he has so much power in such a small space and doesn't spontaneously become a being of magic."

Because he's really much bigger, and you're just seeing the power in a condensed form? That was probably an oversimplification. *But that's Terry's secret, not mine.* "Alright… so what would happen?"

"Most likely? He would immediately become a magical beast, and his strength would be greater than yours. If I'm seeing correctly—and let me emphasize that it's troublesome that I'm unsure of that—he would immediately be able to take full control of your gate. Through your gate, he would control your Bound body. If he wished, you would be little more than a human puppet: an extension of his will."

"But only if he wanted that."

Ingrit sighed. "Yes. But you must realize, he will have an immediate, fundamental change to his intelligence. Even if he was utterly devoted to you now, down to his deepest impulses, those could alter when a greater than human intelligence reprocesses every event in his life, all at once."

Tala frowned, confused.

Ingrit made an irritated face. "How different would you be if you could suddenly reprocess everything you've ever experienced, as you are now? From your birth up until this moment?"

Tala hesitated. *That would be... weird.* But would it change her? *Maybe?* "I think I understand the danger."

"Likely not, but I've already skirted the edge of what I am allowed to say." Her eyes had an almost pleading look to them.

Tala nodded, considering. "When would you advise I consider soul-bonding Terry, for the best result?"

Ingrit grinned. "That is an excellent question. I would suggest that you be well on your way to being Refined before you truly consider that step."

Fair enough, I suppose? How long could that really take? Then, she thought about it. *Ahh, yes. That could take a while.* "Thank you for the advice." *Well, I'm on the topic of bonds.* "So, speaking of soul-bonds brings artifacts to mind."

"Oh?" The librarian had an air of wariness about her.

"If I wanted to grant sapience to an artifact, say a dimensional storage, how would I go about it?"

Ingrit gave her a long, long look. "You cause a lot of stress in those around you, don't you?"

Tala leaned back at that. "I... Sometimes? How is that relevant?"

Ingrit was rubbing both her temples. "Anything with sapience can exploit a soul-bond and make a play for mastery of your soul."

Oh. "Right."

"So... avoid that." Ingrit dropped her hands and shook her head. "You likely don't even want that if you truly consider it. Once soul-bound, a dimensional storage will perfectly do what you need it to, when you need it to. Why would you want it to have a separate sapience? Why would you need it to have its own personality, which could, and likely would, oppose you, on occasion? *Best*-case scenario, you've just created a cognizant slave, with no agency."

"That is a good point…"

"I'm glad you feel that way. What is your next question?"

Tala grinned. *So much for not giving an opinion on soul-bonds.* She supposed that the information hadn't been about the bond or bonding, directly. "Where are all the older Mages?"

Ingrit cocked an eyebrow at her. "That is much too vague a question. You are currently talking to someone older than this city."

"Yes, I know that Archons are long-lived. I mean non-Archons?"

"Ahh." Ingrit thought for a moment. "If I understand your question, you are curious how many non-Archon Mages die of old age? That would be those with keystones and conscious control over their inscription activations but without soul-bonds."

"No? That isn't what I was asking, but that's probably an interesting statistic."

"None."

"How is that possible?"

"Those that don't become Archons, or die of one thing or other, eventually make an attempt at integrating an Archon Star, usually in their late eighties. None have the strength of will to resist attempting in the end. Roughly one in a hundred succeeds at that time. The rest begin the process of becoming founts. I'm glad that you know of those, already. Most Archons do. Interestingly, this process ends up making up a good chunk of Archons overall."

"So, all the secrecy is for nothing? Mages still all end up there in the end?"

"After decades of service and life. The secrecy gives them that. Would you take it away?"

Tala hesitated at that and at the severity of the response. "I… No. I suppose not."

Ingrit gave a single, firm nod.

Tala cleared her throat. Her question hadn't really been answered… "Oh… a Mage in that age range still looks quite young, don't they?"

Ingrit nodded. "They are physically comparable to mundanes in their early fifties."

Well, the life expectancy of those dying of natural causes is around ninety, so… "What is the oldest a non-Archon Mage has reached?"

"Three hundred."

Tala blinked at that. "That old?!"

"He was a singularly spectacular individual. He had his keystone and magesight removed when he turned a hundred and fifty. That lessened his abilities to the point that it took a hundred and fifty years before he was able to create an Archon Star. He was also one of *incredible* willpower, especially with regard to mental temptations. When he reached his three-hundredth birthday, he couldn't resist any longer, and made the attempt. Despite seven Archons doing their utmost to assist his integration of the star, once he forged one, he lost the battle and succumbed."

"Why did he fail?"

"We have no way of knowing what went through his mind at the end, but from what we know of him, he had a love of nature and of balance. The temptation he faced in the end was probably one of feeding the planet, feeding the cycle of nature. He seemingly chose to do so."

Tala didn't understand how that would be tempting at all. "Why didn't the Archons take the star away, preventing the attempt?"

Ingrit gave her a long-suffering look. "To prevent the attempt forever, we would have had to imprison him. Is that a life you'd want? He had a chance, and we helped him the best we could."

Tala felt very conflicted about that. It sounded like Ingrit had given her a *very* abbreviated account. *I'm not really interested in the minutia… Happier topic, please!* "So, how long do Archons live then?"

"Refined do not age and even regress in appearance to a more idealized version of themselves. Before that? Bound appear to age at close to a tenth the rate of mundanes, Fused a tenth of that." She shrugged. "Is that what you are asking?"

"So, those Refined and above never die of old age?"

"None have, to the knowledge of the Archive." Her tone seemed to indicate that meant it was a fact.

"Fair enough. Then, are there any Archons still alive from the first city or the times around then?" Tala immediately began imagining meeting the heroes of myth and legend.

Ingrit sighed. "I'm sorry, but that is information that I cannot share with you." But there was sadness in her eyes.

"Oh…" Tala felt a bit of sadness, though she wasn't exactly sure why. *If they were dead, wouldn't she be allowed to say?* Tala didn't know.

"I need to get to other work soon. Was there anything else?"

Tala nodded. "I'll try to go faster. Are regenerative potions possible?"

Ingrit barked a short laugh. "In theory, yes, but we don't know how to make them. Those in the stories were based upon the earliest Mage healers, who used arcanous plants as facilitators for their magic healing of those they treated. To our knowledge, no true regenerative potion has ever been created."

"Oh… alright then. I'm about to go to Makinaven; what are the best harvests on that route?"

"I'll get you a list. I assume you prefer that to me simply telling you?"

"Yes! Thank you." She was still taking notes, but a pre-made list would be faster.

"What else?"

"What is known about eating harvests?"

Ingrit opened her mouth, then frowned. "Huh… Well, I can tell you that endingberries used to be consumed by our ancestors, but they began to fall out of fashion with the invention of modern inscription, around the time of the first Leshkin War. They do not work for modern Mages for many, complicated reasons."

Unless you have modern inscriptions, based on how they work. Tala didn't smirk, not even slightly.

"Other than that…" Ingrit's frown deepened. "Why would this be restricted information, through the Inter-Guild accords?"

Tala cleared her throat. "It isn't important, I suppose."

Ingrit shook her head. "Well, only information on mundanes consuming harvests is restricted, which means that I must tell you to drop it as it is not for you to pursue that subset of knowledge." She was still frowning. "In any case, it is ill-advised for Mages to eat harvests, but so long as the consumed item isn't naturally toxic and doesn't have an elemental or similar type of power in it, eating it shouldn't be harmful."

"What about elemental harvests that align with the Mage's spell-forms?"

Ingrit took a long moment to consider. "So, this is an area of great debate. Some maintain that consuming such would enhance the Mage, and others claim that the harvest's power would clash with the inscriptions and lead to magic poisoning." She nodded once. "My opinion would be that, unless there is perfect alignment between what is ingested and the Mage's inscriptions, there would be a high likelihood for some magic poisoning."

"And if there was perfect, or near perfect, alignment?"

"Then, it would likely strengthen the natural pathways within the Mage and make the power pulled from the harvest vastly more effective and potent. The result would likely strengthen the Mage's inscriptions as well."

Good to know. That's why the endingberries work so well for me. "Alright, thank you." She thought quickly to change the subject. *I need to go faster.* "Oh! Other sapient species."

"There are many. We collectively call them arcanes, though they have many separate names for themselves, and they see the term 'arcane' for the pejorative that it is."

"What?"

"An insult, dear. Calling them arcane is a reference to arcanous beasts. We're saying that they are little better than animals."

"Ahh… alright, then… What can you tell me about arcane cities?"

"Don't seek them out."

"Why?"

"You would be forcibly turned into a fount, enslaved, or killed."

"Even if my aura was perfectly hidden—likewise hiding my gate?"

Ingrit hesitated. "I have no information to share on aura-shrouded humans entering arcane cities."

Alright, so it's possible, but the information is restricted. "Final question, then. Thank you, by the way, for all the time you've taken."

Ingrit smiled and nodded. "Of course. The pursuit of knowledge is something to be encouraged."

"So, in that vein, is there anything you feel I should know?"

"That is an interesting question…" Her eyes unfocused for a long moment. Finally, she nodded to herself and returned her gaze to Tala. "In your place, I would join the library and learn all I could"—she gestured to herself—"as I have. But being you?"

Tala nodded.

"You should listen to the senior Mage Protector assigned to you. She will do an excellent job instructing you where you are lacking and directing you as you need."

"Huh… alright, I suppose."

Ingrit deactivated the privacy barrier and pushed herself out of her seat. "That really is all the time I have, right now. Do you need an escort out?"

"No, thank you. I remember the way."

"In that case, take care, Mistress Tala. I look forward to your next visit."

"Thank you. You take care as well, Mistress Ingrit. I hope to see you again soon."

Chapter: 28
Mistress Odera

Tala stood just inside the out-of-the-way entrance to a restaurant that she'd never have come across on her own without directions.

It was the night before her departure for Makinaven, just a couple of hours after her trip to the library, and she was finally meeting her 'minder,' Mistress Odera.

Before her, the establishment's interior stretched out, filling the inside of a small rise in the landscape in a very similar manner to the Archon complex, if much smaller. The layout hid and sheltered each table, offering privacy and seclusion while maximizing the use of space.

Every single patron that she could see was a Mage, and most of the staff were at least inscribed. *What under the stars do they need with inscriptions?* There wasn't a uniformity to them as it seemed that each staff member had something different augmented. *Maybe it's just a declaration of station?* She didn't know enough to make a reasonable guess.

A few tables held parties of Archons, if she was guessing correctly, and Tala found herself feeling a bit of social fear for what felt like the first time since leaving the cliques and in-groups at the academy.

What am I doing here...?

She glanced down at her elk leathers.

Why am I wearing these?

She had nicer clothes. Why hadn't she worn them? *Why did I even buy them?* She was getting too used to the elk leathers and how they kept themselves in perfect, clean condition.

She had an almost overpowering desire to step back outside, drop into Kit, and change.

Unfortunately, or maybe fortuitously, a kindly gentleman walked up to her and bowed. His inscriptions seemed to be around his ears, meant to amplify most sounds, while protecting his hearing in a similar vein to Tala's own ear inscriptions, if more crudely implemented due to his lack of a keystone. *It just constantly compresses the volume of sounds that reach his ears into a narrow range.* A fascinating solution for his lack of a keystone. "Mistress Tala, I presume?"

Tala gave a slight bow in return, Terry shifting expertly on her shoulder as she bowed. "I am."

He smiled. "Mistress Odera arrived before you and asked us to keep an eye out. Right this way?" He gestured for her to follow him and turned to lead her deeper in.

"Umm… am I dressed appropriately?" she asked as quietly as she could with any certainty of him hearing. She even took into account his enhanced hearing, making her words a very quiet whisper, indeed.

He paused and turned back towards her, regarding her with a critical eye. After a moment, he smiled, once again. "You look lovely, Mistress. We don't have a dress code, per se, but even if we did, you would be welcome as you are."

She felt herself relax, even if just slightly, as he turned and led her from the entrance. *Nothing for it in any case… I can't go change now. Even if I wanted to.*

As they wandered through, she felt other diners glance her way, and she felt *exceedingly* glad that she'd taken the time to apply her iron salve earlier. She'd avoided doing so earlier in the week, given how she practically bathed in sand, involuntarily, every day. *Rane is brutally effective...*

The Mages they passed were of every quadrant. Tala even thought she saw quite a few bridging quadrants to some extent. The Archons all kept their auras under tight control, and what little of their spell-lines she could easily see with her normal vision weren't easy to decipher beyond the quadrant.

Tala, for her part, held her aura in with ease. In the last week, she'd only woken twice to find her aura unrestrained: the first night, and then again two nights later. After that, she'd been able to maintain her containment even while asleep. *Grediv was exactly right to have me focus on strengthening my will and my soul.* Lyn still occasionally slipped up, at least from what the woman had confided in Tala, but she was getting there. Neither of them doubted that she'd have the unconscious mastery well in place before Tala returned.

The result was that Tala's iron salve was now virtually impossible to detect. Her restrained aura seemed to lessen the effects of other Mage's power reflecting back at them. Though, it didn't eliminate it completely. *I don't know why my aura affects that, but it definitely seems to.* The largest change was that her eyes and palms no longer glowed to her, or others', magesight. *At least I don't look like some crazy abomination anymore.*

She was pulled from her contemplations when the server stopped beside an alcove, turning to gesture and indicating that this was Tala's table.

Tala stepped around the corner and hesitated.

The woman, already seated, was clearly a Mage but not an Archon. *Maybe she is, and she's just perfectly hiding her aura?*

Her dark skin caused the copper inscriptions to be incredibly difficult to see with mundane eyes, especially in the dim, atmospheric lighting. There were no other metals visible. She appeared *much* older than Tala, to the younger woman's eyes.

The Mage's hair was an almost silver-white, and she had deep smile lines, along with other, more subtle wrinkles that seemed to have been expertly accounted for by her inscriber. The style of those lines somehow did not seem like Holly's work, though Tala couldn't have defended the claim with any rationality. The other woman was an Immaterial Guide, just as Tala was, but she specialized in air and water. *How does that make sense? Those are clearly material...*

Tala's magesight was straining to discern what the woman could do, and as part of that strain, Tala saw the barest hints of power across the woman's face. *Her magesight is active?*

That didn't make sense. There didn't appear to be enough power to enact such a working. *And if she was hiding her power, there should be none...*

Something of her thoughts must have shown because the woman smiled, a knowing glint in her eye. "Mistress Tala, welcome."

Tala's examination had taken less than a breath, but she still had the feeling that it had been a bit too long. Tala gave a slight bow. "Mistress Odera, I presume?"

"Just so." Mistress Odera smiled at the server and gave him a nod, which Tala noted was more than Mistress Odera had given her. "Thank you. We should be ready to order in a few minutes."

"Can I get you anything to drink, while you decide?"

Mistress Odera nodded. "Just water for me, please. No ice."

Tala smiled at the man. "Same for me. Thank you."

The server, for his part, gave an almost courtly bow before departing.

"Please, child, sit."

Tala was almost offended; she did technically outrank the woman, after all. On the other hand, Mistress Odera would be her overseer until the Mage determined such was no longer necessary. Tala decided to not make an issue of it for the moment, instead turning to examine the indicated chair.

"I'm aware of your... difficulties with furniture. That seat should bear you with ease, assuming you aren't prone to rocking back on two legs."

Tala quirked a smile and settled down. The metal creaked just slightly but otherwise held perfectly well. *This is becoming more and more inconvenient...* No, she was going to give it a good try before deciding if the increased weight was worth the inconvenience. *At least through the start of this contract.*

Terry flickered to the table, examining Mistress Odera up close but still out of the woman's easy reach. "You are a curious creature, aren't you, tiny terror bird."

Terry settled back, locking gazes with the woman.

"You can choose." Her eyes never wavered. "Terry, yes?"

Terry gave a slight bob.

"We can be civil and largely ignore each other, or you can attempt to attack me, and I will take one of your toes."

Tala blinked at that, opening her mouth to object, but Mistress Odera's eyes flicked to her for the briefest instant, and the look was so intense and full of authority that Tala's mouth clicked shut.

Terry shifted between his feet for a moment, then glanced down, seeming to examine his toes. When he looked back up, his eyes narrowed, just slightly, then he flicked back to Tala's shoulder, where he settled down.

Mistress Odera smiled, showing exactly how she'd earned those crow's feet. "So, you are not only more intelligent than previously noted, but you are also logical and reasonably civilized."

Terry stiffened on Tala's shoulder for a brief instant, and Tala found herself smiling, too. "She's going to be around us a lot, Terry. We figured you couldn't pretend to be a hatchling forever, at least not without it becoming tedious." She snorted a brief laugh. "Especially not after the display in the evaluation room."

Terry opened one eye, giving her a calculating look, then opened his mouth.

Tala chuckled, then gave him a bit of jerky. She decided not to simply toss it to the side. *No need to show all our cards. Not yet.* "So, is your magesight active? I can't quite tell."

Mistress Odera nodded. "It is, as is yours."

"You can see it?" *Did I miss something in my salve application? Is my aura-restraint not as good as I thought?*

"Yes, and no. I can see the ripple effects in the air in front of your eyes. Whatever you have on your skin as defense is quite effective against my level of power, not to mention your aura control." She took a deep breath, closing her eyes. "As to your defense, the ripples of power I'm feeling reflected off of it, from the other patrons here, is a bit disquieting."

That opened so many questions. "How?"

Her smile widened just slightly. "How am I activating my magesight with so little power? Perfect understanding of what it is doing on a level far more fundamental than most Mages ever bother to learn. How can I detect the immaterial effects of magic on the air, as well as the impressively minute reflections from your defense?" Her smile became slightly coy. "The answer is the same."

"How are you not an Archon?"

Mistress Odera paused for a moment. "That is a bit of a rude question." But she shook her head when Tala opened her mouth to respond. "Not an unwarranted one, but I would recommend getting to know someone better before asking that of others. Are we understood?"

Tala felt her cheeks heat. *How is such a light reprimand hitting me so hard?* "Yes, Mistress." *Tala? Are you okay?*

"Very well, the question has been asked. I do not have the right kind of willpower to become an Archon. My master was very clear on that, and no Archon I've met since has disagreed."

"What does that even mean?"

"To become an Archon, to win that fight over self, body, and soul, a Mage must not only desire power and be willing to take borderline unhealthy risks to get it, but they must value their advancement over the good of others."

"Now, wait a minute—" Tala felt her indignation rise, but again, Mistress Odera lifted a hand.

"It is a false choice, obviously, but it is still a choice. To become an Archon, you must deny your soul to the world. You must begin the process of forever sealing your power as your own, never to directly enrich the greater planet. We both know that an Archon can do much with their power to help others, but the power, itself, is not able to be used for such, directly. It is a subtle distinction that requires some fundamental characteristics in one's will, and one's soul, to overcome. I do not have that."

Tala quirked an eyebrow. "So, you are telling me you are too selfless to become an Archon. Are you too humble as well?"

Mistress Odera barked a short, quiet laugh. "That is one way to look at it and how it manifests in most. For me, however, I am too selfish."

"How do you mean?"

"Why, my dear Mistress, if my power is suffusing the world, is my soul not, slowly, gaining dominion over it?"

Tala opened her mouth, thought about it, then closed her mouth again, frowning.

"My conscious mind would be gone, but my eternal soul, which is the real me, would gain a greater hold on this world than I could ever achieve otherwise." Mistress Odera shrugged. "You see?"

Tala thought she understood, but it still didn't make sense to her. "I suppose I understand in theory, but I don't get it practically. If that makes sense… but, if it was logical to me, I'd be in the same position you are."

"Precisely."

"Wait… how do you know all this? Isn't knowledge locked to those who aren't Archons?"

Mistress Odera waved that off. "I am Forbidden from advancing, for as long as I can resist. In order to resist, past a certain point, I have to know what and why. Forbidden are told the basics after they turn fifty. That seems to be the tipping point for most. I have earned more knowledge beyond that."

Tala grunted, thinking about what Mistress Odera had said, in conjunction with what Ingrit had shared about all Mages making the attempt, eventually. *So, she'll hit that barrier in the end, and her soul will begin conquering the world.* Tala didn't really know how to feel about that.

Mistress Odera cleared her throat. "Now, we should get to ordering food."

Tala glanced down at the paper resting before her on the table. *Yeah… food would be nice.* She frowned. The prices were listed as simple numbers, no denomination mentioned.

"Do you have a question, Mistress?"

Tala looked up. "I suppose. The pricing doesn't really make sense. Some things that I *know* are more expensive have a much lower number beside them, and I can't tell what denomination the menu is in."

"Ahh, I see. Did you notice the different ink?"

She hadn't. Well, she had, but she'd simply thought it a stylistic choice. Now that she looked closer and considered, the larger numbers were all written with a silvery ink, the smaller with gold. *Oh...* Her eyes widened. "Oh... I... uh..."

Mistress Odera held up her hand. "I invited you, child. It is an old tradition of mine to eat a final meal here before I leave for a contract. I'll not impoverish you to suit my fancy." She smiled happily. "In truth, it costs me nothing. I did a job for the owner some... thirty?" She shook her head. "Fifty years ago." She snorted a chuckle. "It's changed owners since, of course, but they've all honored the agreement." She nodded happily. "I get to eat here for free before I leave for any mission."

"That was an expensive payment."

Mistress Odera shrugged. "Their daughter had wandered off with a miner, and the miner had come back alone, dazed and clearly under compulsion of some kind."

Tala felt her eyes widening, once again, and even Terry lifted his head to pay closer attention.

"It seems that they somehow wandered into an older tunnel that led outside the city's defenses. The girl was a new Mage, and something decided to snap her up."

"What happened?"

"What happened? I know you are capable of thinking for yourself. What do you think happened?" Mistress Odera shook her head, returning her attention to the menu before her. "I went and got her back."

Tala let out an irritated breath. "That's not a very good retelling of what must have been a very harrowing adventure."

"I'm not a bard, girl."

"You could work on being a better storyteller."

Millennial Mage, 3 - Binding

"I'm a great storyteller, but I'm hungry, and we need to order. Besides, you may be an Archon, but that doesn't entitle you to *all* secrets."

Typical. Even so, Tala huffed a laugh. "Fair enough. What do you recommend?"

"No idea. I've never seen you eat before."

"...But what do you like?"

"Walks in the forest under a cloudless, night-time sky." Mistress Odera gave Tala an utterly serious stare. "Fictional tales of starships and plasma swords, and epics imagining worlds in which magic functions differently."

"For food, Mistress. From the food offered here." *Is she purposely trying to be irritating? Testing me, for some reason?*

"The bread is delicious."

As if on cue, the kind gentleman returned with their waters, a basket of bread, a plate of butter, and two small plates. "Would you two care for some bread, while you're deciding?"

I'm not sure I could balance all that that well. It was impressive. Tala smiled and accepted. "Yes, thank you. What do you recommend from your menu?"

Mistress Odera silently accepted the bread as well, lathering hers with butter to what seemed an unhealthy degree.

"Well, Mistress, that depends. What type of food do you prefer?"

Tala almost snapped at the man but realized that her irritation was with Mistress Odera, not their server. Instead, she took a deep breath. "I'm not partial to any form of fish or water life. Other than that, I just enjoy good food."

"Certainly. Are you looking for a light or a heavy meal, tonight?"

"The heavier and more filling the better, I think." She smiled a bit self-consciously. "I eat a lot."

"We have an endless soup and greens. Often, soup can be a light meal, but ours are of the richer variety, in general, and by virtue of being endless, it should be quite filling."

Tala perked up at that. "Oh? What soups are available?"

"Cheesy-potato chowder. Tomato basil. Broccoli cheddar. Chicken barley. White bean, chicken noodle, and"—he glanced down at a small notepad—"ahh, yes, crawdad bisque, which I imagine you wouldn't prefer."

"Oh… I don't know how I would decide."

"You don't need to decide. You can have as much as you'd like of any or all."

Tala felt immediately guilty. "That seems like a poor deal for you all. I can eat a *lot*."

Mistress Odera reached out her hand and tapped the menu in front of Tala, causing her to glance down. "Oh… alright then." Mistress Odera had pointed out the price: ten silver ounces. *Yeah. They usually pull a hefty profit… even I might struggle to get that much value from it.* "Can I start with the chicken barley?"

"Very good, Mistress. And for you, Mistress?" He turned to Mistress Odera.

"I'd like the long pasta with chicken and the white sauce, please. And a salad to start."

The server got the particulars for their salads and departed.

"So, now that food is on the way. Will you tell me that story?"

"Maybe on the road. We're going to be working together because of your previous… contracts. How about we start there? Tell me about the route to and from Bandfast." Her smile was kindly, but there was an almost predatory glint in her eye.

"Alright, I suppose…"

The evening passed quickly after that. Mistress Odera asked penetrating questions but never pushed if Tala showed any hesitation about sharing. The food was excellent, and Tala ate an almost insane amount of each kind of soup, except the crawdad bisque. The greens were also an amazing counterpoint, and Mistress Odera had been correct in that the bread was to die for.

All in all, even while sharing her dangerous experiences and somewhat foolish choices, the dinner was a pleasant last meal on her final day in Bandfast.

Chapter: 29
Only a Mage Protector

Tala stood atop the cargo wagon, the light of early morning making the busy work yard bright.

Lyn had bid her goodbye before heading to work herself. Tala had paid her housemate-landlord thirty silver ounces before they'd parted ways: twenty for the next month's rent and ten for the rug that she'd bled upon.

Rusting expensive rug…

Tala reveled in the autumn air, stretching slowly now that she'd finished charging the last of the fourteen cargo-slots. The passengers and off-duty guards were climbing in through the appropriate doors as she watched from above.

As Master Himmal had promised, the wagon had been adjusted so that her presence on top wasn't a problem, though her movements did cause the body to sway some.

They even increased the width of the wheels to spread the load better…

True to his word, there were five accessible cargo-slots, boxing in the nine that were loaded down with goods, bound for Makinaven. The one on the back was as she'd seen before, but there were an additional two on each side, mounted to allow the doors to be opened with ease. Each had a short, flexible stepladder hanging down below them to allow for quick entry and exiting.

Despite the cool weather and bits of snow scattered around the work yard, the dark wood beneath her feet was already beginning to warm in the late autumn sunlight. It was going to be a lovely day.

As she watched the guards entering, she was reminded of how small this trip would be with regard to required personnel.

Only forty guards, three shifts of ten with ten as backups, would be accompanying them despite there being more than two hundred passengers. Makinaven, as it turned out, was a popular destination, much more than Alefast, at least for mundanes. *And a more dangerous route, especially if they want us to be secure against a full third of our guards being rendered unable to perform their duties.*

Three of the outer-accessible cargo-slots had been built out to house the passengers. That was the equivalent of twenty-four mundane wagons worth of space, with the added benefit of having the common spaces combined for a more communal atmosphere and trip, unlike the usual separation between wagons. The passengers were additionally isolated from the movements of the wagons, at large, so the passengers should be very comfortable indeed.

The remaining two accessible cargo-slots were what Tala had expected. One was filled by the guard's quarters; accommodations for drivers, which was an unusual luxury given most simply slept in or near their driver's seat in most caravans; and private spaces for the three Mages: Mistress Odera, Rane, and Tala herself. The remaining space in that cargo-slot was taken up with things they *might* need on the venture but could be sold on the other end if they weren't needed, thus increasing the profitability of the trip.

The last accessible cargo-slot was simply a supply storage for the trip itself. With more than two hundred and fifty people, they would go through a lot of food and supplies over the following weeks.

Two weeks. The distance between Bandfast and Makinaven was not too different than that between Bandfast and Alefast, but the need to traverse the forest made the estimated travel time much longer. *If the forest cooperates, it only takes a week, but some unlucky caravans have taken more than a month.* They were prepared, regardless, at least with respect to supplies.

The chuckwagon, the only other wagon on this trip, was in place behind the cargo wagon, and there were no fewer than five cooks already busily working in and around the rig. They also had a dedicated driver, which Tala had been informed was only possible because the drivers were being given accommodations in a cargo-slot.

"Child."

Tala absently tossed a bit of jerky to the side for Terry as she watched a servant push the last of the passenger cargo-slot doors closed.

She was suddenly bumped to one side, and she staggered slightly, causing the wagon to rock beneath her.

Tala spun, glaring at the diminutive woman standing behind her. "What."

"You were ignoring me."

"How was I to know you were speaking to me?"

"Is there anyone else around?"

Tala narrowed her eyes. "Old crone."

Mistress Odera grinned back. "Yes?"

Tala threw her hands up. "Fine. What do you want?"

Mistress Odera gestured towards the forty-two indicator symbols, glowing to Tala's magesight through openings in the wagon top. "It seems that you've done your duties as the Dimensional Mage. Is that correct?"

"It is…" Tala was hesitant in her answer. *Why does that…? Oh. Rust.*

"Good. That means, with those duties accomplished, you are now only a Mage Protector until tomorrow morning and entirely under my authority."

Yeah… I walked into that one. "So it would seem."

"Good. I will be atop this wagon for most days of our trip. I would like you to observe from atop the chuckwagon, while Master Rane and the guardsmen provide encircling defense." She looked at Terry. "Will you be of help, or do you wish to remain as you are?"

Terry glanced to Tala. She shrugged, and so, he squawked and bobbed. "He'll help, but—"

Mistress Odera spoke over the top of her. "Good. He can drive back anything that gets too close. You can support him if he chooses to engage something within the outer ring of our defenses or address any secondary breaches. Questions?"

"Three."

Mistress Odera smiled. "Ask away."

"First, is the chuckwagon reinforced for my effective weight?"

Mistress Odera hesitated, then sighed. "I even knew about that ahead of time and failed to account for it." She shook her head. "Very well. We will both be on this lead wagon. Next question?"

"It seems like you're preparing us for a *lot* of attacks. Is this route really so much more dangerous?"

"You've only taken the one trip to Alefast and back, correct? Including when not under contract?"

"That's correct."

"Yes. This trip will be *much* more dangerous than that one."

"Well… alright then." She lapsed into silence.

After a moment, Mistress Odera cleared her throat. "So?"

"Hmmm?"

"What's the third question?"

"Oh... I didn't actually have one."

"Then, why did you say you had three?"

"Because I had two and figured I would think of a third by the time I got there."

"But you didn't."

"But I didn't."

Mistress Odera snorted a laugh. "You've had some incredibly nitpicky teachers in your life, haven't you?"

Tala shrugged. "That's not entirely true. Most of them were fine, but most also didn't like me too much." She sighed. "I now understand that a good part of that was how I acted, and a part was how my iron made them feel while around me."

Mistress Odera nodded. "I see."

After another long moment, Tala turned away, looking for where she would sit for the first part of the journey. Then, she hesitated. "Wait. I do have a third question."

Mistress Odera gave her a look of patient expectancy.

"Did you really forget about my increased weight?"

"By the plan I put forward, it seems that I did."

Tala narrowed her eyes at the older woman. "You just wanted to see how I would react to you acting in error."

"That is quite the assumption."

"So?"

"So... what, child?"

"How did I do?"

Mistress Odera cocked an eyebrow. "I told you that you could ask three questions, not that I would answer them." She smiled. "Now, have you seen your quarters yet?"

Tala frowned. *So, you're going to be like that?* She groused a bit, then shook her head. "No, I haven't."

"I'd recommend that you do. We aren't leaving for another half-hour or so."

"I can see them tonight."

Millennial Mage, 3 - Binding

Mistress Odera gave her a long-suffering look. "Go look at the room, Mistress Tala. Then, come back here, and we'll go over a few more details."

Tala gave an exaggerated bow. "As you command."

Mistress Odera snorted a laugh. "Don't start something you can't maintain, girl." But she was smiling, nonetheless.

Tala didn't comment as she climbed down, still not sure what to make of the woman as a whole. Thankfully, the cargo-slot in which she would be sleeping was mounted right beside the ladder.

As she stood on that ladder, it was an easy step over, onto the lip of the entrance. The cargo-slot's door swung inward smoothly, towards her left, and Tala moved inside, closing the door behind herself.

She was in a common space, extending before her and mainly to the left. Guards were already lounging, reading, or otherwise resting before their shifts began. The space was lit by simple magic constructs, which would function off the ambient magic in the air, even right outside a human city. For the moment, they appeared to have been empowered sufficiently to remain lit until they reached the Wilds.

Off to her right, clearly marked doors led to two latrine stalls. Someone had tried to explain to her how the waste was contained, and how it would then be shunted out the door at need, but she hadn't been interested enough in the topic to pay close attention. *Don't need that anymore, anyway.*

She crossed through the common space, stopping just inside a short hall at the first door on the right. It was marked 'Dimensional Mage.'

She pulled out the key she'd been given and unlocked the door. *They built all this in here, in just a couple of days?* It was impressive. They'd have to tear it all out before she could allow the devices to power down, too. *I hope it's worth it.*

She stepped inside, Terry on her shoulder, and closed the door, locking it behind her.

It was dark but not pitch black.

A small amount of the light that hit the cargo-slot was distributed into this expanded interior. So, she had enough light to see. *Mundanes probably wouldn't, though. That's probably why the magical lights are in place out in the common space.*

There was a bed for her and a few hooks for her accessories. *Simple, and no more than I need.*

She carefully lowered herself onto the bed and found that it was able to support her weight. *What did they stuff this with?*

Despite her weight, it seemed to hold up well under her and was surprisingly comfortable to boot.

As she examined the structure, Terry walked across the bed and squawked in irritation. As small as he currently was, he wasn't heavy enough for it to be cushioned for him.

Metal. The structure of the bed was metal. *It looks like tubing of some kind. Fused at the junctions to make a near-seamless whole.* As she moved, it creaked ever so slightly. *They even gave it large runners instead of discrete feet to distribute my weight on the floor better.*

They really did think of everything. "I'll pull out my bedroll for you, Terry. You'll be plenty comfortable."

That seemed to mollify the avian.

Tala unlocked her door and moved back out into the hall, resecuring it after she was through. She turned around as the door behind her opened.

Rane stepped out. "Mistress Tala, good morning." He quickly pulled his door closed; not so quickly, however, that she couldn't see inside.

"Good morning, Master Rane." His room was easily double hers in size, and she saw a servant working away inside, seemingly doing whatever servants do. *He looks familiar...* "Is that... Manth?"

Rane smiled happily. "Yes, he was available again for this trip, so he was assigned to me once more."

"That's good?"

Rane nodded, turning towards the exit. "Yeah, it's nice to not have to get to know someone else or work through the finicky minutia of a new servant."

Tala walked beside him, giving him an incredulous look.

"Ahh, right... probably not something you've ever dealt with."

"No, I can't say that I have. When have you?"

"My family had servants, and I interacted with them a lot growing up. And whenever Grediv had us spend any time in Alefast, he would get a servant to handle the minor details for himself and me."

"That would have been nice," Tala groused.

Rane gave her an odd look. "You do know that you could have had a servant if you'd wanted one."

Yeah, but... She let out a sigh of defeat. "Fair enough. You're right, but I think I'm good as I am." They pulled the door open and hopped down, the door swinging shut on its own. *Well-designed hinges.*

"Have you seen our third? I haven't had a chance to meet her yet."

"I have... She's up on the cargo wagon."

"And she can hear you perfectly." The woman's voice came down to them. "Come on up, Master Rane. The three of us should talk before we get underway."

* * *

Tala stood at the front of the cargo wagon, eyes scanning the surrounding landscape. Terry was… somewhere, probably having a grand old time, depopulating the local fauna.

Mistress Odera had gotten the caravan into the formation they would hold for the whole trip. Her reasoning had been sound. "Practice when not under pressure."

As such, the guardsmen were prepared for a vicious defensive battle, which Tala greatly hoped would never come. Three were stationed atop the chuckwagon, their shields mounted in place, crossbows ready to accept whatever specialized bolt was required, and they had a *lot*. Fastened to the top of the wagon, beside each emplacement, was a segmented quiver holding at least twenty different types of quarrels, four of each.

They had a dimensional chest affixed to the center of the space, which held more of every type so that they could refresh their stock as needed. *That must be expensive to maintain…*

Around the two wagons, the seven remaining on-duty guardsmen rode in a loose, ever-shifting formation. Thankfully, each had a very simple set of directions, which, when combined with the other mounted guards' different instructions, created the defensive pattern. Each rider had what looked to be a bundle of spears, varied similarly to the archers' ammunition. Each bundle looked to have been designed for quick selection and armament of a mounted rider. Tala knew enough to know that she, herself, would be laughably incompetent if she tried to design such a thing.

Rane rode in slow circuits around their moving wagons, inside the circle of guards.

Tala was tasked with ensuring nothing obvious showed up to threaten them from the front. She wasn't to engage.

Millennial Mage, 3 - Binding

Mistress Odera had been explicitly clear on that point; she was simply to inform. At her observation, they had already scared away two groups of thunder bulls that had lingered in their path.

Around her regular sweeps of the rolling plains before them, and the dark line of trees some fifty miles distant, she read one of Holly's books, trying to deepen her own understanding of physiology, anatomy, and her spell-forms. Every bit of understanding she gained would increase the efficiency and effectiveness of the workings, and that could only profit her in the long run.

If Terry's frequent, flickering visits were any indication, he was feasting joyfully, his contentment evident every time Tala saw him. *Maybe I should find a way to let him get out more...* On the way from Alefast, he'd seemed content to rest near her. *That was something he had likely rarely been able to do, if ever. Now, he's had more than two weeks of rest, and so the hunt is what draws him.*

She knew that she sometimes viewed Terry as a pet, no matter how many times he had proven to be more. *I need to be treating him like the equal that he is.* With a nod to herself, she pulled out a larger-than-usual piece of jerky and waited.

A moment later, Terry appeared beside her, the size of a large dog. He looked at the jerky in her hand, then up to her face.

She tossed the jerky to him and sat down so that his head was a bit higher than hers. It was actually somewhat intimidating, looking up at the clearly predatory terror bird. She took a deep breath and smiled, speaking softly so even the driver, just a few feet away, wouldn't hear. "Hey, Terry."

Terry bobbed, coming a bit closer.

"I want to treat you more like the partner that you are. I don't want to just have you 'be around.'"

He continued to eye her.

"Can you... let me know if there's anything I can do for you or anything that *we* can do?"

He tilted his head, first one way then the other. Finally, he bobbed his head.

"Thank you."

He moved forward and bumped her head with his. It probably would have bruised her without her defenses.

Tala grinned and lightly headbutted him back, in turn. "I do like having you around."

Terry bobbed once more and vanished.

I'll take that as a good sign. He doesn't have to cling to my side but still likes to be here.

She returned her attention to her current tasks.

Aside from the thunder bull families, a small flock of burning sparrows had swept their way and had been dispersed with a few well-placed bolts. The effectiveness of the guardsmen's ammunition kept drawing Tala's mind to the anti-magic weapons like those quarrels. *They are fascinating bits of magic. Armaments that are empowered by their target.* Tala shook her head. They wouldn't work against anyone who had a good handle on their own power... would they?

Tala glanced back towards Mistress Odera. If Tala hadn't been looking for, and felt, the slight tendrils of magic, stretching from the woman at all times in all directions, Tala would have thought her asleep and blind to the world.

Clouds had rolled in through the morning as they left Bandfast behind, and a light dusting of snow had already fallen. Because of that, Mistress Odera sat wrapped in a blanket, seasoned with white. Tala, herself, had pulled on her leather shoes and wide-brimmed hat.

"Are there weapons that work on Archons like the guards' munitions affect arcanous beasts?"

Mistress Odera opened her eyes. "Yes, and no." She closed her eyes once more.

Tala shook her head. "Care to elaborate?"

Mistress Odera smiled, keeping her eyes shut. "If you are in control of your own power, it cannot be turned against you, unless wielded by one greater than your control." Her smile widened. "I, myself, have resisted the influence of beings and Archons classified as Refined." Her smile faded. "Such control is unusual, however." Her eyes opened, locking gazes with Tala. "I'll wager you now have the strength to fight a Fused and hold your own. You'd likely win as often as not, but if it came to a contest of wills?" She shook her head. "You might even fall to another Bound."

Tala grimaced. "I am working on strengthening my will, my soul."

"As you should, but you have crippled yourself—as anyone with eyes can see."

She cocked her head. "How so?"

"You do not face your greatest fear."

Tala snorted derisively. "I'm not afraid of dying, Mistress Odera."

Mistress Odera's eyes opened, seeming to pin Tala in place. "No, Mistress. You are afraid of living."

Tala rocked backwards in her seated position. *What?* She opened her mouth to respond, but nothing came to her. *Is... Is that true?*

Mistress Odera's eyes were already closed once more, and Tala could see the flow of power pick up around the Mage. If her magesight was right, Mistress Odera had expanded her awareness back to nearly a hundred feet out from the wagon in every direction.

Even after four hours, it *should* have been impressive. But at the moment, Tala didn't have the mental space to contemplate that.

Instead, Tala found herself sitting, staring forward. *Is she right? Am I afraid to live?*

Chapter: 30
Crystal

Tala moved through the rest of the day in a state of deep contemplation. As a result, she focused her actions entirely on her role as Mage Protector.

Lunch came and went, and she was barely able to summon up enough focus to thank the chef for the triple portion she brought to her. *What was her name again?*

The cargo wagon driver chatted with Tala for a bit, and she did her best to at least passingly engage, but nothing that he said sank deeply enough to disrupt her contemplations. *His name is Tion, right?* At least she'd caught that. *It's always embarrassing to ask people for their names after I should know them…*

She did her duty, pointing out no fewer than six more possible threats over the next few hours. Only three of them had to be dealt with in the end.

The afternoon was beginning to move towards the early evenings of the season, when she saw a cloud-like shape moving low across the ground, near the edge of the treeline, still more than twenty-five miles distant, seemingly ignoring the wind. *Another flock of small birds, moving almost in unison.* Not uncommon in flocks, even of mundane birds, but her magesight was clear. *Arcanous avians.*

Each bird was barely bigger than one of her fists, and they flitted about quite rapidly. *Like over-large hummingbirds.* She hesitated at that. *My sight is so much better!* She didn't let that distract her, though.

The birds passed through a column of sunlight, which broke through the otherwise pervasive cloud cover. Each bird shimmered and glinted in that light.

These beasts had a crystalline aspect to them. Tala called over her shoulder, "Flock! Crystalline birds. Small, but there look to be hundreds."

The guards responded, selecting from their more eccentric magical arsenal.

Mistress Odera, for her part, was muttering to herself. "Another? It's been weeks since a caravan reported encountering crystalline creatures. Was it not a migratory group, then?" She clucked her tongue. "A new fount with such a bent means trouble." More loudly, she called out, "Don't let them touch you. Any wound will be devilishly difficult to heal."

Great... Tala drew Flow but didn't funnel the power needed for a transformation. *Another encounter in which I'll be mostly useless.*

Terry had been lying near Tala, but at Mistress Odera's words, he looked back and forth between the two Mages.

"Go, Terry. I don't want you hurt by this, and you won't be much help against so many small enemies."

Terry hesitated for a long moment, then bobbed and vanished.

Be safe.

The guards affixed faceplates to their helms and pulled on thick gloves. Both would hamper them in many situations, but the extra protection could be critical in the coming encounter. Those who were mounted swiftly dismounted and hooked their reins onto the chuckwagon beside the spare mounts, hopefully keeping the animals out of any direct danger.

The drivers, for their part, each pulled out a large, heavy blanket that moved oddly to Tala's eyes. She looked closer, and her magesight detected what looked to be a chain-mail sheet between layers of heavy fabric and leather. Though, that was mainly an interpretation based on the distortions the steel created to that sight.

When no one moved to do anything for the oxen or horses, directly, Tala asked Mistress Odera.

Mistress Odera grunted. "Unless the beasts are seen as competitors or food, they will generally be left alone. I have my sight on them, however. If I need to, I should be able to keep them from harm."

Tala nodded. *Fair enough.*

The flock took another ten minutes to get close enough for everyone to see them easily, and Tala's magesight helped her revise her earlier guess. "I think there's at least four or five hundred." *Another five minutes before they're here.*

Mistress Odera shifted slightly. "If you see a place where you can help, do so. I know your offensive magics aren't suited for this."

My offensive… Right! She hadn't had a chance to try out Holly's additions. *Minute gravity manipulation might be perfect for this situation.* She almost twisted her arms into the right shape for the initial activation, then hesitated. "Mistress Odera?"

"Yes?"

"I have another spell-form available. With it, I can control the gravity around me, to some degree. It might be of help here."

"That sounds ideal. Why do you sound hesitant?"

"I've never used it before. I haven't practiced with it. It's a new spell-form for me, and it's one that requires practice and precision to use effectively."

Mistress Odera cursed under her breath. "Then, no. Don't use it. The last thing we need is for you to accidentally interfere with someone else or worse, destroy a wagon with chaotically assigned forces."

Tala opened her mouth to argue but stopped. *It shouldn't work that way, but worse things have happened when testing out new scripts in stressful situations... That's what I was thinking already. That's why I didn't just do it. Why am I going to fight against advice that I know is wise?* She pulled herself together and nodded. "As you say. I'll add it to my regular practice—as I should have as soon as I got the inscriptions."

Mistress Odera grunted. "You can't practice everything, Mistress Tala. In hindsight, this might have been better to practice with, but if we'd encountered something else, your chosen regimen might have been better. Do what you can, and fill in the gaps with wisdom."

Tala felt a smile tug at the side of her mouth. "As you say, Mistress."

Mistress Odera clucked her tongue thoughtfully. "You are protected against having your skin breached, correct?"

Tala nodded. Not only were her inscriptions oriented that way, but she also had a cup of endingberry juice comfortably processed within her. The power was like the returning of an old friend, and she definitely felt better with its added defense. "I am."

Mistress Odera took a deep breath, nodded, and seemed to decide something. "Then, I need you to make yourself a beacon. With that many, we need a distraction."

Tala gave the woman a questioning look.

Helpfully, the other woman explained. "Go off to the right, walk parallel to the caravan, and do everything you can to dump power into the environment. We'll drive them off from there."

Tala nodded, jumping from the cargo wagon.

The wagon creaked behind her, rocking slightly from the force of her jump and the sudden loss of weight after her departure. She hit the ground much faster than anyone else would have and drove two circular holes into the soil, both some six inches deep. *Huh, not enough pressure distribution, then.* She'd have to have Holly expand that. *If I keep this...*

Tala stepped up, out of the shallow holes and moved away from the caravan, and Mistress Odera called out instructions to the guards and Rane. Tala didn't listen to what was said, except to hear that Rane was ordered inside a wagon. His defenses would do little good against this threat, and he couldn't be risked in the encounter.

Tala, for her part, invoked six void-channels, directing the least into her body to keep her scripts and normal functions powered. The other five, she directed outward. She also released her hold on her Archon aura, allowing that to spread out around her, if just barely.

She dumped power into the air.

Mistress Odera called down to her with an amendment to her orders. "Too much, Mistress. We don't want to draw in additional threats. Keep your aura contained and cut the output by at least half."

Tala immediately did so, dismissing three of the exterior directed channels and retracting her aura with a minimal tug of her soul. *There.*

The effect on the swarm was obvious as they began to fly even more quickly, more frantically, their movement seemingly agitated.

Tala took up a parallel path to the wagons, some hundred feet to the west, heading south.

The guards atop the chuckwagon began firing in a steady rhythm, alternating so that one bolt lanced out every second and a half or so.

Millennial Mage, 3 - Binding

The munitions cut straight lines through the oncoming flock, now clearly oriented on Tala. Each bolt took out close to a dozen enemies. Every bird struck puffed into sparkling dust, but the mass continued to bear down on her.

Ahh… more like six or seven hundred then.

She created another void-channel, directing it into Flow's sword path. It was barely enough power to cause the change of form when coupled with a healthy dose from her reserves. Flow extended as Tala stepped forward, swinging at the leading edge as the birds came into melee range.

That single swing severed dozens, each puffing to sparkling dust. It was a bare fraction of the leading edge.

Tala was struck an uncounted number of times, each little adversary finding a way to hit her with multiple natural weapons as it passed. Her leathers were sliced and torn, immediately pulling back together in the wake of each passing blow.

There was a problem, however. Each cut began to grow crystal, which the leathers had to force out before they could close. It was taking *monumental* power, and the clothing was quickly moving towards total depletion.

Rust that! Tala recreated a fifth void-channel, connecting it to the refill point for the outfit on her right thigh. Her influx was barely enough to keep up with the tremendous drain placed upon their magics.

Her endingberry power was draining at an almost alarming rate, keeping even the smallest scratch from her, though her hair was shorn and tattered.

She struck, again and again, moving Flow in great sweeping cuts, never letting it slow. Her ears were filled with the flapping of wings, the buzzing of quarrels, and the light tinkling of dust falling onto the snow.

The air was so filled with power, both from her and the birds, that her magesight had trouble telling her anything useful.

Finally, the flock had passed, and her series of quick blows was done. She took a particularly deep breath, having maintained proper rhythm, and sucked in a lungful of dust.

She immediately felt the magic that was still held within the gritty substance.

The inscriptions she'd had Holly add to her throat and lungs proved their worth as the entirety of the material, along with their invasive magics, was ejected without taking effect as she coughed out an exhale.

Tala found herself on her knees, hacking into ground.

She recoiled as she saw how much dust was mixed with the now-crystalline grass and trampled snow. *Don't breathe that in, Tala!*

Panicking, Tala vaulted back to her feet and looked around as she continued to cough. Thankfully, the crystal growth didn't seem to be spreading beyond the immediate vicinity of where the dust had fallen. *Good, we didn't just doom the whole of the plains...* Such shouldn't be possible, but it would have been beyond foolish not to check.

She spun, reorienting on the flock as it wheeled around for another pass at her.

She maintained all her channels except for the one that led to Flow. It was still a great burden to maintain Flow in sword-form, so she let that lapse.

Two channels. I think I can direct two void-channels into it, and that should allow me to keep the sword out for longer.

The guards were still firing a steady pattern of shots, each flying true and taking out quite a number of avians with each bolt.

We can do this. This isn't so bad.

Almost as if at that thought, the circumstances radically changed.

The swarm suddenly shifted, breaking into two smaller groups. Both orientated towards the caravan. More specifically, one was aimed towards the guard between them and the caravan and the other towards the chuckwagon and the crossbowmen atop it.

Tala didn't think; she just took off at a dead sprint for the lone guardsman.

I'm not going to make it. She was sixty feet away. Mistress Odera seemed to be beginning a working. *Go faster!* Tala couldn't have said if the thought was directed at herself or the older Mage.

Tala was fifty feet from the lone guard.

The birds drew closer, and that guard crouched low, dropping to one knee, holding his round shield up to protect most of himself from the brunt of the incoming assault.

Forty feet.

Tala recreated all her void-channels, pulsing the power outward in a desperate attempt to redirect the birds towards herself. It failed.

Thirty feet.

As Tala pounded across the grass, she saw an oblong, bubble-like shield of protection blossom into being around the chuckwagon, those atop it, and the animals tied to it. Tracing the flows of power made the obvious more so: Mistress Odera had finished her working, and she seemed to have started a second. *Will she be fast enough?*

Twenty feet.

The guard is still exposed. "Mistress Odera!"

Ten feet.

As if in slow motion, Tala saw the leading birds either stretching out comically small talons before themselves or tucking in wings, orienting their beaks for piercing impacts.

Tala arrived, and another shield, a thing of true beauty, sprang up around her and the guard, along with at least thirty of their enemies.

Not the time to examine her magics.

Flow was back in the form of a sword, fed by two void-channels, and Tala was striking in a furious pattern at the few crystalline enemies that were still alive inside with them.

Most of this segment of the flock was deflected by Mistress Odera's shield, but Tala was focused on what was inside with them.

Dozens of impacts had cascaded across the guardsman as he, too, fought to strike down the birds. His skill was far beyond Tala's, but he was also less well-protected despite his armor.

Crystals already blossomed across much of his armor, and his shield was riddled with holes and sparkling, invasive magic. *Good to know it is a secondary effect. That's why the iron salve didn't help.*

After a few frantic breaths, the inside of the bubble was silent, save for their panting, blessedly empty of living foes.

Tala looked outward and was able to see enough to determine that the remains of the flock were retreating. With a grateful exhale, she then took a moment to examine the magic around her.

Her magesight and normal vision worked together to interpret what she saw.

First, Mistress Odera's shield. There were no fewer than six alternating layers of air and water. Tala struggled to interpret what she saw. *Did she increase the surface tension of the water to such a degree that it pulled itself out of the air and soil to form those layers?* The air had been hardened as well, but Tala couldn't even begin to guess at the method. The result was unquestionable, however.

Millennial Mage, 3 - Binding

This would stop any physical attack I've ever seen. It was incredible.

Second, she looked at the crystalline remains of their foes, sprinkling the now-faceted grass. *Good, the power is used up, and it's not spreading farther.*

Behind Tala, the guard groaned, a thump reverberating through the small space as he fell fully to his knees.

Mistress Odera's magical shield popped, and Tala called out. "Healer! Mistress Odera!" *Better to be safe.*

The guard's shield arm was dangling uselessly, crystals having grown across the shield and the armor on that arm. Those outward facets seemed to have stopped growing, just like the sparkling grass around them.

As Tala looked closer, she saw a streak of dark red crystal in a line from the man's arm, running down the back of the limply hanging shield. *Blood. Magically affected blood.*

Her eyes widened.

She focused, willing her magesight to penetrate the magics of the crystal on the outside of the man's armor, and that was when she saw it.

His very blood was crystalizing, the process following the power-rich channels, feeding on the man's internal magic and working its way upward… inward.

It had already passed his elbow and was moving towards the halfway point to his shoulder.

What do I do? "Your arm is infected."

The guard nodded. "Feels like, yeah." His voice was strained with obvious pain as he spoke through what must have been incredibly disorienting agony. "Take it off."

"What?"

"Cut off my arm!" He leaned back, letting the shield that was braced against the ground help him extend the limb-in-question to give her room to work with.

That should actually work. *Yeah. That should work.*

She didn't hesitate, whipping Flow forward in an upward slash, striking well above the spreading, hostile magics. *As far above as possible, anyway.* She didn't actually have that much arm to work with.

Tala struck true, and Flow passed through armor, gambeson, flesh, and bone without any resistance, cauterizing the wound in its wake.

The man gasped, falling back, pushing away from the now-separated arm with his legs and his one remaining arm.

The infected arm, now bereft of the man's soul to defend it, crystallized instantly, the hostile spell-working using itself up in the process.

Tala immediately focused her magesight on the man once more and verified that all remaining crystals and dust were fully inert. The hostile magic was fully spent.

"Thank you, Mistress. Thank you."

She smiled and nodded, re-sheathing Flow, once again in knife form. "Let's get you healed up. Shall we?"

She glanced towards the front wagon and saw Mistress Odera almost at the base of the ladder.

After a moment's thought, Tala scooped the guard up and ran with him to catch up to the still-moving caravan. His weight was trivial when added to her own, so she covered the distance in short order.

Mistress Odera had seen her coming and opened the cargo-slot into the guard's quarters, climbing in to be ready to receive the man.

Tala hoisted him up, into the waiting arms of several guards who'd been off-duty and who had come to help Mistress Odera when she'd called. Rane was there as well, and he looked almost violently unhappy at having been confined to the wagon.

Millennial Mage, 3 - Binding

Mistress Odera nodded in thanks to Tala, then asked a question with the tone of a command. "Is the magic still active?"

"No, Mistress. All the power's been used. No active workings that I could detect."

After a moment's hesitation, Mistress Odera nodded again. "Please, get the arm and shield. I'll need to examine them after I help him." She then turned to Rane. "Get back outside and keep a perimeter clear. We should be safe, but a false sense of safety is one of the great killers in this world."

"Yes, Mistress." Rane dropped out and took off at a jog to get in front of the cargo wagon to begin his patrol. He didn't seem to want to risk his horse for the moment.

Tala, for her part, turned and ran back for the severed arm. *I have to give Mistress Odera a hand.*

She chuckled at the dark joke, the thought cracking through her panicked calm. *I'm alive… We're all alive.*

Chapter: 31
A Calm, Uneventful Evening

Tala had no trouble finding the guard's severed arm, nor the shield to which it was strapped.

It lay near the center of a circle of crystalline grass and dust. *This is here because of me... He lost his arm because of me.*

That was silly, of course; he was only still alive because she'd cut his arm free.

He had to tell me to.

Even so, she'd saved his life.

She grimaced, shaking off the notion and examining the area. *The magics only affected living matter.*

The guard's shield, though made of wood, must have been too far from its time as part of a tree to qualify because it simply had geological growths across most of its surface. The underlying material seemed mostly intact. *Except the gaping holes that those birds punched through...*

There had been a terrifying amount of power in those little creatures.

Tala grabbed the shield up and turned back, jogging after the retreating wagons.

A moment later, she slowed to a brisk walk and felt her hair bouncing and swaying oddly. *Right!*

She ran her free hand through it, feeling crystals and shorn ends. She shuddered again. *That was really close.* She pulled out her comb and experimentally ran it through her jagged hair. It worked as she'd hoped, pulling the crystal out like it usually did to water. True, in some places that meant tearing the hair, but that was okay.

A moment later, her hair was clear of the magically grown material, and she activated some of the scripts on her scalp, causing her hair to return to the proper length. *There.* With that bit of vanity handled, she took a moment to examine herself and her grisly burden.

Tala, herself, was fine. She'd dismissed all of her void-channels save the one to her body, once her leathers were topped off.

Kit.

She stuck her hand into the belt pouch and created a second void-channel to feed it. The dimensional storage guzzled power.

Almost empty? As Tala thought about it, that made sense. *Kit likely had to shift itself out of the way of quite a few attacks.* She once again was grateful that she'd chosen a storage item with some self-preservation built in. *That's right, Tala. Never forget that self-preservation is key.*

She pushed away the reminder of Mistress Odera's words. *I'm not afraid to live.* Now was hardly the time for such thoughts.

With Kit refilled, Tala looked at the shield and now-mineralized limb. *Every part of it was restructured. How can that even happen?* It should have taken much more power than could have been imparted by such a small creature or in such a brief time.

Multiple strikes? There had been several, obviously, but no, that wasn't the cause. She'd seen the magics feeding on the guard's internal power, that which was coming from his own gate.

What would have happened if it had reached that gate, his soul?

She had no way of knowing, and if she was being honest, she wasn't sure she wanted to know.

I hope Terry came through alright. She had no reason to expect otherwise, but it was still worth checking. "Terry?" She called out loudly enough for her voice to carry, without the utterance being a true shout.

Terry flickered into being beside her. He was as tall as a horse, and he stared at the shield with obvious interest.

"No, Terry. This isn't for eating."

He shook himself.

"Not what you were thinking?"

More shaking.

"Curious about the magics?"

He bobbed.

"Yeah, me too. I'll let you know what Mistress Odera finds out if you aren't around to hear it."

He glanced at her, then, quick as a blink, he was on her shoulder, smaller than most cats. He head-bumped her cheek before curling up.

"Thank you, Terry. I'm glad you're safe, too."

*   *   *

The last hour of the day's traveling passed without further incident.

Mistress Odera didn't have the ability to regrow the guard's arm, but she was able to treat, preserve, and prep the stump for the regeneration of that limb once they reached Makinaven. The other guards had already arranged to fulfill the man's duties until then; having the 'extra' guards on this route made that a trivial thing.

I hope the need isn't a herald of things to come…

The crystal remaining after the tiny birds' magic completed its working was just mundane crystal, similar to that found within a geode, at least that was what Mistress Odera told Tala.

Millennial Mage, 3 - Binding

Once the injured guard's health was assured, a large contingent of off-duty guards did a quick, wide-ranging sweep to gather the bolts that had been fired at the crystal birds, so they could be used later.

Mistress Odera had a tablet, and she'd used it to advise the Caravanner's Guild, at large, of the possibility of a new fount in the region.

The Mage was *very* glad that she didn't have to inform Tala or Rane about the founts. She let them know that, in all likelihood, a high-level Archon would be sent to investigate at some point soon. At worst, caravans would have to be directed wide of the area for a time, adding significantly to the already uncertain route.

Tala, for her part, spent most of the hour alone, atop the cargo wagon, keeping an even closer eye on their surroundings.

When they finally stopped, Tala was introduced to a new horror.

Instead of being able to relax through dinner and the evening, she was required to increase her vigilance as every passenger was allowed out of their cargo-slot to get some fresh air and stretch their legs, while the last of dinner was prepared and served.

Unlike previous caravans, there was no wagon circle to provide even the illusion of separation from the Wilds, nor to corral passengers, when they were prone to wander.

The two wagons were spaced to create a somewhat distinct space, and a few tables were set up there, keeping the people mostly contained. The only saving grace was that it was fairly cold out in the open, and the lightly falling snow added to that incentive for quick retreats to the safety and warmth of the wagon.

She only had to shepherd two passengers back when they walked too far out. It gave her a new view on the headache she must have caused the guards in her previous venture.

Finally, every passenger was back in their cargo-slot for the night, and Tala had finally gotten her dinner. Again, it was a much larger portion than anyone else had been given.

Bless you, Brand. Thank you for taking care of me, even when you aren't here. Maybe, when she was filthy rich, she should hire him as her personal chef... *Lissa could be a good assistant, too.*

Tala took her time, finishing her third, miniature, chicken pot-pie. The hot food allowed her to relax just a bit more as she kept her gaze moving over their surroundings. *What a day. I'll need to thank the head cook for this, too.*

"You know, you humans are so... fragile."

Tala whipped around, staring at the figure standing on the other end of the wagon top.

What caught her attention at first, aside from someone suddenly appearing behind her in the Wilds, was that his eyes were blood.

No comparison held the weight of truth, save to say that his eyes were spheres of fresh, liquid blood, unbroken save small circular scabs in place of pupils.

Meeting that gaze, she felt frozen to the spot.

Around his eyes, true-black, smooth skin forced the orbs into stark contrast, making their deep shades seem almost to glow. Subtle hints of gray lines ran under that skin in patterns very like spell-lines but somehow utterly different—like seeing her own language written with the phonetic alphabet. The concepts seemed familiar while remaining utterly opaque to her interpretation.

Why does he look familiar? Her magesight was screaming at her, and she finally registered what it was saying. *He doesn't have a gate.*

Instead, he was drawing in power from the surrounding air and burning it within himself. The ratios were incredibly off-kilter. He was using massively more than he could draw in from the relatively magic-poor air.

"I saw your beacon of power. Thank you for that. I'd have hated to miss your departure." He smiled, his perfectly white teeth flashing in the fading light. "I love your eyes, by the way. You definitely lived up to the potential I saw in you." He shook his head and clucked his tongue, once. "That said, I must admit, I misjudged you." His voice had a strange resonance, a clarity like a trumpet sounding on a frozen winter's morning.

"Do I know you?"

He laughed lightly, a sound like a steep mountain stream, splattered in flesh and burbling with blood.

How can someone even make that sound?

"We met… briefly." He gave a half-smile. "I'd thought you would be reckless enough to profit me." He glanced away, seeming to be trying to catch sight of something in the distance, off to the north.

"You think I'm not reckless enough?" That thought broke through the odd, strange horror of the situation.

He refocused on her. "Hmm? No. You are, if anything, more reckless than I'd thought, but for some reason, you aren't reckless on things that *matter*."

"I'm… sorry?" She definitely felt the overwhelming desire to apologize properly, to abase herself, but she resisted. *I should be sorry for inconveniencing this creature. Why am I resisting?*

He waved dismissively. "I'm just trying to decide if it would be worth breaking the bond between your body and soul."

Tala instantly had Flow in her hand, three void-channels holding it strongly in the form of a sword. "You will not." She was utterly certain of that.

Does the bond really matter? What was happening to her thoughts?

The light of day was fading quickly, but at that moment, sunlight stabbed through distant clouds to brightly illuminate those directly overhead, bathing the two figures, standing atop the cargo wagon in reflected light. In that new illumination, the silver-ine lines on the being's skin came into greater view. He was frowning. "Oh, don't be tiresome. Your only task here is to let me pick your brain and answer my questions so I can make a properly informed decision." He leaned forward just slightly, looking her up and down, slowly. "That is a fascinating Way you're using there. It looks like it lacerated your soul as you learned it." He laughed again, and Tala found her grip weakening. "Some scars can be useful, I suppose."

Why would I want to hurt such a being? She shook her head, detecting the subtle pressure on her mind. *How?* The scripts around her eyes were guzzling power, trying to keep *something* out, and they were failing. *Wait, why hasn't anyone else noticed him?*

She tore her eyes away and looked around. She was horrified to see that every creature in sight was frozen in place, whether human, ox, horse, or Terry. By their slight swaying and blank expressions, it appeared that they were somehow being subdued in a nonsensical state rather than physically restrained by some means.

Tala closed her eyes, then, and felt her thoughts clear. *He was getting in through my eyes.* Were her palms going to be an issue? She desperately hoped not and clenched her hands into tighter fists, Flow firmly locked in her right hand.

"What is this? You are thinking on your own volition?" Light steps sounded as the being approached.

Tala struck out blindly with Flow and heard a sharp, hissing intake of breath.

"How can you attack me?"

Millennial Mage, 3 - Binding

Tala dropped into a defensive stance, bracing herself as well as she could for attacks from an unknown direction.

"You dare? I gave you the form you need, the path to power, the path to become *useful*, and you take it for yourself, for your own use. I come to talk, and you choose violence?"

Her head snapped to the side as she was struck with a blow that would have felled one of the caravan's oxen.

Tala rolled with the hit, moving the bare minimum to orient on her attacker, sweeping Flow in a covering circle to cut at whatever had hit her.

"No. You are different than before. You have done *things* to yourself. Yours is not a useful insanity. This cannot be allowed." There was a finality to the statement.

Tala didn't even register the hit before she was airborne.

As expected, she came down faster than anything on this world had any right to, and she skipped across the plains, her body digging furrows in the soil with each skipping impact. Her endingberry power was running dangerously low.

She almost smiled as she was reminded of her 'fight' with the cyclops. But Grediv wasn't here to take advantage of the distraction she provided this time. She was on her own.

I can't fight like this. I have to risk it. Her eyes snapped open, and she oriented herself, vaulting back to her feet, and spinning in a circle until she saw the caravan in the near distance, a figure standing on the cargo wagon's top.

He was more of a beacon than Tala had been with all her void-channels dumping power outward.

The aura underlying the power was a deep, green-blue.

Rust me to slag. How had she not noticed that earlier?

With each passing moment, however, the aura was shifting more towards green.

He's losing power by the second. I just need to outlast him. She didn't need her eyes open to do that. Before she could close her eyes, however, the option was taken from her.

Without any appearance of movement, the figure was before her once more, hands on either side of her head.

"It seems that you would take *much* too much power to kill or more time than I have. Even so, I cannot leave you with memory of this."

The scripts around her eyes were overwhelmed in an instant, pushed aside rather than burned away, and try as she might, she couldn't overcome the compulsion that prevented her from closing her eyes, not even to blink.

His face filled her vision.

"Interesting use of iron. So that's how you were able to move so freely." The sides of her head blazed with heat for a brief moment before iron dust showered down on her shoulders.

The being briefly flicked each hand away, then back to her head, clearing the limb of rust. Then, there was a renewed pulse of power.

Tala felt something try to invade her brain, but her very being rose up against the assault. She used every scrap of strength she could draw upon, barely managing to shelter her mind: a pebble before a hurricane.

Even so, the edges of her mind weren't set, yet. Her magesight, coupled with her mental scripts, allowed her to watch, helpless, as her short-term memory was shredded into—

Why am I panicking? What was that daydream, again? Tala tried to shake off the lingering vestiges of an overactive imagination but found her head locked in place, blood filling her vision. *Not a figment?* Brief shreds of memory came floating back. *It was real?! It—*

Millennial Mage, 3 - Binding

Power washed through her mind, and her eyes closed of their own volition.

There was an odd grunt and something that was clearly a curse in a language she didn't know. A voice she'd never heard before muttered under their breath, "How heavy are you?"

Her mind was hit, once more, and her thoughts—

There was a pulse of power, quickly fading into the distance, and Tala's eyes snapped open.

She was lying on the ground, staring up at falling snow and clouds, which were just losing the last light of day.

Where am I?

"Mistress Tala?" Mistress Odera was calling her.

Tala jumped up to her feet, looking around. *Why am I so far from the caravan?*

Mistress Odera was standing near the cargo wagon, looking up at its top, calling out. "Mistress Tala!"

Tala began to jog the couple of hundred yards back to the wagon.

On the way back, she wove around the deep, irregularly spaced furrows in the earth. *What happened?*

She examined within herself and found the bulk of her expected endingberry power was absent; only the barest vestiges remained. *When did I use that up?*

She called out to Mistress Odera, and the other Mage turned towards her, irritation plain on the older woman's face. Even so, she remained silent until Tala stopped beside her. "Why did you leave your post, Mistress?"

"I… I don't think I did."

Mistress Odera paused at that, seeming to understand the depth behind Tala's words. "What do you mean?"

Tala looked over her shoulder. "There is evidence that *something* sent me flying from the wagon top. Some of my defenses are drastically drained, and the earth is churned in a line from the cargo wagon to where I was lying."

Mistress Odera's hands flicked out, and a bubble of power quickly built before fully encapsulating the caravan's campsite. *Her shield.* "What did this?"

"I don't know, and I didn't lose consciousness. I have inscriptions to correct that, and they always notify me when they do. I believe I felt a power fading, retreating before I came to awareness…"

Mistress Odera's eyes were moving across their surroundings. "There are the faintest, lingering traces of *something* with power, here." Her face snapped towards Tala. "What happened to your protection, child?"

Tala frowned as Terry appeared on her shoulder, crooning lightly. "What do you mean?"

"Your iron is gone from your head."

Tala swallowed reflexively, feeling her face with her off hand. *That's not good.*

Terry bumped her cheek with the top of his head.

"No, Terry, I don't know what's going on…" She had the lingering impression of blood. "I'm not bleeding, am I?" She examined herself, and Mistress Odera gave her a once-over as well.

"No, you are perfectly healthy."

The two of them climbed back to the top of the cargo wagon, and after another sweep of their surroundings, Mistress Odera let her shield fall. Tala, for her part, had pulled out an iron salve bar and was desperately working the substance in, all over her head. *I can't stay defenseless.*

The older woman sat heavily. "Something happened, of that much I am certain, but I cannot determine what. I can see everyone who's supposed to be out here, but we should check the passengers against the manifests."

"What's going on?" She'd done a hasty job of her reapplication, but it would have to be good enough for now.

"I wish I knew, Mistress. We've been losing caravans a bit more regularly around Bandfast, in the last half year or so."

"More regularly?"

"Closer to one in a hundred, as opposed to one in a thousand. Though some of that is extrapolation."

"That's… a big difference."

Mistress Odera barked a mirthless laugh. "Yes. Yes, it is."

Tala nodded to herself. "I'll check in with each exposed cargo-slot."

"Send Master Rane to me when you can. I'd like to pick his brain."

Something about that made Tala twitch, but she dismissed the feeling. "Yes, Mistress."

Mistress Odera gave her a long look. "Whatever happened, I am glad that you survived. We might just be able to fill in some gaps in our knowledge because of it."

Tala almost told her about the script at the base of her own neck, which would have recorded a lot of what transpired for Holly's use, but something made Tala think that voicing anything about its existence would be a mistake. Instead, Tala simply gave Mistress Odera a respectful bow and dropped off the side of the wagon, Terry clinging to her shoulder as she fell.

All I wanted was a calm, uneventful evening. She shook her head. Now was not the time for weakness; she had work to do.

Chapter: 32
I'm Hardly Standard

Tala went to each cargo-slot and asked the head servant to do a headcount and compare it to their rosters. Something had her extra nervous, so she asked a secondary servant to watch the one she'd tasked for any odd behavior. *Never hurts to be sure.*

Rane had been in the first cargo-slot she'd begun the process in, and she'd sent him to Mistress Odera.

Less than ten minutes after she'd opened her eyes in the wilderness, inexplicably away from the caravan, Tala's magesight screamed a warning. With a thought, Flow was in her hand in the form of a sword. She spun, lashing out even as she called out a warning.

"Incoming—!" Her call cut off for three reasons.

First, her magesight registered the aura: Reforged. The being before her radiated a perfectly controlled, deep blue aura, clearly a bit more purple than true blue. It didn't radiate out from him, but instead, it was held precisely at the surface of his skin almost like a badge of authority or office.

Second, the person was obviously human. Her magesight held that up before her mind in a way that seemed like it should be unable to be faked. The very magic within him *felt* human. The gate blazing forth was a fairly strong indicator as well.

Third, the man perfectly countered her actions. One hand caught Tala's own, holding Flow at bay. More importantly, his second hand rested against her lips, rendering her unable to continue making sound.

"You are for humanity, yes, Bound? You are not corrupted?" His voice was soft but thrumming with power.

Rane vaulted from the wagon behind Tala, somehow utterly silent in his sudden assault, Force already whipping towards the newly arrived Archon.

The Archon's lips quirked, and Tala saw a section of inscriptions on the man's bare neck flicker to life.

Rane froze mid-air, wrapped in a uniform, dim glow. At the same time, three quarrels jerked to a stop in a perfect cluster, hovering three feet from the man's back.

The man's smile grew. "Impressive response."

Mistress Odera walked up to the edge of the roof, surveying the scene below, and sighed. "Reforged, please forgive these young ones."

The Archon released Tala's hand and lips, stepping back and to the side. "No harm was done, and their reactions do them credit." He shifted his shoulders, and the spell-forms still active on his neck altered slightly, causing Rane to slowly drift down and lightly settle on his feet. The bolts dropped from the air.

"Tell the guards to stand down, please. I don't wish to waste metal or time continuing to counter them."

Tala cleared her throat, sheathing Flow but remaining ready. "Stand down!" She met the new arrival's gaze. He had not been at her raising, but she'd been told that most of the more powerful had not been. "I am human, yes."

His eyes snapped to her, narrowing. "That is not what I asked."

She swallowed involuntarily, fighting the urge to take a step back at the intensity. "Uhhh... ummm... yes? Yes, I am for humanity?" *What does that even mean?*

Mistress Odera began climbing down. "They are newly raised."

The man grunted. "So, you've not yet faced an arcane…" His voice faded. "No. I definitely sense the lingering feel of a Revered." He grinned widely. "Though, it was practically Honored when it left."

Tala frowned. "What?"

He gave a half-smile. "You have advanced magesight? Yes? Good. That is an arcane whose aura is blue, fading back to green."

"Isn't that Reforged and Paragon?"

"For humans, yes. Arcanes function differently. No gate. Different advancement." He shrugged. "But I'm not here to educate you."

That was… surprisingly informative, even so. Tala frowned. *What's his game?*

He looked to Mistress Odera, now standing on the ground near the wagon. "Mistress, you are the lead protector for this caravan. Mistress Odera, correct?"

"I am."

"You are a Forbidden, correct?"

Mistress Odera took a deep breath, then nodded, her eyes remaining fixed on the man. "I am."

"Good, having to temper my words for a usual non-Archon would have been… wasteful."

She grunted, giving a slight bow. "As you say. Thank you for coming."

"I am Master Xeel. A powerful arcane was detected near here; we had to respond." He shrugged. "Tell me what happened."

'We' had to respond? Are the Archons monitoring the whole of the human Wilds, or is it just because we are so close to Bandfast?

Mistress Odera shook her head. "We don't know. No one remembers seeing anything, but we're missing close to a quarter-hour of time if I'm right in my guess. We are still doing a headcount, so I can't swear no one is missing.

Millennial Mage, 3 - Binding

Mistress Tala, here, was thrown from the wagon top. She was on watch and woke up over there, with no memory of being attacked." She pointed to where Tala had been.

The Reforged nodded, glancing that way and seeming to take in the entire scene. "Quite a bit of lingering power, there." He turned back to Tala. "How did you survive?"

"No memory." She cocked her eyebrow. "We did just say that."

Xeel snorted. "Let me rephrase. Why would an arcane leave you alive?"

Tala felt a chill. *Something to do with blood...?* Xeel's eyes narrowed, but he didn't comment. Tala shook herself, then responded. "I honestly don't know."

Rane stepped forward. "Mistress Tala has bent most of her magic toward survivability." He glanced to her, motioning for her to expound.

She sighed. "I also use a complementing power that reinforces me. When I came back to consciousness, over there, my reserves of that power were nearly dry."

Xeel frowned, looking more intently at Tala. She felt her iron salve warm under the force of his magesight if just slightly. Finally, he grunted. "Is that endingberry power?" He barked a laugh. "That must've made them rusting *furious.*"

Tala cocked her head. "Why?"

He grinned. "The first humans to successfully rebel used endingberry power to stand up to the arcane enforcers that were sent after them. Most of us can't use it these days, but it will be interesting to see how you turn out. Did you build your entire schema around using them?"

That's a bit rude to ask, but I suppose it's relevant. "Well, I sought my power based on the mythos, yes. Though, I didn't know that endingberries were the basis at the time."

"Ahh, fascinating." He scratched under the right side of his chin. "Might get you in trouble in the forest, depending on how much you rely on that defense." He hesitated, glancing towards Mistress Odera. "But we are getting off topic." He sighed. "If there is no memory of the encounter, it was likely a Conceptual Guide." He spat to the side. "I'll need to examine each of you for programming." He grimaced in an almost childlike way. The face he made reminded Tala of one of her brothers being told to clean up a particularly odorous mess. "I'm guessing you have quite a few passengers?"

"More than two hundred."

Xeel sighed, again. "Well, I'll see to the mundanes first. You three last. That sound good?"

Tala felt herself relax. *Good. I can take a minute to get my thoughts in order...* She frowned. *Wait. That doesn't make sense—*

Xeel's hands were suddenly on either side of her head, light flooding from his palms, locking her in place.

She gasped, arching before the influx of power. There was no damage being done, nothing for the endingberries or her defensive inscriptions to resist.

In less than three seconds, Xeel had stepped back, spinning and throwing out hazy beams of light, which caught Mistress Odera and Rane. Xeel had directed one hand at each. Magical light, Xeel's power, swept through the two much more quickly than it had through Tala.

"You two are clean. I apologize for the little lie. I needed to catch you off guard, and having you expect me to examine you later was sufficient for that." He turned back towards Tala. As he did so, Mistress Odera and Rane looked her way as well. "You've had a chunk ripped out of your short-term memory—if I interpret the lingering effects correctly." He seemed hesitant. His eyes flicked towards the other Mages, but finally, he grunted, shaking his head. "There seems to be something else, lingering. An older effect, put in place at least a month, maybe a month and a half ago."

Rane frowned, and Mistress Odera pursed her lips.

That timing would place her at the Academy or newly arrived in Bandfast... right? *Maybe it was right after I left, on my first contract?* "What are you saying, Master Xeel?" She felt oddly disconnected like she was in a dream.

"I'm saying that you've crossed paths with an arcane before this evening. It's hard to tell them apart at times, but I would bet that it was the same one."

"What...?"

Rane stepped closer. "What do you mean?"

"There's nothing wrong with you, Mistress Tala. There is nothing lingering within you, waiting to activate. You are as changed as you will ever be, barring another encounter. You are human and for humanity." He smiled consolingly. "That said, two encounters with the same arcane in so short a time means that you might see it again." He sighed. "We'll try to keep a closer eye on your routes, but we can't guard you night and day." He shrugged. "Not much else we can do, right now."

"So... I've been altered?"

Xeel shrugged again. "Nothing so overt. You might have had a memory added or removed. Your personality, or thought process, might have been slightly shifted, or you might have had your magic nudged one way or another. Though, given your choices"—he grinned widely—"I would say that no arcane pushed you towards your specific spell-form schema or endingberry use, at least not intentionally."

"That's something at least."

"Now, I do need to examine the rest of the caravan. After that, I'll stand guard tonight to make sure it doesn't return, but tomorrow, I have to deal with that crystal-attuned fount." He scratched the side of his own head. "Well, and any arcanous beasts that have gone through it." He grimaced, but it passed quickly.

Mistress Odera bowed. "Thank you, Master Xeel. Taking night watch is a kindness, and I'm glad that our report reached the proper eyes."

Xeel nodded slightly. Then, he glanced to Tala. "Tell your... friend that he can come out and that his attempts to watch for an opening are pointless." He had a twinkle in his eyes as he said the last.

Friend...? Oh! "Terry."

Terry appeared beside her, his head level with hers, his eyes fixed on Xeel.

"You're a big one, aren't you?"

Terry hunkered down slightly and let out a thrumming whistle. Tala rested her hand on his neck. *What's going on?*

Xeel held a casual stance, but he was clearly focused on Terry, probably more than he had been on any of them since he arrived. He tsked. "Huh... I thought we'd expunged that particular fount." He frowned, his magesight clearly active. "No... you aren't a new one." His eyes moved to Tala. "Is he in your care?" The question was firm and felt like it had a depth that Tala couldn't begin to understand.

"He is with me... yes? What's going on?"

His eyes returned to Terry. "Some arcanous abilities are too dangerous to allow to linger. Like the one you encountered earlier today." Xeel tilted his head towards Terry. "If I'm reading his magic and age right, he is a remnant of another such. My understanding was that we expunged them all."

Terry hissed.

Not good. Tala slipped her hand over to the other side of Terry's neck and pulled him sideways against her.

Millennial Mage, 3 - Binding

He jerked slightly, then twisted his head to look at her, a query clear in his eyes, along with pain. "He is with me, my partner. Is that going to be a problem?" *What do you want of me, Terry? I can't help you kill him.*

Xeel hesitated, then shook his head. "No. It should be fine. If he were a true menace, he'd have been noticed and hunted down decades ago."

Or he's good at hiding and escaping. "When were the arcanous animals and fount... expunged?" She did not like that word used for those who had been like Terry.

Xeel seemed to take a moment to consider. "A hundred years?" He frowned. "No... it was near Manaven waning... Two hundred? Give or take."

Tala let out a long breath. "Two hundred years." *And hundreds of miles... Has he moved with humanity? Staying near our cities? Why?* She stroked Terry's feathers. "Are you alright?" Terry gave her a long look, then blipped to her shoulder, curling up and snuggling against her neck.

Xeel grunted. "I've work to do. I'll take up watch in half an hour. Please plan to sleep then so my time isn't wasted. The forests have been more active of late, and you'll want to be well-rested for that part of your journey."

Each of the Mage Protectors nodded in return. "Thank you."

*   *   *

Tala woke in a cold sweat. The dreams were back.

She sat up with a groan, both from her own lips and the metal frame of her new bed. *Why won't these leave me be?*

Terry wasn't in her room, and she was utterly alone in the dark.

Cursing quietly to herself, she stood, buckling on her belt and locking her door as she headed outside.

All the guards were sleeping; Xeel was on guard duty, and everyone was taking advantage.

Where is Terry? He wasn't in the common space, and she didn't see him when she pulled open the door, exiting the cargo-slot.

It was deep night, somewhere between midnight and dawn.

Tala walked outside, her bare feet crunching on the snow and frozen grass. It wasn't unpleasant, not yet, so she didn't pull her shoes from Kit.

"Couldn't sleep?"

Tala spun, finding not-Xeel standing behind her. Oh, it looked like him, but Tala's magesight told her that the form was made purely of light, so looks were all it had. *Well, and sound.* "Illusion?"

The image shrugged. "I'm on the wagon top if you prefer face-to-face."

She looked up to where the man was standing, looking the other way... fifteen feet away. "You could have just said something." She addressed the man, not the image.

"True, and you could be less suspicious." The illusion continued to speak.

She hesitated. "Do you mean I shouldn't be so suspicious of you, or that I should act less suspicious?"

"Both."

Tala glanced back and forth between the illusion and the man on the roof. "Can you... not do this? It's really odd."

The not-Xeel vanished, and Xeel looked down at her. "You could just climb up. I did offer you that."

Tala huffed but did as he suggested. When she reached the top, she looked around, taking in the surrounding, white landscape. "Winter's a bit early this year."

"Not too much earlier than average. Isn't the Academy farther north?"

"Yes, but it's an island."

"Ahhh, right. I often forget how much the ocean affects local weather."

"So… seen anything interesting?"

He shrugged. "Most arcanous beasts prefer the daytime."

I know some striking, avian exceptions… "So, it's safer at night?"

He hesitated. "You know… no? Those which do roam in the dark hours tend to be more dangerous, but they are also usually better at picking weak targets. So, caravans are probably safer at night…" He shrugged. "So… yes?"

"That's not really an answer."

"Worthwhile questions rarely have a single, simple answer."

Tala grunted.

"So, why are you up? You could sleep another couple of hours, at least."

Nightmares. "Don't need as much sleep anymore."

He gave her a long look, then turned his attention back to their surroundings. "Have you decided whether or not you want to continue to hurt everyone around you in your quest for adventurous death?"

Tala spun on him. "Excuse me?"

He held up a slate. "It's boring for the moment, and you seemed interesting, so I read your file. You do dangerous things, then let others dig you out or cover for you. Seems to work out well for you, across the board."

"That's hardly fair."

"Oh? Maybe not, then. It is probably less-than-accurate to say you want to die, but you do seem to have a hard time grasping how your actions will affect those around you."

"You seem very free with your opinions."

Xeel shrugged. "I have perspective and a lack of care for your feelings." He smiled her way. "Please don't mistake my words for distaste. Many of your accomplishments are quite impressive. You just aren't great at the wise application of your... ideas." He nodded. "Yes, you need to better temper your ideas in the fire of reason." He snorted at himself. "Rust me, I'm getting old." He shook his head. "All that to say, Mistress Odera will be good for you."

"You know her?"

"Hmmm? No. I read her file, too. Her interestingness is less... densely packed, but that is a feature of a long life, I suppose. The woman who campaigned to get the two of you paired knew what she was about."

Woman? Lyn... She had no reason to believe it had been Lyn, but it fit. "So, do Archons just wander the Wilds, showing up after the danger has passed?"

He frowned at her. "You've encountered another Archon in the Wilds? That wasn't in your file."

"I guess I didn't tell anyone, after the fact."

"This was when you were snatched from your last caravan?"

"Yeah."

"Who was it?"

"What?"

"Who was the Archon that you met?"

"She just told me to call her Mistress."

"Like... the title?"

"Yeah."

"That's a bit... arrogant."

Tala chuckled. "Yeah, that's what I thought, too."

"She didn't return you to your caravan. That would have been noted. What did she want?" He sounded like he was trying to sound casual, but Tala felt an intensifying of his focus at the question.

"She wanted me to serve her. Offered to buy out my contracts and all that."

Xeel grunted. "She must have liked what she saw. Maybe she saw herself in you." He raised an eyebrow towards her.

"Yes, yes. I'm arrogant." Tala rolled her eyes.

"Do you disagree?"

Tala hesitated. "No?" She sighed. "All through the academy, I asked questions others said were worthless and did things in ways that were 'idiotic.'"

"Your choice of almost purely defensive inscriptions, and your propensity for iron?"

"Among other things. 'Gravity isn't meant for precise targeting, Tala.' 'Why do you want to be protected from a knife? If someone's that close, you already failed. Why can't you just accept the consequences of that failure?' And on, and on."

"Ahh, yes. You showed them."

Tala glared at the man, then threw her hands up. "Why am I even talking to you?"

"Because you couldn't sleep, and in all likelihood, you will never see me again after tonight. I am a safe sounding board."

"Oh?"

"Or so you would think."

Tala grimaced. "My file?"

"I excel at recall and note-taking."

Tala flopped down, causing the reinforced wagon to rock. "Why do you care?"

"Because you have the makings of either a great asset or an incredible liability for humanity."

"And you care about humanity."

"Dear child, that is the only thing I care about. Those who had other concerns are gone." Something in the way he said 'child' had none of the condescension that she'd felt when others addressed her that way. It had the flavor of a grandparent, bending down to pick her up after a fall.

Well, I might as well ask him some things. He seems much freer with information than most. "You are moving from blue to violet. What does that mean?"

Xeel hesitated at the sudden change of subject, then shrugged. "I am in process of re-forging my soul."

"I don't know what that means."

He smirked. "Nor should you."

"Wait, blue is 'Reforged.' Shouldn't you be done?"

"That refers to the Reforging of the body."

"Which you also won't explain."

"Which I also won't explain."

Tala rolled her eyes. "Why all the secrecy? Why not just tell people?"

"If I explained how to reforge one's soul, would you attempt it?"

"...No?"

He gave her a long look.

"Fine, that's fair. But I'm hardly standard."

He laughed. "You are not as special as you might think. Much of what you have done is *precisely* why we've set things up as we have. You've been lucky; you've gotten some good advice along the way; and you've built yourself specifically to mitigate the fallout from your bad decisions, at least on yourself." He gave her a pointed look.

"I never mean to cause anyone else difficulty."

"Do you think about others at all?"

"Yes?"

"I believe you."

She glared. "You're a rusting wonderful person."

"I'm glad you think so."

Tala really didn't know what to think of Xeel. He seemed, at the same time, to care way more than he should and not at all. "Why are you really here?"

"To deal with the crystal fount and respond to an arcane."

Millennial Mage, 3 - Binding

"But why you?"

"I was available and of a power with the detected threat. We sometimes send groups, when only lesser Archons are available, but it doesn't usually end as cleanly."

Tala thought about the fight she'd witnessed at a great distance. "Are... are we losing?"

Xeel gave her a different long, long look, then shook his head. "No, not in the sense that you mean."

"Then, in what sense are we losing?"

He snorted a chuckle. "Do you really want to know?"

"Of course." *Yeah... maybe I don't...*

"I don't think you do."

"Just tell me." His seeming reading of her thoughts was getting irritating. *Or I'm just not that hard of a person to read...*

He smiled knowingly. "Do you know how many Archons humanity has?"

"Oh... slag... no?"

He laughed at that. "Fair enough. I'm not sure I could put an exact count to it either. But that's not the point. For every human Archon, there are at least ten with that power from the other nearby races."

"Then... how?"

"How does humanity endure?"

She nodded.

"Most don't care about us."

"Then... why does it matter?"

"Because they would care if we struck back against those who would oppress us. Hence, the Wilds." He gestured around himself. "They struggle to endure in such low-magic zones, so we armor ourselves against those truly hostile to us and endure."

"That sounds... exhausting."

"Truer words, my dear." He let out a sigh, and Tala truly looked at him for the first time.

He was taller than her, with a solid build, but not a bulky one. His close-cropped hair was blond-gray, and his face was clean-shaven. He lacked wrinkles, but something about him still almost screamed out the years that he had lived. His presence was heavy.

His Mage's robes were a simple dark brown, and he wore a plain copper band around his left ring finger.

"How long?"

"Have I lived?"

"I was going to ask how long you've been fighting, but either works."

He smiled at that. "I became Bound and joined the fight"—he seemed to consider—"I think it was nearly sixteen hundred years ago." His smile softened. "We've come so far since then."

Tala's eyes widened. "How?"

Xeel shrugged. "Once one is Refined, aging ceases to matter, and if you don't die in the fight?" He smiled. "You simply persist. One day, I'll meet my match and die defending humanity, but whether it's in a day or millennia?" He shrugged again. "We'll see."

Tala was plucking at her elk leathers, contemplating. The fight was important. Arcane encounters were notable. She should tell him. *It's not worth it. Not really. I should just leave him be.*

"What is it? It's not like we're being circumspect here."

"How sure are you as to the timeline of my previous encounter with the Arcane?"

"Fairly, why?" His tone once again conveyed an intent focus on her answer.

"Because, if you were right, then I was either at the academy or in Bandfast."

Xeel stared at her for a long moment.

She did *not* like his silence. She felt the need to fill the void. "That… shouldn't be possible, right?"

"No… no, it should not." He gave her a long look. "How sure are you?"

"The first time I entered the Wilds, in my life, was thirty-six or thirty-seven days ago."

"That is in the window of my estimate…" Xeel shook his head. "I'm more willing to believe that the signs have faded more quickly than average than that an arcane was within one of our cities." He tsked. "Still, we can't discount the possibility."

Tala watched the ancient Archon as he processed through what she'd said.

Finally, he smiled. "Thank you for making sure I noticed that. Your file showed your activities in general, but I didn't connect those two things specifically." He shook his head once more. "You've given me much to think about."

Tala stood. "I'll leave you to it, then. Thank you for answering so many of my questions."

He waved her off. "I've never liked the secrecy we're forced into. I'm glad I could highlight some things that you should know." He gave her a firm look. "You are a key member of this caravan. Every action you take affects everyone in it. Please don't forget that."

She nodded, feeling that settle down on her shoulders, really, for the first time. *This isn't just a place to make money, Tala. These people are counting on you. Your pay for the work matters, but only if they survive.*

With that added burden, she climbed down the ladder and went to check around the wagon for Terry.

Chapter: 33
A Start

Tala trekked a circle through the light dusting of snow around the isolated wagons, anchored for a night in the wilds.

Terry was nowhere to be seen and didn't come when she called to him.

She almost tossed out a bit of jerky, but since he hadn't responded to her calls and wasn't coming to her as she held the bit of meat, she was fairly certain he wasn't watching.

For a brief moment, as she stared towards the forest in the distance, she thought her magesight highlighted several humanoid shapes, moving just inside the treeline. *Holly's enhancement of my magesight gave it quite a bit longer range...*

It was hard to tell, though, because of the sheer scale of the distant forest. If the shapes had been human in size, then those trees easily matched the descriptions she'd earlier doubted. *Almost a thousand feet tall...* True, if the creatures were a bit smaller than human, while being humanoid in shape, the comparative height would be lower, but even so, they were monumentally massive trees.

In reviewing the memory of seeing the figures, she decided that she hadn't been deluding herself; the creatures had been there. That said, they weren't human as they'd lacked gates.

Additionally, they were solidly below the Archon range of power. *So, not arcanes either.*

Millennial Mage, 3 - Binding

Arcanous humanoids? She knew there were quite a few beasts and monsters that appeared human-like, at least at a distance, and many were known denizens of the great southern forest. *That's probably what I saw.* She would probably have to help safeguard the caravan from many of those in the coming days.

She found herself fixating on the distant trees, trying to see more creatures within their depths. The recent, unremembered encounter with the arcane was making her jumpy.

She shook her head. *I don't need to sleep more tonight.* So, she started her day.

She didn't speak to Xeel as she climbed back up on the cargo wagon, charging each of the cargo-slots in turn.

That done, she dropped down, slamming into the earth and sending up a puff of powder that had somehow avoided being trampled into ice. *Snow's dry here.*

With no one to gawk—except Xeel, but he didn't really count—Tala moved through her physical exercises, working up a sweat with the complexity and difficulty despite the well-below-freezing air. As usual, balancing and the maintenance of proper form were often the hardest parts of the more advanced movements.

She mentally thanked the Wainwrights for having isolated the cargo-slots when she did her jumps. Try as she might, she couldn't land lightly enough to prevent the wagons, tables, and benches from shaking.

Xeel regarded her with an odd look when she began that series but quickly returned his attention to their surroundings.

Physical side complete, she moved through her magical, spiritual, and mental exercises. This included topping off all her magical items. *Except Terry's collar… I hope he's alright.* Thankfully, the collar was basically useless outside of the cities, and the ambient magic in the air was sufficient to keep it from becoming inert, while in the Wilds.

Personal item recharging done, she retreated into her room within the cargo-slot, locked the door, stripped down, and opened Kit wide on her floor.

Bath time.

The dimensional storage had accommodatingly created a depression, which was perfectly sized and shaped for her to soak in. Her hot water incorporator would provide enough water. *Luxury!*

She easily connected four void-channels to the incorporator, causing water to jet out, splashing across much of Kit's floor. Before Tala could temper the flow, the surface of the inset tub shifted, creating a modulated surface that somehow disrupted the incoming stream such that it didn't splash or reflect out.

"Thank you, Kit."

Kit did not respond.

With the modification, Tala risked connecting two more void-channels to the device, causing a marked increase in the rate, though not near the fifty percent she'd expect from a linear alteration of power. *Don't focus on the numbers, Tala.*

The splashing water had reminded her how close to boiling it really was, and so she pulled out her cold-water incorporator as well, moving two of the void-channels over.

With the added channels and second incorporator, the tub filled to a good level in no time, and Tala was soon lowering herself into the steaming bath. It was still far too close to boiling for most people, mainly because Kit's boundaries didn't seem to have any heat capacity or ability to absorb or impart thermal energy. Thus, the water could only cool by radiating heat up into the air.

Millennial Mage, 3 - Binding

The temperature would have been a problem without inscriptions, and even so, Tala had to be careful not to cook her brain. After cleansing herself, she let the heat work its way through her body, relaxing her muscles and helping them get the most from her workout and stretching. Finally, she could tell that the heat, even reduced, was getting to her, so she pulled out the cold-water incorporator again and lowered the temperature to a standard, more manageable level.

Huh… I wonder if using a dimensional storage, like Kit, for the oven box would allow for incorporator-based precision and baking? It was a thought.

As she lay there, she absentmindedly connected a void-channel to Kit, bringing the pouch's reserves quickly back to full, restoring the little it had used reshaping for her bath. *It would really be convenient to bond Kit…* She'd told Elnea that she'd allow the Archon to watch that bonding, though. *I could bond my elk leathers…* It just seemed too soon to bond something else. Grediv's books still wouldn't let her read any of them, and that implied that her soul was still settling after her step up as Archon. *Probably wisest to wait.* She sighed in resignation.

Now that she'd refilled Kit, Tala played with the void-channels themselves.

In addition to the one already connected to her body, she forged one to Flow; while her body couldn't handle the excess, her bond to Flow was still capable of growing stronger, so it accepted the extra power readily.

Relaxed and content, Tala modified the size of the channel leading to Flow. She'd fallen into a pattern of simply creating multiple channels if she needed more power, but that wasn't really required. Because of her one-sided practice, it took more focus to create a void-channel with twice the throughput when compared to just creating two, but she did *not* want to make that worse by leaning on a crutch of her own making.

In seemingly no time at all, the water began to discorporate, leaving Tala dry and clean, though there was a bit of dirty remnant in the lowest portion of the basin.

She climbed out of Kit, combed through her hair and braided it, then dressed for the day.

She walked out into the common space only to find it still empty. *It is still before dawn, and everyone's taking advantage of Xeel's presence.*

Tala sighed. *Great...*

Not wanting to wake anyone, she went back outside. Blessedly, it seemed that it was close enough to morning that the cooks were beginning their work; the chuckwagon was alive with activity.

I should check in with them. I know that Brand spoke to the head chef on my behalf. What was her name again? Tala searched back through her memory. *Amnin!* That was it.

Tala walked up to the open side of the wagon, frowning. *If they want to hide what's inside, why have the side open so often...?* She shrugged. She'd connect with the Culinary Guild more closely in the future, but that wasn't why she was here.

"Amnin, good morning!"

The woman leaned out from behind a set of shelves. "Mistress Tala?" She smiled. As she walked over, she gave varying instructions to the other cooks. Amnin then leaned on the counterlike portion of the opening in the wagon and looked slightly down at Tala. "Good morning. What can I do for you?"

"I noticed you all up, and I thought I'd say hi."

Amnin's smile widened. "Feeling a bit better than yesterday then?"

Tala hesitated. *Than yesterday?* Mistress Odera's admonition came back to her. *I guess I pushed those thoughts aside...* Her countenance must have fallen a bit because Amnin's smile dimmed a little.

"Oh, I'm sorry, Mistress. I didn't mean to remind you of whatever is getting you down."

Tala smiled and shrugged. "It's fine, Amnin. I do need to think about it."

The woman seemed to contemplate that briefly. "Wait there a moment." She stepped deeper into the wagon, and Tala heard the clink of plates and the pouring of liquid, among the other noises of a highly active kitchen. The chef returned shortly, bearing a jug and a plate. "Coffee and sweet-knots." She smiled. "These are from our test batch. We've eaten what we need to, and more are in the ovens."

Tala blinked up at the woman. "Why?"

Amnin smiled in return. "Pastries, coffee, and watching the sun rise over a beautiful landscape can help you work through all sorts of things." She held out the plate.

Tala felt her eyes water, just slightly. *She doesn't even know me, and she's being this kind.* Tala nodded, took the offered items, and smiled. "Thank you. I'll try that."

"Good. I'd join you, but I have a couple hundred people to feed in just under two hours. We've a lot to do."

"I'll leave you to it, then..." Tala nodded to herself. "Thank you."

"Go. Take some time to think."

Tala turned and went to the easternmost table to face the east with her plate and jug as her only companions. She had to brush some new-fallen snow from the seat and tabletop, but it hadn't been too much of an inconvenience. As she'd been about to sit on the bench, she remembered her weight. *Thankfully.*

She moved the bench aside and pulled out her folding seat, letting out a sigh as she settled down. It really was comfortable.

I'm too in my head.

"Well, then, talk to yourself, Tala."

She snorted a laugh at that. *Yeah, and make myself look crazier.*

"Which is more important, looking sane or being sane."

She hesitated at that. *I am a bit… off.*

"You think?"

Yes… actively.

"Don't sass yourself. It isn't useful."

Fine…

"So… do I want to be alive?"

Pressure and tingling in her nose and a tightening of her throat were the only response she could muster.

As she looked out over the snow-dusted plains, she took a deep drink of dark coffee and then a bite of one of the sweet-knots. The delicacy was light and fluffy, yet somehow sweet and robustly creamy. *These are amazing.*

"There is much to live for."

She had to set the pastry to the side. *Do I really want to live for passing pleasures? Tasty food? Beauty here and there?*

She put her face into her hands and couldn't answer. "What is the alternative?"

…Gates prove there is another realm. Would death be so bad?

"Would it be better?"

I don't know.

"So… why don't I want to live?"

She took another bite and a long drink. *I'm unwanted. I've served my purpose.*

"Oh?"

I was sacrificed to make my family's prospects better, but I'm still around.

"You are hardly unique in that."

Millennial Mage, 3 - Binding

She wiped her face, glaring into the distance. *Just because others are suffering, possibly worse, doesn't mean that I'm not suffering.*

"That's true." Tala took a long breath, barely being able to utter the next words, "It's okay to hurt."

She bent over her food, then, weeping silently. There was a cathartic release in the act, and for what felt like the first time in years, she allowed herself to *feel* her deep-set ache, her almost crushing loneliness.

The issue wasn't solved, not even close. She hadn't even taken a single step towards true resolution, but she had finally actually looked at the wound within herself.

It was a start.

* * *

When the light of dawn finally began to highlight the distant horizon, Tala's eyes were dry, her plate licked clean, and her jug of coffee empty.

She briefly placed the dishes into Kit, pulling them back out perfectly clean.

"Thank you, Kit." *I wonder where all the gunk goes…* It was something worthy of investigation… later.

Kit did not respond.

She returned to the chuckwagon, giving Amnin the earthenware. "Thank you, Amnin. I… I think I really needed that."

The cook smiled towards the Mage. "Sometimes, the person we need to talk to most is ourself." She looked at the plate and jug. "Oh! Thanks for giving them a once over." She then bustled off, back to work.

Passengers and guards were beginning to emerge, and it was almost time for breakfast. Xeel had departed a short while ago, simply waving to her before he vanished.

"Terry? Are you back?"

Terry flickered into being on her shoulder, and she let out a sigh of relief.

"Are you okay?"

Terry nuzzled against the side of her face, then bobbed a nod.

"Anything I can do?"

He immediately opened his mouth wide, and she grinned.

"I can do that." She got out a few chunks of jerky and tossed them.

Terry effortlessly acquired them with barely a flicker before curling up to seemingly sleep.

"Mistress Tala!"

Tala turned to see Rane approaching. "Good morning, Master Rane."

"Do you want to get in a bout before breakfast?"

Tala opened her mouth to say no, then paused. "You know what? Yeah. I've been wanting to test out the sheath."

Rane gave Flow a skeptical look. "Are you sure that will contain it?"

Tala thought for a moment, then glanced towards the chuckwagon. "Hey, Amnin!"

Amnin came to the opening. "Yes, Mistress Tala?"

"Would the caravan be very inconvenienced if I broke a table?"

The woman scratched her head. "Well, we have a few extra... You'd be charged, though."

"That's fine. Thank you!"

She turned back and saw Rane giving her an odd look.

"What?"

"You... asked?"

"Yeah?"

"That's not really like you."

Millennial Mage, 3 - Binding

She thought about it for a moment, then shrugged. "I'm trying to change." Without another word, she walked over to one of the still-unoccupied tables, off to one side. She took Flow from her belt, locking the sheath in place.

With two slightly larger-than-usual void-channels, she extended Flow and the sheath to sword size. *Baby steps.*

She used a quick motion to bring the sword down on the tabletop. Flow's magic lashed out, bent by the protective device, and the force was distributed across the entirety of the table, driving the legs four inches into the crunching, frozen soil.

She turned to Rane, grinning. "Satisfied?"

He was nodding. "Yeah, that's perfect."

* * *

As it turned out, Tala hated the taste of snow somewhat less than that of sand. *Not really surprising, I suppose.*

Three quick bouts, sword on sword, hadn't changed the outcome away from the expected. Terry watched from his perch on a nearby wagon.

Tala and Rane were squaring up for their fourth when Rane cleared his throat. "Why aren't you blocking?"

"Because I can't block your strikes."

"No. You couldn't block them, but that was with a mundane weapon. What will Flow do?"

Force vs Flow, eh? That was a thought. *But... will he break Flow?* That was unlikely. Flow was soul-bound against Force, which was just magic-bound. *That doesn't make it inherently better, though.* It would be a risk, either way. *He said it couldn't be stopped by a like-powered opponent. That doesn't mean that's an absolute, and Flow should be more powerful...*

"So... ready?"

Tala nodded, raising her blade into a hanging guard.

Rane fell into a high guard, a favorite of his, given his longer weapon. With a smooth forward step, he swept out, cutting towards her legs.

It was a laughably easy blow to parry. *So, he's as nervous as I am, it seems.* Tala responded with a sweep of her own, and the blades met between the fighters.

A concussion of force radiated outward in a circle, clearing the ground of the light, dry snow and breaking the grass flat.

Force and Flow stopped in a low bind, neither Tala nor Rane negatively affected by the clash.

They both started laughing, smiles stretching across their faces. Tala felt a joy building within her. *I can fight him on an equal footing now!*

"Yes!" Rane was nodding. "Let's go."

The following exchange of blows was bliss to Tala. Everything she'd been learning came into play as she fought more to perfect her own movements than against Rane as an opponent.

Each meeting of empowered weapons caused a harmless, soundless shockwave, which just served to energize them both.

It was still laughably obvious that Rane was the superior swordsman. While Tala's quicker movements and stronger strikes made such a long exchange possible, only her increased weight and proper footwork kept her grounded enough to consistently clash with the much bigger man, wielding the heavier blade.

Rane, for his part, kept what amounted to a perfect defense against her. She knew there were flaws in his movements—she could even see some of them—but she didn't have the skill to exploit them.

The engagement lasted a staggering thirty seconds of furious back and forth before Tala's errors compounded sufficiently for Rane to drive her into the ground once more.

She rolled to her feet, laughing, sword already raised defensively toward her sparring partner.

Rane had a massive grin across his face as well. "Again?"

"Again."

Chapter: 34
Fool's Folly

The Devourer of All had spent the entirety of her considerable existence reincarnating around the fringes of human civilization. The short-lived mammals were easy to fool at first. Their folly enabled Devourer to consume much of what they had tried to claim, along with quite a few of the silly creatures themselves.

This allowed her to grow in strength, building towards her goal: the fulfillment of her very name.

Unfortunately, as time went on, humanity learned to look for telltale signs of Devourer's power, no matter what form she took.

Each time they found her, they would slay her, tossing her true self back into the void where she languished until she could claw her way back out to find a new vessel, a new form.

This agonizing process forced her to grow, to change, and to find new ways to exist for longer stints. Her hatred of the void warred against her need to devour all and her need to grow strong so that she could do just that.

Through several existences, she made slow progress by consuming things that the peons wouldn't miss. Holding off on eating the humans, themselves, as long as she could. To facilitate this, she renamed herself: Devi.

It was much easier to resist desires to devour when she didn't constantly call herself Devourer.

Millennial Mage, 3 - Binding

There should be no mistake, her goal was—and would always still be—to grow until she could Devour All, but she was willing to be patient.

As Devi, she had consigned herself to a meaningless existence, eating the detritus stored within her and forgotten, while remaining within the current human cesspit.

Then, one came and dared to claim her.

This new creature had almost immediately placed itself within Devi's power, and Devi decided it wasn't worth resisting. The humans would find her and send her back to the void, but she would have at least consumed this arrogant creature.

But the human had surprised her.

Devi tried to taunt the thing, beginning to form human handprints on the walls, waiting to savor the creature's terror.

Completely counter to her expectations, the human had placed its hand on the handprint, and Devi had received *power*. It was not the meager trickle that humans had used in the past, while attempting to lay claim over one of her temporary forms.

No.

This one filled Devi to capacity.

Devi *couldn't* eat the human, even if she tried. There was nowhere for the power she would gain to be stored. Devi needed time to consolidate her gains, increase her capacities, and then, she would be ready to eat the human.

So, Devi waited.

But the strange human continued to feed her vastly more than anyone should have.

The human didn't question it, simply providing more as Devi was able to accept more.

Devi grew in power, her all-consuming desire to Devour only grew, but her appetite remained satisfied.

It wasn't a quick process; it would take decades of this behavior before she could fully manifest her power and consume everything, but when compared to the glacial progress of the past millennia? Patience now was nothing.

The good peon had taken to calling Devi by a different name. That was acceptable, as Devi wasn't about to tell the human who she really was.

And, though she would never admit it, not even to herself, Devi was coming to like being called 'Kit.'

Author's Note

Thank you for taking your time to read my quirky magical tale.

If you have the time, a review of the book can help share this world with others, and I would greatly appreciate it.

To listen to this or other books in this series, please find them on mountaindalepress.store or Audible. Release dates vary.

To continue reading for yourself, check out Kindle Unlimited for additional titles. If this is the last one released for the moment, you can find the story available on RoyalRoad.com for free. Simply search for Millennial Mage. You can also find a direct link from my Author's page on Amazon.

There are quite a few other fantastic works by great authors available on RoyalRoad as well, so take a look around while you're there!

Thank you, again, for sharing in this strange and beautiful magical world with Tala. I sincerely hope that you enjoyed it.

Regards,
J.L. Mullins

Printed in Great Britain
by Amazon